THE CLOUD COLLECTOR

ALSO BY **BRIAN FREEMANTLE**

BRIAN FREEMANTLE

THE CLOUD COLLECTOR

THOMAS DUNNE BOOKS
ST. MARTIN'S PRESS ⚎ NEW YORK

THOMAS DUNNE BOOKS.
An imprint of St. Martin's Press.

THE CLOUD COLLECTOR. Copyright © 2015 by Brian Freemantle. All rights reserved. Printed in the United States of America. For information, address St. Martin's Press, 175 Fifth Avenue, New York, N.Y. 10010.

www.thomasdunnebooks.com
www.stmartins.com

The Library of Congress Cataloging-in-Publication Data is available upon request.

ISBN 978-1-250-06623-7 (hardcover)
ISBN 978-1-4668-7381-0 (e-book)

Our books may be purchased in bulk for promotional, educational, or business use. Please contact your local bookseller or the Macmillan Corporate and Premium Sales Department at (800) 221-7945, extension 5442, or by e-mail at MacmillanSpecialMarkets@macmillan .com.

First Edition: November 2015

10 9 8 7 6 5 4 3 2 1

For Camille Colon, my über-fan and friend

AUTHOR'S NOTE

I am grateful to Simon Taplin and Jeff Kightly for technical guidance in the writing of this book. Any errors result from my misunderstanding of that guidance.

The mystery of how he [Osama bin Laden] kept in touch with his followers was at least partly solved yesterday by U.S. intelligence officials . . . to send an e-mail bin Laden would type a message on his computer, copy it to a flash drive and hand it to a courier who would then drive miles to a distant Internet café. The courier would then send the e-mail from the café, making it all but untraceable.

—Report of a CIA briefing on how Osama bin Laden controlled
Al Qaeda from his Abbottabad, Pakistan, lair,
London Times, May 13, 2011

I think it's a violation of human rights. . . . It [the use of drones] means you assassinate people without bringing charges, without finding them guilty, and in the process inadvertently causing collateral damage, that is the killing of completely innocent people who might be in the neighborhood.

—Former U.S. president Jimmy Carter,
London Times interview, July 4, 2012

THE CLOUD COLLECTOR

THE FORENSICALLY ENHANCED CLARITY FROM SUCH A NEGLECTED CCTV was remarkable. Closing the blinds of the CIA's Langley viewing room into semi-darkness helped. The original TV camera on the wall of the single-storey winos' bar had been ten yards from the assassination, which was another advantage. The target car, a bumper-crumpled, windscreen-cracked Ford with a red offside front wing that didn't match the rest of the faded blue paintwork, came surreally into the silent picture from the left of the screen. It wasn't hurrying, slowed further by vehicles haphazardly parked on either side of the street: it was still too early for traffic restrictions or people. The front passenger had his window down, arm on the sill. The wristwatch was a heavy mix of dials, control knobs, and numerals that would have glowed in the dark or been legible underwater.

The Ford driver found a tight space just before the telephone stand and put another dent in the bumper shunting into it. The passenger rolled his window up, but didn't get out. Neither did the driver or the scarcely visible third man in the rear. All three were heavily bearded. No-one appeared to be talking. A time counter had been superimposed on the screen: it registered six and a half minutes past five before the two men in the front got out and walked, still not talking, to the telephone. Neither attempted to get inside the hood. The driver rested his arm against the telephone ledge to keep his watch in front of him. Like the other man's, it had a lot of dials and knobs. Both men physically reacted to what must have been the incoming ring. One man grabbed the receiver, crowded beneath the hood by the other, preventing either from becoming aware of the ambush until the man they'd left in the Ford emerged from its rear, waving and obviously shouting. By that time the three who'd come from an unobtrusively parked fawn Toyota were close enough to fire point-blank. They did so precisely, bringing both men down with body hits and finishing off with single head shots. The other Ford passenger was running, and one of the hit squad broke away in pursuit but almost at once accepted that the intervening distance was too great and gave up, walking casually back to the other two bent over the bodies, rifling through their pockets. They straightened, laughing, as the returning man reached them. All three walked unhurriedly back to the Toyota and drove off in the direction of the Capitol, obediently halting at a red stoplight just visible to the CCTV.

'So how does it work?' demanded Charles Johnston, the newly appointed CIA director of covert operations.

Jack Irvine knew that having gotten this close he couldn't afford any mistakes. He could not give this unknown man the slightest excuse to cancel, question even, the operation on which he'd worked so hard for so long to the exclusion of girlfriends, any other social life, even his belovedly restored but now neglected '92 Volkswagen. His operation—*his*, no-one else's—had to be preserved, and he'd do everything and anything to ensure that it was. The Anacostia video provided the proof that it worked.

As the cliché went, pictures were worth a thousand words and words were what Irvine intended to limit. Neither Johnston nor the other two men with him needed to know the full details of what he'd achieved as a National Security Agency highflier roaming way beyond Iran's official Halal Web site to discover its use of unrestricted, anonymous cyberspace darknets.

Irvine said, 'It's anti-terrorism, using the Internet—Facebook and chat rooms—as the jihadists use them: how bin Laden himself used them. And Al Qaeda and every other militant Islamist, anarchist, and would-be terrorist is still using them.' It had echoed impressively when he'd mentally rehearsed it. Spoken aloud, it hadn't sounded quite so good; neither had the hesitation in his voice.

'How?' demanded Johnston. He was a large, heavy-featured man of self-protective conformity whose suits were always grey, shirts always white, and ties always plain. At that moment those heavy features were expressionless, betraying nothing.

'Taking terror to terrorists: we hack into their traffic, manipulate it. . . .' Irvine, who despite the abandoned jogging routine was an athletically slim man suited to jeans, T-shirts, and loafers, gestured towards the now-blank screen. 'Atrocity-planning terrorists killing other atrocity-planning terrorists with no collateral damage: no dead, innocent civilians and children caught up in a Reaper drone attack; no accusations against our military. All are identified by the NSA from overseas intercepts leading us to individual groups within the United States. Proof of intended terrorist attack is never obtained from illegal phone, computer, or radio wiretapping or hacking in this country.' Irvine again indicated the screen. 'That's not our first success. If we can't create an internal war, we alert Homeland Security or other enforcement agencies overseas.' He was covering all the obvious objections, Irvine knew, disappointed there was virtually no reaction from the covert-operations director.

'So that's how it's different from the NSA's Prism Project and the Brits' Tempura programme of 2012 that got us so much heat. We hunt, don't wait?'

'Exactly!' agreed Irvine, acknowledging that Johnston had tried to prepare himself. Irvine was sure there was still no danger of his being found out.

'And what we've just seen is the result of an already-sanctioned feasibility trial?' pressed Johnston, ever cautious.

'Officially designated Operation Cyber Shepherd,' confirmed Irvine.

'I've already established a NSA team at Fort Meade; they're waiting to be briefed.'

Johnston jerked his head in the direction of the dead screen. 'What about the guy that got away?'

'Ismail al Aswamy, an Iranian in the U.S. on an expired student visa.' Irvine looked sideways at James Bradley, the operation's CIA supervisor, who continued studiously to ignore him. 'Jim assured me Aswamy's ours whenever we want to take him. For the moment we're ready to follow wherever he leads us.'

'What's the body count so far?'

'The two you just saw taken out brings those eliminated here to a total of five. The other three were in Boston. Anti-terrorist police in Rome, Italy, have a group we've identified under surveillance. We've given the UK a lead in a town there called Bradford; no playback yet.'

Three and a half thousand miles away, in the Thames-side headquarters of MI5, its diminutive Director-General was even more curious at a lack of results.

His critics saw David Monkton's reluctance to delegate as the man's most obvious failing, while his matching number of supporters judged it his major attribute. In an organization as large and as complex as Britain's counter-intelligence service, delegation was operationally imperative. Monkton, whose life was tightly structured on self-imposed rules, evolved an equally reluctant compromise. He insisted upon daily, not weekly, updates on priority-designated cases from his divisional directors and carried out unannounced, unpredictable spot checks upon what he considered inadequate briefings.

This practise would uncover the nightmare scenario feared by every Western intelligence agency since 9/11 and 7/7.

2

DAVID MONKTON CONDUCTED THE MEETING NOT FROM HIS inherited desk, which he knew to be too large for someone of his stature, but by moving around the river-view suite, sometimes, such as now, out of his visitor's sight. Re-emerging, the MI5 Director-General went to a much-smaller side table upon which he'd spread the dossier retrieved earlier. Without looking back to Jeremy Dodson, his operations director, Monkton said, 'Why didn't this intrigue you as much as it intrigues me? As it *should* have properly intrigued you!'

Dodson, who'd actually consulted reference books for the diagnosis, decided Monkton's behavior was a classic example of a Napoléon complex, the insignificantly small man's constant need to bully. 'The police are adamant there's no link whatsoever between what came from America and the murder.'

'Which police? Special Branch? Scotland Yard's anti-terrorist division? Who?'

'A combination,' avoided Dodson uncomfortably. He shouldn't have left himself so exposed.

Monkton collected the file and finally returned to his over-sized desk, leaning forward over it and smoothing into place his immaculately trimmed toothbrush moustache that didn't need smoothing. 'I don't understand that answer, as I don't understand too many other things. Let's go back to the very beginning, to when we got the alert from the National Security Agency.'

The operations director breathed in heavily, only just preventing it from becoming a sigh. 'Fort Meade picked up some low-level Pakistani chatter and followed it to Germany. It included the name Roger Bennett with an indication that he was British, and so they passed it on to the Government Communications Headquarters at Cheltenham.'

'Who, quite properly, following established procedure, passed it on to us, which in practise means you. So tell me, what did you do? That's what I really want to know.'

'I strictly followed established procedure by passing it on to Scotland Yard's anti-terrorist unit,' recited Dodson. It wasn't going to be enough, he knew.

'And left it there, as someone else's responsibility?'

'No!' denied Dodson, the forcefulness just short of impertinence. 'The Yard traced Bennett to the London School of Economics; he'd dropped out and returned to his home in Bradford after two terms. He apparently knew Arabs there, but there was no evidence of radicalization or of his attending a mosque in Bradford or anywhere else. The Yard is overstretched, as you know. They judged him too low-key to justify an intercept warrant on his phone or any other electronic equipment.'

Monkton let an accusing silence build. 'There was a Pakistani connection: positive suspect chatter. You have the authority to apply for an electronic intercept warrant.'

'The Yard passed it on to the local police,' tried Dodson desperately.

'Who are now trying to find out why and how Roger Bennett ended up in a Bradford alley, stabbed to death and with half his tongue cut out.'

'Bradford police are investigating it as a gang killing. They have Bennett as a petty criminal, not a terrorist.'

'Did he have a criminal record?'

'In his late teens. Robbery with violence and aggravated assault.'

'Which I don't see in this file,' persisted Monkton, tapping the papers before him.

'It had nothing to do with terrorism.'

'Who, then, was making contact with him from Pakistan, through a German intermediary? And why was he on NSA's suspect airways list six months before he's found murdered?'

'I don't know,' miserably conceded Dodson.

'But I want to know,' insisted Monkton. 'Use proper channels to reach the chief constable, seeking his authority and assistance to clear up something we don't understand, that sort of approach. I don't want anyone believing their toes are being trodden upon or their territory invaded. And I don't want any media leaks.'

'I'll avoid that,' promised Dodson.

'I'll be extremely disappointed if you don't. And I'm already disappointed enough as it is.'

"Thanks a fucking lot!' protested Jack Irvine as the door closed behind the head of the CIA's covert division.

'You got a problem?' mildly queried Harry Packer, NSA's liaison director to the Agency. He was a bespectacled, balding man with the stoop of someone uncomfortable with his height, determined physically as well as figuratively to keep well below the parapet until he'd worked out the personal benefits of this operation. So far, he believed they might be considerable, and to climb out of the toilet into which his personal life was being flushed away, he needed all the benefits he could get.

'I think not getting any support or input from your two guys with whom Shepherd is being worked is a problem, yes,' said Irvine, over-emphasizing the irritation. 'I also think I was set up as the fall guy if Johnston scrapped the whole operation.' He'd done the right thing, holding back until now:

he still had the back channel to the CIA deputy director if Johnston changed his mind. He'd marked both as promotion-positioning backwatchers manoeuvring maximum advantages from Cyber Shepherd.

'But he didn't scrap it, did he?' James Bradley, Irvine's CIA counterpart, smiled. 'There wasn't a chance in hell of Johnston cancelling something already approved by our recently elevated deputy director. Johnston's ass is Teflon-tempered.'

Conrad Graham's promotion created the vacancy Johnston now occupied following belated recognition of Graham's role establishing the joint National Security Agency/CIA task force that devised, with the Israeli Mossad, the Stuxnet cyberwar weapon. A worm that without detection overrode already-installed computer control programs, Stuxnet was introduced into Iran's uranium-processing facility at Natanz in late 2010 and unknown to its Iranian operators alternated between fast and slow the intended centrifuge rotations sufficiently to disrupt Tehran's atomic development.

They wouldn't mock if they knew how much he'd gained from Stuxnet, Irvine thought. 'So why the big silence?'

'Shepherd's your baby: you didn't need any help from us setting it all out for the new man,' said Bradley, a carelessly crumpled bachelor fattened by microwave TV dinners and whose invariably tightly buttoned jackets concertina-creased over yesterday's shirt. 'I thought we'd established the rules of engagement: you handle all the clever cyberspace shit. I pick up when everything gets down to ground level: a perfect combination.' And one that was going to get him a $2,000 grade hike, reflected Bradley.

'That made us little more than observers today,' endorsed Packer. 'What *could* we have contributed that you couldn't explain better?'

'So what did you observe?' Irvine mocked back, even-voiced.

'New guy on the block, feeling his way in, is all,' said Bradley.

'And now it's time to move on,' hurried Packer, determined to get away from the CIA's Langley headquarters in time for that night's poker, upon which the monthly alimony depended.

'I'm coming up to Fort Meade fully to brief the team,' announced Irvine. 'Meade is where the facilities are, from where we're going to get the leads.'

'I'll make the arrangements,' undertook Packer, a career bureaucrat, not a cryptologist, who'd already decided to associate himself with all that was safe—and probably documented—and to steadfastly avoid anything and everything that was not. Staff movements were his responsibility, and he was apprehensive that Irvine's relocation to DC might prove too expensive.

'That would be a contribution,' said Irvine heavily, but then wondered why he'd bothered: he was going to keep them at a greater distance than they imagined they were keeping him. Looking to Bradley, he said, 'We haven't talked about al Aswamy.'

'What's to talk about?'

'You pick up when everything gets down to the ground,' irritably echoed Irvine. 'We still don't properly know how important he is.'

'He's locked in our box and we've got the key,' guaranteed Bradley. 'You look after your side, I'll look after mine.'

That's precisely what he intended to do, thought Irvine.

'Arrogant son of a bitch!' declared Bradley, generously pouring Jack Daniel's for both of them. They'd finally moved from the viewing room to the man's mission-assigned office, which had corner-window views out over the Virginia forest as far as Rock Creek Park, although the Potomac was hidden in the intervening valley.

'He's the best Arabic scholar at Meade, never known an encryption he couldn't break, and he works a computer like Chopin played the piano,' enthused Packer sycophantically, gauging he had a maximum of thirty minutes before he needed to get on the road. 'And Conrad Graham judged him invaluable on Stuxnet.'

'Which very obviously Irvine believes, too,' said Bradley, settling behind his desk. 'Important maybe, invaluable, no. This is a crusade against Islamic extremism, not a reputation-building exercise or redemption effort for the fuckups of his father.'

'He talked about his father with you?' asked the surprised Harry Packer, who'd imagined he'd be the only one to check out Irvine's background.

Bradley shook his head. 'Came up in all its sorry detail during his background check: hell of a mess. Sure as hell don't want to be caught up in a repetition.'

'That's hardly likely: this is altogether different.'

'It's got the potential.'

'Everything we do, either here or at Fort Meade, has the potential for disaster,' Packer argued back, more for his own reassurance than the other man's. Shaking his head against a refill, he said, 'What about Chuck Johnston?' Today had been their first personal encounter.

Bradley considered his answer. 'Word is that there's never been a decision, right or wrong, with his name on it.'

A responsibility-avoiding principle he also studiously observed, Packer recognized. 'This hasn't got his name on it. Conrad Graham signed off.'

'That's why I knew Johnston wouldn't pull the rug from under us.'

'Still right to handle it as we did.'

'Don't want anything to come up and bite us in the ass, do we?' invited Bradley, adding to his own glass.

'Absolutely not.' He'd be back in Baltimore soon enough, Packer decided. He had a good feeling—a winner's feeling—about tonight.

'I've made all the necessary police approaches: gone back to Scotland Yard and GCHQ, as well. There's nothing beyond what you've already seen,' Jeremy Dodson told Monkton. 'And I've drawn up a list of officers if you want us to get physically involved.'

'I definitely intend our getting involved,' said the Director-General, for once behind his overwhelming desk. 'And I've already decided upon an officer.'

Dodson hesitated, covering his awkwardness by retrieving the sheet of paper he'd already pushed partially across the desk. 'You won't be needing this, then?'

'No, I won't be needing that.'

'I've still got time to brief him this afternoon,' offered Dodson hopefully.

'I've already done that, too.'

3

'SO MI5 IS RECRUITING WOMEN NOW!' THE DESK PLATE IDENTIFIED
Edward Pritchard as a detective superintendent. The undisguised impli-
cation was that the employment barrel had been scraped from its absolute bottom, including splinters. The wall behind the man was a collage of
overseas police-force pennants and framed photographs of foreign events
all featuring Pritchard in the foreground.

'They have been for a long time now.' Sally Hanning smiled, contemptuous of the chauvinism of the man who sat with both hands cupping a
bulged gut, as if it needed support. It would have been charitable, which
she rarely was, to think its burden was the reason for his not standing when
she'd entered the room.

'Actually licensed to kill!'

'No,' she said, impatient with the condescension. 'Just to get easily irritated by irrelevant nonsense. Your chief constable promised every assistance. And that he'd send you a memo setting that out.'

Pritchard's superciliousness slipped. 'What, precisely, do you want?'

'That promised assistance. I'd like to see the full case file on Roger
Bennett, be updated on what progress there's been about a possible Pakistani terrorist connection, and hear whether it had any connection with
his murder.' Sally smiled again, happy at the abrupt change in attitude.
'In fact, I'd like you to talk everything through with me from the very
beginning.'

'I'm having the case file copied; it'll be ready before you leave,' said the detective chief stiffly. 'There's no connection whatsoever between Bennett's killing and any Pakistani terrorism. Apart from what was passed on from America, which only amounted to half an A4 page, there's absolutely nothing to substantiate a Pakistan connection to the man. We didn't find any mosque he attended and therefore no evidence of any conversion or interest in Islam.'

'What assistance did you get from Cologne?'

'Cologne?' queried Pritchard blankly.

'The contents of that half A4 page were routed through Cologne,' Sally pointedly reminded him. 'Are the German details in the file being copied for me?'

'I've just told you we don't believe Bennett was involved in terrorism.'

'Are you telling me you haven't had any communication with Cologne?'

'It wasn't necessary. Bennett was a petty crook, nothing more.'

'Why do you think he was killed, had his tongue cut out?' broke in Sally, irritated at the returned dismissiveness.

'He was a thug, small-timer imagining he was big-time,' recited Pritchard wearily. 'Offended someone who'd watched too many Hollywood films and didn't like something Bennett said. We've got a lot of lowlifes of too many nationalities in Bradford, all fighting among themselves. Roger Bennett isn't any loss to the community.'

'I don't understand your remarks about the tongue cutting and Hollywood movies?'

Pritchard gave an exaggerated sigh. 'All those Hollywood films about the Mafia: what happens to gangsters who shoot their mouths off.'

Sally didn't immediately respond. 'We're discussing possible Middle East terrorism. Tongue cutting is for a different sort of offence there.'

Now it was the police chief who remained briefly silent. 'You weren't born in this country, were you?'

'No,' confirmed Sally, with no intention of satisfying the man's curiosity. She'd inherited her Jordanian mother's olive complexion and Chanel-chic,

small-busted figure, and her blue-eyed natural blondness from her English father.

Again Pritchard waited, but when she didn't continue, he said, 'What
is it a punishment for?'

'Mostly dishonour.'

'I'd say that's the same thing.'

'There's a big difference,' insisted Sally. 'You know the lowlifes with
whom Bennett mixed?'

'None that know anything about his killing. Or who'd tell us if they
did.'

'What about family?'

'He didn't have any. Only son, mother died in the nineties, father nine
months ago, when Bennett was at college in London.'

'There were surely schools or colleges here he went to before graduat-
ing to the London School of Economics?'

'Got there from a probation-rehabilitation scheme after convictions for
violence; would have gone to jail, where he belonged, if the save-the-world
evangelist couple he held—and stabbed—at knifepoint hadn't pleaded in
court for leniency to save his soul for God. People in the parole office ran
a book on how long he'd last in London. His probation officer won thirty
pounds, bought drinks all around.' Pritchard looked pointedly at his watch.

Sally relaxed back in her chair. 'Where did he live?'

'In whatever gutter he woke up in. There was a room at a hostel, but
it's been emptied now, of course.'

'I'd like to go through everything from the crime scene that you're still
holding: clothes, what he had in his pockets, stuff like that.'

'You can help yourself to whatever you want.'

'And an officer to take me to the hostel to see if there's anything Bennett left behind.'

'You can have anything you want,' repeated the man, shuffling inef-
fectually to stand, to end the encounter. 'Is that all?'

'Unless something else comes up.' Sally smiled. When it did, she'd decide to take Pritchard's offer literally.

Jack Irvine's chosen team was already assembled in the smallest of the first-floor conference rooms at the National Security Agency's sprawling Fort Meade complex.

During their work together on Stuxnet, Irvine had recognized Burt Singleton—around whom it was said the NSA had been built—not just as one of its foremost cryptologists but as one of its most innovative thinkers. Marian Lowell, who positioned herself two rows farther back from Singleton, was an equally revered legend, a married-to-the-agency professional whose encyclopedic memory virtually made unnecessary the meticulously maintained research that Irvine believed to have shortened by months the final development of the Stuxnet worm. On either side of Marian, mother hen protecting her chicks, sat Shab Barker and Akram Malik, American-born grandsons of two Pakistani immigrant families whose respective hotel and leisure empires made possible Yale and Harvard educations with magna cum laude mathematics degrees. Proud of their American citizenship—the family name of Bibi had become Barker, Shabaz shortened to Shab—they'd also inherited a pride in their ancestry, which they considered shamed by the terrorist complicity and corruption of Pakistan.

'Marian's given me three-to-one against our finally hearing what the hell's going on,' declared Singleton, a flop-haired man who hid his prowess beneath a convincingly adopted Louisiana-ole-boy accent to match an appearance of constant perplexity. The elbows and cuffs of his jacket were leather patched, and the cord trousers puddled over scuffed combat boots.

'You should have held out for ten.' Irvine smiled back, grateful for the man's unwitting icebreaker. 'But first you're going to hear an apology. We're going to run a highly classified project, Operation Cyber Shepherd, partnered with the CIA, who until now has insisted on my working with them on a need-to-know basis. What you're being told today you should have been told earlier, and I'm sorry you weren't.'

There were frowns between Singleton and Marian but no immediate challenge, which Irvine had half expected.

'Some things came up during Stuxnet that didn't specifically contribute to that project,' continued Irvine. 'They did, though, give me an idea that I ran past Conrad Graham, then the CIA's director of covert operations. He approved my exploring them as a possible operation, which for a time I did as a research project.' Irvine stopped, again risking an interruption he didn't want and fortunately didn't come. 'It's important for all of you to understand that everything you've so far done at my request was properly approved and authorized.'

Irvine was conscious of renewed looks between Marian and Singleton. The two Pakistani Americans still gave no reaction.

'It's a CIA-financed operation, headed by a covert-division supervisor named Jim Bradley. Harry Packer's the liaison officer from here,' went on Irvine. 'Everyone in this room has the highest security clearance, higher probably than a lot of the CIA people working on the periphery of what's involved. We're not on the periphery. We're at the very core, the people making it work, and I don't want it continuing as it has until now.'

'I don't think I do, either,' intruded Singleton at last. 'I'd like what at the moment sounds like nonsense properly explained, right now!'

'We'd all like that,' insisted Marian. 'Our employment contracts are with the National Security Agency, not the Central Intelligence Agency, by whose operating procedures none of us is bound.'

Irvine had forgotten Marian held a corporate law degree. 'That's why we're having this meeting.'

'To make the Stuxnet sabotage work we had to get to the Programmable Logic Controller of Iran's Natanz and Bushehr facility computers,' reminded Irvine. 'Which we couldn't, not by direct hacking. The Iranians had anticipated the danger of an Internet connection. Their nuclear PLCs weren't connected but ran independently. Our only way in was to hack the personal computers of the Natanz and Bushehr scientists to create our botnets—or Trojan horses or spiders, whatever you want to call them—the moment they put their memory sticks into their otherwise protectively isolated mainframes . . .'

Marian and Singleton were nodding in recollection. Barker and Malik were both pressed forward, easily following the explanation.

'Israel's Mossad had a lot of personnel file details on the Iranian and Russian technicians at Natanz and Bushehr,' picked up Irvine, his earlier tension easing. 'Israel also have equipment similar to our own algorithm capacity and our dual random-number generators.' Irvine cleared his throat, wishing he'd brought water into the room with him. Looking to Singleton, he said, 'Am I making myself clear?'

'I'll let you know if you don't,' said the man with obvious reservation.

Was it just an irritation at not being included from the beginning? wondered Irvine. Or was it deeper than that, the resentment of someone twenty years his senior believing he should have been the project leader? 'Once we got into the personal PCs, we automatically gained access to every name—and computer—on each PC's contacts list, multiplying our botnet trawl. They were careless, these guys; had every excuse to be, I guess. They were inside what was supposed to be the most secure facility in the entire country. No-one could get to them, read their mail, which was why they wrote in clear, never encryption. I read a hell of a lot, we used a hell of a lot. There was one guy I picked out early on, signed himself Hamid. Came to believe that at another time in another Cold War he'd have been described as a commissar. Hamid didn't close down after Stuxnet so I went on monitoring him in my own time back at Meade; tried to follow his communication routes, which started to go through cutouts, although too often still unencrypted. His using the anonymous darknet chat rooms didn't surprise me. Facebook did. It took me a year to hack into all Hamid's cutouts—as well as Hamid's shared darknet account—to be able to follow the traffic both ways, although not quite as long to realize that Hydarnes, his shared Tehran account, is that of a covert-operations division of Vezarat-e Ettela'at va Amniat Keshvar.' Irvine paused, preparing his denouement. 'We have our own Trojan horse deep inside, totally without Tehran's knowledge or suspicion.'

Singleton interrupted disbelievingly, 'You got us *inside* Iran's espionage service!'

'An active subversive operational unit of Vevak,' qualified Irvine, using the acronym. 'From that one discovery and the botnets we installed from the address-book links, we've established that they're heavily using Facebook when they leave their darknet concealment to get into the West.' The hesitation was again intentional, for effect. 'And it hasn't stopped with social networks. Through darknets I've got into chat rooms. I think we've got a handle on at least two, maybe three, darknets regularly visited by Al Qaeda groups in Arabia, Yemen, Pakistan, the Maghreb, Europe, and here.'

'All that has emerged from social networks!' questioned Marian Lowell, an angular-bodied woman whose blue-dyed hair was lacquered into a protective helmet and who always wore business suits. Today's was brown check, with a belted jacket.

'A lot of it,' confirmed Irvine. 'Don't forget we didn't then fully appreciate how social networks would be used to avoid censorship and security controls in the Maghreb revolutions of 2011. Then it was to publicize regime change. Think of the opposite. What better concealment can any sort of terrorist group have than to be among millions upon millions of social-network users, until now hidden from us, too, despite our worldwide signals intelligence-sharing with Australia, New Zealand, Canada, and the UK and our bilateral exchange agreement with the UK. It's the equivalent of double, even triple encryption with double, even triple anonymity.'

There was a contemplative silence. Singleton stirred as if to speak, but before he could, Barker said, 'Okay, so we're ahead of the game. We can alert counter-intelligence to prevent the attacks before they're mounted. That's our job; what's different with what you're doing?'

From anyone else Irvine would have considered the question sarcastic, but not from Barker, a soft-voiced, gentle-mannered man confronting a regretted teenage addiction to hot dogs, hamburgers, and molasses-soaked waffles with a self-devised white-fish, nut, and herbal-drink diet that contributed nothing to any weight loss but substantially to discomforting flatulence.

Irvine breathed deeply, preparing himself. 'We're not stopping when we identify a planned attack. We hack into the planners' computers, add or remove or alter their messages—sometimes leaking to rival groups, intruding Shia or Sunni hatred—to turn one against the other.' He paused. 'So far two groups have destroyed each other instead of innocent Americans . . . innocent civilians anywhere.'

There was utter silence for several moments. Then Singleton said, 'I want to know a lot more than that.'

'You picked up a private Facebook message to Boston six months ago that originated from Syria,' reminded Irvine. 'I got a botnet into the Boston recipient's laptop. He was a Syrian immigrant. The CIA found an Al Qaeda suicide video in his apartment when they made a quick in-and-out intrusion. He'd formed up with two others, both Palestinian-born Americans with Hamas-based relatives in Gaza, all part of the Hamas–Al Fatah reconciliation.'

'I don't remember arrest publicity,' complained Singleton. 'When's the trial? On what charges?'

'There wasn't a trial. I followed the Syrian-led group through their Facebook cutouts into their operational e-mails. They were buying weapons for Hamas through Mexican suppliers, shipping through Colombia on a drug-supply route. I introduced an e-mail through Colombia to the gunrunners' Gaza control, showing they were operating a weapons-supply business on the side. All three got taken out by a Hamas hit squad.'

'So we're setting up our own Murder Incorporated and you're inviting us to become part of a botnet hacking group to operate it?' Singleton calmly asked.

'Absolutely not,' rejected Irvine, anxious to introduce the carefully prepared justification. 'We got bogged down in an illegal war in Iraq, we got bogged down in Afghanistan—where no invader has ever won a war—and we've crossed too many borders of too many countries clandestinely fighting terrorists. And what's the universal condemnation against America every time? Collateral damage, killing or maiming civilians. We identify a target in Pakistan, a Predator drone drops its bombs or fires its missiles, kills two or three terrorists—if we're lucky—and wipes out twenty innocent old men, women, and children. You know our kill score of innocents so far in Pakistan? Three thousand and rising. And with every one of those innocent deaths also dies every hope of our ever winning hearts and minds and stopping America from being the most vilified and hated nation on the planet. This way there's no collateral hurt. Those we trace who don't kill each other we pursue and punish, legally if at all possible. No dead innocents, no America Go Home banners, no American-flag burning.'

'Didn't we leave loose ends in Boston?' relentlessly persisted Singleton.

'Again, very definitely no!' insisted Irvine, believing he was winning the inevitable moral argument. 'Through the Syrian we got to two more whose supposedly hidden Facebook exchanges claimed Al Qaeda affiliation. The FBI has the entire group under blanket surveillance—with court-approved wiretaps on cell phones, landlines, and Internet connections—until this new Al Qaeda–affiliated group and other associates are identified. From the Colombian Facebook traffic there was a steer to the three-man Boston assassination team. The Boston assassination trio are based in Miami; their day job is acting as the conduit for a cocaine cartel working out of Medellín. Everything's now with the Drug Enforcement Administration, who didn't have the Miami three flagged until we told them.'

Marian said, 'I logged other partial penetrations, following the guidelines you set for us. How many more fatalities have there been with your intervention with those?' Once again it wasn't an accusation.

'Two in Washington, a month and a half ago,' responded Irvine. 'Both were Americans, former infantry who'd done four tours between them in Afghanistan. Came home not just disillusioned but anti-U.S.; converted to Islam and met their recruiter, an Iranian named al Aswamy, in an Arlington mosque. I got that from al Aswamy's Facebook. He was using a binary code, half-encrypted on his private Facebook wall, the other half on a different time and day by cell-phone texts, read properly only when the two halves were put together. There was also a reference to another radicalized Muslim group in Annapolis; they'd apparently rejected al Aswamy after he made a recruitment approach; they'd identified him as a Sunni. They were Shiites.'

'I got their cell number for you,' remembered Barker.

'Which was all I needed. Al Aswamy was routing through Pakistan's Islamabad on a darknet to conceal his Tehran control. I hacked back into his Facebook traffic and his cell and reversed al Aswamy's original message en route about recruiting the Americans. I added that they'd been dishonourably discharged from the U.S. infantry after an incident in Sangin in which two Shia girls were raped before the entire family were shot dead. It was an actual atrocity that occurred in Afghanistan, without any arrests. I also added, as if in reply to al Aswamy, that in view of the Annapolis rejection he anonymously leaked to U.S. authorities that they were planning a terrorist attack and sent it as an apparently misdirected e-mail.'

'That would have used al Aswamy's e-mail address, as well as whatever identification he'd let them have when he originally approached them?' predicted Marian.

'That's how it worked.'

'But not with one hundred percent success,' challenged Singleton. 'You said the two Anacostia Americans were killed. Al Aswamy's the leader; what happened to him?'

Irvine smiled at the prescience. 'He got away and I'm damned glad he did. The two Americans were hit at the very moment they were to get instructions for an attack, although we didn't know that at the time. We only discovered it when we got the recording of their broken telephone conversation, five words: *The attack is to be . . .* We've gotten more since. But not enough. Just that it's still to be staged, but not where or when. Or precisely by which newly recruited group.'

'You're right,' said Marian Lowell, even-voiced. 'We haven't gotten enough by a very long measure. What are you doing about it?'

Singleton unexpectedly answered, 'The Facebook account and separate Internet addresses you're having me monitor are al Aswamy's, right?'

'Right. And they begin on Halal and route through darknets from Iranian intelligence.'

'What if they use a different Vevak route to Facebook that we don't have?' demanded Marian. 'Or call from a landline or cell we're not aware of for the second part of a binary code? Or use any other sort of PDA we don't know about and aren't listening to? We're wide-open on this!'

Irvine said, 'You're forgetting the Trojan horse I've got in the Tehran system. Anything protectively routed from al Aswamy would eventually go through the Tehran router in which I am embedded. I'd know the minute it arrived: the computer alerts are tied to my cell and that's permanently on wherever I am. Additionally—and obviously essentially—al Aswamy is under the tightest twenty-four-hour, CIA surveillance. We couldn't have missed anything, *can't* miss anything.'

'We're relying on just one electronic source, an interrupted telephone call,' Singleton objected. 'I'd like a secondary confirmation.'

'So would I,' supported Marian at once.

'So would we all,' agreed Irvine, uneasy at the opposition from the two whom he considered the strongest of his team. 'You tell me how often we've had two sources positively to be sure of a terrorist act.'

'We guess or surmise rather than be sorry after an event,' argued Marian. 'You're talking about an attack you *know* is going to take place. You surely can't wait for the entire picture before we move: you pick up al Aswamy, you prevent an attack you've got evidence is going to take place. Waiting creates an unnecessary risk.'

'Al Aswamy doesn't move without our knowing. We don't get something soon, I'll reconsider. I'll give it another week.'

'This is going to be a totally cohesive group from now on, isn't it?' queried Singleton.

'Of course.'

'Everyone's going to know *everything* that's happening?' persisted the man.

'It can't work any other way now,' confirmed Irvine, illogically wishing there were, reluctant as he was even to have had to disclose as much as he had to those he implicitly trusted and upon whom he relied for Operation Cyber Shepherd to work.

Marian said, 'What's the CIA's contribution to all this, apart from the half-assed need-to-know stupidity?'

'Financial,' replied Irvine easily. 'It's their budget, not ours. Additionally, when we isolate a foreign source or group, their guys on the ground, wherever that is, have to provide the backup for our manipulation. Likewise, here in America.'

'What if the contacts here are Americans?' seized the woman. 'The Supreme Court has ruled it's illegal for the CIA to operate against American nationals within the United States.'

'But not upon foreign nationals in the United States,' argued Irvine. 'If it's an all-American group we move against their contacts overseas and turn the American end over to Homeland Security.'

'The CIA has a code-breaking facility,' Singleton pointed out. 'What's our liaison with their division?'

'None,' said Irvine. 'This is a specialized unit performing a very specialized function.'

Marian said, 'I've never heard of a joint operation like this before.'

'There hasn't been one like this before,' said Irvine.

'That's what worries me,' said Singleton.

Marian turned to the man. 'I'm not paying out on the bet.'

'I don't expect you to,' said Singleton.

Irvine was fifteen minutes early for his meeting with Harry Packer, but was ushered immediately into the liaison director's office for a glad-handed greeting. Before Irvine properly settled himself, Packer said, 'I know I stayed out of it—and told you why—but between the two of us, I thought that was one hell of a presentation at Langley, Jack.'

'Thank you,' said Irvine guardedly. This was only his second meeting with the man and Irvine regarded this encounter as an assessment.

'What do you think of Johnston and Bradley?' It was important Packer identify the strengths and weaknesses of everyone with whom he was now linked. He wished to hell he'd better identified the strengths and weaknesses of those who'd taken $500 off him after the Langley session.

'Cautious, maybe,' suggested Irvine. 'Thought there might have been a little more enthusiasm for what could be a career-builder for them.'

'That's what I thought.'

A man of other people's opinions, judged Irvine. 'You foresee a working-relationship problem?'

'Too early to say,' avoided Packer. 'But that's why I think it's important for you and me to work close together: make sure they don't steamroll us, just because they're financing the whole thing.'

'How, exactly, do you see our working to avoid that?' asked Irvine uneasily.

'I'm not suggesting we're constantly in each other's pockets,' quickly qualified Packer, eager to rig his selective-information safety net. 'I know the CIA better than you do, can recognize the curveballs quicker than you. I'll watch the DC manoeuvring, you keep me technically ahead with the code-breaking.'

Irvine couldn't have established the boundaries keeping the other man as far away as possible better himself! 'That sounds just fine.'

'And I want you to know, Jack, I don't have any reservations about how successful this operation is going to be.'

'That's good to hear.'

4

SALLY WAS THE ANGLICIZED NAME FOR SELWA, A CHANGE SHE'D introduced within a month of her parents' assassination. Unbeknownst to both she'd never liked the hybrid of an Arab name with her English father's surname: from her early teens she'd thought it appeared that she was undecided about which of the two cultures she bridged. It certainly did not reflect a rejection because of the atrocity, although it obviously coincided with her being moved from Amman to London. That relocation—and the initial unwelcome safe-house precaution—had been imposed by MI5 in its initial mistaken belief that its Jordanian network was being targeted by a militant Islamic Al Qaeda faction or the newly emerging IS. In the year it took for the truth to emerge—that her parents had been the unintended, wrong-place-at-the-wrong-time victims of Hezbollah cross-border informer retribution—MI5 had recognized its Arab-language deficiencies and drawn heavily upon Sally's complete bilingualism. Six months after that, customary background vetting foreshortened because of her father's station-chief credentials, Sally officially joined MI5's Arab division. The only suitability examination to which she was subjected was psychological, to determine if she'd suffered mental trauma from the circumstances of her parents' murder. The conclusion was that she had neither emotional disturbance nor generalized Arab antipathy: the official verdict was "exceptionally well adjusted, at every psychological level."

A further finding of that psychological profile was that Sally Hanning's mental strength and resilience translated into a stubborn personal independence against authority in general and a refusal in particular to unquestioningly accept information even from supposedly professional or qualified sources.

Sally didn't consider her encounters with Detective Chief Superintendent Edward Pritchard or his deputed sergeant who'd escorted her to Roger Bennett's hostel to be either qualified or professional. Which was why, to prevent any warned-against secret-service publicity, she'd used the inherited authority of the sergeant who originally escorted her to return to the hostel alone later the same afternoon. It took her less than thirty minutes to recover Bennett's computer from a locker the earlier, dismissive police search hadn't found, and which she, in turn, didn't bother telling the police chief about before leaving Bradford.

Before doing so Sally followed correct procedure, having Thames House officially advise the Government Communications Headquarters, Britain's equivalent of America's NSA, of her cross-country journey to Cheltenham. A slightly built, quiet-spoken man whom Sally guessed to be no more than ten years older than her, was waiting when she got through the protracted security procedure at GCHQ. He told her his name was John, which she knew it wasn't. She introduced herself as Sally because her name would have been on London's notification to match her MI5 accreditation documents.

'London said you wanted some technical help with the Bennett alert from America?' he greeted, looking at the encased computer as he escorted her to a small, windowless interview room on the same ground-floor level. Sally knew she was still only in the outside perimeter of the communications hub.

'I want this hard drive examined for deleted material that might connect with what came from America,' elaborated Sally, putting the computer on the table between them. From his side John placed a slim, unmarked manila folder next to it.

The man frowned. 'It wouldn't have been difficult for Bradford forensics to have done that for you, without your coming all this way.'

'I want it done professionally, properly.'

'How soon?'

'Today. Bennett's dead, murdered. There's been a lot of time wasted.'

'We didn't know he'd been killed. The police didn't tell us. Our involvement was limited to intelligence traffic, nothing more.'

'Can you check everything on the hard drive today?'

'Working from the date of the known American interception?'

Sally hesitated. 'We could initially go forward from there. We might need to go backwards, depending upon what we find. My guess is that there was earlier traffic that wasn't intercepted.'

John opened his folder, reading aloud: ' "Invite the brothers to the celebration." ' He looked up. 'It certainly reads as if there was something earlier. Let's start from the date of this transmission, see how and where we go from there.'

'The Bradford murder file had that message in unencrypted English. Was that how it was originally intercepted by NSA? Or was it encrypted?'

John went back to the file. 'It was in English, on the private link from a Facebook account. It was encrypted in what amounted to little more than a schoolboy code: figures plus one for corresponding letter in the alphabet to decipher. Bennett would have had a crib to read it. It would have provided virtually instant translation.' John smiled and looked up. 'At first we agreed with America that the encryption was something incredibly clever, something we hadn't come across before *because* it was too simple!'

'So there won't be any translation difficulties if there's more, using the same encryption?' She'd need to run a passport search, Sally reminded herself. There hadn't been one among Bennett's personal belongings she'd sifted through in Bradford or in the hostel computer locker. With one realization came another. 'What did you do here, after getting that one message? Did you monitor the German sender's computer address? And Bennett's?'

John returned to his folder. 'Bennett's message was intercepted from a Cologne Internet café. The account was in the name of Mohammed, which has to be the most generic Arabic name. We installed a monitor for a month. We put Bennett's electronic address on a watch list, also for a month. After that we checked with Thames House, who said we could lift both.'

It wasn't just Bradford police who'd screwed up, Sally recognized. It might have helped if she'd at least had an indication from London that she was picking up a botched case. Edging the computer towards the man, she said, 'Can we get started, to see how much time we might have lost so far.'

'If there's more and it's encrypted Arabic, it'll take longer than what's left of today; the code will have to be broken and the Arabic translated. Sometimes there are words or colloquialisms too close in definition to give the instant translation you want.'

'My mother was Jordanian,' disclosed Sally. 'I'm totally bilingual. Even with a difficult translation I could get a gist sufficiently for a general impression. And Bennett's from a background that makes it doubtful he'd know any Arabic.'

'So we could be lucky.' The man smiled.

'Luck would be a bonus.' Sally at once regretted the rare self-pity; she didn't even believe in luck.

Marian Lowell got to the commissary early, determined to get their already-chosen table from which they couldn't be overheard. Burt Singleton came in as she was setting out her Caesar salad. He scuffed awkwardly with his tray from the service line and remained standing.

'The sole's come off my boot,' he complained.

'Don't do another home repair; buy new at Kmart.' She was conscious of the occasional smiles and looks from other early diners, aware of the gossip that she and Singleton were longtime lovers. It wasn't true but it didn't bother either of them.

'Maybe I should.' He unloaded his plate of meat loaf and put both their empty trays on a nearby waiter stand. Coming back to the table but still standing, he said, 'Well?'

'I've been through every legal hearing in which the agency's been involved in remit transgressions, particularly under Nixon and Bush. As well as through all the textbook references I could locate. I couldn't find anything that even came close to this. And hacking isn't a crime, by our definition; that *is* what our remit is, entering other people's communications without their knowledge or permission, although I've never considered myself working as part of a botnet.'

Singleton began to eat. 'I couldn't find a definite legal bar, either. But it's pretty well set out that NSA doesn't perform field operations.'

'Jack covered that very specifically. Any fieldwork or humint retrieval is carried out by the CIA. And since 9/11 the courts have returned ambiguous rulings against us when we've been accused of wiretapping and bugging here at home, despite Signals Intelligence Directive 18 specifically prohibiting it without a warrant from the Foreign Intelligence Surveillances Court.'

'Washington commandment handed down from Mount Sinai: "Nothing's wrong or illegal until you're caught doing it," ' recited Singleton, quoting the in-house cynicism. 'Don't forget the 2013 uproar over our Prism Project precisely to monitor Facebook through Britain's GCHQ, for which we gratefully handed over something like one hundred and fifty million dollars. What happens if there's another whistle-blower like Edward Snowden?'

'There'll be another uproar,' accepted Marian drily, working her way through her salad.

'Can we belatedly object?'

'No,' she said without hesitation.

Singleton pushed his plate away, the meat loaf half-eaten. 'According to our contract terms, we could simply withdraw. We didn't know what we were doing during the initial period.'

'You mind taking that meat loaf away?' said Marian, a vegetarian. 'It smells disgusting.'

'Tasted disgusting, too.' Singleton transferred the plate to the waiter stand. 'I asked what you're going to do.'

Marian didn't reply at once, chasing the last crouton around her dish. 'I'm not sure where I'm safer, inside from where I'll be able to assess the dangers and accusations before they're made. Or outside, to plead ignorance when it all goes wrong.'

'I'm not sure a court would accept an ignorance plea. Or that ignorance is even a defence.'

'We're staying in, aren't we?' accepted the woman, resigned.

'I guess.'

'But I'll keep looking for something that gives it some legal justification.'

'So will I,' said Singleton. 'Let's hope it doesn't have to come from our trial lawyers.'

James Bradley prided himself on covering all the bases, which he wasn't able to do with Jack Irvine, and it unsettled him. His difficulty was in having to rely on records and written accounts of Irvine's cryptographic brilliance, unsupported by any biographical material apart from the abbreviated account of the debacle surrounding Irvine's ambassador father, which, realistically, he might have misinterpreted and didn't have any relevance anyway.

There were, of course, the obvious practical precautions such as the CIA surveillance he'd imposed upon Irvine and his Fort Meade team. Bradley looked up from the list of CIA internal-security officers he was forming to watch over Irvine and the operation, halted by a sudden doubt about Harry Packer's reliability. Shouldn't Packer be added to his personally compiled list? Bradley asked himself. Unquestionably, he concluded. He'd read somewhere that knowledge was power, and he was going to emerge from all this with more power than anyone suspected.

5

JACK IRVINE GOT HIS CELL ALERT HALFWAY BETWEEN WASHINGTON and the National Security Agency's installation at Fort Meade and was momentarily undecided between turning back or continuing. Calculating the next available turnaround intersection to be three miles farther on, he decided Meade was closer and kept driving.

Burt Singleton was waiting in the foyer of the main building. 'We followed it back through the cutout chain—all the way to Hydarnes.'

Irvine said, 'We're in business!'

'What's the significance of the domain name?'

'Hydarnes was a legendary Persian warrior; for *Persia* now read *Iran.*'

'What ever happened to Hamid?' asked Singleton, remembering the domain name of Irvine's first darknet interception.

'One day he just wasn't there anymore.'

Under Marian Lowell's supervision, the thirty-six-hour occupation of their assigned office following Irvine's formation briefing was only obvious from the newness of its furnishings. A wall-mounted selection of clocks showed world-time variations, from which daylight working times could be calculated. The display was above a cabinet-enclosed television, adjacent to another wall of filing cabinets, fax machines, photocopiers, transmission machines, and a separate scanner. A third wall was shelved almost to the ceiling: three racks were already filled with index-arranged mathematic, cipher, and encryption manuals in a range of Asian, Arabic, and Western languages, and another shelf was full of matching indexed dictionaries, idiomatic lexicons, and thesauruses. The only practical furniture was the individual desks for each member of the team—Marian's marked by a vase of red bud roses—topped by the highest-powered NSA desktop computers, each with even larger mainframe connection capability. One of the fully operational desks, in the centre of the rest, was for Irvine, who ignored it.

Instead he said to Marian, 'Where are the others?'

'Shab's taking a trial algorithm run. Akram is on the Dual EC DRBG generator, trying a random-numbers search.'

'So it's a different encryption?' anticipated Irvine, turning back to Singleton.

'Everything's different. Islamabad's no longer in the loop. Initial Halal routing this time was an encrypted text to Sana'a. From Yemen the link went through darknet cutouts to a Facebook account in Baghdad.' Singleton paused. 'And from Baghdad we've lost it.'

'No forwarding link?'

Singleton shook his head. 'We're obviously embedded now in the Baghdad account, but there's been no onward activity. We only know it's for al Aswamy because it originated from Vevak.'

'What about al Aswamy's Facebook account at this end?'

Marian gestured towards the computer on her desk. 'I've had your botnet open from the start. Nothing.'

Irvine finally went to his desk, but sat on its corner, not the chair. 'The different routing is an obvious precaution, after the Anacostia ambush. I always expected it would start from Tehran: that we'd follow from there to any new account al Aswamy set up.'

'You want coffee?' invited Marian from a Cona setup Irvine hadn't seen in the filing-cabinet corner of the room. She'd already poured two mugs and held the pot over the third.

Irvine nodded acceptance as Singleton said, 'Maybe we blindsided ourselves. They could have switched to something else, human couriers or flash
drives, for instance, like bin Laden used from Abbottabad.'

By *we* the man meant *you*, Irvine knew, taking the coffee from
Marian. 'I told you the CIA's got al Aswamy in a box. He can't make a
move we don't know about it.'

'Don't you think you should give Langley the heads-up about this?'
suggested the woman, behind her desk now.

'This isn't three hours old yet,' protested Irvine.

'We know from the phone call after the Anacostia ambush that there's
an operation going down somewhere. And we've intercepted an encrypted
message, as yet unbroken, from an electronic address of the Iranian intelligence service from which al Aswamy takes his orders,' argued Singleton. 'That's enough for Langley to move.'

'We've got time!' insisted Irvine.

'This isn't what we've been formed to do; we can't sit on this,' came in
Marian.

'We're not going to sit on it!' insisted Irvine, refusing to recognize the
weakness of his not reacting immediately. 'We're going to give Shab and
Akram time on the computers. If it defeats them—and us, because we're
all going to work on it, too—then we'll alert Langley.'

'By the end of this day if we don't crack it,' persisted Singleton.

The man was right, Irvine knew. 'By the end of the day,' he capitu-
lated.

'You've upset a lot of people,' complained Jeremy Dodson the moment the
secure telephone connection was established.

'Who?' sharply demanded Sally, irritated at having to wait over an hour
for a temporary desk and telephone.

'I had the GCHQ security director on, querying your authority for what
you wanted.'

'They had my official accreditation and authority ahead of my arrival here!'

'It's not the sort of request they're accustomed to, and they're nervous after all the whistle-blowing exposure in 2013,' said the MI5 operations director. 'And a Detective Superintendent Pritchard's claiming you left with official police evidence.'

The complaints were being set out as accusations, Sally recognized, wondering if Dodson was trying to generate a personally protective smoke screen against the mistakes she'd already isolated. 'The computer?'

'Yes.'

She'd obviously unsettled the arrogant bastard more than she'd imagined. 'They hadn't discovered its existence to make it part of any police evidence! And Pritchard told me I could have whatever I wanted of Bennett's property. He'll have to do a damned sight better than this to save himself from a disciplinary enquiry. Did you confirm that I had it and where I was with it?'

'Of course I didn't. I said we hadn't been in contact, didn't know where you were, and that I'd get back to him when you made contact. He said he was taking it up with his chief constable.'

That risked creating the publicity of MI5 involvement the Director-General had forbidden, Sally immediately recognized. 'I'm following a disastrous catalog of professional mistakes and cock-ups that could end as precisely that, a very real disaster that should and could have been prevented. I want you to have several things done for me as quickly as possible while I'm stuck here. And I'd appreciate you, personally, getting back to Pritchard to tell him what I've just told you, using those precise words. He's to do nothing whatsoever, something he's very good at, until he hears from me.'

Dodson didn't respond at once, and when he did, the uncertainty was obvious. 'Are you seriously suggesting there's a terrorism danger here!'

There wasn't sufficient justification for that, Sally acknowledged. 'I believe there's every indication.'

Once more there was initial silence. Then Dodson said, 'What else do you want done?'

Sally had compiled her list to fill time while she waited for the desk assignment. She reminded the operations director that the leads to be immediately followed to the Cologne conduit were in the NSA's initial communiqué and dictated every relevant detail to trace a passport in Roger Bennett's name from the incompetently maintained Bradford crime file.

'This is going to take time,' said Dodson.

'Time's what we haven't got,' warned Sally, wondering if she was going to have anything to substantiate the exaggeration of connecting Bennett's death with a terrorist threat at the end of the GCHQ examination.

Independent of each other Irvine and Singleton followed the same algorithm search that had partially defeated Barker, both double-checking their effort after their partial failure. Irvine decreed an assessment session. Marian provided fresh coffee.

'Let's start from absolute basics,' said Irvine. 'It's obviously algebraic.'

'Encrypted by someone or some group who'd know a search for its algorithm would be the first move if it were intercepted,' agreed Barker.

Singleton sighed. 'Do we really have to be *that* basic! It's an intelligence-generated encryption, from our equivalent in Iran. So they'll be good, the best Tehran can find. They've been hit, here, but they don't know how or by whom, except that Anacostia looks gang-related, not an attack by law enforcement: that's our advantage. They wouldn't expect our level of expertise. But they'll still have put a lot of professional effort into protecting their traffic with cutouts and double or treble encryptions. We know from the partial Anacostia interception that they're going ahead with whatever attack they're planning. How many English letters can we reasonably get so far from the original Arabic?'

'Three,' at once replied Marian, who'd maintained the tentative, insufficient deciphering.

'But they're not positives,' protested Barker. 'They appear to work in some sections but not in others.'

'Multi-algorithms,' declared Irvine. 'The letter-to-number or symbol transference is limited, changing at intervals, either fixed or irregular.'

'I agree,' said Singleton.

'It's Facebook, not Twitter,' Marian pointed out. 'Even without being able to read it, I'd say from the length that it's attack instructions.'

'I haven't forgotten the urgency,' said Irvine, recognizing the direction of the discussion.

'Akram's not going to be able to contribute at this stage,' predicted Singleton.

'You're right,' confirmed the tightly bearded man, entering the room after an hour at the random-number generator. 'I've got some numbers for alphabetical substitution, but they fit in some parts but not in others.'

James Bradley answered his phone on its first ring.

'We've got a problem,' announced Irvine.

'Serious?'

'It could be.'

Sally Hanning's concern deepened far more quickly than either she or Jeremy Dodson anticipated. Forty-five minutes after her short-tempered exchange with MI5 headquarters in London, the GCHQ official she only knew as John returned to her temporarily assigned office to announce that nothing remotely resembling a coded message had been deleted from the hard drive of Roger Bennett's computer.

'Which is why it's been so quick,' said the man. 'What has been deleted is inconsequential. Seems to have gambled a bit: dog- and horse-racing tips, stuff like that.'

'You've kept it all?'

'Of course. We're running printouts right now, assuming you'd want to go through them.'

'I do,' said Sally at once. She was sure she hadn't over-reacted to her finding of the computer, but where else was there for her to look for what she was sure was a terrorist outrage in the making! 'Was text all there was? No pictures? Film?'

The man shifted awkwardly. 'There were some photographs. A film.'

Sally frowned, aware of the man's discomfort. 'What's wrong?'

'They're pornographic.'

Sally gave no open reaction, conscious of the man's embarrassment. 'Have you copied them all?'

'Yes.'

She nodded to the television in the corner of her temporary office. 'I'd like to go through the printed text and still photographs first, before looking at the movie. Can it be watched on that screen?'

'There's a DVD facility. Can you work it okay?'

Sally recognized the apprehension that she might ask him to operate the player. 'I'll manage.'

'And now you want us to work backwards through the hard drive from the date of the NSA interception?'

'I thought we'd agreed that.' From the relieved smile she knew she was right about playing the disk.

'There isn't a great deal on the earlier part of the hard drive, but you might want to book into a hotel in the town.'

Sally shook her head. 'I've grown to like the room, don't want to leave it until I find what I want. I'll wait here until you get the rest of the stuff.'

Sally spread out everything John had so far retrieved, working methodically. She separated the electronic messaging from the pornographic stills, leaving the DVD to last, isolating potential inconsistencies in the printouts on her second reading. Sally added to her curiosity list on her third reading. When he returned after two hours, John confirmed her guess. He reported they were halfway through the remainder of the hard-drive examination and, less embarrassed than before, that it included another pornographic movie. It took two more hours of intense study of the pornography for Sally to make the connection between the still and movie pictures. Her immediate excitement had nothing to do with the sexual content and was balanced anyway by her completely objective acceptance that although her discoveries could easily be assembled into a circumstantial presentation of a crime, it provided absolutely no indication of what, where, or how that crime might be attempted.

It was past nine that night when her GCHQ escort finally returned to Sally's room, with the second DVD download and the sheaf of printed-out electronic messages.

'I'm afraid you're going to be disappointed,' he apologized.

'Maybe I won't be.'

She watched for ten minutes, oblivious to John's discomfort behind her, before she suddenly said, 'Oh my God!' and snatched out for the telephone.

She calmly dictated her identification number and password when she was connected to the MI5 Watch Room at Thames House, even-voiced although authoritative when demanding to be patched through to Jeremy Dodson with the assurance that she was calling from a secure telephone.

When the man answered she said, still totally controlled, 'I've got it! It's nuclear!'

At that precise moment, just over three thousand miles away at the National Security Agency complex at Fort Meade, Maryland, Jack Irvine took the telephone call for which he'd anxiously been waiting.

James Bradley got on the line: 'It's more than a problem. It could be a goddamned emergency.'

6

'HOW THE FUCK COULD IT HAPPEN!' DEMANDED IRVINE, CARELESS of Marian Lowell, in whose presence cursing was forbidden.

'I'm waiting for the agent-in-charge to get back here. All I know so far is that we've lost al Aswamy as of thirty minutes ago.'

'Bullshit! Tell me what happened!' Irvine was aware of the looks passing between Marian and Singleton: the other two were concentrating entirely upon him, all their automatic random-search programs initiated. Belatedly Irvine switched to speakerphone.

'The son of a bitch kept to routine. Left the Ely Place apartment around noon, walked the usual route to the Dubois take-away for the lamb kebab, which he ate on the premises, then went directly back to Ely Place.'

'Didn't it occur to anyone that the routine was established for a reason!' broke in Irvine, exasperated.

'I'm rehearsing the obvious questions, too,' rejected Bradley. 'Al Aswamy left Ely Place at four this afternoon and took the crosstown bus, with our guys on it with him. He rode all the way to the old post office building. Got straight off the bus and onto the pillion of a Honda 250 cc that had followed from somewhere along the route.'

'Your guys didn't have vehicle backup?' groaned Irvine, exasperation turning into incredulity.

'No.'

'What about the registration?'

'It all happened too quickly.'

'Jesus!'

There was a brief pause from the Langley end, where Bradley was bunkered in his locked office, the occupancy slot reading IN CONFERENCE. He was sweating profusely, his normally tightly buttoned jacket discarded, shirt collar open. 'We fucked up big-time. Satisfied?'

'Fighting among ourselves isn't going to help,' cautioned Burt Singleton.

'Who's listening to this!' The irritation at his having made a public admission echoed in Bradley's voice.

'Speakerphone. Me and the team,' said Irvine.

Whose was the greater mistake, his and his surveillance team's, or Irvine and his cryptologists'? If there was some way to recover, which at the moment he couldn't foresee, he'd have to work hard to shift the majority of the responsibility on the NSA, Bradley calculated. 'What chance is there of picking things up from your end?'

'We're routing high-velocity random programs,' said Irvine. 'But the Facebook account in Baghdad is dormant.'

'Talk words I understand!' protested Bradley.

'Think of Baghdad as a PO box number, a place for receiving mail,' lectured Irvine with forced patience. 'It received today's coded message from Yemen. The Baghdad operator, Taliban or Al Qaeda, copies it—typing it onto another, separate computer that has no electronic connection with the Facebook receiving machine. The link is broken: we can't follow it. It's downloaded from the new computer onto a flash drive, a memory stick, to be sent from an Internet café without leaving any trace to a sender or a recipient.'

After another silence Bradley said, 'So we're entirely dependent on your breaking the code?'

'We can't rely on that being sufficient until we read the message. It might be incomplete, not giving us enough information. We need to find al Aswamy.'

'What about al Aswamy's cell phone; you're tapping that, right?' demanded Bradley, searching for wiggle room.

From his desk Singleton said, 'It's not currently switched on. There haven't been any e-mails or voice mails.'

'There must be another way!' insisted Bradley, hoping it didn't sound like a plea, which it was.

'Al Aswamy!' exclaimed Irvine in abrupt awareness. 'Was he carrying anything when he left Ely Place, a bag or an obvious computer case maybe?'

After the third confused silence of the day from Langley, Bradley said, 'I don't know.'

'For fuck's sake, find out!' yelled Irvine.

An official GCHQ car, with a security-cleared driver, enabled Sally Hanning to keep in cell phone contact with London throughout the journey. Sally had known Director-General David Monkton would be with Jeremy Dodson when she arrived at Thames House just after midnight. She hadn't been told of a third man.

'You convinced us sufficiently to call in the Cabinet Secretary,' announced Dodson, as he introduced Sir Peregrine North, a grey-haired, patrician-featured man whose soft handshake matched a marshmallow voice.

'Have you warned Sellafield?' Sally asked at once.

'Maximum alert, army units on standby,' confirmed Dodson just as briskly. 'Let's hope you're not mistaken.'

Dodson very much hoped she would be, Sally knew. 'After all the bungling there's already been, let's all hope I'm not,' she retorted, ignoring the differing expressions between North and David Monkton. 'What about identification from the photographs I had wired from Cheltenham?'

'Have you any idea how big the terrorist suspect list is!' protested Dodson.

'I didn't ask how long the list was.' She was being peremptory, verging on impertinence, Sally accepted.

'Which leaves us with the rest of your evidence to assess,' urged Monkton.

'And to act upon it quickly if you're right,' emphasized North, infusing urgency into his muted voice. 'There's been considerable emergency mobilization with nothing to substantiate it apart from your conviction.'

'Is there a screen with a DVD player?' asked Sally, aware of Dodson's satisfied smirk at the Cabinet Secretary's reservation.

'Waiting,' said Dodson. He was still flushed from their irritable exchange and knew it.

To the other two men, Sally said, 'You probably already know that the photographs I sent from GCHQ are pornographic. So are the DVDs I want you to see. I'm not uncomfortable; please don't be on my account.'

The viewing was set up in an anteroom to the Director-General's office, chairs already arranged. The three men sat. Sally remained standing and said, 'What you're going to see could be dismissed as teenage obscenity or average stag-night entertainment, which is precisely what I believe it was intended to be mistaken for were it intercepted: the sort of stuff that's on a lot of computers belonging to men of Roger Bennett's age and background. He was twenty-one, remember. . . .' She turned to the television. 'Here's the first. It had been wiped, but GCHQ recovered it from the hard drive.'

On the screen appeared a pastoral scene—hedgerows, a country lane, cows in a distant field—with a sound of birdsong. Into the frame came a group of Western-dressed men and women, all Caucasian. Some of the men were darker, more Mediterranean complexioned than the others; two of them were bearded. Three of the women had the same dark colouring. The group came to a crossroads and had an animated although mostly inaudible discussion in what nevertheless sounded like English. One of the darker-skinned men pointed, without comment. Unquestioningly the group took the indicated direction. The film cut to a hedged field, in which the women in the group were laying out picnic rugs and food hampers but being jostled by the men into feigned wrestling that quickly degenerated into supposed rape, two blond-haired women held by some of the men for the pleasure of the others.

Sally abruptly stopped the DVD, putting the disk on rewind before turning back to the room. 'What did you see?'

'Filth,' said an even-redder-faced Dodson, looking for agreement from the Director-General, who ignored him.

North said, 'I presume the significance was in the background? They took the direction of the street sign to Seascale, the nearest village to Sellafield.'

'And the signpost had the county identification of Cumbria,' endorsed Monkton.

'Sellafield,' confirmed Sally, 'scene of a disastrous fire that destroyed a reactor and released 750 tcrabecquerels of radioactive material into the atmosphere, including dangerous iodine-131 that can be absorbed by humans. That closed-down reactor still contains fifteen tons of uranium fuel that can't be finally decommissioned until 2037, according to the information I accessed from my iPhone on the way back here.' Neither Monkton nor North was betraying any embarrassment or outrage at the film, she saw as she started the DVD again.

Almost at once Sally freeze-framed the rape scene, using the remote-control zoom to enlarge as much as possible the features of a man who still remained indistinct, almost hidden at the rear of the watching group. 'I believe this man is our murder victim, Roger Bennett. And hope that identification will be confirmed when the film is subjected to better forensic enhancement.' Sally moved the zoom, isolating the bearded, direction-choosing man and two blond women. 'Remember these particular faces.'

She unfroze the film but stopped it again at the fake orgy. 'Look particularly at the faces of the two blond women who are the supposed victims and the man at the signpost who is one of the rapists. They seem almost anxious to show their facial features.' She stopped and extracted the disk, replacing it with another. 'This is the stills collage that I had individually transmitted from GCHQ for the comparison with known or suspected terrorists. There are twelve in total, and in all the two bearded men and the two blondes predominate. I'd guess the still photographs were taken on the same day as the first movie: the discarded clothes are the same, and I think we might be able to date it by enhanced photo-analysis. They might be naked, but both men and the smaller of the two blondes are wearing elaborate wristwatches, which might have a calendar facility. I don't know what significance it might have, but I think it's worth forensically testing. I also suggested there should be very careful analysis of every piece of dialogue, beyond the usual porn-movie grunt and groan, that can be recovered from the first film and the one you're about to see.'

Sally changed disks again. 'Different day, because there are different clothes discarded and it's consensual sex this time, which isn't the intended focus. And the Roger Bennett figure doesn't appear. There's no mistaking the establishment in the background: it's the positive identification of Sellafield, the first British nuclear-processing site to produce weapons-grade plutonium-239.'

She finally turned off the television, picking up the printout bundle from the side of the television table. 'These are the entire textural content of the hard drive that was wiped before the NSA interception and what remained afterwards. There's nothing of obvious significance, but there is what I consider a peculiarity. A substantial amount of the text material is gambling tips, horse and dog racing. At least six are specifically inter-esting: they show no sender locations, apart from coming from a German Internet source, meaning they were sent from anonymous memory sticks. That was how Bennett got the message that was picked up by NSA.'

Sally waited for a reaction, but none came from the three men fac-ing her. Hurriedly she went on, 'I believe what I've recovered indicates an imminent attack upon the Sellafield nuclear installation. If it succeeds—certainly if it causes a nuclear leak—it'll rank with 9/11 in New York or 7/7 here in London—'

'Stop!' broke in North, at last. 'On precisely *what* are you basing these assumptions!'

Sally saw another satisfied smirk from Dodson. 'The presence of the man I believe to be Roger Bennett, whose personal and police photographs I've studied. And the memory stick e-mails from a German source, from which the NSA interception emanated.'

'We don't know that the e-mails you've isolated *are* from the same German source, that they're even *from* Germany!' seized Dodson, exaggerating the incredulity. 'It isn't sufficient for you just to *believe* that one hazy image could be Roger Bennett to have raised an alarm like this; we'd need more than that even if it were Bennett. I think we should consider standing down.'

'I didn't decree the alarm level, although I think it's justified,' defended Sally. 'It's the middle of the night now; it would be inconvenient as well as a mistake to reduce or withdraw what's been put in place until the full forensic examinations are completed.'

'The longer we leave the emergency in place, the greater the danger that there'll be an information leak, screaming headlines, public panic, and embarrassing parliamentary explanation,' persisted Dodson.

'Better a false alarm than the screaming headlines and public panic that would result from a nuclear leak we'd failed quickly enough to prevent,' said Sally.

'A drawdown at this hour is impractical,' decided Monkton. 'We'll give forensics until the morning.'

'But no longer than the morning,' stressed North. 'I fear we've cried wolf here.'

The Director-General answered the anteroom extension to his personal internal telephone, listening without interruption and remaining momentarily silent, head bowed. He replaced the receiver and turned back to the others. 'The man at the street sign is Hasib Hussain, but in Germany he calls himself Horst Becker. He tops their most-wanted terrorist list.'

Dodson's face was ashen.

7

'WE'VE GOT HIM!' PALPABLE RELIEF WAS IN JAMES BRADLEY'S voice.

'No, we haven't,' refused Irvine, concealing his similar feeling in front of what remained of his blank-faced audience. After the conclusion of the first exchange with Langley, Barker and Malik had left to compare the minimal transliteration they believed already achieved from the ongoing random high-velocity sweep.

'We've got an area,' insisted the CIA man.

'We enhanced the signals search for his cell phone and computer after your surveillance supervisor finally remembered that al Aswamy was carrying a computer sack,' persisted Irvine. 'The signal was traced somewhere in Brentwood, Northeast DC, but it was too faint for coordinates. The area's still too big. And presumably he's still got his motorcycle transport.'

'It's a good enough location to put in a new team.'

'Try to make it a better crew than the last one,' said Irvine heavily.

'I've briefed them personally,' assured Bradley, reluctant to capitulate again, but conscious of his weaker position. 'We'll find the son of a bitch, and this time we won't lose him. You staying at Fort Meade tonight?'

'Of course.'

'I'll be here at Langley. That's where to find me.'

'We need to meet tomorrow, whatever happens,' said Irvine. 'Your field-work has got to be better than this.'

'All of those things and more. Let's talk in the morning, assess where we are. Fix a meet then.'

'You're right,' agreed Burt Singleton, as Irvine replaced the receiver. 'This is a bad start that could turn into a full-scale disaster. We've already gone over our agreed deadline: the other Homeland Security agencies should be brought in first thing tomorrow.'

'I know.' Irvine paused. 'It went too well and too easily in the beginning, made us forget there'd be setbacks.' Made *me* forget, he mentally corrected himself.

'That's the flaw,' picked up Marian Lowell. 'It only needs one glitch. There's a straw to clutch at if the cell and computer signals stay in Brentwood. I can't think of an obvious target there.'

'What reason do we have for believing al Aswamy's still with his phone or computer?' punctured Singleton. 'From the bus-and-motorcycle routine, he suspects he's under surveillance, taking precautions at least. Wouldn't the obvious evasion be to lay a false trail by dumping them?'

'If he were doing that, he would have left both turned on, to give out a stronger signal,' argued Marian. 'He's being cautious, is all. He'll be imagining it's a gang dispute with the Annapolis group.'

Barker and Malik filed back into the room. Malik shook his head, not needing to say anything. Barker said, 'Looks like a long haul.'

'I'll sleep over, too,' decided Singleton. 'Keep on top of the signals check.'

So far the team had every reason to doubt his leadership, Irvine accepted; now Singleton had even elected himself the protective guardian.

Unlike their American counterparts, Italian carabinieri, Special Forces units, and the anti-terrorist division of the CISR, Italy's security service, were well prepared. Within a day of receiving the NSA warning of a potential attack, they'd traced the Internet café just off the via Ludovisi to which the original suspect e-mail had been sent from Cairo and attached monitoring intercepts on all its terminals. The café was also put under physical surveillance. CISR code-breakers, equipped by the original NSA interception with the domain code, took only half a day deciphering the next transmission from Egypt. It identified the Colosseum as the symbolic target to be rigged on a linked chain of charges set to explode at the height of the following day's tourist excursions; the expectation was that people who survived the blasts would be crushed beneath the total collapse of the remaining complete wall of the two-thousand-year-old structure.

The Italian military-led operation in the event of the attack materializing was devised in two days. To avoid detection by the still-unidentified terrorists during the day of the possible attack, a hundred Special Force commandos in civilian clothes infiltrated the ancient amphitheatre in twos and threes among the guided tourist groups. Their bags and backpacks contained AK-47 rifles and Beretta handguns. Another thirty army engineers, in civilian overalls, went in as apparently part of the permanent maintenance staff. As well as more weaponry, their tool bags and backpacks contained infrared night-vision scopes and heat-seeking sensors as well as heavy battery-generated floodlights and special noise equipment.

The buildup was matched outside the structure. During Rome's frenetic evening rush hour, unmarked cars and vans began gradually moving into position on all approach roads, with backup squads radiating out behind them. Each was connected by dedicated radio link in addition to open-channel conference telephone facilities. The entire outside of the Colosseum was under night-vision infrared surveillance. Two helicopters were on take-off standby in the Borghese Gardens.

The attack began precisely at 2:30 a.m., at timed intervals, down the via Claudia in four vehicles, a lead car and three vans carrying their explosives, detonator caps, and connection cables to ensure a simultaneous detonation sufficient to destroy at least a hundred yards of the still-intact outer wall overlooking the area where tourist coaches disembarked their passengers.

Two men in the lead car were instantly visible on the external infrared surveillance, silently alerting those waiting in ambush both inside and
outside the Colosseum. The moment the two got out, both carrying heavy
satchels, their vehicle moved away towards the shadowed Nero Park. Despite the infrared facility it was impossible to see the tools with which
the two worked on an entry door into the Colosseum. It opened as the
first of the following vans approached down the via Claudia. From the
rear three men emerged, formed a chain, and transferred equipment
sacks into the monument. As the first van followed the car into the park's
shadows, the second van arrived to continue the explosives transfer, followed
by the third to the vacant unloading area.

It was completed by 3:30 a.m.

The vehicle drivers spaced their return from the parking area, the last
two lingering at the door through which the others had already entered,
checking all the outside approach roads. The telephone alert that the entire group was inside was duplicated over the radio. Initially only four Special Forces teams moved. One squad completely blocked the door through
which the terrorists had entered with a large, multi-spiked control barrier ironically similar to some of the outwardly spiked fighting machines
manipulated by gladiators two thousand years earlier. The other groups
blocked every other possible exit with identical barriers.

At another silent command, the remaining anti-terrorist specialists and
police moved into place, totally surrounding the huge amphitheatre from
the outside.

The interception was perfectly coordinated. At a radio signal, the arena
floodlights and those carried in earlier burst on simultaneously with those
outside. Simultaneously, too, the decibel-shattering scream of psychological-
warfare sirens erupted. The Special Forces and police were earplugged
against the disorienting noise. The deafening cacophony drowned the brief
exchange of gunfire, in which only one of the intended bombers was slightly
wounded. Twelve out of the total of twenty attackers surrendered without
a fight.

The attempt to destroy Rome's most famous antiquity created an international furor, heightened within hours—to America's discomfort—by confirmation of the wounded man's identity.

Sally Hanning got back to Thames House by nine, having showered and changed and showing no trace of only having had three hours sleep. Neither did the meticulous David Monkton, who'd slept at the MI5 headquarters. To Sally's well-concealed bewilderment she was ushered into the anteroom in which, four hours earlier, they'd watched pornographic films. The previous night's television table was now laid for breakfast, two chairs set in readiness.

Looking at Sally's overnight bag, Monkton announced, 'I've decided against your going to Sellafield.'

'It's my case,' immediately protested Sally.

'Which is acknowledged in the official commendation I'm attaching to your file today.' Monkton buttered his toast. 'The operation becomes physical interception now: SAS Special Forces and police snatch squads.'

Sally sat where Monkton indicated and poured coffee but ignored the food. 'What happens if there's no attack?'

'The cordon stays in place. Cleaned-up facial photographs of the groups will be issued to Special Branch and anti-terrorist units at every port and airport exit in the country. There's no government decision this early about publicly issuing the pictures, which is what the German anti-terrorist agency wants. . . .' Monkton looked at his watch. 'There's a German squad getting here in two hours. They've been trying to get Horst Becker, aka Hasib Hussain, for the past year: he was the leader and the only one to escape from a terrorist bombing in Hamburg that killed ten people last October.'

'What about territorial rivalry?' presciently asked Sally, pouring herself more coffee.

Monkton shook his head. 'The arrest will be ours. It's inevitable, I suppose, that Berlin will seek extradition, but Becker's not an adoptive German national as far as I know. It's a matter for the attorney-general and home secretary. We'll certainly have a precedence claim.'

'What precedence?'

'The Germans are suggesting Becker might have killed Roger Bennett. Those the police did catch and arrest after the Hamburg atrocity describe Becker as someone who enjoys killing.'

'What about the indistinct photograph on the first porn movie?' demanded Sally.

Monkton allowed a bleak smile at the persistence. 'Forensic came back an hour ago. They're putting the possibility that it's Bennett at seventy percent.'

'And the e-mails?'

'Still being assessed.'

'Why Bennett?' reflected Sally, helping herself at last to a croissant. 'And why kill him so publicly? If he hadn't been murdered and his body dumped so publicly the terrorists could easily have got to Sellafield.'

'They almost did,' reminded Monkton. 'And it's only speculation that Becker or anyone else in the group *was* involved in the killing. I'm equally curious at how and why a petty criminal like Bennett—which is what he was, certainly not someone with any political ideology—came to be with these people in the first place.'

Was this breakfast and this conversation—and not letting her complete the case, which was the normal procedure right up to a prosecution—some kind of test? wondered Sally. 'Let's keep in mind that forensic are stopping short of a positive identification, but run with the hypothesis that it is Bennett. The only reason for his inclusion has surely to be that he *was* disposable: brought in to serve some purpose but to be discarded after that purpose was achieved.'

'You've already flawed your argument,' insisted the Director-General.

'Disposable, sure; but why would professional terrorists leave the body so publicly? Wouldn't they sink it in a reservoir, bury it in a landfill, anything to avoid attracting attention until after the attack?'

'He did something wrong, and he needed to be made an example of.'

Monkton nodded cautiously. 'Still leaves unanswered why he was involved in the first place.'

'Identification,' Sally continued to speculate. 'Becker came from Germany, maybe with others. Let's surmise that Bennett, who must have had a passport that we haven't yet traced, was a link man between a terrorist group here and Becker and maybe others from Germany.'

'That has possibilities. But there are still some gaping holes.'

This had to be a bizarre test, Sally determined. 'But then Bennett did something wrong.'

Jeremy Dodson's arrival stopped Monkton's response, although the operations director did not immediately speak, clearly as surprised as Sally at the breakfast preparations. After several moments Dodson said, 'None of our in-house specialists can make anything that's relevant from the gambling messages. I've gone back to GCHQ for help and—'

'I did that already,' interrupted Sally. 'They described these sorts of exchanges as kids' stuff; they couldn't determine significance.'

'Kids don't attack nuclear installations,' rejected Dodson, not bothering to conceal the resentment.

'Which is why it's so clever: everything is done or phrased to be dismissed,' retorted Sally, contemptuous of the man's attitude. 'What about the particular e-mails that I drew attention to?'

Dodson coloured. 'I marked them for specific attention by GCHQ.'

'That wasn't my question. Did they come from the same Cologne Internet café as the NSA intercepts!'

'Those IP addresses without sender identification did come from the Cologne Internet café,' pedantically confirmed Dodson, stone-faced.

'That gives me something to work on if I'm not going to Sellafield,' said Sally. In addition to constantly watching her back against Dodson's retribution, she thought.

Just after four in the morning Jack Irvine translated sufficiently to give them a partial message. It was predicated on colloquial Gilaki—one of the predominant Iranian languages—but further disguised by Dari dialect phrases and terms. He didn't initially wake the snoozing Singleton for help, wanting to decipher the entire encryption himself, but he admitted defeat just before dawn. Once awake, Singleton took a while to recognize the rhythm, needing the reference manuals more than the younger man, but refreshed by his rest he made quicker progress. It was Irvine, though, who guessed at a further Dari encryption as the words began to formulate.

'Now all we've got to do is work out what it means,' agreed Singleton, looking down at the translated message:

Fourth first in the war and first to the brothers.

8

SALLY HANNING WAS AS CONFUSED AS MI5'S HEAD OF OPERATIONS but hid it better than Jeremy Dodson, who throughout the breakfast encounter limited himself to yes or no responses whenever possible and minimal mutterings when it wasn't. To Monkton's final instruction—that anything, no matter how seemingly insignificant, be immediately taken to Sally—the man only just managed a head jerk, refusing verbally to acknowledge his messenger-boy function.

Sally was irritated, too. She was officially the Sellafield case officer—which justified her receiving everything, although not that Dodson be the courier—and regulations required that if at all practicable, case officers should be present at the conclusion of an operation. Here it would have been both easy and practicable, incurring no physical risk whatsoever, for her to remain at some safe control point. She also didn't like being used as the pawn in whatever humiliation Monkton was inflicting upon the head of his operational division. Dodson clearly featured to some degree in the failure to respond earlier and deserved reprimand or censure, but today's episode was childish, pulling wings off a fly to stop its annoying buzz. It was positively distracting, determined Sally, as she settled back into her unexpectedly returned office. She stored the unneeded overnight bag by her single filing cabinet, pulling out a lower drawer to accommodate the blotter, filing trays, and her favourite photograph of her dead parents from her desk to create space to arrange the printouts of the betting tips recovered from Roger Bennett's computer. Lastly, determined against any distraction, she turned off her computer and cell phone and told the switchboard she didn't want any interrupting external calls. Twenty-six printouts were in the computer's standard 12-point, Times New Roman font. Additionally, overnight a second set of printouts had been greatly enhanced at MI5's north London forensic laboratory. Neither location nor date for any of the horse or dog-track meetings had appeared on the slips, which seemed to have been scanned onto an e-mail from a selection of newspapers and tipster magazines. Obfuscation, Sally reminded herself: nothing intended to be understood as it was actually represented. What message or messages could be hidden among horse-racing and dog-track meetings? A lot. Each slip selection held variations of three to four animal names, which usually extended beyond a single word. The longest was five: sixteen horse races, ten dog-track events. All printed in English, so presumably all English meetings. No, not necessarily: animals ran under their English names at foreign events. Sally separated the horse selections from the dog recommendations and tried to make out something—anything— significant by merging or combining words or minimal phrases. She gave up on the fifth horse race. It would need a computer—and more days than they might have left—to cross-compile every possible computation and at the end still likely achieve nothing. Sally's mind was blocked. The slips *had* been subjected to the highest degree of computer analysis on the state-of-the-art specialized equipment at GCHQ. The switchboard ban was against incoming, not outgoing, calls, she decided.

It took a full thirty minutes to satisfy Cheltenham security of her identity and that she was talking on a guaranteed secure line before she was connected to the man she knew only as John.

Before Sally was able to query the faint reception echo, he said, 'We've obviously been told about Sellafield. We're on top alert, so this call's being recorded and simultaneously listened to.'

Who'd raised the Cheltenham alert, Monkton or Dodson? 'Tell me what checks you carried out on the betting slips.'

'Trigger-word comparisons,' replied the man at once. 'We made three programs, one ASCII for Roman-letter transliteration, one Arabizi Arabic, and one classic Arabic, of familiar greetings and farewells, a range of Arab religious reference, words like *Al Qaeda, Roger,* and *Bennett*—both separately and together—*Sellafield,* and atomic and nuclear terminologies.'

'What's ASCII?'

'Computers can read numbers, not letters,' responded the GCHQ official, eager to display his expertise. 'ASCII is the numeric code for Roman script. The original was IPv4, which divides into thirty-two bits that include separating decimal dots. When everyone up to and including their herders for their yaks began buying computers, capacity had to be increased to satisfy demand. IPv6 was developed in 1995 with 128 bits.'

'Arabizi's colloquial Arabic, right?' queried Sally, wanting to make some contribution.

'We call it chat-room Arabic. Classic Arabic is obviously the written version. All three were run through high-velocity supercomputers, scanning at a thousandth of a second, seeking a match or combinations of the words on the slips for an alternative translation from what they appeared to be. There was nothing.'

'What else?'

'We're locked onto Bennett's computer address, although we know you have it, to intercept any further messages from Germany from anyone who might not know Bennett's dead. And we're monitoring the Cologne Internet café.'

'And?'

There was a pause from Cheltenham. 'What else did you expect?'

'Could you build another programme from the betting slip names to find the locations and dates of the horse- and dog-racing meetings?'

'That's not how we work,' mildly protested John.

'But could you do it, with the facilities you have there?' pressed Sally, curbing the impatience.

'It's technically possible, yes.'

'And having done that—and getting the complete race cards—could you get the first-, second-, third- and fourth-place winners if the events have already taken place?'

'What significance, what connection, are you looking for?'

'I don't know,' confessed Sally emptily. 'But there's *something*. There has to be: everything on that computer has or had a purpose.'

'Stay on the line,' ordered the man.

Sally did, straining to pick up any of the discussion obviously taking place, but heard nothing.

'Your instincts have been good so far,' said John, coming back on the line.

'You'll do it?'

'I'll come back to you if there's anything.'

'Today?'

There was another hesitation. 'I hope so.'

Sally welcomed the reference to instinct, not luck, although for the first time ever she accepted that luck wouldn't have gone amiss.

Luck was very much on Charles Johnston's mind, three thousand miles away in his Langley office. Outside his door glowed the red DO NOT DISTURB warning. All calls were on hold for him to properly evaluate the heaven sent, career-protecting approach he wouldn't have anticipated in a million years. His response couldn't be delayed, though. It had to be today, within the hour; because of the time difference it was already afternoon in London, and it was imperative the request wasn't extended to anyone but him.

E-mail or telephone? E-mails created electronic trails. Telephone conversations could—and certainly would from his end—be recorded, but security was guaranteed between sender and recipient; he felt safer with telephones. It came with another absolute essential: every exchange was strictly one-to-one.

The connection was quicker than Johnston expected. He'd gathered up what he thought might be necessary from the minimal briefing dossier, but wasn't properly ready with his recording system when David Monkton came on from London.

'An unexpected surprise, hearing from you after so long,' Johnston greeted, hurriedly activating the machine.

'Good of you to get back so quickly. Wasn't sure the e-mail address I had would still work after the transfer.'

'It worked just fine.' Johnston had met Monkton the previous year at a NATO security conference in Brussels, before Johnston's transfer from the CIA's Profiling and Analysis division to covert operations.

'Congratulations at the promotion.'

'Thanks.' Johnston frowned, inherently cautious. 'Didn't expect the news to have reached London.'

'We've got an efficient embassy in Washington.'

Too efficient, thought Johnston. 'Your e-mail referred to terrorism?'

'It's an imposition,' apologized Monkton in advance. 'You're the only person I know at the proper level. What I'm looking for is an introduction to whomever I need to talk with in the FBI, Homeland Security, or NSA. And I'd appreciate guidance on which of the three I should go to.'

It *had* to be the UK alert from the National Security Agency, decided Johnston, satisfaction at his initial guess surging through him. 'That's a pretty wide canvas. You want to be a little more specific?'

'From one of your NSA intercepts we're now going to be able to prevent a terrorist attack on one of our nuclear installations. I've got an idea I want to talk through with the person in Washington who's controlling those intercepts. I'm guessing NSA, but I don't want to waste time going to the wrong place. There've been too many public problems involving all of us, haven't there?'

It was scarcely taking a chance, reasoned Johnston, picking the slip from the open dossier. He could always row back, excusing what he said as a misunderstanding about another totally different operation. 'Did that intercept read, "Invite the brothers to the celebration?" '

The silence from London lasted several moments. 'That's exactly how it read.'

'You're talking to the person who's controlling those intercepts.'

Johnston had correctly guessed the subject of Monkton's call, but the thirty-minute conversation that followed was completely different from what Johnston had imagined, so much so that to keep the eagerness from his voice he at times stayed with single-word responses to reassure Monkton that he was still on the line. Johnston's longest contribution was to insist that his co-operation was dependent upon everything's remaining strictly between the two of them and conducted solely by telephone until he decreed otherwise.

'Your project, your rules,' agreed Monkton.

The thwarted attempt to kill hundreds of tourists in the destruction of one of the world's greatest antiquities was obviously the biggest international news story of the day. It escalated with the mid-morning journalistic scoop disclosing the wounded man's identity and escalated even further with Al Jazeera showing on both its Arabic and English-language channels a terrorist video sent to the station in advance of the Rome attack.

The film opened on a split screen, one-half showing an official portrait of Giovanni Moro to establish that the long-haired, tightly bearded man on the opposite half of the picture was unquestionably the grandson of Aldo Moro, the two-time Italian prime minister assassinated in May 1978 by Italy's Red Brigade terrorists.

Giovanni Moro spoke in impeccable English from behind a desk in an undisclosed room. The predominant, greatly enlarged photograph on the wall behind him was of his grandfather's body as it had been found in the boot of a Renault 4 on Rome's via Michelangelo Caetani. Beside that major photograph was a slightly smaller although clearly visible picture of a man its caption referred to as Steve Pieczenik.

In a level, unemotional voice Moro said he had obvious personal as well as ideological reasons for his rejecting his country to live in exile in the Basque country of northwest Spain, and for his converting to Islam to embrace it and its opposition to the American-dominated West. His grandfather had literally been sacrificed in a plan orchestrated by the CIA—an intelligence organization matching in evil the then-Russian KGB and now its FSB successor—to prevent the Italian Communist PCI party from gaining a coalition position in the Christian Democrat government of the day.

The man gestured to the second photograph, claimed to be that of Steve Pieczenik. This man, declared Moro, was the then-U.S. State Department official sent from Washington to mastermind the killing. 'So blatantly arrogant were the U.S. government and its pernicious Central Intelligence Agency that this man Picczenik openly admitted the crime,' continued Moro. 'He went on public record to boast, "We had to sacrifice Aldo Moro to maintain the stability of Italy." What he really meant was to maintain the United States' control of the affairs of Italy, a determination it retains to this day throughout the world, particularly against Islamic countries.'

Moro was issuing the video for publication in the event of his death or capture, concluded his diatribe. If he was captured alive and put before a court, he would use the trial as a platform from which to illustrate further examples of America's manipulative global interference.

The U.S. State Department's premature denial, within an hour of the Al Jazeera Qatar transmission, was directly and just as promptly contradicted by 1987 television news footage of Pieczenik actually making the quoted admission, adding a diplomatic dimension to an attempted act of sensational terrorism.

Charles Johnston wasn't sure if the current Colosseum attack and past incidents, both ultimately traceable back to the covert operations directorate, were a personal danger or potential benefit, but self-protective as always he ordered a full copy of the Al Jazeera transmission and the complete case records of the Aldo Moro killing. He took it as another sign of good luck that no-one had tried to retrieve the records ahead of him.

Five hours earlier Akram Malik, the new American, had put forward his suggested deciphering, which Irvine hesitantly accepted at Burt Single ton's announcement that al Aswamy had turned his computer and cell phone on.

'He could be getting ready to move!' said Marian.

9

'WHAT'S THE MOST QUOTED EULOGY FOR GEORGE WASHINGTON?' rhetorically demanded Malik. 'That of General Henry Lee—that Washington was "first in war, first in peace, and first in the hearts of his countrymen." What's beaten us all night, until now? The three different encryptions for the word *first*, then changing again the *f* and the *t* in *fourth* to stop us from getting a match with the letters in the following repetitions is as clever as hell.'

'Isn't it all *too* clever as hell from an Arab source, throwing our own history back at us?' queried Shab Barker, also thinking like the American he had become.

'I don't think so,' said Marian Lowell. 'I'm reading it—interpreting it—as proof that it's coming from NSA's Iranian equivalent, which I thought we'd already agreed was the level of expertise we're confronting.'

'Can't we get signal coordinates from al Aswamy's computer and cell, now that he's turned them on!' demanded an anxious James Bradley, on the open line from Langley. 'I got people on standby, ready to move.'

'We're trying to make out the coordinates, for Christ's sake!' snapped Irvine, encumbered by the telephone headset that left him hands-free for his computer. They were all wound tighter than springs; he didn't care that his tension was obvious to the rest of his team.

From the computer station from which he was monitoring the increased signals, Singleton said, 'I'm worried al Aswamy's deflecting attention from however they're moving to a target elsewhere.'

'They've only been turned on for four minutes.' Irvine tried to calm down. 'I'm into his Facebook and the cell: the first key he hits, I'll know.'

'It's the Washington Monument, matching the arrogance of the Pentagon and the White House attempt of 9/11!' insisted Malik. 'The monument is actually in the White House sight line: the Oval Office would be hit by the shock waves of an explosion. The "fourth" referred to in their message signifies their move, in what they consider their war. Its success will be the "first" for their group.'

'I'm not waiting any longer,' insisted Singleton.

'We're not,' agreed Irvine. Into his mouthpiece he said, 'We're going to warn Homeland Security.'

'I already did, thirty minutes ago,' admitted Bradley. When he'd tried to notify Charles Johnston, a secretary told him the covert operations director couldn't be interrupted until further notice.

'It'll be total lockdown,' predicted Irvine, taking off the headset, in which he felt vaguely ridiculous. 'An hour from now it'll be on every news channel you can think of.'

'Which is what it should be if the monument—with the White House in range—is the target,' said Malik, considering the alert his vindication from the initial doubt of the others in the group.

'What if it isn't?' demanded Irvine. 'Al Aswamy will know now he's being officially tracked, so he'll abort any alternative. And we'll lose him from this end.'

'Losing him from this end is better than risking whatever might have happened in downtown Washington in full sight and blast range of the White House,' said Singleton, not looking away from his computer screen.

'Not if their suspicion goes as far as believing it's at our level,' persisted Irvine.

'You sure you're looking at this from the right perspective, Jack?' Marian frowned, crossing to where the man sat. 'It isn't us five and a few at the CIA, Superman and his elves, battling global terrorism into imploding: "Hallelujah, Gotham City's saved!" We're a minuscule part of a microcosm, working an idea that had some early success—according to its doubtful justification—an idea that I, personally, still have some problems with. You waited too long on this. You've still risked God knows what and God knows how many lives if al Aswamy's target isn't the Washington Monument and he manages an atrocity someplace else. And if he does, I'm walking away from this because I think you're on an ego trip for some personal reason and have forgotten what our function is.'

'And in those circumstances, I'm walking with her,' added Singleton at once.

'I'm on NBC,' announced Shab Barker, looking away from his computer screen. 'They've just cut into the *Today* show with a news break: major terrorist alert in Constitution Gardens and the Mall. White House is in lockdown, as you predicted.'

'And the targets are moving!' declared Singleton, hunched back over his screen. 'Both signals, but . . .'

'I've got them on my screen, too,' came in Bradley, from the speakerphone.

'I've got a coordinate for Rhode Island Avenue and Utah . . . ,' cried out Malik, his voice trailing towards the end.

'And Rhode Island and Windom,' finished Singleton. 'However many there are, they've split, going in completely opposite directions.'

'I'm sealing Rhode Island Avenue in both directions,' reported Bradley. 'Got helicopters up, full liaison with Homeland Security, everyone involved who should be involved.' Which included the CIA director, Bradley added to himself.

Al Aswamy's cell phone was found an hour later, wedged in the roof-mounted luggage rack of a Volvo heading into Washington. The computer had been lodged among a beet crop bound for Annapolis in an open-backed Toyota flatbed. Both vehicles had refueled at a gas station on the DC boundary.

At just after two that afternoon, English time, Jeremy Dodson arrived at Sally's office, pointedly entering without knocking. Fluttering the papers he carried, Dodson said, 'Forensic enjoyed the blue movies.'

Sally sighed. 'What did they find?'

'Nothing. Complete waste of time.'

Sally took the report from the man, skimming through its findings. Only one of the date windows she'd isolated on the wristwatches for particular examination showed a full legible number under maximum photographic enlargement: 31. Only a single digit—3—had been recovered from the chronometer of the second man. Reflected sunlight from the woman's watch face had destroyed any possibility of a date being visible. Sally put the report aside, looking up to the man, who'd pulled a chair forward from the wall and appeared comfortably seated. 'The thirty-first is today's date.'

'July had thirty-one days, too,' retorted Dodson. 'So that's when your porn movie was made, if you're trying for a significance. And the other guy probably had the correct date, too, just missing the one.'

Nothing was to be gained by talking to this man, Sally recognized. 'Is there anything else?'

'I'm hoping you'll tell me.'

'Tell you what?'

'What the hell's going on! Did you include me in your complaint about Bradford?'

Sally raised her hands in a warding-off gesture. 'I don't know what you did—or didn't—do about the original NSA warning. I'm not interested. Far too much *wasn't* done following the warning, which is why I've officially complained about Bradford. I'd expect there will be an internal enquiry, whatever the Sellafield outcome. I'm not interested in that, either. I certainly haven't filed any personal complaint about you. If you're curious about this morning's breakfast with Monkton, I don't know what the hell was going on there, either. Which *does* interest me. When I find out what it is, I'll deal with it by myself, for myself, which is how I suggest you handle your uncertainties.'

Dodson stared back at her for several moments, seeking a reply. 'I see,' he finally managed inadequately.

'So *is* there anything else?'

'You haven't heard about Rome?' Dodson stretched the incredulity

'Obviously not, if it happened in the last twenty-four hours,' said Sally impatiently. 'I spent it isolated here, trying to work out what I've missed.'

'There was an attempt to blow up the Colosseum; a relative of Aldo Moro's is involved. There's no other story on the news channels.'

But there was.

Sally's office television came on as she tuned in to security-distanced helicopter footage of the White House and the eerily deserted surrounding area, occupied only by police and emergency vehicles, with a voice-over account of the president's aerial evacuation to Camp David and the threat of an imminent terrorist attack.

Instinctively Dodson said, 'Good God!'

David Monkton responded on the first ring. Sally said, 'It's tonight. It was planned as a concerted global attack.'

Which it had been.

And would almost certainly have succeeded at Sellafield if the nuclear facility hadn't been on the highest alert. The attackers came in from the sea, the weakest security point. There were twelve, in two rigid-bottomed ribs running at minimal speed on muffled outboard engines, which stopped yards from the beach silently to coast in on what momentum was left. To reduce any noise further, the ribs were lifted, not dragged, up onto the beach. All twelve wore black coveralls, backpacks, and gloves. Their faces were cork-blackened behind night-vision goggles, also black. No words were spoken: all commands were hand-signaled to marshal the group into two lines—a lead man slightly ahead of each—to move up the beach.

The perfectly coordinated trap snapped shut when they were midway between the shoreline and the beach top. High-powered lights—blinding to night-vision infrared—burst on from a solid bank at the beach head, the signal for matchingly powered spotlights to blaze on from the Special Boat Service ribs that had followed in from the sea and now formed an unbroken line at the water's edge. The white light was completed from above by three helicopters instantly launched from inside the Sellafield plant to hover overhead. The surrender instructions, in English and German, were sufficiently amplified over the rotor noise to be clearly audible.

The disorientation was almost total, the blinded group snatching off their goggles and stumbling into each other in panicked confusion. Only three attempted any recovery, removing short-barreled Uzi automatic weapons from their backpacks as they discarded their goggles. Still blinded by the intensity of the light, two fired automatic bursts in the direction of the repeated surrender instructions. There was no overwhelming return fire. Three single marksmen shots brought down the two who'd fired; the third dropped his weapon and obeyed the new amplified instructions to separate from each other before prostrating themselves on the beach. Stun grenades—twelve to achieve temporary unconsciousness in such an unenclosed area—were dropped from the hovering helicopters. Several in the group were stirring, groping about uncertainly, but again sufficiently disoriented to be disarmed and restrained with wrist and ankle bindings.

The terrorist attack had commenced at 3:00 A.M., the significance of which had only taken Sally Hanning minutes to realize when, during the assault, she received the full details of the horse and greyhound selections from GCHQ.

That recognition fit all the other missing pieces of the failed jihad jigsaw over the following twenty-four hours.

10

THE POLITICAL DECISION, REACHED THAT SAME DAY BY PERSONAL telephone link between president and prime ministers, was to claim the failure of the three attacks proved the overwhelming Western supremacy in its war against terrorism. What wasn't agreed on in the hurry for public reassurances was a commonly worded statement.

In its exaggerated satisfaction at unexpected international admiration, Rome boasted its total crushing of all terrorist activity and ridiculed Giovanni Moro as a politically confused anachronism, inadvertently diminishing Washington's discomfort at its cynical abandonment of an Italian politician for similarly anachronistic reasons. At a glad-handing CIA/State Department meeting at Langley, chaired by Deputy Director Conrad Graham, Jack Irvine—while still not disclosing his Vevak entry—successfully argued that to divert Iranian suspicion of the level of their penetration, their public declaration should indicate the global plot had been detected by Britain's GCHQ. Charles Johnston, the outsider from the president's private praise, tried to get his involvement recognized by disclosing in a memo he security-limited to the White House and Irvine the secondment of a British MI5 officer to Operation Cyber Shepherd, correctly guessing it wouldn't be challenged in the euphoria of the moment. That euphoria was mirrored in London, despite David Monkton's irritation at Washington's identification of GCHQ and MI5. It was mitigated, however, by the recognition of London's speed in unraveling the international coordination of the attempted attacks; Sally Hanning's contribution was acknowledged, by name, in a strictly restricted memorandum circulated to the White House and Downing Street.

Sally's quickly realized significance of the horse-racing forecasts—coupled with the set-in-advance 31 date on what turned out to be Horst Becker's watch—was her ultimate breakthrough. The 31 showed not just on the Sellafield porn film but on the watch Giovanni Moro very visibly wore on his Al Jazeera video. Moro's watch also registered a three o'clock time, as did that on Becker's accomplice on the Sellafield film.

The forecasted winner of the three o'clock race at Rome's Capannelle meeting on the thirty-first was Centurion Revenge. That for the three o'clock at Maryland's Laurel Park for the thirty-first was Washington Demise. The matching time and date prediction for Cumbria's Carlisle racetrack was Atomic Disaster.

The fitting, concluding irony was that none of the predicted winners placed.

At Sally's persistence, as the day progressed, the computer found among Giovanni Moro's belongings and al Aswamy's computer were subjected to the same forensic examination as that of Roger Bennett. Both hard drives contained the same intended horse-racing mockery. The major discovery was the identification of Moro and al Aswamy on the porn movies.

It would take more than a month before every strand confirmed the extent of the global conspiracy and established al Aswamy's leadership role.

The more immediate, culminating sensation that day was the discovery during an obvious security check of two forty-pound bombs, constructed to Afghanistan IED design, within twenty feet of each other inside the Washington Monument. Both were primed by cell phone attachments to detonate when called from al Aswamy's BlackBerry: only the two detonator numbers were stored in its memory.

'You going to admit how totally fucking lucky we were?' Burt Singleton demanded of Jack Irvine. It was the first time the man had ever cursed in front of Marian Lowell, who once again didn't protest.

'No!' refused Irvine, drained of any satisfaction at the personal congratulations at the Langley meeting by the unimpressed reception of the Fort Meade team he'd briefed over the previous thirty minutes. 'I delayed too long before reverting to Homeland Security procedure. That's a mistake that won't happen again. Nor, hopefully, will the CIA lose a target like they lost al Aswamy. But we recovered and that didn't happen despite us: it happened through the professionalism of what we do and how we do it—*your* professionalism. From today, from today's meeting at Langley, any uncertainty's gone about Cyber Shepherd and its continued operational existence. We're a confirmed, active unit that the president himself knows about.'

'Does the president also know that we've lost al Aswamy, who from my reading of everything you've told us from today's assessment is a top-level Iranian agent moving freely not just around America but around the world—which obviously means different identities supported by different passports—organizing international attacks?' said Marian.

'Of course State took that on board,' said Irvine, exasperated at their lingering doubt at the justification for what they were doing. 'Today's meeting was a review of what we know of an ongoing situation, with still more to come out. But it was obvious Tehran is going to be hung out to dry diplomatically when we get more from Italy and the UK.'

'I don't think Rome's statement was well phrased,' suggested Shab Barker, tentatively offering a Muslim mind-set reaction. 'These were major, coordinated state-sponsored acts of terrorism, more so even than 9/11. There's a lot of jihadists and fundamentalists who'll read it as a challenge.'

'That's my assessment, too,' supported Akram Malik, savoring the acknowledgement at identifying the Washington Monument target.

'And State's view,' confirmed Irvine. He looked at Singleton. 'You can add Rome's mistake to your list.'

'I'm not making lists or issuing challenges, just trying to establish parameters,' dismissed the older man. 'On the subject of which, how was it between the CIA divas?'

'Strained,' judged Irvine, shrugging. 'The White House congratulations were to Conrad Graham for approving Cyber Shepherd. Until his announcement of a UK involvement, Johnston was virtually a sidelined observer.'

'What about that UK involvement?' pressed Marian. 'Whose idea was that?'

'What I know, you know,' said Irvine, shaking his head. 'That's why Harry Packer stayed behind in Washington, to find out more.'

'But it's MI5, not GCHQ?'

'That's what Johnston said.'

'So it doesn't directly impact on us like Tempura and hacking the telephones of world leaders did?'

'I supposed I'll have some contact at Langley,' said Irvine. He went to Singleton again 'I went into the Tehran botnet before I came down today. It's dormant.'

Singleton indicated his illuminated screen. 'It still is. I expect it to stay that way, don't you?'

'Locating al Aswamy here in America is down to Homeland Security and the FBI now. We stay with the Vevak botnet, permanently monitoring.' Irvine hesitated, the lack of response burning through him. 'Who knows,' he continued, concentrating on Singleton, 'maybe our luck will hold,' and wished he hadn't the moment he spoke.

'What more practicably have you got in mind?' asked Singleton, refusing to rise to the remark.

'What we've today been overwhelmingly sanctioned to do: move on, find more. Destroy more.' Irvine hoped this time the pause was better planned. 'I'd like to think you're all still with me in doing that.'

Barker and Malik smiled in reassurance, Malik actually nodding. Singleton and Marian Lowell remained expressionless.

'What you achieved, in such a short period of time, was remarkable,' opened David Monkton. That afternoon's one-to-one encounter in the

Director-General's river-view office was more formal, but the diminutive man still avoided the embarrassment of sitting behind his expansive desk, instead pacing around his office as if physical movement were part of his thought process. Twice he'd stopped close behind her, once with his hand on her chairback.

'Thank you,' said Sally inadequately. The Thames House rumor was that the bachelor Director-General was a misogynist, which made the very idea inconceivable, but it would have been easy to imagine that the man was working up to some physical approach. She was more curious than alarmed at the possibility.

'There've been a lot of high-level exchanges between Downing Street and Washington; your contribution's been made very clear,' said the man from somewhere behind her.

'That's extremely generous.' And a potential procedural breach, she thought: individual officers were never identified, under any circumstance.

Monkton came into view but ignored his chair, perching instead awkwardly on the front edge of the desk. 'What would your reaction be to my appointing you my director of operations?'

Sally was unaware of instinctively pulling her skirt farther to her knees until she was actually conscious of doing it and stopped, irritated. 'I'd appreciate the confidence, but it's not a role in which I've ever imagined myself. I've always considered myself a field officer, like my father.'

'Which is what you've overwhelmingly proven yourself to be and why I've changed my original intention.' Monkton smiled, a quick on-and-off expression. 'I'm attaching you, nominally, to our embassy in Washington. But you won't be working from our *rezidentura*. You'll be attached to the covert CIA unit that got onto the Sellafield attack in the first place. Will you have any personal difficulty with the posting?'

'Absolutely not,' said Sally, covering her surprise.

'I'd hoped there wouldn't be.'

She came forward in her seat, her concentration absolute. 'They've already agreed to this?'

Monkton's smile was longer this time. 'Without any hesitation.'

'Why so quickly?'

'I know, very slightly, the covert operations director in overall command of the unit.'

That wasn't sufficient reason, Sally decided. 'So you approached him? They didn't come to us?'

'Approached him accidentally, initially. And before you put so much of Sellafield together as you did.'

Which made the acceptance of an outsider even more difficult to understand. 'Who's my case officer?'

'Me, quite separately from the *rezidentura*. This is a totally restricted operation.'

More interoffice resentment, accepted Sally, who knew Jeremy Dodson had seen her pass his office on her way to this meeting with Monkton. 'What's my brief?'

'To find out how they did it. We almost missed out on Sellafield. I don't want to get that close to disaster again.'

Monkton surely didn't believe the CIA was casually going to share some secret route or source! Sally said, 'I can leave right away.'

'Be very careful.'

She'd need to be, Sally guessed.

All three sat unmoving in the covert director's suite, each mentally circling the other for the greatest territorial advantage.

'We could scarcely have imagined presidential approval,' opened James Bradley, establishing the high ground.

'But that's what we've got,' insisted Harry Packer, striving to keep the satisfaction from sounding too obvious. He'd had a personal congratulations from the White House: the name Harry Packer was known to the president! He hadn't missed a trick so far, now that Irvine's relocation costs had passed unchallenged. A lot of rungs—all with the very necessary salary increments—in Meade's promotional ladder were still to be climbed.

'As long as you continue to justify it,' qualified Johnston, distancing himself. 'What's the progress with al Aswamy?'

'Highest Homeland Security priority,' insisted Bradley. 'Every appropriate agency involved, top of the FBI Most Wanted list. Picture selection on every TV newscast tonight, in every newspaper tomorrow.'

'You think it's possible to entrap someone like al Aswamy, whom we now know to be a major Iranian terrorist, in a country the size of America, with the length of its seacoasts and land borders with Canada and Mexico?' said Johnston.

The other two men shared a hesitation. Point up the defeatism, Bradley decided. 'No, but we've sure as hell got to try, along with all the other agencies.'

Packer said, 'And we've still got our electronic trace.'

Johnston shifted, preparing himself. 'Unfortunate that you lost him when you did.'

The cocksucker had them under surveillance! seized Bradley. Why hadn't his own watch team picked up the tail!

'We didn't lose him electronically,' exaggerated Packer. Johnston was covering his ass against any later accusations.

'But you haven't got him in the bag.'

'We identified the Washington Monument—with its proximity to the White House—as the target,' insisted Packer.

'And risking the leak wasn't a difficult decision for me to make,' came in Bradley. 'I'm sure you would have confirmed it had I been able to reach you earlier than I did.'

'It's got to be us who gets al Aswamy, not another Homeland Security agency,' insisted Johnston.

'How do you intend this UK participation to work?' demanded Packer, more interested in the future than the past.

'She pulled together all we so far know about the combined attack,' said Johnston, also welcoming the subject change. 'She'll have useful input.'

'She?' questioned Packer.

'Middle East background, like your guy,' said Johnston, who'd withheld the gender at the earlier, larger meeting. 'Name's Sally Hanning. Jordanian diplomat mother, father an MI5 station chief in Lebanon, Turkey, and Syria; both died in a Hamas ambush. She's bilingual in Arabic, Oxford educated . . . the whole works.'

'It's just been proved, if proof were necessary, that we're confronted with a state-sponsored conspiracy, not an independent Islamic group,' said Johnston. 'We'll benefit from someone with her sort of background to compare with Irvine's assessments.'

'Working under whose jurisdiction and control?' at once demanded Packer, anxious for as much insider knowledge as possible: the protection that presidential approval bestowed also carried with it greater official scrutiny. He didn't want his fucked-up private life to emerge.

'Ours here at Langley,' assured Johnston. 'Her brilliance is in analysis, not cryptology. If we'd had that analytical assessment available earlier, we might now have al Aswamy in custody.'

'What do you think?' asked Harry Packer thirty minutes later, in Bradley's office, a bottle of Jack Daniel's open between them.

'Putting his own person in,' judged Bradley cautiously. He needed time, a lot more information, to make a proper assessment. One immediate decision was not to tell Packer of his suspicion of Johnston's surveillance. Which reminded him he had his own group to confront.

'Maybe you can turn her into becoming our person,' said Packer hopefully.

'Always good to have a joker in the pack.'

11

JACK IRVINE WENT THROUGH THE HIGH-FIVES RITUAL AT THE OVAL
Office video feed for individual presidential praise—as well as the required Georgetown champagne pit stop on the way home—but throughout
it all his mind, and his imagination, were in the past. It wouldn't have
been a video feed if his father had succeeded as he'd deserved to succeed.
It would have been a full-blown White House ceremony, his father centre
stage at the president's side, the Arabs in whom he'd misplaced his trust
completing the historic group, the door to the secretary of state's office wide-
open for his occupation.

As he entered his Owen Place 'safe house' apartment, taking a Miller
Lite instead of champagne from the refrigerator as he passed, Irvine wondered if the few who knew or who vaguely remembered his father's be-
trayal would make the connection with what had happened today. Irvine
doubted it. Too few people knew and even fewer cared; success, however
manufactured or hyped, was to be associated with in Washington, DC,
never perceived failure. Only he would ever know, or need to know, that
he'd dedicated today to his father: the day but not its implications. In practical reality today was his, an event he'd earned for penetrating the in-
nermost core of Iranian intelligence, and he was going to use it to every
possible benefit. From today his was a voice—and a name—that would
be listened to. From now on those with whom he'd unwillingly been assigned, without choice, knew that whatever their designations or titles,

he was their equal, not a subordinate to be patronized, as he believed Johnston and Bradley and even Packer had imagined they could treat him.

It was essential he remain objective, Irvine acknowledged; stay with
Miller Lite, not aspire to champagne. Burt Singleton *was* right: they had
been fucking lucky. And Shab Barker and Akram Malik were right, too:
the attempted but overly exaggerated political reassurances of outright anti-
terrorist victory would fuel a fundamentalist challenge they'd confront,
with attacks even more spectacular than those so narrowly—so fucking
luckily—averted. And Ismail al Aswamy, a far more important figure than
Irvine had initially imagined, was still free potentially to mastermind
them.

Irvine picked up another beer on his way to the computer bank that
had been his first installation after his transfer from Fort Meade. It com-
prised two protective firewall terminals programmed instantly to self-
destruct at attempted intrusion. Additionally there were special USB
barriers perfected at Meade. The mainframe was linked, on a dedicated
secure line, to the Shepherd office in Maryland. Irvine's cell phone was
additionally linked, on a separate dedicated and USB blocking line, to alert
him to any enemy-targeted activity, no matter how slight, when he was
away from either his Meade or Owen Place stations. The Owen Place machines could not operate independently and could only be activated after
a signal from Fort Meade by a sequence of commands between all three.
Disconnecting or severing any power lead or umbilical link between the
three triggered automatic destruction as well as sounding an alarm at Fort
Meade. Irvine changed the three hard drives each month after transfer-
ring their contents to a storage cloud.

Irvine settled comfortably in his wingback chair, dismissing the passing
thought of a third beer, fingering his way instead through the keyboard
labyrinth. The system operative, he embarked upon another slightly less
complicated entry into the carefully hidden botnets that completely concealed his trawling Internet presence, particularly inside the anonymous,
underground darknets. The primary priority for such concealment was to

establish the bots in countries with lax or disinterested cybersecurity; best of all were those countries whose governments actively sponsored commercial intelligence hacking. China was Irvine's first choice in which to stable his Trojan horse, actually in a Ministry of Commerce site in Beijing. There was the familiar blip of satisfaction at the easy entry, with no flashback alarm or barrier. Irvine moved on just as smoothly—and unobstructed—into his second cutout, embedded unknowingly to the Yemeni government in its Finance Ministry Web site. From Yemen he moved to his operational bot deep within Moscow's Interior Ministry. Irvine's domain name was Shamil25@akhoulgo.org.ru, the final initial letters identifying its internationally recognized Internet Protocol registration through an unwitting shipping company in St Petersburg. Irvine chose Russia for its haphazard Internet security, and the name Shamil as bait. Imam Shamil was a Muslim warlord who led a three-year uprising against czarist expansion in the northern Caucasus in 1825.

'Move on, find more, destroy more,' Irvine said to himself; for the moment the White House had to be ignored. The way now was back, not forward: back to Moscow Alternative, a darknet site with a number of shared subcatalogs that he'd found in the computer contact lists of two of the Anacostia group he'd penetrated after discovering Ismail al Aswamy's recruitment approaches, before learning of the man's importance or, ultimately, of Vevak's Hydarnes domain. One of those subdivisions was called Object. Another was Action.

On his first entry into the Action forum he invoked the devout *Inshallah*—if God wills it—in Arabic before agreeing in English to an insistence posted by an anonymous Vladimir that America was 'the Devil's crusader.' To be labeled or accused of being a crusader is the most vilifying accusation that can be leveled against a man in the Arab world. No responses had been posted on his wall, and Vladimir had not appeared in the chat room again during Irvine's following visits, which had been intermittent because of the concentration upon the other, obviously more productive targets. During those infrequent visits, though, he'd had two offers of sales of Russian military weaponry, both including grenade and hand-held rocket launchers, and engaged— only once and then briefly, to avoid the unlikely attention of an official Russian monitor —in another one-to-one exchange with Enslaved, who was recruiting volunteers for bomb attacks in Moscow in protest against continued Russian oppression in Chechnya.

Irvine finally got another beer from the refrigerator before computer hopping to his eventual St Petersburg concealment. He scrolled quickly through the Moscow Alternative subcatalogs to reach Action, recognizing none of the previous tag names with whom he'd had contact. He decided against an immediate phishing trip, instead offering his sublisted Shamil25 identity as bait, setting himself a thirty-minute time frame. And waited. There was a bite after twenty-five minutes. The sender domain was Anis@ mukhtarbrigade. Irvine instantly identified the significance. Anis is a Libyan name. Omar al-Mukhtar was one of Libya's most famous historical freedom fighters. Anis opened with *As salamu alaykum,* 'peace be upon you.' The message, in English, read, *Where have you been?*

Irvine replied with the peace invocation before replying, *Travelling.*

Anis wrote, *Was there sunshine in the desert?*

Not all the time, responded Irvine, paraphrasing the Arab proverb without directly quoting it. His computer was on automatic save, for the exchange to be code analyzed later, although Irvine doubted it would provide anything useful this soon.

Travel is sometimes better in the cold of the night.

The three attacks were scheduled for 3:00 a.m.! But it would be an inconceivable coincidence for this to be a reference to the al Aswamy conspiracy. Irvine wrote, *Unless there are unseen hazards.*

Always to be guarded against, came the response.

But not always possible to avoid, risked Irvine. He shouldn't press any harder, build too much—build *anything*—on this, but most important he shouldn't frighten off whoever Anis might be.

Journeys can always begin again if the will exists.

It sounded like another proverb, but Irvine didn't recognize it this time.

As it does exist, lured Irvine.

Marg bar Amrika, came the Iranian diatribe.

Death to America, echoed Irvine in English.

Inshallah registered on Irvine's screen, which then blanked.

'Fuck!' Irvine said aloud.

Charles Johnston decided his newly formed relationship with David Monkton—hopefully to be continued through Sally Hanning—was emerging to be his ace in the hole. Two hours earlier the MI5 chief had provided more than Johnston would have imagined possible to assemble in such a short time.

According to the UK dossier, Horst Becker had instantly been named by frightened members of the Sellafield attackers as the psychopathic killer of Roger Bennett, selected by Becker to be the disposable to-and-fro gofer once the three groups had been assembled. But the killing—and leaving the body as a warning to others in the conspiracy—had been ordered by Ismail al Aswamy when Bennett attempted to blackmail them after realizing the extent of the conspiracy. According to the Sellafield confessions— corroborated within the following hour by three statements from the arrested Italian group—al Aswamy had boasted of organizing other units for an already planned and rehearsed global jihad.

Johnston prepared his memoranda with care, timing its circulation and ensuring all its recipients were listed on every copy to avoid any later accusation of the manipulation that he was, in fact, orchestrating. The White House chief of staff headed his distribution list, followed by Homeland Security and the State Department team that had attended that day's joint meeting. Those he dispatched by courier. The remainder, to Conrad Graham, Bradley, and Irvine, he held back until the last internal mail drop, which wasn't collected for delivery until 9:00 P.M., by which time he knew all three would have left the building.

Sally Hanning completed in a single day the formalities of closing down her Pimlico apartment, arranging the redirection of what little personal mail she received, and fixing drawing arrangement through Washington's Connecticut Avenue branch of HSBC, her London bank, through which she established direct-debit settlements for the few continuing bills. She collected from Thames House the up to-the-minute running dossier on the Sellafield investigation on her way to Heathrow Airport for the last flight of the day, picking up a selection of British and American newspapers from the Special Branch unit permanently based there, who'd extended the helpful colleague courtesy by getting her upgraded to first class.

On the plane, the adjoining seat was unoccupied, removing the difficulty of her openly reading MI5 material with triple security classification in public surroundings. Al Aswamy's claim to be masterminding other impending attacks would cause official panic, Sally knew. But she was reading an interrogator's paraphrasing, not a verbatim transcript. If the word had been *boasted,* it could conceivably have been just that, empty braggadocio. But only *just* conceivable. It was vital that the near-hysterical publicity—more sensational in the English than American newspapers beside her—hadn't in any way indicated the NSA's original interception. Sally skimmed the sensationalism, knowing more than the self-proclaimed security correspondents, reading more closely the diplomatic reactions. There was total European Union condemnation of Iran, with unanimous support for the emergency UN Security Council debate America was instigating. Russia and China were indicating they would introduce their veto. Italy, Germany, and France were recalling their ambassadors from Tehran for consultation. During an emergency debate in the British Parliament, three MPs described the attack on Sellafield as an act of war.

Sally left until last her Washington introductory file, belatedly curious at being attached for the first time to an overseas British embassy. In the Alice in Wonderland fantasy world of espionage, in which every host country knows every embassy intelligence officer, each of whom knowing their counterpart in every other embassy, the cover of Nigel Fellowes, MI5's Washington station chief, was assistant trade attaché. His half-framed, coloured studio portrait showed a flaxen-haired, tightly mustached man in a country tweed jacket over an unmatched Eton tie. Attached beneath it was a printed-off personally addressed computer assurance to her that he was looking forward to her arrival, with a promise to do what-ever he could to help.

Sally hoped the promise was genuine, although she didn't really care if it was or not.

'Totally confidential?' queried Harry Packer, feeling the first stirrings of unease.

'There's a contract provision for that,' insisted Burt Singleton.

'I know.'

'So that's what this is going to be, a strictly confidential meeting?'

'Of course, if that's what you wish.'

'I do. There's no disloyalty to the team.'

'Understood. So what's the problem, Burt?'

'I believe Operation Cyber Shepherd is illegal.'

'For Christ's sake, Burt, you all got praised by the president himself!' exclaimed Packer, carefully using *you* instead of *we*.

'That doesn't make it legal. Nixon and Bush broke the law all the time.'

'You want the full exoneration?' demanded Packer.

'With its acceptance signed by you, as the authorizing officer.'

Shit, thought Packer. His name would be on a paper trail if the shit hit the fan and everything became public.

12

NIGEL FELLOWES HAD WORN THE SAME TIE IN THE INTRODUCTORY dossier, and it still clashed with his broadly striped, dark blue suit that Sally usually associated with big-bonus City bankers. As he walked across the vestibule of the British embassy on Washington's Massachusetts Avenue, Sally saw he was both slimmer and taller than she'd guessed from the head-and-shoulders portrait. He reached her with both hands outstretched to enclose hers: 'Welcome to the capital of the free world, welcome, welcome . . . although October is the harbinger of winter here, and when it gets to November, you'll know what winter is.'

The softness of his hands was accentuated by their clamminess, and she was glad when he released her. 'I'm not here on vacation. And it wasn't necessary for you to get up this early.' The plane had been delayed by headwinds, but it was still only seven fifteen in the morning.

'Early birds catch the worms and all that sort of thing,' said badly clichéd Fellowes, picking up her cases. 'What's it to be, the apartment that's ready for you in the compound or a get-to-know-each-other chat?'

'I managed to sleep on the plane,' exaggerated Sally. 'Why don't we talk.'

'First-class!' enthused Fellowes, setting off deeper into the embassy, identifying various sections as they passed. Sally nodded but didn't respond, deciding to keep the encounter short, thirty minutes tops. More people were in the corridors and open-doored rooms than she expected, but then she remembered the five-hour time lag between London and Washington, DC, and guessed that 7:15 a.m. hadn't been at all early for Fellowes.

Sally's impression upon entering was that the MI5 *rezidentura*, on the second floor, was inadequately small. The narrow outer office, at that moment unoccupied, she assumed to be for a secretary, led into a suite only slightly larger than her own at Thames House. There were two unidentified side doors but no obvious corridor to the remainder of the section.

Fellowes dumped the cases directly inside the door but didn't go on to his immaculately uncluttered desk, instead putting himself between it and one of the unmarked doors. 'My eagle's nest!' he announced. 'The main *rezidentura* is downstairs, closer to the communications room. But according to London, yours is a very special assignment.' He opened the closed door with a flourish, flicking on the strip lights. 'Your office, with everything you'll need: computer, secure telephone, copying facilities, Reuters-wire links. Anything missing can be installed in twenty-four hours.' With another flourish he gestured to his desk. 'And here's where I am, always available as I promised in my note. It's going to be a perfect working relationship, which I thought we'd establish more fully at dinner tonight, if you're not too jet-lagged.'

Sally went slowly to the already-set visitor's chair and didn't hurry settling herself, using the moment to get her responses in order. She'd already decided Fellowes was a posturing caricature, probably assigned more for his diplomatic than espionage capabilities—for which others in the *rezidentura* could doubtless compensate—but she didn't want a repeat of Jeremy Dodson's distracting antagonism. 'What's London told you of my being sent here?'

'Precious little,' mildly complained Fellowes. 'Obvious confirmation of its sensitivity, of course. Just the broad outline of it involving the three attempted attacks and that you were pivotal in their prevention.'

'No running case notes?'

'No details at all.'

'What about my case officer?'

The smile stopped just short of patronizing. 'Me, naturally! I'm head of station here.'

'That's been confirmed by the Director-General?'

'Of course it hasn't! It doesn't need to be. It's standard operational procedure.'

Why the hell did Monkton play these stupid games! 'Nigel, I don't want us to get off to a bad start,' Sally began cautiously, nodding to the now open-doored side office. 'And I thank you for all the trouble you've obviously gone to, fixing up my own office. But I've been ordered to deal directly with the Director-General, no-one else.'

The flush of anger that began to form on his face while Sally spoke was complete by the time she finished, the colour heightened by the blond ness of the man's hair. 'I don't accept what you're telling me!' he said, discarding the earlier affectation. 'If you're seconded to my *rezidentura*, you come under my authority. Those are the regulations.'

'I'm not aware of the regulations, but I can appreciate your difficulty,' soothed Sally. 'It's possible I misinterpreted Monkton's instructions. Why don't you message him right now and get everything clarified while I settle into the apartment?'

'You mean you're not accepting my authority!'

'I mean that to resolve any misunderstanding, which might well be *my* misunderstanding, I'm asking you to clear my terms of reference here with the Director-General.'

'I've got every intention of doing just that!'

He'd meant it as a threat, Sally knew; it sounded more like the class bully about to take his football home because he hadn't been made team captain. She'd only used up fifteen of the thirty minutes she'd allowed for the encounter, she realized gratefully.

Jack Irvine listened just sufficiently to James Bradley to ensure he didn't miss anything beyond what the CIA man had already told him, his concentration instead upon the significance of Charles Johnston's sidelining Bradley, which was reducing the man to near apoplexy.

If it was true that what had so far been prevented was only the beginning of a global terrorist onslaught, then losing al Aswamy was a disaster whose consequences were difficult to quantify. It reduced presidential congratulations and sycophantic backslapping to a piss in the ocean, a level to which he'd already relegated much of the earlier euphoria.

'Isn't there something a little more important than your being bypassed?' he interrupted the other man.

'What do you mean?' demanded Bradley, halting the diatribe.

'For Christ's sake, it's surely obvious what I mean!' Irvine said, careless of his irritation. 'We've got corroborated information from terrorist detainees of further terrorist attacks, and all you've talked about since I got here is being kept out of the loop overnight. Don't you think it would be a good idea if we concentrated upon what's really important, which is finding the guy who's masterminding those other intended hits!'

Bradley remained strangely still in his overstrained jacket, his face equally creased, head sideways in exaggerated curiosity. 'Am I missing something here?' The voice was that of a schoolteacher addressing the class buffoon.

'Missing it completely. We left a loose end.' Irvine hesitated, momentarily undecided. '*You* and *your* chosen team left a loose end, and if that loose end isn't tidied up double-quick, I'd say you're going to be sidelined a hell of a lot more than you are being now. But I don't intend to be sidelined and see a functioning anti-terrorism operation get flushed down the toilet. You missing anything of what I'm telling you, Jim?'

'I don't believe I am.' Bradley sat at last. The schoolteacher's voice had gone.

'You heard from Packer?'

'He's on his way. Should be here in an hour.'

'Was I to be included in whatever you plan to discuss?' demanded Irvine.

'Of course.'

Irvine didn't believe the man. 'That's good to hear.'

Both men were glad for a telephone interruption. Bradley picked up and didn't speak until the end of the call, saying, 'I understand. He's with me now,' before replacing the receiver. To Irvine, he said, 'A meeting at two, the deputy director's suite. You're to be there.'

'That's good to hear, too.' Still at a top table, Irvine reflected, and at once wished he hadn't because it was how Bradley's mind would have worked.

'Holy shit!' was Burt Singleton's response when Irvine finished talking.

'Spraying in every direction,' agreed Irvine. He sat lounged back in his Langley office, the telephone cradled in the crook of his shoulder.

'They got any leads to al Aswamy up there?'

'Not as of twenty minutes ago, when I left Bradley. Conrad Graham's called a crisis meeting.'

'At least Vevak haven't taken al Aswamy's site down.'

'You checked this morning?' There had been nothing when Irvine had logged on from Owen Place.

'And with you, last night.'

'You did . . . ?' began Irvine, but he stumbled to a halt, answering the question before asking it. 'You hacked me!'

'Hardly hacking when I've already got every available ASCII access code to get past your firewalls, but, yes, I guess it qualifies as that.'

Irvine didn't respond at first, his reactions colliding. The first was in-dignation, which was instantly confronted by the affronted hypocrisy at having had done to him what he practised every day as a profession. If he were a professional, why hadn't he detected what was happening? Why hadn't his firewalls been triggered? Because Singleton, with the IP codes, was a professional, too, Irvine supposed; a better professional. 'Were you going to tell me?'

'I just did.'

He was at risk of being talked into a corner, Irvine recognized. 'When did you start piggybacking?'

'From the beginning, obviously.'

'Through the cutouts then?'

'How else could I have been with you from the beginning? You haven't concealed them since telling us about Shepherd.'

'So what's your judgement about al Aswamy's Vevak site still being up?'

'I'm hopeful. But cautious.'

'What about Moscow Alternative?' tested Irvine.

'Curious, aren't you?' tested Singleton.

'Of course I'm curious,' said Irvine, discomfited by the questioning switch.

'About what, exactly?'

This really was verbal arm wrestling. ' "Where have you been?" ' Irvine quoted.

The pause now was from Singleton's end. 'I couldn't believe you'd missed it—didn't want to believe you'd missed it—but I'm glad you didn't. You engaged with Anis before?'

'No.'

'Has he been listed there before?'

'Not on the Action subcatalog. Can't remember him on any other darknet, either.'

'You're sure?'

'Positive.' Singleton was still leading, Irvine accepted.

'What about Object?'

'I don't remember Anis being there, either.'

'Or Moscow Alternative?'

'It's a long catalog. I don't recall it.' Irvine wasn't any longer lounged back. He was holding the receiver now, slippery in his hand, feeling—sure he was sounding—totally ineffective.

'So how do you read that?'

'There's not enough to read, not yet.'

'But you're going back?'

'Of course I'm going back.'

'It could be a come-on, a poacher-turned-gamekeeper entrapment.'

'I realize that. So could leaving al Aswamy's site up.'

'Why'd you piggyback me, Burt?' abruptly demanded Irvine, impatient with the minuet.

'Having someone riding shotgun is never a waste of time.'

'You know I wasn't detected, I—both of us—would have seen it before the cutout destruction.'

'Not chased this time,' agreed Singleton. 'But if al Aswamy's site was being monitored by Vevak, they'll have your electronic fingerprint.'

'Which will lead them straight to the second cutout, which will destruct before it can be recorded, with another cutout still in reserve.'

'It's impressive protection.'

'You'll tell me if you come along again, won't you?'

'Before I do it,' promised Singleton. 'Looking forward to hearing the outcome of this afternoon's meeting.'

'So am I.' Irvine guessed at last why Singleton had electronically shadowed him. The man—maybe Marian and the other two as well—suspected he was being sidelined. Which was, Irvine reflected, how he himself had felt before the earlier confrontation with Bradley.

'I shouldn't have been put in the situation,' protested Sally.

There was a hesitation from the London end of the security-guaranteed connection. Sally was boxed in a claustrophobically small, soundproofed cubicle in the embassy's communications room. She wondered how difficult it was for David Monkton to remain at his desk for a telephone conversation this long; maybe he had a cordless phone, to enable him to do just that.

Eventually Monkton said, 'My instructions were quite specific.'

'To me. Not to Fellowes. It's caused unnecessary friction.'

There was another pause. 'Which has now been resolved. The *rezidentura* is to provide everything you ask for but you communicate directly to me, both verbally and electronically. It's to be an absolutely restricted case file, shared with no-one at the embassy, up to and including the ambassador. And if there's difficulty with the ambassador, tell him to channel all his queries through the Foreign Office and the foreign secretary, whom I'll be personally briefing.'

Now Sally hesitated. 'You surely can't believe this embassy is insecure?'

'If any of the information we're getting from the Sellafield and Italian prisoners becomes a reality—which I hope to God it doesn't—there's going to be chicken-coop panic and conspiracy theories up to and including Martian invasion with Armageddon finally upon us,' lectured Monkton. 'And some of that panic and those conspiracy theories will be engendered by supposedly levelheaded diplomats and intelligence agencies talking to other supposedly levelheaded diplomats and intelligence agencies, each anxious to provide just that little bit more than the others, to justify their existence. MI5's function is to advise the government of what dangers truly and genuinely exist, totally without embellishment that might lead to the wrong reaction or conclusion. That's what I want you to provide, information and analysis and judgement without any embellishment, which you overwhelmingly proved yourself capable of doing not just with Sellafield but by making the connection with Rome and Washington. That's why I've tolerated the insubordination with which you began this conversation.'

'Which might have been avoided if it had been explained to me earlier,' persisted Sally, despite the warning.

'Now it has been,' said Monkton briskly. 'Have you made contact with Johnston?'

'The message I got was that he's at a meeting but will return my call as soon as it ends.'

'He spoke to me earlier, asking for any overnight developments.'

Sally frowned. 'Are there any?'

'No. I told him you'd be making contact.'

She had to ask, insubordinate or not, Sally decided. 'You intend maintaining separate contact with Johnston?'

'Of course I do!' said Monkton at once. 'It'll give us two sources from which to ensure that we're getting as much as we can realistically imagine they'll share.'

Which made good, pragmatic sense, Sally conceded. 'Isn't this too serious for territorial nonsense?'

'You're the last person from whom I expected that degree of naïvety.'

Shit, thought Sally. 'I'll try to avoid it.'

'I hope you do.'

13

THE PENDULUM SWUNG COMPLETELY FROM COMMENDATION TO condemnation. That afternoon there was no White House TV link, no West Wing staff presence; the largest Homeland Security contingent was from a disgruntled FBI, closely challenged by a State Department group. There were altogether too many individually to identify beyond department or organization-table designations.

'Let's get the latest update,' brusquely opened Conrad Graham.

The demand was directed at his successor. His preparations completed, Charles Johnston didn't hurry, looking pointedly instead to James Bradley as if the responsibility for losing Ismail al Aswamy were personally that of the field supervisor. Satisfied the unspoken accusation had registered, Johnston said, 'There's nothing positively new to take the search forward. But I've already got a preliminary analysis of what we've had from the Brits and the Italians.'

Johnston had headed the CIA's Profiling and Analysis division before this new appointment, remembered Jack Irvine. He couldn't imagine the man would contribute a worthwhile analysis this soon.

'With what result?' Graham frowned, his similar doubt obvious.

'There are four separate disclosures of more attacks from the UK detainees,' noted Johnston, setting his own pace. 'And they are separate, taken individually from three men and one woman kept apart from each other to prevent any collusion over their stories. Each, predictably, worded their account differently, but the essential facts remained identical—at different times in the buildup to Sellafield, al Aswamy talked of six other already chosen and attack-rehearsed targets, three in the U.S., the others in Europe. No definitive location for any of them. The Italians also kept their prisoners apart. Two talked of other attacks. Again, of six, three in America, three elsewhere, the attackers already trained. Again, there were no specific locations."

Irvine thought Bradley overdid the impatience., Johnston at once capitalized, stretching his pause for the other man's anticipated interruption. Forced into making one, Bradley said inadequately, 'We already know all of that, don't we?'

'What about the significance?' immediately returned Johnston, seizing the unexpected opening.

Bradley was lost, guessed Irvine. As was he, as well as quite a few others judging from the facial expressions around the table.

Conrad Graham broke the impasse. 'Let's quit the guessing games, start talking straight, okay!'

'The initial analysis is that the similarity of the prisoners' accounts makes the threat credible: that there are definitely going to be further attacks unless we stop Ismail al Aswamy,' declared Johnston, once more looking directly at Bradley.

'Where the hell's the evidence for that!' challenged Conrad Graham.

'Six people separated from the moment of arrest—two of them additionally distanced by the thousand miles between London and Rome—all telling the same story, with virtually no deviation or embellishment,' insisted Johnston.

'That's not evidence of anything!' disputed Bradley, emboldened by the deputy director's doubt. 'Aswamy was blowing smoke, trying to impress everyone with what a big important guy he is. We've got to get him, sure. But there's not enough to make predictions about more attacks.'

'Trying to impress everyone with what a big, important guy he is!' echoed Johnston. 'Ismail al Aswamy trained three terrorist groups—one still running loose here in America—to attack an iconic American monument, a British nuclear facility, and Italy's most famous antiquity. You really think he needed to prove to anyone that he's the current numero uno?'

'Is this discussion applicable right now?' intruded a heavily built, immaculately suited, black State Department delegate. 'We've got matching information we need to treat as positive threats until it's proven otherwise. So we've got to maintain the ongoing high-security status in all three countries. But if we're going with psychological profiling, how sure are we that bagging Aswamy is the answer to the problem? He wasn't personally there in the UK or Italy when the hits were attempted. The attacks could go ahead whether or not we get the son of a bitch.'

There was a silence, people seeking opinions from other people rather than offering their own. Too many people were here—quite irrespective of their security clearances—to disclose details of Operation Cyber Shepherd, Jack Irvine decided.

Conrad Graham once more broke the logjam. 'I don't think at this stage we can be sure of anything. And for that reason, quite apart from the analysts' input, we've got to go along with al Aswamy being the key to future outrages: cut the head off the monster and it all dies with him.'

This was futile, Irvine thought. This supposedly coordinated—in reality, totally *un*coordinated—assembly had been brought together for a later media release to satisfy the public that they could sleep safely in their beds at night, without a single member having an achievable proposal to confront the crisis. The check he'd made fifteen minutes before entering the room showed the Vevak botnet still undetected, and there'd been no activity alert from the computer-linked cell phone in his jacket pocket. But to disclose the botnets existence would be seized upon in the desperation permeating the room as the best hope of re-locating Aswamy. Which it couldn't be. It was inconceivable that Iran's seasoned intelligence apparatus would contemplate again using a Control route linked to the loss of three global spectaculars.

Was he entitled—empowered— –to make such an arbitrary decision to keep secret the Vevak penetration? Irvine asked himself, conscious of Harry Packer's questioning look from beside him, mirrored by that of Bradley from the CIA group opposite. Leaning sideways to Packer, Irvine said softly, 'I'll take any queries.'

'You think there's a possibility of another chance interception, Jack?' questioned Graham, seeing the exchange. 'For Christ's sake, give me something positive to sort this mess out!'

Chance interception, seized Irvine, recognizing his escape from any later accusation of withholding the Vevak coup. 'No, I don't, not in the time frame we're considering here.' Irvine came to an awkward halt as an idea began to formulate, but forced himself on while he resolved the other abrupt thought. 'It'll obviously remain our highest priority, and with so many people involved in Italy, the UK, and here we've got to hope Tehran will believe their intended sensations failed because of a human leak or infiltration, not from a NSA intercept, and re-open electronic communication with Aswamy. But if they do, they'll bury it as deeply as it's technically possible. We're not likely to get anything new anytime soon.' The second pause was for breath to articulate the idea now clear in his mind. 'But there's surely something practical we can do? A million bucks got us Saddam Hussein in his desert hidey-hole. And twenty-four million dollars got us bin Laden. Why don't we offer another bounty, up there in the millions, same relocation promise for the person who comes forward to lead us to al Aswamy? His crew *is* still loose somewhere in America; a couple of million bucks and a new life could put a hell of a strain on an adopted ideology.'

A positive stir went through the room, Conrad Graham pushing back into his seat in physical satisfaction. 'Why's the obvious always so obvious that no-one sees it?'

'Let's not confine it to the U.S.,' Johnston bustled in. 'Through the MI5 officer I've got seconded here and the close relationship I've established with MI5's Director-General, we can widen the bounty offer to the UK.'

'Why stop there?' demanded the immaculate State Department

spokesperson, enthused by a practical suggestion. 'We can get our embassies to push it throughout the European Union.'

'And the Arab states,' encouraged Irvine. 'Tehran's still a pariah regime in the Middle East.'

An assembly line had virtually formed, Irvine observed, to register on the official record in support of a substantive idea. Charles Johnston was thinking the same, conscious of the palpable relaxation around the room. He forced his way back into the discussion with the announcement that Sally Hanning, whom he didn't name, would coordinate the debriefings of the UK detainees' supposed knowledge of new attacks after the debacle of the CIA's losing al Aswamy. And then produced his carefully prepared denouement.

Matching further CIA analysis, he went on, the British suspected that some, if not all, of the four, in their custody claiming additional attacks knew more, possibly even the attack locations, though they had been denying it. As of that morning following the publication of the terrorist's photograph, there had been 1,230 possible sightings of al Aswamy, resulting in 580 arrests. That provided a bargaining lever, reciprocal access for the MI5 agent to those arrested in the U.S. in exchange for the British four being made available to U.S. interrogators. He'd use his special relationship with MI5 to make that request, Johnston promised. But London and Berlin were already in a jurisdictional dispute over Horst Becker, the leader of the Sellafield assault. At the moment, London was guaranteeing every debriefing co-operation except personal access.

'We go with the bounty proposal,' abruptly concluded Conrad Graham, turning to Johnston. 'And keep pressing for access to those who are talking. A million bucks might be more attractive to them than a rendition flight to one of our amenable persuasive friends.'

Charles Johnston was at the door when Sally entered his office and courteously led her to its side annex, where easy chairs were arranged around a low table upon which a coffee tray was already set. He remained standing until Sally settled herself. She was glad he hadn't clung as tightly to her hand as Nigel Fellowes.

Finally sitting, Johnston said, 'I'm sorry about the delay. It turned into a long meeting.' It had also taken him a good half an hour to get rid of his lingering anger at failing to make the impressions he'd intended.

'A development!' hopefully demanded Sally. It really would be new if there was. There'd been no indication from David Monkton when she'd telephoned London an hour after what she knew to be Johnston's morning call to London.

'A lot of empty talk, going around in circles,' dismissed Johnston. 'We're going to put a million-dollar bounty on al Aswamy, with a witness-protection promise to anyone who leads us to him. I'm going to press Dave to put it to your four to see if it'll unlock any doors.'

'It's worth a try,' agreed Sally, although doubtfully.

'It got us Saddam Hussein.'

Obediently following Monkton's suggested approach until she formed her own objective route, Sally said, 'My director greatly appreciates this degree of co-operation.'

'It's going to work out just fine. Which it's got to, with something this big. That's why we're glad to have you aboard. Dave's told me how you led the way.'

How would Johnston respond to being called Chuck? idly wondered Sally, deciding the man's flattery was a good enough opening. 'My advantage in London was being at the very centre of things, able to assess the raw intelligence ahead of any other analysis or pre-conception.'

'Which is what you're going to have here: everything channeled through me.'

It was uncomfortably like a reprise of the Nigel Fellowes encounter, which she had to block from the outset. 'I'm not fully clear how Cyber Shepherd works in practise.'

Johnston paused, belatedly offering coffee that Sally didn't want, but she insisted on pouring for them both to show unfelt deference, intent on manoeuvring her own version of co-operation. 'How Cyber Shepherd works?' she prompted.

Johnston's response still wasn't immediate. Eventually he said, 'A tight unit: the inner core's headed by a NSA whiz kid, working with a CIA control. It's an Agency—which means me—covert operation.'

It was little more than confirmation of what she'd already inferred, but Johnston's vague generalization was to prevent her from getting a true picture of the operation from any inadvertent mistake he might make. It was her moment to generalize to get the potential difficulty out of the way. 'An operation that pulled off a hell of a coup isolating what turned out to be three attacks.'

There was another pause from the man. 'With the exception of losing al Aswamy.'

He'd introduced it, not her, Sally recognized, relieved. Which didn't sync with his earlier effort to impress. 'Mistakes happen.'

'This one shouldn't have happened. And it sure as hell wouldn't have if I'd taken over this job a week or two earlier.'

Now it synced. Which direction could she safely follow? Feed the ego, she decided. 'And if we'd had al Aswamy the threat of six more imminent attacks might not be so great. I can understand the problems you had with today's meeting.'

'The only practical discussion, apart from the bounty, was the initial assessment I had our analysts here carry out. I was grateful for Dave's heads-up with that, of course.'

Sally had been curious if the man was going to more openly refer to his independent contact with the Director-General, but now that he had, she wished she understood what Johnston was alluding to. 'I'm not sure I'm keeping up with you here.'

'The matching accounts of further attacks confirming that they're genuine, not empty boasts by al Aswamy.'

Monkton hadn't said that! Certainly not to her. The reference had virtually been a dismissive afterthought illustrating the hysteria of some European security services at the prospect of further outrages on their soil. Sally remembered Monkton's warning of diplomatic and intelligence-service exaggerations in times of national crisis: *MI5's function is properly to advise the government of what dangers truly and genuinely exist, totally without embellishment that might lead to the wrong reaction or response. That's what I want you to provide.* She said, 'My director-general didn't put it to me as strongly as that. I took it as a description of the over-reaction in Europe to the threats, not a confirmation of them.'

Johnston's face briefly tightened, then relaxed. 'Profiling and Analysis was my division until very recently. I know their abilities and have a lot of respect for their judgement. They think the similarities strongly indicate genuine attacks.'

Because that was the assessment they were guided towards, guessed Sally, mentally flagging the exchange for her next conversation with Monkton. Time to get back to the more immediate objective. 'This tight, inner core unit is based here at Langley, right? Everyone moved down from Fort Meade?'

'You've done your research, know where the National Security Agency is.'

Along with millions of cyber buffs from age eight upwards who knew Google wasn't the sound made by a newborn baby, thought Sally, weary of the facile patronizing. She shifted in her seat, slightly smiling in expectation, saying nothing.

Finally Johnston said, 'Split. All the interception stuff starts over in Maryland. Control's up here, answerable to me.'

'There's no-one from NSA here?'

The face tightened again, longer this time. 'The whiz kid I spoke about; worked on the Stuxnet sabotage of the Iranian nuclear facilities. Came up today with the bounty idea. Diplomatic family, spent all his life in the Middle East until college here; knows it like the back of his hand.'

'Not American?'

Johnston, who'd labored his answer to deflect her, frowned. 'American diplomatic family.'

It still wasn't the direct answer she wanted. 'Working from here or Fort Meade?'

Now it was Johnston who paused. 'Both. He's got an office here but spends time there, where the technical facilities are.'

'My security clearance has been verified and accepted, hasn't it?'

'Of course.' Johnston frowned. 'You wouldn't have gotten past the gate if it hadn't been.'

Sally's smile widened. 'No impediment to my meeting the inner-core guys down here then? Or up at Fort Meade, either?'

'I can't authorize access to Fort Meade.'

'But you can here, can't you? It's your operation,' seized Sally. 'It really is essential to be as close as possible to the raw-material source, remember.'

'Of course you should meet them.'

Not easy but then again not as difficult as she'd expected it might be, reflected Sally. Something else was surprisingly much easier on her drive back into Washington, and the concentration it required delayed a proper analysis of her conversation with Johnston. She was chilled, her mind momentarily frozen in disbelief, when the possibility occurred to her, but then she refused to accept it because it couldn't be possible. Or could it?

'The son of a bitch hung me out to dry in front of the largest fucking Washington audience he could find!' fumed James Bradley. 'Bastard; cocksucking bastard!'

Neither Irvine nor Packer said anything, watching the fury-driven man stride from place to place around his office, picking up and putting down unfocused-upon objects, too agitated to remain still.

'It's on the written record, all there in print. It'll go beyond Graham to the Director himself. Anyone need a fall guy to dump all the shit on, they got it now.' Bradley punched his chest, further crumpling the buttoned-up jacket. 'Here's the target; just pull the fucking trigger.'

'There's almost six hundred people already in the slammer, and that'll quadruple by the day when the bounty is announced,' reminded Packer. 'We'll get al Aswamy from among them.' He hoped. Packer had seen his personal recognition by the president as his guarantee of promotion through the NSA executive to financial survival, but had been worried by the absence of White House staffers at the meeting.

'That wasn't how I heard what the Bureau jerk-off said,' refused Bradley. 'The way I heard it, every jerk-off and his dog are calling 911 if they see a guy in a beard and a bedsheet, and all of us know that the last thing al Aswamy has got now is a fucking beard and kaftan. And you're right about the bounty. There's going to be a roundup of more people than you can shake a stick at for al Aswamy to hide behind.'

'There were as many photographs with the beard airbrushed out,' said Irvine, searching for a contribution. 'And a million bucks might ring the right bell.'

Disregarding the effort, Bradley said, 'I could sure as hell have done with more help from you, too!'

'What goes around comes around,' reflected Irvine, vindicated by the man's earlier abandonment. 'I gave a completely honest answer to Conrad Graham's intercept question.'

'There was time before the meeting for us to talk about the bounty idea.'

'I didn't have the bounty idea before the fucking meeting!'

'You could have talked up your chances of catching a transmission again,' persisted Bradley, changing tack. 'What the hell are your guys doing up there at Fort Meade apart from scratching their asses!'

'We're the last of the last of the conceivable chances of finding him again, for Christ's sake!' insisted Irvine.

'He's got to speak to someone, somehow!'

Bradley was flailing around like a blind man swatting bugs. More quietly but with his anger growing, Irvine said, 'Of course he's got to speak to someone. He's probably doing it right now, from wherever the hell he is, which could just as likely be from a bazaar in Islamabad as from a cell phone in Lafayette Park across from the White House. We found him for you once, Jim. We played him like a puppet and did a lot of collateral terrorist damage. And then your guys lost him like a bunch of amateurs, and it was on your watch, which is why you're getting the heat. And I'm not going to let any of my guys get burned by that heat.'

'What the hell's that mean!'

'Exactly what every word meant. Your watch, your ass. Don't try to off-load it. We can't do any more than what we're doing now.'

'What do you think of Johnston's analysis theory?' intervened Packer to defuse the confrontation, his decision to distance himself from Bradley confirmed.

'It's bullshit,' dismissed Bradley, finally sitting at his desk. 'He just wanted to sound like he was taking everything forward, which he didn't.'

'Who knows?' Irvine shrugged, disinterested.

'You think Cyber Shepherd can survive?' Packer asked him, voicing another concern.

'With changes,' predicted Irvine.

Bradley turned sharply at the remark but said nothing.

14

'JOHNSTON'S ALREADY BEEN ON,' DAVID MONKTON SAID AT ONCE, hurrying through the perfunctory greetings. 'How was the meeting?'

Sally hesitated in her cramped cubicle in the embassy communication room, hopeful the remark indicated more immediate openness than Monkton had so far shown. Establish the parameters, she decided, confirm the hope. 'What time did he call?'

Now the Director-General hesitated at the unexpected response. 'Four fifteen, your time.'

'I left him at four ten. He was anxious to get in first, wasn't he?' And Monkton was still at Thames House at 10:20 p.m. London time, she calculated from the cubicle clock set on English time.

'We're in the middle of a crisis,' reminded the man, unwittingly meeting Sally's reflection. 'Did he appear pressured, face-to-face?'

'He's very positively distancing himself from the loss of al Aswamy. Actually insisted it wouldn't have happened if he'd been in place earlier, so there's clearly some responsibility-shifting going on.'

'He tell you about the bounty?'

This is encouraging, thought Sally. 'Said it was the idea of the NSA cryptologist assigned to the operation.' There was no reason to mention the Middle East diplomatic background. It was only of curiosity interest to her, nothing at all to do with her professional assignment.

'Working *how?*' seized Monkton. 'What's different from normal NSA activity?'

'We didn't get that far. But I am going to meet him and the CIA supervisor heading the unit, so I should find out.'

'When?' demanded the Director-General. 'We're never going to be side by side with whatever they're doing, but I want to be as close to Johnston's shoulder as it's possible to be. He's got to go on believing we've got stuff he needs to stay just that far in front.'

Confirmation she scarcely needed that she was piggy in the middle, acknowledged Sally: roasted if she got it wrong, farmyard queen if she got it right, whatever *it* was. Sally eased her shoes off against the chair leg and felt a stocking ladder.

'What about the bounty?'

Sally frowned at the phrasing: Monkton wasn't giving her any leads. 'They've worked in the past for America. Us, too, although not quite on the same publicity scale.'

'He give you a figure?'

'No.'

'He claimed the CIA paid twenty-four million for bin Laden. When I told him our intelligence was that it went directly to finance Al Qaeda, who'd decided to sacrifice someone past his sell-by date, Johnston said so what, it made the right headlines.'

'It answers your question about pressure, doesn't it?'

Monkton laughed approvingly. 'The State Department are going to press European governments to make big-dollar commitments as well, to make the eventual pot impossible to refuse. And for us to dangle the carrot right away in front of our four particular detainees.'

'You think our government will go for it?'

'It would be a reward for information leading to the eventual arrest and conviction of al Aswamy, which is quite different from paying a ransom, which we officially don't do. And publicly it would look like positive action, which Downing Street's anxious to be seen taking.'

'When do we pay ransom?' demanded Sally, continuing the cynicism.

'Whenever it'll get people back alive,' answered Monkton without hesitation.

'You believe our four know more than they've so far admitted?'

'It's possible, although they haven't moved their initial claims forward. Johnston wants us to make them available for American interrogation.'

'In England?' questioned Sally, practically before the man finished speaking.

'America.'

'That means extraordinary rendition: torture somewhere.'

'Probably,' accepted Monkton in flat-voiced agreement.

'Are you going to hand them over?'

'I'm not, I understand the approach is also being made by the State Department to the Foreign Office, which makes it a political decision.'

London would go along with that, too, Sally knew. With that acceptance came another awareness. Monkton was now telling her *everything*, if not directly then by inference. Taking the man's lead, she said, 'We got any harder information of new attacks?'

'We never had *hard* information in the first place, only what the four told us without anything to substantiate what they're saying.'

'That's what I told Johnston. He's arguing there'll definitely be more, according to the analysis division he used to head, based on what our four and the two in Italy are saying.'

'You believe he said that at the crisis meeting?'

'Yes.'

'He told me State were there. It'll be spun back as a definite possibility through the Foreign Office.'

'He didn't tell you about the analysis?'

'He asked if there was anything more from the debriefings; that was how he got round their being handed over for American questioning. You think yours was a good first meeting?'

'I didn't expect him to agree to my meeting people in the active unit, so I consider it a good start.'

'How do you gauge that?'

'I don't, not yet. He made a fuss about being the man in charge, in control of everything. He won't be if I meet the active unit by myself, will he?'

'*If* you meet them by yourself,' heavily qualified Monkton.

'We'll have to see.'

'How's it at the embassy?'

'I'm only using the communications room and the compound apartment.'

'No contact beyond Fellowes?'

'Not even that, since the first day.'

'It'll come soon, now that the State Department are dealing with the Foreign Office.'

'I haven't forgotten what you told me.'

'It's been a good start,' assessed Monkton.

'Let's hope it continues that way,' said Sally, doubting that it would.

Nigel Fellowes was waiting directly outside when she emerged from the cubicle.

Jack Irvine switched the telephone to voice mail, slid the additional interior security bolt into place after double-locking the door to his CIA office, and finally slipped the colour red code into its outside slot, isolating himself to reflect on the day. Having made the only positive contribution at the Homeland meeting, he should, he supposed, feel some personal satisfaction. But he didn't. Conrad Graham was right: offering a bounty was *too* obvious, and for none of the other supposed professionals to have come up with the idea ahead of him verged on the unbelievable. Equally absurd was the blame-gaming between Charles Johnston and James Bradley, which was anything but a game. Al Aswamy *had* been lost on Bradley's watch, and Bradley had to take the fall if sacrifice was inevitably demanded.

Inevitable, that is, until five minutes ago and the arrival of the internal e-mail at which he was now looking, addressed not only to him but copied to James Bradley, setting a time the following day for both of them to meet the British MI5 agent, named for the first time as Sally Hanning. Or could it merely be a postponement of the inevitable? Irvine wondered, recalling Johnston's heavy inference—unchallenged by Conrad Graham—that the woman would monitor the Cyber Shepherd fieldwork. If the infantile disputes continued between the two, Bradley's humiliation would be compounded by having to confront the woman who'd be overseeing his every decision. What about me? questioned Irvine. All the indications so far were that the woman was a field operative, not a cryptologist. So what practical purpose could there be in his meeting her? Every purpose, if it achieved his overriding concern of keeping Cyber Shepherd alive. And the way to do that was to build upon the operation's already proven success: locate new intended outrages to manipulate and destroy terrorists as sensationally as they'd so far prevented those they'd already uncovered.

It was time to return to the momentarily untapped Moscow Alternative.

Burt Singleton picked up on the first ring, not speaking until Irvine finished his account of that afternoon. Then the man said, 'You call that a crisis meeting!'

'I don't. They do.'

'That doesn't overwhelm a guy with confidence.'

'Al Aswamy doesn't need to do anything else, does he? He's got us and half of Europe in lockdown panic just by walking away.'

'That could be the extent of the threat.'

'I know.'

'What's the bounty?'

'It hasn't yet been internationally agreed.'

'It's worked in the past,' conceded Singleton. 'Any heads rolling, for losing the son of a bitch?'

'Not yet.'

'We still in business?'

'Why shouldn't we be?' Irvine questioned back, discerning the expectation in the other man's voice.

'Thought maybe there'd be a pause until things settle down.'

'There's no pause,' insisted Irvine. 'We continue with our part of the al Aswamy hunt by monitoring the Vevak site. I'd like you to handle that, with Shab and Malik on standby to help. I'm going to spend time in the chat room we haven't properly explored yet.'

'What about Marian?'

'I need her available to help me with the chat room, as well as sifting anything that might look promising from our general target interceptions. I want to see if we can expand those. Shab and Malik could help there, too.'

'And we'll liaise all the time?' demanded Singleton, concerned that Irvine might keep him out of the loop because of the doubts he'd expressed.

'All the time. You know that's the arrangement.'

'When are you next up?'

'Maybe in a day or two. We'll see what develops.'

Irvine guessed Marian would pick up the gist of his conversation with Singleton, but cautious of her feeling left out, he patiently went through his account of the afternoon for a second time.

'The bounty response lines will be blocked by every con man with a faint pulse,' predicted the woman.

'They already are, before the amount's even been announced.'

'And we go on as before?' she questioned, confirming Irvine's belief that she'd been close enough to Singleton to overhear most of their earlier exchange.

'Hopefully better than before,' said Irvine briskly. 'You've read my chat-room download?'

'Of course I have,' said the woman stiffly.

'It was a rhetorical question, not a doubt of your professionalism: you're on the team *because* of your professionalism,' said Irvine more stiffly, wearied by the perpetual suspicion of both Marian and Singleton and determined against the sort of stupidity existing between Johnston and Bradley. 'We got the Moscow Alternative darknet through the contacts list of the Annapolis group who killed two of al Aswamy's team. So we know that group is an active cell who kill and who talk on the Action subcatalog of Moscow Alternative. I want us to talk to them, too, to get their trust and pick up any hint or indication of any attacks they might be contemplating or get involved in. I want you to organize an IP code search on the random-number generator. If necessary, extend it through our Echelon tie-in with Britain's GCHQ, who did damned well with al Aswamy, and Canada's CSE. You and Burt can divide Shab and Malik between you to share the workload.'

'That all?' The cynical stiffness now was at the rebuke stage.

'No. You know the botnets I've already set up to get into Moscow Alternative. Get into the subcatalog using my Anis domain botnet. Create a repetitive programme to download every name listed on the wall over a twenty-four-hour period that we can compare not just with the Annapolis list but every other address we've got on record.'

'What are you going to be doing?' persisted Marian.

'Working on it with you as soon as I finish what needs to get done up here.'

Sally Hanning had forgotten about the heel-to-thigh ladder in her tights until she felt the coldness of the chair she was ushered into by Giles Podmore, who had solicitously been waiting directly inside the door of his embassy office, as Charles Johnston had been a few hours earlier inside his door.

'It's very good to have you with us, Ms. Hanning.' Podmore, pink faced, plump, was scarcely taller than Sally, who thought the man could have modeled for the *Just William* comic books that her grandmother had inexplicably sent every Christmas to whichever embassy her father had been stationed. The cherubic smile he was now giving would have suited the illustration, too.

'I'm here on a very specific assignment.'

'We can well understand that.' Podmore continued to smile. 'And I want to assure you right away that every help and assistance the embassy can offer is at your disposal.'

'That's very kind.' Sally smiled back. 'But my embassy needs are minimal: just the communication facilities and the convenience of a compound apartment.'

'I'm sure there are some social possibilities you might very much enjoy.'

'Thank you, but I don't imagine I'll have a lot of time for socializing.' Protocol decreed she comply with Fellowes's summons outside the communications room, knowing he was relaying it from the ambassador, but she wished she could have avoided this. She had to make contact with Johnston in thirty minutes and didn't want to create any excuse for the man to change his mind about her meeting the coordinators of the unit or the NSA cryptologist.

'Quite so,' bustled Podmore. 'You're going to be extremely busy, involved, I appreciate. But my ambassador has asked me to arrange some time within your busy schedule for contact between us: the ambassador, myself, and of course our Mr. Fellowes. And let me say at the outset that we appreciate our meetings will have to fit into your schedule, not ours.'

She breathed in deeply. 'I must repeat that mine is a specific, strictly governed assignment. I am instructed by my director-general to tell you that all information about the ongoing search for the missing terrorist, Ismail al Aswamy, and any wider aspects of the investigation have to come from your usual contacts with the American State Department, who we know to be fully involved, or any other source through which Mr Fellowes works.' She wished it hadn't sounded as if she were reciting from a head-master's school report but hoped the formality would cut short a pointlessly protracted argument. Podmore would have been warned by Fellowes, but Sally was impressed by the man's portrayal of bewildered outrage.

Podmore did not speak immediately but stared at her in wide-eyed, feigned amazement. Then he said, 'This is ridiculous . . . totally unaccept-able. We're talking about the *ambassador*! You can't refuse the ambassa-dor.'

'I was advised to tell you that if you felt the need to protest, it should be done through the Foreign Office, which is being fully briefed by the Director-General. That briefing will also include everything in which I am involved, here in Washington.'

'There will certainly be the strongest protest, both through the For-eign Office and personally to your director-general,' threatened Podmore. 'And I expect you to hold yourself in readiness for further meetings be-tween us.'

'Of course.'

With less than ten minutes before her scheduled call with Johnston, Sally headed to her unused office. After a jump of satisfaction when he told her of the eleven o'clock meeting the following morning, she was then quickly disappointed—although objectively not surprised—that Johnston stipulated the encounter would be in his office.

Fellowes, at his immaculately clean desk when she opened the link-ing door, asked, 'What's it feel like to commit suicide?'

'Painless.'

15

THE BOUNTY OFFER WAS POLITICALLY ORCHESTRATED TO ACHIEVE the maximum impact. America led at midnight eastern time, with $12 million. The United Kingdom's carefully timed £2 million was next, and by varying breakfast times the following morning the European Union's euro contributions brought the total to $20 million. Every televised and newspaper announcement was accompanied by genuine although technically sharpened photographs of Ismail al Aswamy, as well as enhanced facial images of the man without his beard—some retaining the moustache—from several generated angles.

Government anti-terrorist ministers announced their contributions in eight European countries, including Britain. In America it was declared by the head of Homeland Security. He was accompanied in television studios and at a general press conference by the deputy director of defence and the directors of the FBI and CIA. The timings of the declarations were coordinated. The accompanying statements, intended to be reassuringly calming, were not.

The political needs of each country to show concerted resolve achieved the opposite. The FBI director misdirected the tone by declaring al Aswamy number one on the Bureau's most wanted list; every agent in the country was specifically assigned to the manhunt. At 1:30 A.M. in London the anti-terrorist minister was unable to properly read his auto-cue and repeatedly referred to an overwhelming scourge of international terrorism and ad-libbed that Interpol, which is a police information-disseminating system with no operational capability, was mobilizing an armed, continent-wide force authorized to use "ultimate force," inevitably translated as a shoot-on-sight edict. From Berlin, consumed by the Sellafield seizure of the man wanted for the Hamburg massacre, came the positive assertion that al Aswamy was the hitherto unidentified successor to Osama bin Laden, which was seemingly doubly confirmed within thirty minutes by France. The Parisian spokesperson suggested that specialized army forces were on standby with police units protectively emplaced around such iconic landmarks as the Eiffel Tower and the Arc de Triomphe. In Italy, its government basking in public approval for saving the Colosseum, the flood finally spilled over the dam. Sufficient details of the Iranian-sponsored international structure of Al Qaeda were being disclosed by the would-be perpetrators of the Colosseum outrage so as to totally destroy the organization's existence. Also emerging from those disclosures were al Aswamy's further intended attacks, none of which would now succeed.

Throughout two continents a slew of supposed media and intelligence specialists analyzed the individual government statements—initially intrigued by their nocturnal timing from America's midnight announcement—and concluded with assessments far more closely correlated than the individual countries' disconnected efforts. The $20 million confirmed that al Aswamy *was* bin Laden's successor as the ultimate leader of the disparate Al Qaeda. That was further confirmed by the magnitude of the three failed attacks: had they succeeded, they would have been far greater than the 2001 Twin Towers atrocity. The ambivalence of the Italian statement clearly indicated that the new targets were unknown. Al Aswamy and the terrorist group he led were still at large in America, but that Europe was contributing to the bounty proved the assaults were going to be global. Which further proved that Al Qaeda had regrouped into an international force capable of striking globally. Sellafield was a clear indication that one—or even more—of the forthcoming atrocities would involve a nuclear weapon.

'What the hell's going on?' demanded Sally in her morning telephone contact with London, the monitoring TV in the embassy communications room loud enough for her to hear the continuous news coverage.

'Everything that I was afraid would happen,' replied David Monkton.

Sally delayed leaving the compound apartment until the last possible moment, expecting the meeting to be cancelled, and drove out to Langley waiting for the cell phone call that never came. She entered Johnston's office with five minutes to spare. The two men she'd come to meet were already there, their chairs forming a vague semi-circle completed by Johnston at his desk. They reminded her of the three wise monkeys, although ready rather than reluctant to see, hear, and speak of evil. Or were they? Their body language was scarcely that of a combined team: each seemed to want space from the other. Her already positioned chair made her their focus, like a job applicant, which by a long stretch of imagination she supposed she was. If the seating arrangement was meant to unsettle her, it didn't work.

She'd correctly identified the two strangers while she was still standing, before Johnston's introduction. James Bradley's tightly corseting suit looked as if he'd uncomfortably slept in it, which considering the unfolding mistakes of the previous night was a distinct possibility. The handshake was overly firm—which she anticipated and so didn't flinch—but at the same time dismissive, matching the fixed expression with which he was now regarding her. He probably had more reason than she did to be uneasy, Sally supposed, remembering her previous day's conversation with Johnston. As the CIA supervisor, he would be held directly responsible for the failure of al Aswamy's surveillance. Jack Irvine, by comparison, hadn't attempted any finger-crushing nonsense and instead smiled an even-toothed smile and said, 'Good to meet you,' as if he'd meant it, even if he didn't.

Sally put him at at least six feet two, the height accentuated by a slimness she guessed to be more naturally than athletically achieved. The freshly laundered chinos were barely creased, and the deep blue George Washington University sweatshirt looked fresh, too. He wasn't wearing socks with the loafers.

Johnston said, 'Well, what do you think of what's happened overnight?'

As of an hour ago Johnston hadn't spoken with Monkton, Sally knew. 'The leak of further possible attacks was inevitable, with so many people involved in so many countries. But it shouldn't have happened this way. It was ridiculous to pander to individual country posturing instead of centralizing the bounty offer, and even more ridiculous to let the announcements run like an all-night film, which is precisely what it's turned out to be, a Hollywood catastrophe movie. The biggest error was the ignorance it showed. Al Qaeda isn't a cohesive organization with al Aswamy at its head, like an army general. We all know it's a collection of disparate cells, only very loosely connected.'

This wasn't what she was there for, but Sally accepted the previous night couldn't be ignored. Bradley's face had initially tightened as she'd begun talking, but he relaxed by the time she'd finished without having referred to the missing Iranian.

'What about you?'

Bradley too obviously didn't expect Johnston's direct question. Recovering badly, he said, 'It's kind of a mess, but everyone in the world will know what al Aswamy looks like now. Twenty million will get him.'

The demand for Bradley's opinion hadn't been part of whatever preparation there'd been before her arrival, Sally guessed. So it *was* the continued humiliation of the man. She said, 'Last night's damage can't be undone.' The remark wasn't compassion for Bradley: she wanted to get to the purpose of this meeting, not play a CIA who-did-what-wrong game.

'What about you?' persisted Johnston, coming to Irvine.

There was no surprised reaction. Without any hesitation Irvine said, 'What more is there to say? It was a screwup, from a bad start to a worse finish, and now there's worldwide panic, and al Aswamy, Tehran, and every half-assed terrorist in every cave, hole in the ground, ashram, or mosque is risking cardiac arrest laughing so hard at not having had to do a goddamned thing to generate that panic. So why don't we talk about something else, something constructive?'

Irvine enjoyed the restrained but approving smile from the woman, though he was still adjusting to her presence. He hadn't thought about what she would be like, hadn't thought anything about her beyond that their encounter was delaying his getting to the Moscow Alternative chat room. But he'd briefed everyone at Fort Meade beforehand and had his cell phone in his pocket. He could spend a little more time here.

There was definitely a Middle East connection, he decided. If Sally Hanning was her real name—and during his first week at Langley he'd learned exchanged names were rarely if ever birth names—she'd had mixed parentage. Caucasian features, so the most likely was a Western father—British even more likely because she'd been accepted into Britain's MI5—and a Middle Eastern mother. Milked-coffee complexion, deeply blue eyes, blond hair fashioned to Western shortness, maybe five feet eight, maybe an inch taller. Didn't fit a Maghreb profile; farther north than Israel—the strongest contender—Syria, Lebanon, or Jordan. Flawless face, flawless body, catwalk couture, in-your-face confidence. Not the right combination, came the abrupt caveat. Another first-week lesson: professional intelligence agents didn't exist. They were never there, never seen, never remembered: like ghosts, they didn't cast shadows, didn't photograph, neither on camera nor in mind. Sally Hanning was break-your-neck-turnaround beautiful to look at, which he was having a hell of a job steeling himself from too obviously doing, glad at that particular moment he didn't have to try so hard because she'd picked up on his remark.

'Why don't we do that?' snatched Sally. 'There's nothing we can do or say that's going to affect anything else at this moment, is there?'

'I'd hoped there might have been something,' said Johnston, refusing to be hurried. Still talking to Irvine, he said, 'Something you might have come up with?'

Moving in the right direction, thought Sally: it actually sounded like an easy transition into what she was there to hear.

'If there'd been anything, anything at all, I wouldn't have waited until now to tell you,' disappointed Irvine.

'I haven't spoken to London yet today?' switched the covert operations chief, implying the question as he turned back to Sally.

'There's disbelief at what happened last night, nothing more,' replied Sally shortly, determined to force the pace as well as the direction. 'Perhaps we can talk about what part I can play in the Shepherd operation?'

Bradley stirred. 'Yes, that's what we're here to talk about.'

Sally thought she detected some resentment, which wasn't so easy to understand. There was no authority, no way, her presence could affect him.

Johnston said, 'Shepherd's a specialized operation, targeted against terrorist groups using social networks, predominantly Facebook. We identify, isolate, infiltrate, and misdirect.'

Too generalized, too glib, assessed Sally, at once; go along with it, prise it out a scrap at a time, she told herself. Overly generalizing in return, she said, 'Isn't that what NSA does anyway?'

Both Bradley and Irvine frowned at the demand. Johnston came close and said, 'Identifying, certainly; more suspecting, maybe, before passing it on as we did with Sellafield and the Colosseum, in Rome. But we confirm the suspicion when it directly affects America.'

Better, but not by much, thought Sally. 'And having isolated and confirmed the suspicion, the CIA infiltrates?'

This time Irvine didn't frown. Bradley did, though, and Johnston came closer than before. With a vague hand gesture to Irvine, the man said, 'You want to come in here, Jack?'

'It's not physical infiltration. We do it electronically—' started the cryptologist.

Sally broke in, 'Hacking?'

'Yes. You up to speed with that?'

Sally shook her head but didn't speak, wanting everything to come from one of the three.

'We don't do it direct: we get into other sites, without the account holders knowing, and from the first go into a second and from the second go into a third. They're our firewalls. Our targets can't ever get past them. They self-destruct the moment they're detected. There's no danger of our being detected.'

'And access all their planning; get ahead of them?'

'Exactly.'

Shit! She shouldn't ask questions that only got single-word answers; there'd even been a hint of a patronizing smile from Johnston. 'Where and how does misdirection fit in?'

For the first time Irvine hesitated. 'It gives us logistical time to get the CIA in position.'

Sally was conscious of a facial relaxation from Johnston and Bradley. Keeping her attention more on Bradley than Irvine, she asked, 'What happened to the Washington Monument logistics?'

'We weren't properly in position when the media leak happened,' said Bradley hurriedly.

'Which won't happen again,' said Johnston just as quickly.

They were treating her like a fool, Sally decided; shut up or put up time. 'I came here, was accepted here, on an understanding between you, Mr Johnston, and my own director in London that I could make a contribution to Operation Cyber Shepherd, as I made a contribution to an intended assault upon an English nuclear installation. I was able to do that because I was at the absolute centre of the investigation, able to fit the pieces together—'

'We're aware of your success,' intruded Johnston.

'I'm not trailing success stories,' dismissed Sally impatiently. 'I'm setting it out solely to illustrate *why* I was able to achieve it, *why* a potentially fatal leakage of nuclear material was stopped.' She looked directly at Bradley. 'If al Aswamy is controlling other attacks, through other groups, and some of those we've detained in Britain and Rome know more than they've so far admitted, you could well get al Aswamy for twenty million dollars. But getting him doesn't guarantee that none of his other targets won't be hit; every indication is that he's too committed to disclose them even if he's seized. And it wouldn't reduce the threat if he is caught and gives up every location. One of his groups could—and probably would—get through. Which again isn't any guarantee that a catastrophe will be prevented. That twenty million dollars and all the hysteria it's generating is a direct challenge to enough jihadists and fundamentalists to stage outrages entirely unconnected with al Aswamy and anything he might or might not have planned.'

'We know that,' persisted Bradley.

There wasn't the resentful attitude of the beginning, judged Sally. 'I'm reassured, which I haven't been up to now.'

'You are here by invitation,' threatened Johnston stiffly.

Almost too far, Sally accepted warily; no farther. 'To do what! Work how? With whom? At what level?'

'You'll work here, at Langley. Through me,' said Johnston.

A virtual repeat of the Patrick Fellowes charade, Sally recognized; confirmation of what she'd feared from the outset. 'With access to all the raw intelligence, as and how it comes in?'

'Eighty percent arrives in Arabic,' said Irvine, staging a personal experiment.

'Which I have,' responded Sally, seeing an opening. 'I could work with your linguists if there are any dialect or regional difficulties.'

It confirmed Irvine's first impressions, but he hadn't expected the reply. 'We'll sort any problems out as and when they arise.'

'You're a linguist?'

'Some Arabic,' minimized Irvine, aware of the concentration from the other two men.

'That could work well, with both of us being here at Langley.' She'd pushed the promises well beyond what Johnston had been prepared to accept, Sally thought contentedly.

'We'll sort out the details,' Johnston tried to qualify.

She already had if she was quick enough, thought Sally. But she could allow a few more minutes. 'While we're sorting things out, I'd like the surveillance that's been put on me since yesterday lifted. And please don't tell me it was for my own protection. The amateurs you assigned need far more protection than I do.'

Jack Irvine had enjoyed Johnston's discomfort at Sally's dismissal of the surveillance just slightly more than the inquest that immediately followed, although he believed he'd eventually convinced the covert operations director that he'd have no difficulty concealing the contentious aspects of Operation Cyber Shepherd. Today's episode compounded his increasing belief that the only way to preserve the operation was to completely bypass Johnston and Bradley and appeal directly to Conrad Graham—the original and enthusiastic authorizer—to reorganize the CIA supervising structure.

His phone finally vibrated as Irvine entered his CIA office, stopping him just inside the door. Marian said, 'Shab's sending you the full e-mail, but I wanted to give you the heads-up right away.'

'What!' demanded Irvine.

'Akram's made a connection with Anis on the Action subcatalog: there's an ongoing exchange right now. And we've got three other possibles going through the number generator.'

'Tell Akram—' Irvine instinctively began, but stopped short of appearing unsure of Malik's ability.

'Tell him what?' demanded the woman.

'Tell him well done.'

'You coming down?'

Irvine hesitated. 'Seems you're doing all right without me. I can monitor Akram from here.'

'How's it going?'

'Not as good as it's obviously going with you.'

———

Sally's frustration at taking ten minutes to exit the labyrinthine CIA building was doubly compounded by being told, when she was finally able to make a cell phone call from her car, that David Monkton was in conference. She transferred the call to Jeremy Dodson and demanded she leapfrog any other held calls once she made secure contact from the embassy, refusing any further conversation on an open line.

When the embassy connection was made and without any greeting, Sally blurted, 'Have you spoken to Johnston?'

'No.'

Got in first! she thought. She could be the manipulator, not the manipulated.

Monkton listened in customary silence. When Sally finished, he said, 'Yes, I can do that. And there's something else.'

'What?'

'The government has made a political decision.'

'Oh,' said Sally in immediate understanding. Monkton was being protectively ambivalent to allow them both a pedantic legal denial if it ever became a public scandal: the Sellafield detainees were—pedantic again—MI5's responsibility.

'Don't approach Johnston until tomorrow. I want to give him time to calculate his reliance upon us.'

For such an inconspicuous, insignificant-appearing man, David Monkton was a true Machiavellian bastard, she decided. 'There's something else from this end, too. I'm under permanent CIA surveillance. Started directly after I left Langley after my initial meeting with Johnston. I demanded today that it be lifted, but I don't expect it to be.'

'Do you want me to raise it?'

Sally hesitated. 'No. Let's see what happens.'

16

JACK IRVINE WAS SWEPT BY AN ACHING FRUSTRATION AT eavesdropping on Akram Malik's chat-room conversation with Anis, his hands initially hovering involuntarily over the computer keyboard through which he'd gained remote access to the younger man's machine at Fort Meade. Irvine had entered Akram Malik's computer with its page register at three, preventing his reading the already-scrolled-up beginning of the conversation until after the disconnection. That Malik had sustained the exchange for that long had to mean that Anis did not suspect the person to whom he was now talking was not the Shamil25 to whom he'd spoken the first time. Although he'd never experienced or seen definitive proof— and therefore didn't subscribe to it—the legend persisted among a number of professional cryptologists that some were so proficient in their art that they could recognize differences between keyboard transmission patterns purporting to be from the same sender, a technique that *was* established with Morse-code traffic in the Second World War. Irvine reassured himself that if such prowess existed beyond acknowledged key counting, it would be at Vevak level, not that of Anis. A more objective suspicion was a differing command of Arabic, which again was unlikely. Arabic was Malik's second language, as it was Irvine's.

Irvine came into the exchange on an incomplete Anis response to a post from Malik that Irvine could not see. What Irvine was able to read was *baubles of the Great Satan.*

The bounty? Irvine immediately wondered.

Malik: *If a flea had money it would buy its own dog.*

They were talking in euphemisms, recognized Irvine, who knew the proverb.

Anis: *A friend that you buy for money will be bought from you.*

Definitely the bounty, determined Irvine. But after almost three pages tiptoeing on a private, one-to-one link, he would have expected—hoped at least—that they would have progressed to more direct exchanges.

Malik: *As easily perhaps as an enemy.*

Irvine tensed forward, expecting a disconnection, imagining Malik held by matching fear. Then . . .

Anis: *Depending, of course, upon the price of both.*

Malik: *And how it is dispersed.*

Malik was doing well, decided Irvine. He didn't think he could have done better.

Anis: *Perhaps among many.*

What the hell did that mean? questioned Irvine, struggling for the response he would have attempted.

Malik: *But for a single cause.*

He wouldn't have chosen that remark, thought Irvine worriedly.

Anis: *Which requires the strength of many.*

Malik: *An army of sheep led by a lion would defeat an army of lions led by a sheep.*

The perfect response! gauged Irvine, again recognizing the aphorism.

Anis: *Which army would you join?*

The invitation to commit! identified Irvine, once more physically leaning towards his screen for the Fort Meade response.

Malik: *Lions led by lions.*

Anis: *Who would welcome you.*

Malik: *I am honoured.*

Anis: *Marg bar Amrika.*

Malik: *Marg bar Amrika.*

Anis: *Inshallah.*

Malik: *Inshallah.*

Irvine didn't risk entering Malik's screen, unsure if Anis had closed his connection. Marian Lowell answered the telephone and said Malik wasn't immediately disconnecting either for the same reason, although it appeared that Anis had gone. Singleton came on the line, agreeing at once that Malik had handled the conversation perfectly.

'What about Shab?'

'Still number crunching. No luck this soon; unrealistic to expect there could be. I'm obviously concentrating on the Anis IP code.' There was a hesitation. 'You can see Akram's disconnected now. I'll put you over.'

'You did a hell of a job,' at once praised Irvine, finally scrolling back to the beginning of the computer conversation with Anis.

'Thank you,' Malik said modestly. 'I was lucky to sync with his thinking.'

'Luck didn't come into it. You had a handle on it from the start. So how do you read it?'

Malik hesitated, reluctant to endanger the praise by a misjudged remark. Finally he said, 'We're being groomed for something.'

'Right on the button. We're going forwards, no longer backwards. I'll be with you in just over an hour.'

'And I've downloaded two other IP domains to target,' said Malik, bringing up a new page. The first was Mohammed@homagebridge with a YE country code, denoting Yemen. The other was Nek@dangerrange. The country code, NG, identified the registration country as Nigeria.

'Why these two?' asked Irvine.

'They came into the room immediately after Anis. And they approached me,' said Malik. 'Both IPs were originally in Arabizi.'

Objectivity is the primary mind-set of a man obsessed with self-preservation, and objectively Charles Johnston acknowledged, without distracting rancour, that he had been totally outmanoeuvred by David Monkton. Or possibly by Sally Hanning. More objectively still, by the two of them. But only he knew that, would ever know that. With the merest tweaks the setback could—and most decisively would—be reversed into an unquestionable coup amid the otherwise tail-chasing panic to find Ismail al Aswamy.

The woman had to be his focus. She'd manipulated their first meeting to get what she imagined to be open-book access to Irvine and was obviously the conduit to Monkton, who'd emerged a far-harder hard-ass than he'd anticipated. His disadvantage was that he needed them, both of them. Was he adept enough to outmanoeuvre the manoeuvres? Remaining rigidly objective, Johnston conceded that he wasn't sure; worse, if the woman—who'd always suspect deception because of the business they were in—saw as much as a shadow of double doubt, they'd beat him again, and the next time it might not be as easy to reassert himself as the ringmaster.

He had a conduit of his own, Johnston abruptly remembered. Sally Hanning would accept what Jack Irvine told her far more unquestioningly than from him. Not the ideal solution but the best available for the moment, until he could devise something better.

'Hi! Remember me!' uncomfortably gushed Sally, forcing the brightness. Monkton's 'no contact' edict didn't include Jack Irvine.

'Who is . . . ?' began Irvine, disorientated at the cell phone intrusion within minutes of his arrival at Fort Meade.

'After this morning's arrangement I thought—'

'Sally.' He stopped, recognizing her voice. 'I'm not at Langley now. You're on an automatic telephone switch system. I'll be back—'

'What's happening at Meade?'

'I can't talk now. I'll be back tomorrow. I have to go now.'

'Who the hell's Sally?' demanded Burt Singleton, as irritated as Irvine at the intrusion.

'The Englishwoman who Johnston's so impressed with: the one who pulled everything together in the UK.'

'I didn't think she was going to be any part of what we're doing here?' challenged Marian Lowell.

'She isn't!' said Irvine, his irritation at the confrontation turning inside the room. 'Let's get back to what I came down for.'

'I think we've talked ourselves out here,' said Singleton. 'It looks like something's going down, but I've got an uneasy feeling about it.'

'Like what?' demanded Malik, resentful of his coup being doubted.

'A feeling is all.' Singleton shrugged.

'Maybe it'll help if I get the other access codes,' said Shab Barker.

'And I break into Anis's to get some idea of who he really is,' said Singleton, sensing the other man's discomfort at not having contributed anything so far.

'I've come out of the chat room,' reminded Malik unnecessarily. 'You want to take over or for me to go on?'

'I couldn't have done better than you did today; none of us could. You go on,' said Irvine, who'd made the decision on the drive down from Washington.

'When?' pressed Malik. 'Immediately, like later tonight or tomorrow? Or maybe wait a little?'

'Damned if we do and damned if we don't,' mused Irvine. 'I'd like to let in a little slack. But in the current Washington hysteria we need something positive to justify our continued existence.'

'Tomorrow then?' Malik pressed, determined to prevent any misunderstanding.

'Early,' decided Irvine emphatically. 'Let's see if he's testing us like we're testing him. Log in around dawn. See if he's waiting. Or if anyone else takes over or joins the discussion. If you don't get a ping by nine, nine thirty, come out.'

'You telling Washington about this?' demanded Singleton.

'There's nothing to tell them yet.'

Marian Lowell waited until she was being driven home by Singleton before asking him, 'Would you have gone in so soon?'

'No,' said the man shortly.

'So you think Irvine's taking shortcuts to save his precious project?'

'Something like that.'

'Worried?'

'It won't be our faces it blows up in, will it?'

'That's DC diktat.'

'It's contagious, like a plague.'

'I could have scanned all this to the embassy restricted to Your Eyes Only,' protested the Records supervisor at Thames House, at the end of their forty-five-minute exchange.

Which wouldn't have kept it from Nigel Fellowes, suspected Sally, from the seclusion of her compound apartment. 'There's a reason. I owe you.'

'I hope it's worth it.'

'So do I.'

17

HAMBURG WAS THE INITIAL TARGET. SEPARATE DEVICES WERE
linked to explode in sequence beneath the three main fuel-storage tanks in
the port, but only the first properly detonated, and the resulting blaze did
not spread to the other two. Four ready-for-shipment containers were destroyed. Six firemen were injured, none seriously. The names of Ismail al
Aswamy and Horst Becker were included in all three anonymous calls to
Hamburg police within an hour after the explosion, claiming Al Qaeda
responsibility. The second assault came an hour later with the detonation of
phosphorous-packed bombs beneath two of the support legs of the Eiffel
Tower, ridiculing earlier French-government guarantees against any terrorist act upon national monuments. Here again, no-one was injured, but
the ferocity of the phosphorous heat caused substantial burn-pitting to
both support struts, which now needed extensive metallurgical examination.
Ismail al Aswamy was named in the three Al Qaeda claims. The timer
malfunctioned on the bomb secreted in a pod of the London Millennium
Eye, although the detonator flared sufficiently to ignite its canvas holdall.
Had it exploded during the Ferris wheel's thirty-minute rotation, the capsule would have been ripped from its mountings and potentially thrown as
many as thirty trapped people into the Thames. Some would inevitably
have drowned. Instead the malfunction left substantial forensic material
and sufficient eyewitness descriptions of two men hurrying from the sabotaged capsule for three different photo-imaging reproductions.

David Monkton waited until Sally transferred to the security of a communications-room cubicle for their twenty-minute conversation. She was able to watch an hour of CNN updates and to shower and dress before Charles Johnston's call.

'I've been waiting,' said Sally, unsure how her carefully planned day was going to be disrupted. That she was being involved so immediately was encouraging, though.

On this second occasion Sally got to the covert operations director's office ahead of anyone else, guessing when they finally arrived that Johnston had given them a later arrival time in the hope of learning more about the London episode in the thirty minutes they'd been alone together. Which he hadn't. She'd used the time against the man, seeding what was to come with the vaguest suggestions of intelligence gains over any losses, but stopping short of expanding on what they might be. She and Monkton had agreed during their predawn discussion that the failed London attempt — and their equally agreed assessment of the other two — added to their potential negotiating advantages. Monkton would automatically have known of her earlier archive search, but it had been absolutely essential that she'd told him then rather than during their later, scheduled morning contact. Sally was passingly disappointed when only James Bradley and Jack Irvine finally arrived, but at once balanced the regret with the thought that it might make it easier to concentrate upon Irvine, which had been her original intention after her records search. He'd obviously been stressed, impatient at her interrupting whatever was happening at Fort Meade the previous evening.

'You've seen all there is to see of the overnight escalation?' greeted Johnston in oddly weary resignation.

That didn't chime with their earlier conversation, despite her determined avoidance to be specific, thought Sally. Was that unprofessional misinterpretation or a weak attempt to prompt her immediate intervention? She remained silent.

'What is there beyond what's on TV?' demanded Bradley, bringing the attention upon Sally by putting the question directly to her.

Centre stage earlier than expected, Sally accepted: an easy beginning, giving them all the chance to settle. 'We've lifted a lot of forensics in London. And despite their both being hooded, we've got good images of two men who left the pod in which the bomb was planted. They're being put through terrorist photographic records, have been for the past three hours. The proof that they are the would-be bombers is unarguable. We're enhancing a CCTV film for definitive facial identification, but enough remained of the holdall for a positive facial match with what one of the men carried onto the wheel. And there's fingerprints to top it all off.'

'They rode it?' demanded Bradley. He was predictably straitjack-eted in the same tightly buttoned and even tighter creased suit he'd worn before, and Sally didn't think the shirt had been changed, either. His nervous fidgeting was more obvious, with a lot of discomfited foot shuffling.

'To plant their explosive,' confirmed Sally. 'It takes at least half an hour, sometimes longer depending upon the number of passengers, to make one complete revolution. They had plenty of time to secure it under the seat.'

'It answers the questions about al Aswamy, doesn't it?' pressed Johnston, increasing Bradley's unease.

To openly show Johnston up didn't serve any purpose, least of all hers, Sally decided. 'Why don't we set out those questions, make sure there aren't any misunderstandings between us?'

Johnston and Irvine frowned. Bradley, the most pressured, said, 'For Christ's sake! There's only one question and that's surely been answered! Al Aswamy *has* set up other attacks and these were the first three!'

'You hear any chatter to support that, Jack?' Sally asked.

The phraseology more than the unexpectedness of her question sur-prised Irvine, who blurted, 'No, there hasn't,' before wishing he'd given himself more time to formulate a response. With no alternative, he went on, 'I spoke to Meade this morning. There's been nothing from the usual sites that are the quickest to carry genuine Al Qaeda claims.' There'd been no approach, either, from Anis to Akram Malik's pre-dawn return to the Action chat room.

'Nothing's been registered by GCHQ, either,' disclosed Sally, mentally crossing off an intercepted transmission hurrying Irvine to the NSA the previous evening. 'And the naming doesn't fit the pattern, does it?'

'No, definitely not,' recovered Irvine. Brains—if he'd needed proof— as well as beauty, for which he didn't need any more proof, either, decided Irvine, studying the woman. He hoped the darknet reaction to the overnight attacks—and more particularly a possible re-emergence of Anis— wouldn't keep him from the planned meeting with Sally.

'What happened to the need to avoid misunderstandings?' complained Johnston in clumsy irony.

Sally intentionally ducked the question, deferring to Irvine; he had to be brought in, flattered, and the other two would more readily accept the opinion of a fellow American. And it was another chance, albeit slim, to get an indication of what had so fully occupied Irvine the previous night. The code-breaker said, 'There's customarily very quick Internet traffic about any outrage Al Qaeda genuinely sponsors from Yemen's affiliated Ansar al-Sharia and al Shabaab in Somalia, as well as some Pakistani groups. That traffic's usually on Arabic media and broadcasting sites we permanently monitor. We didn't pick up anything overnight; still hadn't when I spoke to Meade forty minutes ago. Sally's just told you the UK didn't pick up anything, either. And there's a pattern to the Al Qaeda declarations, which doesn't fit here. Genuine Al Qaeda claims never name individuals, as al Aswamy was named during the night, with Horst Becker's added in Hamburg.'

Intent upon getting the slightest indication that her previous night's hunch had some basis, Sally concentrated upon Jack Irvine's Arabic pronunciation as he talked: definitely Middle East, not Gulf peninsula or Maghreb, she determined. Not sufficient to confirm her suspicion about Irvine's personal background, but an indicator that she could be right.

'You telling us these weren't organized terrorist attacks!' demanded Bradley hopefully.

Time to re-enter the exchange, establish her presence. Sally said, 'No, I'm not suggesting that at all, and I don't believe Jack is, either. The MI5 assessment is that the attacks were too quickly combined and badly carried out terrorist operations, the one in Germany—probably carried out by remnants of Becker's original group—just slightly more professional than those in France or England. But that alliance wasn't with al Aswamy or orchestrated from Tehran, which is the assumption we were supposed to make to fit a global campaign.'

'That's the evaluation I'm offering, too,' confirmed Irvine.

'NSA's considered evaluation or just yours?' challenged Johnston.

'Mine, to be included in any NSA submission requested by Homeland Security,' insisted Irvine.

'And is it just your judgment?' pressed Johnston, turning back to Sally.

'What I've set out is also the opinion of my director-general; the MI5 assessment is being submitted today to the government and anti-terrorist committees, prior to the prime minister's statement to Parliament.'

Johnston was momentarily silenced by her answer, the effect Sally intended. 'Is that what he's actually going to say?' pressed the man.

'I believe the thrust is to be that despite the anonymous claims, there is no definitive evidence linking the London attempt to al Aswamy or Iran, and therefore no proof of a concerted, well-organized global terrorist campaign,' paraphrased Sally, conscious as she spoke of the visible surprise on the faces of all three men—particularly Irvine—at her apparent high level of knowledge of government thinking. Sally knew from their earlier preparations that David Monkton would confirm that inference when Johnston spoke to him, which she had no doubt the man would do immediately after this meeting.

'You think that's enough to reassure people there is no international jihad?' questioned Johnston, his tension easing. 'They're still acts of terrorism.'

'It won't reassure everyone; conspiracy theorists are always waiting in line,' conceded Sally, wanting to move on. 'But there are more than enough disparities to make the case for the majority. And there are other possibilities involving al Aswamy.'

'What!' immediately seized Bradley, coming forward in his chair.

Sally staged the hesitation, wanting to register uncertainty in Johnston's mind. 'There could be further reciprocity between our two services.'

'What's that mean?' persisted Bradley.

'There's been some discussion about prisoner access'

'With your Sellafield detainees?' demanded Johnston, the tone and the immediate facial colouring betraying his ignorance of the higher-authority Washington request

'Everything's still at a very preliminary stage: it's not as straightforward as my coming here,' said Sally, avoiding the positive answer but wanting to imply her personal participation. 'Technically their custody is MI5's responsibility: we're conducting the interrogations at the moment.'

'And you are aware of these discussions?' pressed Johnston, as she'd hoped he would.

'I'm included in the consultations.' Come on, she thought, give me a way in!

Irvine said, 'Seems like we're looking to you for quite a lot of co-operation?'

Good enough, decided Sally. 'That's what we've agreed to, isn't it? Total co-operation and intelligence exchange of everything?'

'Yes,' said Johnston. 'That's our agreement.'

Jack Irvine only just held back from snatching for his muted cell phone, pressing into his chair to suppress its vibrating alert. He said, 'I'm sure it's going to work out just great.'

James Bradley said nothing.

'He broke his own record: you could scarcely have shut the door behind you,' timed Monkton.

'He ended the meeting straight after I mentioned prisoner exchange,' said Sally, back in the uncomfortably familiar communications cubicle. 'I'm sure Johnston didn't know.'

'So am I, although he obviously didn't admit it. Conrad Graham's not doing a lot for morale.'

'He's doing a lot for ours, though.'

'The PM took our lead for his Commons statement. And Berlin is dismissing any link between Hamburg and al Aswamy.'

'What about bounty response?'

'No-one's bothering to count public-report sightings anymore. None we've got in custody have broken rank yet.'

'How are you judging that?'

'I want to think that the threat was an empty bluff, to achieve the reaction it has, but I'm keeping my options open. Nothing on al Aswamy?'

'Not as of an hour ago, when I left Langley.'

'Have we done enough to keep you in the loop?'

'If it's about al Aswamy, yes. If they get him, they'll believe their immediate problems are over and want to tell the world. I'm still not learn ing anything about Cyber Shepherd: certainly not sufficient to understand what it's been set up to achieve.'

'You sure you're right about Irvine?'

'Not at all. It's still a hunch, a feeling without anything more to it than the name and a Middle East connection, which could just be coincidental. But I don't believe in coincidence.'

'Pity there isn't a photograph.'

'It would be an old one.'

'The ambassador's protested to the Foreign Office at how you're being allowed to operate.'

'We expected that.'

'And Records have complained at your insistence upon having the material you wanted dictated on an open line instead of being scanned over. They claim it risked security.'

'It would have been scanned to the communications room. Fellowes is the bureau chief, known and acknowledged. I'm not. I don't believe the scan would have been sent solely to me, even with an Eyes Only restriction.'

'What would the name have meant to Fellowes, even if he'd read it?'

Sally was damned if she was going to be pressured by the man as he'd harassed Jeremy Dodson and God knows how many others. 'Not a lot, to begin with. But what if he'd bounced it off one of his CIA or FBI friends on the cocktail circuit? And they'd asked around among themselves and discovered a resented MI5 officer—on an assignment her ambassador isn't allowed to know about—was asking about a disgraced former ambassador?'

Monkton was silent for several moments. 'I don't want to provide ammunition for continuing complaints.'

'Neither do I.'

There was further silence before Monkton said, 'I thought you had a meeting with Irvine today?'

She hoped Monkton hadn't regarded the exchange as a contest. If he had, it was too bad. 'He's calling me; promised it will be today, sometime.'

'I'll wait to hear,' ended Monkton, replacing the receiver in London without any farewell.

Wait was all that she could now do, accepted Sally. And if she was right that the soft burr she'd heard from Irvine's direction at the end of the meeting had been a muted cell phone, it might be a long wait.

Burt Singleton's remotely accessed screen came into focus as the man picked up his telephone at Fort Meade. Instantly recognizing the images on his screen, Irvine said, 'Tehran's back on?'

'Loud but not clear,' confirmed Singleton. 'Idrid@righttime.dj— Djibouti's a first—is a new domain in the Action subcatalog. Not on our watch list, either. And we haven't encountered the code before, either. Obviously it isn't broken yet; it's not going to be easy getting repetitions. Like the two that Malik picked up, it was originally in Arabizi. It was switched into Roman script at a Sana'a Facebook account. Which is where we lost it. I'm guessing a public-facility receiver, maybe a teahouse.'

'Something—al Aswamy, most likely—is moving, from a message concentration like that!' said Irvine.

'No trail after Sana'a. The bastards have well and truly learned the memory-stick trick, haven't they?'

'It's their job,' said Irvine pragmatically. 'And ours to beat them at. How do you rate our chances?'

Irvine imagined the shrug that went with the pause from the other end before the man said, 'Is it that twitchy up there?'

Now Irvine frowned, discomfited at so unwittingly conveying the attitude at Langley. 'I'm trying to keep our part of the operation afloat.' Which might not be Singleton's ambition, he thought, remembering the man's initial reaction to his complete explanation of Shepherd.

'*If* it's to al Aswamy, we might pick up a response *if* the messages require responses, and *if* by the time we do that we've broken the new code, and *if* that reply establishes a route, and *if* that route doesn't get broken by another memory-stick transfer . . .' The pause now was for effect. 'To save you the trouble, that's five *if*s.'

'I kept up with the count and take your points,' said Irvine. 'No reappearance from Anis?'

'Akram wants to know what to do.'

'Go back into the room,' decided Irvine. 'Try one of the others you've isolated if Anis doesn't show. And if Anis does turn up, tell Akram to wait for him to make the approach.'

'You going to say anything about the re-activation?'

'Not until we know more.'

'What have you got to tell me!'

'The Brits aren't linking last night with a continuing al Aswamy campaign: they think they were opportunists, jumping on a bandwagon.'

'Can't see how that helps a hell of a lot.'

'What you've just told me could change a lot of things,' said Irvine, deciding against disclosing the potential prisoner access—and the inevitable rendition—to someone who already questioned the legality of what they were doing.

'Is the British gal co-operating?'

'On a political level she's giving us more than we're giving her because we've got fuck all to give!'

'You going to tell her everything about Shepherd? GCHQ might have come across today's code.'

'It's a thought,' begrudged Irvine.

'Then think it,' urged Singleton. 'Jesus had disciples, remember?'

And one of Snow White's little helpers was named Grumpy, thought Irvine.

'Didn't think you were going to call,' greeted Sally.

'Got caught up in something,' said Irvine, who like the rest of the Fort Meade team had failed to understand anything of the new Iranian code. 'Didn't think I'd still be at Langley.'

Clumsy avoidance or even clumsier seduction pitch? Immaterial questions: she had him on the line, literally, and she wasn't going to let him get away. 'It's only a little after seven. I don't consider it late.'

'We could meet in town.'

Seduction pitch, she isolated; better, on balance, than heavy-footed avoidance. 'Why don't we do that?'

'There's a touring Boston Philharmonic at the Kennedy Center or jazz in Georgetown. We can eat at either.'

'Georgetown,' she chose at once. 'Let's eat first.'

'There's an Italian place on M Street and Wisconsin: Francesco's. Eight o'clock?'

18

SALLY WAS THERE BY EIGHT FIFTEEN, DETERMINED TO BE FIRST. But failed. Irvine had beaten her by what she guessed from his half-empty beer mug to be several minutes, maybe as many as ten if not more. Sally resolved the awkward hiatus of his rising to greet her simply by sitting down without offering a handshake or cheek to be kissed, which she guessed to be his open-armed expectation. The jeans were those he'd worn earlier, but the casual-necked, button-up polo shirt and Ivy League blazer, complete with heavily embossed, fake club badge, replaced the sweatshirt. Suspecting the preparations, Sally had changed, too. Her indigo Gucci silk shirt contrasted against the designer-faded jeans but matched the Chanel pumps. A cologne miasma smothered her Dior eau de toilette, so she guessed he'd showered as well.

Sally thought, Zero for trying too hard, minus even that for over-confidence.

Irvine thought, Good-bye empty bed, fingers crossed against my receiving a cell phone alert that spoils it all. Gesturing around the crowded restaurant, he said, 'Much more conducive than Langley.'

'Conducive to what?' Rules of engagement from the outset, she determined.

Right off the block, Irvine decided, encouraged. 'Getting to know each other, working together. That's the idea, isn't it?'

'Very definitely my idea. Is it yours?'

The waiter's arrival broke the moment. Sally ordered valpolicella. Irvine shook his head against more beer. Struggling for the innuendo, he said, 'Do you take the lead in everything?'

A lead she had to get absolutely right, she reminded herself, ignoring the clumsiness: professional business before private curiosity. 'I appear to be providing all of that without getting anything in return.'

Her obvious reference to the earlier Langley encounter momentarily confused him, but if those were the motions she wanted initially to go through, it was fine by him. 'What other way is there except from you guys? All we've done is fuck up big-time and create an international crisis. And we sure as hell don't want to talk about that.'

Sally suggested they order when the waiter returned with her wine, guarding against interruptions. Not waiting for his agreement, she took linguine with clams. After a brief hesitation, Irvine chose veal and a bottle of the wine she was drinking.

Sally said, 'I don't want to talk about any of that, either. What I want to talk about is a secret covert operation conducted by a very select code-breaking unit that was pretty damned successful before the CIA fucked up, a fuckup that wasn't the direct fault or responsibility of that unit.'

Irvine looked sharply around the adjoining tables before coming back to her, genuinely off-balance. 'You've forgotten we're in a public place, for Christ's sake!'

'A very noisy public place. There are only two tables that could conceivably over-hear us, and I've tried very hard since I got here to catch a single word that either couple has said. And haven't. We said "fuck" three times—that makes it four—and there hasn't been the slightest reaction from any of them, which there instinctively would have been even though it's an utterly meaningless and inoffensive expression outside of monasteries and nunneries and probably not even there. From now on we can talk in generalities that wouldn't mean a thing if overheard. So let's stop fucking about—there, I've said it again and no-one flinched—and you tell me what's so special or different about what you're doing from what NSA does all the time but which no-one is telling me, despite a supposed agreement. And despite, also, an exchange bargain that might solve your embarrassment.'

She hadn't been first off the block in the way he'd hoped, and his false start could have disqualified him, Irvine acknowledged. But it was recoverable. He smiled broadly and said, 'That sure was one hell of a speech!'

'Any part you didn't quite understand? I do re-runs.' Easy, she warned herself. He was back on track; she didn't want to stir resentment.

'I think I got it all.' Why hadn't he gone back up to Fort Meade to continue the code search instead of subjecting himself to this!

'So do I get it all in return?'

She really did have them by the balls, Irvine conceded, glad he'd already thought everything through. Fort Meade was occupying more of his thinking now than thoughts of an empty bed.

She'd off-balanced him, Sally decided; she had to maintain the pressure, not give him time to recover. 'We can talk as we eat,' insisted Sally as their food arrived. '*You* can talk as we eat.'

Irvine did both carefully. Sally had pushed aside her plate long before he finished but didn't immediately respond, looking directly at him as if expecting more, mentally filtering the explanation for what he *hadn't* told her. Eventually she said, 'You locate a questionable Facebook and satisfy yourselves it's a terrorist route by hacking into it? Getting in gives you the sender's complete contact list? The identifications increase with every interface that group has with others: suppliers, sympathizers, government links? You infiltrate misinformation, and if or when you get enough to indicate a possible attack, you press the button and stop it before it happens?'

'Take your prize from the top shelf.' Irvine smiled, believing he deserved one, too. If he wrapped this up soon, he could still go down to Meade.

What *hadn't* he told her! Sally wondered again, not smiling back. 'Tell me about the misinformation?'

Irvine shrugged, disinterested. 'Slipping stuff in here and there, creating distrust or suspicion, turning them against each other.'

Possible sensitive spot, detected Sally; certainly an unthinkingly weak response. 'Is that what you did with al Aswamy?'

Too close, Irvine recognized; still not a problem though. The trick would be to avoid lengthy answers that she could pick at. 'In the beginning.'

She gestured the waiter to clear the table, shaking her head in refusal to anything more without consulting Irvine, who stopped the man before he could leave to order coffee and brandy he didn't want. He didn't ask Sally if she wanted to change her mind.

'Tell me more about that,' persisted Sally, ignoring the petulance as she'd ignored the earlier innuendo.

'Followed his contacts list; leaked Sunni to Shiite and vice versa.'

Sally easily hid the satisfaction, hurrying on before Irvine could reflect upon what he'd said. 'And created chaos?'

Irvine shook his head. "They broke away from what they were planning, certainly. There was some infighting.' Which was virtually the truth, dependent solely upon interpretation.

'What's al Aswamy?' she asked, taking the chance.

'Shiite.'

She had enough information! Sally determined triumphantly. But to cut off at once would be too obvious. 'What about last night?'

'Last night?' hedged Irvine.

'Sounded as if there was something going on at Fort Meade?' Would he finally mention the muted cell phone call she'd heard?

'We thought there might have been something,' allowed Irvine cautiously. 'We're still working on it.' Singleton's frustration had stoked the distracting guilt that was now crystallizing in Irvine. He definitely shouldn't be here, doing this. He should be at Fort Meade working grids and graphs and computers and randomly generating number sequences with the rest of them, not sexually fantasizing over someone who could probably scarcely wait to get home and wash her mouth out for uttering a forbidden word.

'Involving al Aswamy?'

'Too early to say.' He'd be wasting time going all the way to Fort Meade now, he determined, his mind switchbacking just as he was wasting his time here to no purpose. He could be back at Owen Place in thirty minutes, remotely accessing what Singleton and the others were doing, making it clear that he was on board.

'Anything our GCHQ could do to help?' His attitude had changed. Had he realized his mistake?

Irvine shook his head. 'Nothing that would make any sense; nothing that would make sense to anyone yet.'

It had to be an enciphered code they couldn't break. But if they hadn't broken it, how could they suspect it? Obviously from its source. Al Aswamy's control had been very publicly identified. 'Iran makes sense.'

'So would your backing off just a little,' began Irvine, finally losing his temper, and continuing as far as 'I've told you . . .' before his cell phone vibrated. Sure he hadn't paused but speaking slightly louder, he finished, '. . . everything there is to know, so why don't we call it a day?'

'Don't you think you should take that call?'

'You let me look like an asshole!' accused Charles Johnston, his anger worsened by Conrad Graham's delaying their meeting this late into the evening.

'It's higher than me; higher than you,' said the deputy CIA director. 'Everyone's hunkered down after all the shit there was about rendition after 9/11 and Guantánamo. We've got to be careful.'

'I'm supposed to be heading the fucking operation!'

'I've just told you it's gone wider than that now. There's too much in the public domain. Now it's damage limitation on what we're going to do about it.'

Johnston hesitated, trying to peel away the nuances. 'You mean I'm no longer involved?'

'I mean you and your guys are part of a bigger operation, making every possible contribution, but that some things are being negotiated higher up the chain,' said Graham, impatiently looking at his desk clock.

Off the responsibility hook, judged Johnston. Which was what he himself wanted. But not to be marginalized. Remembering his morning session with Sally Hanning, he said, 'When are we going to get our guy from the Brits?'

'Still being negotiated. That's what we've been discussing upstairs until now, how to make it work.'

The motherfucker didn't know! realized Johnston. 'The conditions seemed pretty straightforward to me.'

Now it was Graham who hesitated, no longer occupied with the desk clock. 'What are you talking about!'

'We get a British prisoner to interrogate when the Brits are satisfied their gal is getting access to everything here. And I mean—and they mean—everything.'

'Why the fuck didn't you tell me this before?'

'Those higher up than me didn't keep me in the loop, remember?'

Sally sat unspeaking in the passenger seat of the '92 Volkswagen in its Canal Street lot, for the first time that night not trying to lead. Irvine remained silent for several minutes, staring down at his phone's text window. She could see a message, but wasn't able to read it from the intentionally awkward way he was holding the cell phone. Still unspeaking, he turned the phone off and put it back in his pocket.

Keeping the exasperation from her voice, Sally said, 'Anything I should know about?'

'There's a volume of traffic we can't read: a pattern.'

'What are you going to do.'

'Go back to Langley and give a warning.' More quickly than I did before, Irvine thought.

'I want to come with you.'

He hesitated. 'Why not?'

Sally twisted briefly in her seat to see if her followers were in place as they crossed the Key Bridge back towards Langley and exploded into laughter.

'What the hell . . . ,' Irvine said.

'You haven't been left out.'

'What are you talking about?'

'I picked up my surveillance the moment I left the embassy, itemized the cars around the restaurant—where you already were—when I got there. Your watchers are in line behind my watchers watching us. Gives you a warm feeling, being so well protected, doesn't it?'

How could things go from the president's calling him Harry to hell in a handcart? thought Packer. *Because* of that presidential recognition he would still have been okay, the way the others were still okay, if that asshole Burt Singleton hadn't pissed his pants and filed the formal disagreement declaration against Cyber Shepherd. Now he not only had to acknowledge an official document in writing but comment upon it before lodging the complaint with the counsel's office. He wouldn't hurry, Packer decided. If al Aswamy was detained and the threatened outrages prevented through Irvine's team—including Singleton—two floors below, the man's protests could be judged for what they were, pant pissing. Packer's problem was not knowing what to do if al Aswamy wasn't caught and there was an atrocity on American soil.

19

THEY WOULD OBVIOUSLY HAVE MET EARLIER, IF ONLY TO AGREE to her presence, and it clearly wasn't the full crisis committee. But it was still a far higher table than that at which Sally or David Monkton had expected her to sit. In addition to Conrad Graham there was a man she knew without introduction to be retired admiral Joshua Smith, director of Homeland Security, who sat facing her. He was flanked on his left by FBI director Frederick Bowyer and on his right by State Department deputy secretary Wilbur Denver. Charles Johnston, Bradley, and Jack Irvine were spread out farther around the oval table. Immediately behind Graham was an official recording bank of two stenographers, supported by four sound technicians independently keeping a backup audio transcript.

Everyone visibly showed the tiredness of a much-interrupted night that had only allowed a maximum of three hours' rest between various meetings, which had included arranging this limited gathering and a conference call between Sally, Monkton, and an anxious, promise-guaranteeing Johnston.

Conrad Graham concluded his formal introduction of Sally by identifying her as the MI5 officer who'd prevented the attempted UK attack and whose experience—'your thinking and your analysis of this worldwide Al Qaeda assault'—they considered invaluable. Sally acknowledged the tight-faced nods from the three new government officials, fully aware as she did so that it was an unthinkable concession for an agent from another intelligence service to be co-opted at such an echelon. Inconceivable, that is, but for the largely self-induced panic from which everyone was feeding. In addition there was the benefit of their having a readily available scapegoat for inevitable mistakes.

'Where's your evidence for an attack!' demanded Smith, an indulgently large, red-faced man.

Graham deferred to Irvine, who twice cleared his throat in surprise before saying, 'There's a pattern. A buildup of traffic that matches what we discovered when we reverse-analyzed the volume that preceded the previous attacks, not just here but in the UK and Italy.'

'You intercepting this new traffic?' picked up FBI director Frederick Bowyer, a diminutive, round-faced, round-bodied cottage loaf of a man, frowning in similar doubt.

'Some. We haven't yet deciphered it.'

'My bureau needs to be involved if there's an attack within America,' insisted Bowyer. 'That's our remit.'

'Let's establish if there's going to be one or whether we're crying wolf here,' said Smith.

'I'm formally registering the responsibility,' insisted Bowyer.

'It's registered,' promised the Homeland director.

Was Irvine crying wolf? wondered Sally. He hadn't gone into detail during their various exchanges during the night, but she'd expect more than what he was offering now.

'If it's al Aswamy, we can get the son of a bitch!' intruded the guilt-heavy Bradley. 'We can trace him through his e-mail address!'

'No, we can't,' refused Irvine. 'Al Aswamy's not using the e-mail address we had; he knows it's not secure anymore. He actually left his computer on a beet delivery truck, remember?'

'So you're telling us you believe there's going to be another attack, but that we *don't* know where, when, or how! And that we don't have a chance in hell of finding out!' demanded Wilbur Denver.

'Yes,' said Irvine flatly. 'The only chance we've got of locating al Aswamy through his e-mail traffic is to intercept another message that we can read and then follow to its end. Or in reverse, catch one of his to Tehran.'

After a long moment of receptive silence, Denver said, 'There's got to be a public warning!'

Admiral Smith turned to Sally from a cupped-hand exchange with Bowyer and said, 'We need your detainee! Now!'

We want your experience, your thinking, and your analysis, recalled Sally, all watch-and-wait resolutions discarded. 'What you need is a lot more considered thought and far less knee-jerk panic.'

The brief silence this time ranged between surprise, astonishment, and affront. Smith's face became redder. With difficulty he said, 'You have a point to make?'

'Several,' replied Sally, hurrying past the outburst. 'It would be the worst possible mistake to renew a public alert linked to an apparent new threat. What would it achieve? More panic to compound the hysteria created by a ridiculously high bounty producing a response too great properly ever to be analyzed—conceivably, even, overwhelming any real sightings or locating information.'

She was being too forthright, Sally realized, but she was too committed now to bite back the words: everything that David Monkton had warned her against. As well as being too negative. There had to be a balancing, positive contribution. She wished at that moment that she could think of one.

'It's my opinion, my judgement, that the most recent attacks weren't anything to do with al Aswamy or Al Qaeda,' Sally resumed. 'Al Aswamy is our concentration; he's state sponsored, Al Qaeda connected. Which means it's organized, well planned, despite our managing to intercept and prevent the three original attempts. Al Aswamy wasn't in direct command in Italy or the UK. He had to rely on others, who weren't as good as he is. Which he knew and possibly made provisions for, in the event of their failing.'

'What the hell are you talking about now!' demanded Denver, irritated at the criticism of his new-alert suggestion.

'It isn't professional for the leader of a current militarily organized group to discuss future operations in which that current group isn't involved; not even if they *were* to be involved,' set out Sally simply. 'It endangers those intended operations if they are caught, which both groups were in Italy and the UK.'

There was another punctuating break. Johnston said, 'You're contradicting yourself. You started off saying al Aswamy's a professional, now you're saying he's not.'

'I'm doing nothing of the sort,' corrected Sally, welcoming the proposal at last formulating in her mind. 'I'd consider it extremely professional to insure against the failure of something you can't personally command by carefully planting stories of further operations—'

'Planting!' seized the FBI director. 'You saying you don't think any more attacks are planned! Where's your evidence for that?'

'I don't have any evidence for that,' admitted Sally easily. 'I'm simply putting forward an alternative to what everyone's convinced themselves is going to happen, something that's also completely unsubstantiated by any evidence.'

'What about this!' demanded Irvine, gesturing with his own message copy.

'Indeed, what about it!' echoed Sally, waving her own slip as if answering a flag signal but then reading from it. 'Addressed to Hydarnes, Persia's— now Iran's—legendary warrior.' She hesitated, realizing her own oversight or again something further she hadn't been told. 'What was al Aswamy's operational addressee name on the original intercept?'

'Jamshid . . . ?' responded Irvine, turning the identification into a question.

'Another legendary Iranian warrior king,' completed Sally.

'Precisely why I said an hour ago that if al Aswamy isn't still operated by Hydarnes, then there's another cell we don't know anything about and have every reason to worry ourselves shitless,' said Irvine.

Sally looked down momentarily at the paper slip, folding it into concertina strips. 'Iran's the third-largest Internet user in the world—in addition to its own Halal or darknet Web usage—isn't it?'

'Yes?' confirmed Irvine, still questioning.

'What level of expertise and competence would you put them at, compared with NSA?'

Irvine hesitated. 'Maybe a tad short in actual technology. Operationally about equal. They recovered far more quickly from our Stuxnet malware than anyone expected, years earlier, in fact.'

'Tehran planned a world spectacular, as spectacular had all three succeeded as America's 9/11 or Britain's 7/7. One failure, one possible electronic interception, would professionally be built into that planning. I've already suggested how al Aswamy might have expected it. But if I were sitting in Tehran, analyzing how all three misfired'—Sally looked at Graham—'and don't forget you've asked for my analysis ... I'd conclude that three failures are too great a coincidence to be simply unlucky. I'd suspect that my communications chain's been compromised—'

'And if I were sitting beside you in Tehran, I'd close it down!' Irvine fought back.

'Because you think like a cryptologist, not as an intelligence officer who spends most of his or her time second- and third-guessing what your opponent is doing or might be doing,' capped Sally. 'Second- or third-guessing means working out how you lost three out of three operations to prevent your losing any more. What I'd do in Tehran is bait a hook—continuing the warrior code names, which almost makes it too obvious a bait—and cast it into cyberspace, counting the number of cutouts it passes through to discover how badly I've been compromised. Hydarnes was still on the Halal net at Cairo. If you react with a warning, it'll tell them you're that close. By successively reducing the number of cutouts, it'll also tell them if you're getting even closer still. And throughout all that time the panic and chaos already generated by twenty-million-dollar bounties and describing al Aswamy as public enemy number one will be compounded by renewed official warnings.' Sally intruded an emphasizing pause. 'Terror achieved without even bothering with a terrorist act. A perfect misinformation coup.'

'That's total hypotheses, from start to finish!' dismissed Joshua Smith. The uncertainty in his voice didn't match the intended rejection.

'No more than believing what the detainees are saying, which at the moment is nothing,' retorted Sally.

'You can't seriously be arguing that there shouldn't be a fresh public warning,' persisted Denver.

'I'm totally serious in arguing just that, and I've already told you why,' insisted Sally.

'I don't want to be told what we shouldn't do!' complained Smith. 'I want to hear what we *should* do!'

'Play the misinformation game against them,' declared Sally shortly.

'Go on,' urged Smith hopefully.

'You've got media sources through which you leak unattributed stories to spur bad guys into detection reactions, right?' Sally asked FBI director Frederick Bowyer.

Smith impatiently overrode Bowyer's hesitation. 'Of course he has!'

'Use a prestigious one: *The New York Times* or *The Washington Post*. But only one. It's got to be believed. The story is that al Aswamy has been detained and turned, that he's co-operating with the bounty guarantee and a new and safe life in a witness-protection programme. And then have every Homeland Security agency refuse to comment—but not deny—in the media rush to catch up on the story, which will be interpreted as confirmation that it's true. It'll dampen down the public frenzy, which needs capping. More important still could be a response from al Aswamy, desperate to let Tehran know he hasn't defected.'

The stir moved around the table, the frowning Joshua Smith the focus. Before Smith could react, Bowyer said, 'What happens when it's shown to be untrue, if there *is* another attack to prove it isn't true!'

'The story was unattributed; every Homeland agency refused to comment. We're not responsible. So what that it was untrue! It still gives us a chance—and more time—to get al Aswamy.'

'It's still "what if?"' said Bowyer.

'Okay,' said Sally, thrusting back into her chair. 'Someone come up with a better idea.'

'I may have been a little too outspoken,' admitted Sally.

'You were, and I warned you not to be, at that level,' said David Monkton.

Not for the first time Sally wished for more inflection in the man's flattened voice to get a better indication of his mood. 'There was no point in my being here without knowing everything, which in the beginning I didn't. I'm still not sure I know it all now.'

'And trying to take over the meeting was the way to get it?' asked Monkton, heavily sarcastic.

'I didn't try to take over the meeting. I was invited to give an opinion, which I did. And then to put forward a proposal, which I also did: the *only* proposal.'

'That, hopefully, will keep us where we are,' allowed Monkton doubtfully.

'When the meeting broke up, it was only being considered?' qualified Sally.

'There was a fuller meeting immediately afterwards where it was agreed.'

'Was it Johnston who complained about me?' demanded Sally. 'Or someone higher?'

'Johnston. And it hardly amounted to a complaint; it was a comment during a longer conversation.'

'About what?'

For the first time there was hesitation from London. 'They're desperate to get one of our prisoners.'

'I thought that had been decided?'

'I'm delaying as long as possible to keep us—which means you—where you are now.' Monkton paused again. 'There's also further Foreign Office pressure over your independence from the embassy. Have you had any fresh approaches?'

'I got back to a message from the first secretary, asking me to call. I haven't responded, obviously; waited until we'd spoken.'

'Don't agree to a meeting until tomorrow, to give us time to see if your idea is adopted. And when it happens, let's cut the aggression.'

I'll try, Sally thought.

20

THE NEW YORK TIMES RAN THE SEIZURE OF ISMAIL AL ASWAMY—together with his acceptance of a bounty payment in return for co-operation—as a three-inch-deep band across the top of its front page, giving the impression of its being the lead story. Specific details were limited by the need to agree to bargaining arrangements and the amount of the bounty payment with other countries, particularly the United Kingdom and Italy. Al Aswamy had already disclosed the extent of Iranian financial, matériel, and manpower support to Al Qaeda in Mali, Yemen, Somalia, and Kenya. Newspapers, wire services, and television news organizations throughout the world—including Al Jazeera—interpreted the refusal of Homeland Security agencies to comment on or to deny the *New York Times* story as confirmation that it was true. The story was either re-published, with attribution, or re-written without acknowledging the source. Both versions were supplemented by archive material and stock film footage. Understandably the most commonly re-published pictures were of the deserted Washington Mall, Rome's Colosseum, and the Sellafield nuclear plant.

Sally began monitoring the coverage from the embassy communications bunker just after dawn, channel-hopping from American TV to foreign stations to establish the global pickup. Its extent, in such a comparatively short time, surprised her. Al Jazeera's Arabic coverage was greater than on its English-language service and appeared to be the basis for Arab print, radio, and television reportage that appeared throughout the Arabian Peninsula and the Maghreb. There was no coverage from any of the limited media outlets in Mali, Yemen, Somalia, or Kenya, which was predictable. Sally considered Tehran's continued silence sufficiently curious to raise the issue with Jack Irvine ahead of her regular morning contact with David Monkton. Irvine told her there'd been no progress deciphering the new codes. He added that the more senior members of the Fort Meade team weren't impressed with the *New York Times* bait.

Sally was irritated by the dismissal, suspecting that Monkton wasn't, either. The Director-General took her patiently through the forthcoming encounter with the ambassador, insisting that she show the respect that the man would expect. At the end of their preparation Monkton warned, 'Don't get into any details of the bounty offer with the embassy people.'

'I didn't intend to,' said Sally, hoping she'd kept the indignation from her voice. From Monkton's initial silence, she knew she hadn't.

Eventually the man said, 'You clear on everything else?'

'Quite clear.'

'Let me know how it goes as soon as it's over.'

'Of course.'

The Director-General again disconnected without any farewell.

Sally arrived politely early, but Giles Podmore, the first secretary, was waiting, apparently impatiently, in his outer, secretarial office to turn her immediately back out into the corridor. 'Now it's a matter for the ambassador.' His voice changed at the word *ambassador.* Sally wasn't sure if it was out of respect or intended intimidation.

Nigel Fellowes was already waiting outside the ambassador's suite, with the usual uncoordinated neckwear. Sally took the anteroom chair. The two men remained standing. No-one talked; it reminded Sally of awaiting punishment outside principals' offices at embassy schools she'd attended. Even the black Chanel dress over her white blouse would at a stretch have qualified as a school uniform. They were summoned precisely on time. Sally led.

Sir Norman Jackson was a prominent-nosed, heavy-featured man whose thick, white hair was swept back into wings on either side over a pink, polished face. In marked contrast to Fellowes's outfit, the ambassador's broadly striped blue suit perfectly matched the Eton tie.

Sally thought all of it—even the old school ties—pretentious, although predictable, but she didn't expect Podmore to lead the inquisition that came next.

'This encounter is all totally unnecessary!' declared the diplomat.

'I totally agree,' said Sally.

'That is impertinent . . . insubordinate!' accused Podmore.

Just like a principal's office, Sally decided. 'I don't believe it to be necessary, either. My position has been fully explained to both you and Mr. Fellowes.' She switched her attention to the ambassador. 'As it would be to you, Your Excellency, if you speak with my director-general.' As she spoke, Sally saw Podmore's face tighten at what she belatedly realized he'd see as her dismissively going beyond him to the ambassador. Which, she supposed, was exactly what she had done to get this meeting over as soon as possible to get to other things she considered more important than massaging egos.

Podmore went to speak but stopped at a gesture from Jackson.

'I regret what appears to be a problem, which I am anxious to resolve to avoid it affecting your future career, Miss Hanning.' Jackson smiled as he made the threat. The teeth were evenly sculpted.

So much for diplomatic nuance, thought Sally. 'I'd hoped both Mr. Fellowes and your first secretary would have explained the situation to you.'

'Both recounted their conversations with you. I found your explanations totally unacceptable. I will not tolerate any United Kingdom agency sending its officers into—or under—the protection of this embassy imagining they can conduct themselves entirely independently of myself or my senior staff.' Jackson was still smiling his even-toothed smile, his voice level, conversational.

Her early-morning rehearsal with David Monkton had been inadequate, Sally acknowledged, recalling her late father's dictum that one *Your*

Excellency was sufficient subservience. 'My director-general is equally anxious to discuss this matter with you personally, if you've sufficient time in your schedule today.' That hadn't specifically been discussed during that morning's call but it had previously, and Sally didn't see why she should shoulder the entire opprobrium. Which wasn't giving in to bullying: it was being pragmatic. Irrationally Sally was caught by further embassy-school déjà vu. Some of those schools had actually *been* part of the embassy complex, customarily in rooms attached to their libraries, a facility she should have remembered earlier.

'I wanted to give you the opportunity to settle the matter without officially escalating it further, Miss Hanning.'

No, you didn't, was Sally's immediate thought. Why the reluctance? 'I appreciate your consideration.'

'Which I wish you'd reciprocate. What reason is there for your behavior, MI5's behavior?'

'To answer that I again ask you to speak with my director-general.'

'Did you know of the arrest of this man Aswamy before the *New York Times* disclosure?' intruded Podmore.

'Yes,' snatched Sally, seeing the opening. 'As did the Director-General with whom I'm asking you to establish direct contact.'

The two diplomats exchanged hesitant looks. Fellowes frowned, in matching uncertainty, looking to the other two for guidance, which didn't come.

Jackson said, 'It was a Homeland Security disclosure, wasn't it?'

They believed they were being *politically* sidelined! guessed Sally. And Jackson would, in effect, be admitting it by contacting Monkton. 'Can I give my director-general a convenient time to call you today, to make everything clear?'

'Two this afternoon, Washington time.' The surrender was blurted out, reluctantly, to Podmore's visible surprise.

Sally didn't slow when Fellowes caught up with her in the hallway.

She didn't look at him, either, as he said, 'You must have a damned good reason for being as arrogant as you are!'

Never, despite what she believed to be her complete self-honesty, had Sally ever considered herself arrogant. Unhelpfully she said, 'Yes, I must have, mustn't I?'

'I'd hoped it was something about al Aswamy,' said Conrad Graham.

'I wish it were. But I think this is important, too,' said Jack Irvine. It was Sally's interpretation of Tehran's silence at the Aswamy arrest claim, not his. And her original idea. It was for her to introduce, not him.

'No-one likes seniority leapfrogging,' warned the CIA deputy director.

'I don't like being under surveillance,' said Irvine. 'It's either Johnston or Bradley, doesn't matter which. Either would have denied it if I'd gone to them and kept it on, like they've kept it on Sally.'

'You sure they're maintaining it on Sally?' asked Graham, a man of Ivy League neatness still unsure of choosing the greasy pole of Langley promotion over the adrenaline of ankle-holstered fieldwork.

'It was she who picked up mine, as well as her own. And that was *after* she complained to both Johnston and Bradley. Which doesn't say a hell of a lot about your surveillance unit, especially right after losing al Aswamy. To impose it on someone like Sally, a professional, was insane. She seems to have a hell of a lot of clout, and you haven't got your Sellafield detainee yet.'

'You really think she could screw that up?'

'What's the point of taking the risk? Al Aswamy's still more likely to be here in the U.S. than anywhere else. He's your target, not Sally Hanning or me.'

'The surveillance will be lifted, from both of you.'

'And from the rest of my team?'

Graham frowned, head to one side. 'You sure they're being surveilled?'

'Let's cover all the bases at the same time.'

'This doesn't create a precedent,' warned Graham.

'I'm not trying to create precedents. I'm trying to prevent Cyber Shepherd from being thrown off track by something this stupid.'

'I told you surveillance is over.'

'Let's hope it isn't replaced by something just as stupid. Or worse.'

'You telling me something else I should know about?'

'Not yet. If I think there is, I'll write a memo, with copies to everyone. That's the ass-covering system, isn't it?'

'That's the ass-covering system,' agreed Conrad Graham.

The vigil had become monotonous, as vigils always do, eroding its very purpose as it always does. Anis was there on the screen in front of him, with Mohammed's and Nek's presence posted on the screen above him, before Akram Malik saw his target on the Action subcatalog! He blinked, clearing his vision, annoyed at the concentration lapse: the rest of the team were at their screens, unaware. Anis was simply posted, waiting. As Malik was waiting. Should he initiate the contact, which he wanted to do, despite Irvine's warning? Or wait to be approached? He could call him, at Langley, or ask Burt, just feet away, locked into his own Vevak vigil. Marian, even. Or make his own decision, which again he wanted to do: go on proving his right to be part of the elite group. Jack had admitted he couldn't have handled the last encounter any better. And Jack wasn't there, wasn't in contact.

Malik reached out to his keyboard, but before he could touch a key, Anis was there with the essential *As-salamu alaykum.*

Malik hesitated, flexing his fingers, then responded with the obeisance to Allah.

Anis: *Do you agree that the unliftable stone should be kissed?*

Malik sighed at the frustrating familiarity of the aphorism-dependent text, although he hoped an omen was in the friendship proverb. He matched the tone with *A chameleon does not leave one tree unless he is sure of another.*

Anis: *We are sure.*

The rejoinder jolted Malik, his mind momentarily frozen. But only momentarily. He couldn't hesitate, appear surprised or confused into inaction! No more aphorisms, no longer working their way through Arab ambiguity. He replied, *Are we still alone?*

The reply was the arrival of Redeemer on his screen. The newcomer wrote, *I welcome and greet you as a friend.*

Malik: *As I greet you.*

Redeemer: *There are more to encounter.*

Malik: *As I hoped there would be*

Anis: *Have you many friends?*

Malik was conscious of someone at his side and felt Marian's hand encouragingly on his shoulder before he detected her perfume. She said, 'Good! Keep going! Shab thinks he's getting this new guy's IP!'

Malik: *All whom I consider unliftable stones*

Redeemer: *Do you follow the work of al-Ghazali?*

'Shit!' exclaimed Singleton, who'd joined Marian and recognized as Malik did the Moslem denominational test. Marian pressed Malik's shoulder again but said nothing, although she knew the significance, too. Abu Hamid al-Ghazali was the greatest of eleventh-century Moslem philosophers, revered today throughout the Arab world. And a Sunni. Iran, the predominant Al Qaeda sponsor, was overwhelmingly Shia. If he identified himself from the wrong denomination, the moment—his chance—would be lost. Malik hesitated, hands hovering once more, before abruptly writing, *I am more familiar with the words of Ali.*

The hesitation now was from the darknet chat room. Malik remained staring fixedly at his screen, unsure of his choice. Ali was the foremost disciple of the Prophet Mohammed and in Shia prayers is accorded the highest honour by being referred to as the friend of Allah; by proclaiming him Malik had identified himself as a Shia. Neither Singleton nor Marian spoke.

Then ...

Redeemer: *I welcome you to the work we have been called upon to perform.*

Singleton said, 'You got it right! For Christ's sake don't let them go!'

Anis: *Are you prepared?*

    Malik: *As a warrior is always prepared.*

    Redeemer: *Are you really in Russia?*

    Malik: *I can be anywhere.*

There was no immediate response. Then ...

    Anis: *Can you travel?*

    Malik: *Where?*

    Anis: *Europe. Satan's lair.*

    Malik: *Yes.*

    Redeemer: *With companions?*

    Malik: *Possibly.*

    Redeemer: *Are you trained?*

    Malik: *Yes.*

    Redeemer: *Do you have weaponry?*

    Malik: *They can be obtained.*

    Redeemer: *In what quantity?*

    Malik: *What are the requirements?*

    Redeemer: *Considerable.*

    Malik: *Provide a list.*

    Redeemer: *It will come.*

    Malik: *When? I am talking with others who are impatient.*

    Anis: *It will come when the moment is right.*

    Redeemer: *Marg bar Amrika.*

Malik: *Marg bar Amrika.*

Anis: *Inshallah.*

Malik: *Inshallah.*

From his computer station Shab Barker said, 'It's Redeemer@raidtaker, openly with an IR, Iranian identification, and I've got him all the way back to Malmö!'

Illogically, having made the discovery it had not until now occurred to her to pursue, Sally's feeling was of anti-climax.

It had proved remarkably easy, simply cross-referencing what she'd partially obtained from the long telephone conversation with London Archives against easily available American government records in the Washington embassy library. Which Sally could have done anytime, anywhere. That she'd been curious enough to do so now was the result of being, albeit minimally, in an embassy environment and making the connection to the Irvine name from the passing remarks about the code-breaker's Middle East upbringing. All of which amounted to what? Certainly a bizarre coincidence for someone who didn't believe in coincidence. But little else to any practical use.

Taken to its paranoid extreme, it could be argued that her parents would not have died in the aftermath of U.S. ambassador Andrew Irvine's deluded misconception of a Middle East peace process with Yasser Arafat's Al Fatah. But by the same reasoning, they wouldn't have died had they not chosen to cross from Jordan into Lebanon on the very day the fighting began between Hamas and Al Fatah, a direct result of Ambassador Irvine's unapproved and misguided diplomatic initiative. In the current cynicism of the region their deaths were considered collateral damage. Which was not, nor could ever be, her cynicism. Only to herself—and definitely not to the psychiatrists and psychologists whose examinations she'd defeated—did Sally admit an early, unfocused determination to hunt down their killers by joining the security service. Her reaction then at learning

Jack Irvine was the son of the disgraced American envoy to Lebanon would probably have been very different from what it was today. Now she realistically acknowledged the impossibility of ever finding the bomb throwers or the Kalashnikov marksmen. That realism did not mean, though, that she'd emerged from her aching grief, which she'd also concealed from her examiners. It meant she'd created her own impenetrable self-protective firewall from behind which to live.

Confirming Jack Irvine's background had been pointless, a self-indulged distraction; even arrogant, she accepted, remembering Nigel Fellowes's accusation. Perhaps she was adjusting already.

'I asked to be kept in touch, remember?' complained Harry Packer. 'I've been trying to get you since yesterday.'

'We spoke the day before yesterday. There's been nothing on my voice mail since then.'

'I want to speak to you personally, not through voice mail.'

'We're speaking personally now,' said Irvine, irritably shifting the Langley telephone to his other ear. 'What's your problem, Harry?'

'Not being kept up-to-date is my problem.' How much easier would it be if he told Irvine that one of his team wanted out?

'There's no update since we last spoke. If there were, I'd have been the one to contact you.'

'I'm talking about real progress, not all this bullshit stuff. Aren't you picking up *anything*!'

'Nothing that's leading anywhere, not yet.'

'So there is something!' seized Packer.

'When there is, you'll hear about it,' refused Irvine. 'You know where we're working from. We don't see enough of you.'

Motherfucker, thought Packer.

21

JACK IRVINE DIDN'T INTERRUPT BURT SINGLETON, NOT WANTING the increasing irritation— now at being left out—to be obvious. Scrolling through the saved exchange, he said, 'You're right Akram really got a handle on it.'

'So's Shab,' said Singleton with unusual enthusiasm. 'We've got a lot to work on, from the domain IP. It's turning into a great team effort.'

Without my being part of it, thought Irvine. 'Why didn't you call me?'

'That's what I'm doing now!'

'I mean when it was going on.'

'Marian called your Langley number: got no reply or switch-over and assumed you'd picked up the interception on your cell link and were on your way here. And it *was* going on: we handled it.'

'And I'm grateful,' Irvine retreated awkwardly. 'You're a hell of a backup, all of you.'

'You coming down now?'

'Later. There are things to do here first.' Singleton was patronizing him, as Johnston and Bradley had, Irvine decided.

'Seems constantly busy up there?'

He must have been with Conrad Graham when they'd tried to reach him, his alerting cell phone connected to the Vevak botnet and his Langley line on divert. 'Anyone pick up on something they didn't expect?'

'Like what?' demanded Singleton.

It wasn't a bingo night quiz, thought Irvine. 'Sally and I were put under CIA surveillance; not sure if it extended to you guys down there. If it was, it's being lifted by the deputy director. But I want all of you to make sure that it has been taken off. And tell Packer, too—'

'Son of a bitch!' exploded Singleton. 'What the fuck's going on up there?'

'Things you wouldn't believe,' dismissed Irvine, glad he'd redressed the lost balance. 'How do you read Tehran's silence about the bounty?'

'Make a list, close your eyes, and stick in a pin,' said Singleton cynically.

'Look where you're sticking your pin,' insisted Irvine.

'Why should Tehran bother to say anything publicly beyond their denial of the three original attempts? They know we haven't got al Aswamy. They say anything more—or leak denials through their known ally countries—it's a contradiction of that denial.'

'What about Hydarnes?'

Singleton paused. 'I haven't got any further on that; it's my concentration, obviously.'

'Let me give you another stick-pin list. Do you think Anis and Redeemer could be a new, emergency contact and control system for al Aswamy to resume operations? Or, alternatively, an entirely new Al Qaeda group, either for a completely new campaign or to continue what al Aswamy started but can't continue any further because he's too compromised?'

The hesitation this time was longer. 'Jack, this isn't what we do! We intercept Internet traffic between bad guys and break their codes to find out who and where they are for law enforcement and spooks to take over if we can't turn them against each other. Hydarnes could be any one of your speculations or none of them at all, something completely different still.' There was another pause. 'Let me ask you a question in return: Are you bouncing your different choices off me or are they those of the British gal, who, according to my recollection, wasn't going to infringe on our part of the operation?'

'We work from speculative analyses, hypotheses, all the time,' weakly protested Irvine, accepting he'd been outargued.

'I don't have an opinion on any of your possibilities,' positively refused Singleton. 'I know we'll crack Redeemer. He didn't have a self-destruct fire-wall on any of his cutouts.'

'It's darknet traffic. They feel safe, untouchable, and untraceable.'

'It's still unusually insecure.'

'You using my botnets to get to Vevak?'

'You know I am.'

'Thought you might have created some of your own, leave mine open.'

'I don't think we should risk interfering any more with what you've already established.'

'We're safe enough,' accepted Irvine, backing off again. 'It's Vevak I'm linked to. Call me if there's anything elsewhere, okay? I won't again forget to put the Langley line on divert.'

'It's not tit for tat, Jack: you're not being left out.'

'That's good to hear,' managed Irvine, glad his internal telephone broke the conversation.

'You son of a bitch!' erupted James Bradley, as Irvine entered the covert director's office.

'What is it about being part of an operational group that you don't understand!' took up Charles Johnston, so tight-lipped it seemed difficult for him actually to get the words out. He was white-faced with fury, too, in contrast to Bradley, who was heart-attack red. Irvine had expected the confrontation with at least one of the men, but not that it would also include Harry Packer, who sat uncertainly in a side chair.

'The part about paranoid members of that group putting official surveillance on other members not suffering the same problems.' Irvine, still standing, turned to Packer. 'Didn't expect you here, Harry. Left a message at Meade for you to be told the watch was being taken off. Didn't think you'd like it, any more than I or any of the others down there liked or accepted it.'

'Surveillance . . . ? What . . . ?' stumbled the uncertain man.

'You know what surveillance is, Harry? It's what the CIA mount on people, even though by law they're not allowed to impose it on fellow Americans, but do it so badly it's spotted right away and everyone ends up looking like assholes. As everyone's looking like assholes for losing an international terrorist named Ismail al Aswamy.' Irvine went back to the silenced Johnston and Bradley. 'If you looked at your in-boxes this morning, you will have already read the e-mail I copied to both of you in which I was complaining to the deputy director. I also included Sally Hanning in the complaint. She had already protested, very forcefully, as I am sure you'll both recall. You really expect to get a British detainee with their invited representative on a watch list! I don't. Neither does Conrad Graham.' Even as Irvine spoke, he realized he was being way over-the-top, but he didn't care because it felt good to be the shouter.

'I was under surveillance!' demanded Packer, recovering at last although still incredulous. His concern wasn't at being watched, but at the thought of its potentially discovering the financial shit and the ongoing alimony row with Rebecca.

'You're part of an operation carrying the highest security designation—' groped Johnston, still tight-lipped.

'Don't come at me with that necessary-protection bullshit,' cut off Irvine. 'I'm not taking any of it. And I'm not going down the toilet with either of you. I'm going to entrap terrorists, hopefully with people from the CIA whom I can trust.' He needed to take a breath. 'I'm through. Anyone got anything additional they want to say?'

No-one spoke.

Sally's third conversation of the day was a foretaste of the lackluster initiative that was to follow, although it did confirm her earlier guess that the embassy confrontation stemmed from Sir Norman Jackson's fear of being politically bypassed by London as well as by the U.S. State Department and Homeland Security. The ambassador had been mollified by Monkton's supposed disclosure that MI5 didn't believe the Iranian terrorist had genuinely been detained—that it might emerge to be a mistaken identity—and the agreement that the two men should personally liaise daily, to avoid further misunderstandings.

Sally was one of the first of the straggled arrivals for that evening's review meeting. Johnston and Bradley were among the last, both stone-faced, and to Sally's complete disinterest they pointedly ignored her. By contrast Jack Irvine, even later, hurried to the seat next to her, whispering as he sat that he had something to tell her. Summoned first, Irvine told the meeting there had still been no Internet interception connected to al Aswamy. Johnston contributed to the depression by adding that there'd been no practical CIA developments: they were still waiting on access to London detainees. A procession of U.S. department deputies and directors sought answers to the avalanche of demands from foreign government counterparts, intelligence and security agencies, and world media. The repeated answer was to keep stonewalling. FBI director Frederick Bowyer warned future co-operation with *The New York Times* was jeopardized. Another meeting was scheduled for the following day; everyone had to remain on standby for any intervening development.

As the room emptied, Sally said, 'What's there to tell me?'

Irvine said, 'Were you tailed coming here?'

'I didn't pick it up, but I didn't try very hard. I've got a meeting with Johnston in an hour.'

'I went over his head, to Graham. Got it taken off all of us, you particularly. I claimed we wouldn't get our prisoner transfer if it wasn't lifted.'

'You think it will be?'

'Look harder in your rearview mirror on your way back.'

'We didn't really get to the end of all there was to talk about at that dinner, did we?' encouraged Sally, still unsure she'd learned everything about Operation Cyber Shepherd.

'A rain check,' avoided Irvine. 'I'm going up to Meade. My team's there. I need to be there, too, from time to time.'

But not when that time would take him wouldn't extend this late into the evening unless there was a good reason, thought Sally.

22

NO-ONE LOOKED UP WHEN IRVINE ENTERED THE FORT MEADE HUB, and however illogically he felt like an outsider, which he supposed even more illogically was how they probably regarded him; certainly it was the impression he'd gotten from Burt Singleton during their telephone conversation. Marian finally realized his presence, saving him the further awkwardness of having to announce himself.

'Everyone here this late must mean something?' Irvine said, responding to the general greeting.

'Could be something,' said Singleton cautiously. 'That's why we're all still here, waiting to go through it with you.'

'Al Aswamy still tops the league table,' prompted Irvine hopefully. 'As of two hours ago, the CIA had nothing: it's all foxes in the hen coop up there.'

'Nothing here either,' deflated Singleton. 'We're getting the odd letter, but it's not leading us anywhere.'

'Our botnet firewalls are still up: we're not falling into a trap!' pressed Irvine, the satisfaction stirring.

Instead of answering, Singleton gestured to his computer screen, clearly displaying Irvine's intact cutout protection.

'That's brilliant,' enthused Irvine. 'Either way's a winner.'

'Providing we get it right from the moment Vevak's transmission starts,' qualified Singleton even more cautiously.

Irvine thought, annoyed, that he'd overdone the praise, like someone anxious to ingratiate himself. 'I'm missing your point.'

'I'm using your bots, into which we're both still logged, waiting for their next move,' reminded the older man, holding Irvine's total concentration. 'And you're something like twenty-eight miles away in DC, sometimes not able immediately to react, which is how we've got to react when Vevak—or al Aswamy from wherever he is—moves. Down here, I'm set the moment that happens.'

Singleton was right, Irvine at once accepted. There was no benefit, no useful professional reason, for the duplication. But he didn't want to surrender the control. Everything was his. The idea was his and the project was his and its operation was his and the success had to be his; and when others got involved with their own agendas and ambitions and careers, it was his job to protect it. Matching the other man's caution, he said, 'You think we could get in each other's way?'

'Not working together, side by side, moving parallel with them. Reacting separately from each other, with no guarantee of being able instantly to communicate, we're endangering what we're trying to do.'

From the intentness with which they were all looking at him, Irvine suspected that some if not all of this had already been talked through, such as Singleton's earlier remark of Irvine's not being left out and the minimal effort made to contact him when Malik finally got a reaction from Anis and then Redeemer. 'That's the first priority, not endangering what we're trying to do.'

It *was* his operation, his responsibility, Irvine told himself again. He could refuse to surrender control, as his father had refused to delegate: to share anything of what he'd tried to achieve diplomatically, determined to be the peacemaker where so many others had failed. Was that his motivation here, public recognition? Hardly. Cyber Shepherd could never publicly be acknowledged, as he could never openly be identified as its architect. All of which was immaterial, Irvine recognized, dismissing another illogicality to bring himself back to those still looking at him, waiting.

He wouldn't be making any concessions. He'd be showing the mature responsibility of a team leader confident in his position, adjusting to the predictable expansion of a successful project. 'I guess there's more to tell me, but this is how I see this part of it going forward. Still outstanding is al Aswamy, who may or may not reappear through Vevak's Hydarnes site in which we're still embedded and, it seems, unsuspected. What we don't know is whether the new stuff we've intercepted—but not so far broken— is linked to al Aswamy or an entirely new target through Redeemer and Anis.' The concentration was relaxing, no longer challenging, gauged Irvine. 'So here's how we'll cut the cake. You, Burt, will take over the Vevak-Hydarnes monitor. You, Akram, will handle the Moscow Alternative darknet with the Anis and Redeemer postings and its subcatalogs— which I'm still waiting to hear about—with Shab and Marian acting as backup to the rest of you.' Irvine coughed, clearing his throat. 'I'm spending more time in DC than I intended because of al Aswamy. The moment that's resolved, it'll reverse with my being back here most of the time. Until then, whenever I'm in DC, I want to be contacted, day or night, on my cell— which will never be switched off—the moment anything comes from anywhere that needs the sort of reaction Burt's talking about.' Irvine paused gratefully. 'Anyone got an argument with that?'

No-one spoke. Irvine was relieved.

So, Irvine quickly decided, were most if not all of the others. Shab Barker began speaking, rehearsed but unprompted, as Irvine turned to him, appearing at first more anxious to move beyond the confrontation than talk of his pursuit of Redeemer. He'd taken the precautions Redeemer had ignored, assured Barker, establishing self-destruct firewalls in unsuspecting computer systems in Vistula, St Petersburg, and finally Helsinki. From Finland he'd chased Redeemer into the hacked mainframe of Malmö's third-largest fish-exporting company, established almost a hundred years earlier and still controlled by a family directorship. The chain hadn't progressed from there, nor had Redeemer returned to any Moscow Alternative subcatalogs since the first approach. Anis had not returned there, either.

'But Malmö is where it begins and ends,' declared Barker. 'Malmö is where the group is located.'

'Where's the evidence to support that?' at once challenged Singleton, the edge back in his voice.

'I finally got lucky with Anis: randomly different digital selection, randomly different result. I got the numeric code and the IP. While Akram was double-checking it today, I compared it against Redeemer, just filling in time until you got here. They're the same.'

'You didn't tell us while we were waiting with you!' accused Marian.

Irvine was aware of Singleton sitting tight-faced except for an angry tic pulling the corner of his mouth down almost into a grimace.

'Shab and I wanted to make absolutely sure before we started ringing bells,' said Malik. 'It'll be a group privately sharing the same protocol on the Action darknet. Anis was the stalking horse, testing if there'd be any attempt to follow after he made the chat-room approach. Passed us on up the chain when he was satisfied we were genuine, not law enforcement. Redeemer didn't bother with cutouts because he didn't think he had to; he thought he was safe. It's classic darknet macho bullshit.'

There was such a thing as darknet macho bullshit, a lot of it even, accepted Irvine, acknowledging, too, that the delay in attempting to follow Anis had more to do with the distraction of al Aswamy than allaying fear of pursuit, but he shared some of Singleton's reservation.

Marian said, 'It's not classic, and sharing a protocol is not enough on a darknet site to justify your assumption of a Malmö base. The far more likely explanation is that everything was transferred onto a memory stick to be continued from a separate computer. *That's* classic.'

'I would have expected at least one protective cutout,' contributed Irvine.

'That worries me, too,' picked up Singleton, still tight-faced.

'Why should it be worrying any of us?' questioned Marian pragmatically. 'We've picked up something that's worth taking forward. But it's not in our backyard. So we pass it on to the Swedish authorities, as we passed on the UK and Italian intercepts that turned out to be the al Aswamy operation.'

'If I'm wrong, if it's a memory-stick transfer, we don't know if it's going to end up in our backyard or not,' disputed Malik, disconcerted at the opposition.

'We can get into his bot,' reminded Irvine.

'We didn't do that with the intercepts in Italy or the UK,' immediately confronted Singleton.

'We didn't have the protocol at the time to get into either. And we didn't know we were looking at a jihad conspiracy,' came back Irvine, just as quickly. He went to Malik. 'You did most of the hard work and there's no reason to stop now. Hack in.'

All the machines were connected to Malik's by remove access, the screens filling simultaneously with Malik's page.

Marian said, 'A friendly backyard, but still no good to us.'

'Oh yes, it is!' said Irvine. 'That couldn't be better!'

Which couldn't be said for the early part of the evening, he decided, easing the neglected, tappets-clattering Volkswagen onto the I-95 for the unplanned return to Washington. Irvine believed he'd come out as best he could from the Singleton confrontation, but it was obvious to everyone that he'd conceded. It had all been evened out, though, by the Pakistanis' initial coup, which he'd confirmed by approving the hacking of Redeemer's botnet. Irvine didn't believe Shab Barker had only discovered that Redeemer and Anis were sharing the same darknet address shortly before his arrival, any more than Marian Lowell or Burt Singleton. And Singleton's barely controlled annoyance at an announcement he wasn't expecting more than balanced out whatever he'd achieved by gaining total control of the Vevak monitoring.

To what was he returning? wondered Irvine, welcoming the glow of Washington ahead. Conrad Graham's reaction to Irvine's Fort Meade telephone alert of Malik's success had been far more subdued than Irvine expected. The deputy CIA director's initial concentration must have been entirely on the following day's specially convened meeting Irvine had been summoned to attend. At least he now had something positive to offer for a change.

At just past ten thirty, when Irvine got to Owen Place, he abruptly thought of calling Sally. Just as quickly he put the idea out of his mind, irritated that the thought had occurred at all.

23

IT TOOK A FURTHER YEAR OF FIGHTING AND DYING AFTER THE
Vietnam peace declaration before Hanoi and Washington diplomatically
agreed to the shape of the table at which an accord was formally ratified,
recalled Jack Irvine. That absurdity, according to his mother, began her
husband's professional disillusionment, later explained away—for diplomatically acceptable reasons, what else?—as an irrecoverable mental
breakdown. Which of those currently assembled around the deputy CIA
director's conference table was beyond recovery? wondered Irvine, sur-
veying the men opposite. It surely had to be James Bradley, as always
tightly mummified as if in readiness for burial. Johnston was also looking nervously around, inviting reassurance. What Irvine hadn't expected
was being awakened at 5:00 a.m. by Harry Packer, whose NSA position
couldn't be endangered, on his way from Baltimore insisting he wasn't
partnered in internal manoeuvring with either Bradley or Johnston. Irvine
felt comfortable in the knowledge that he was safe, eager to detail to Conrad
Graham the previous night's discovery.

Irvine suspected that Graham staged his late arrival for effect, which
he immediately compounded by announcing that as of that moment he
was personally taking control of Operation Cyber Shepherd. There were
to be no unilateral actions that hadn't first been approved by him, including the choice and delegation of all subsidiary CIA personnel. CIA surveillance upon anyone currently engaged in the operation had been lifted.

None was to be imposed in the future. The open dissent and criticism of the control and command of Operation Cyber Shepherd from virtually every other Homeland Security agency had reached the White House, from where the instructions he was relaying had been issued. There were more than a dozen open threats of exchange withdrawal from foreign intelligence agencies with which they'd enjoyed close and useful co-operation, and *The New York Times* was now leading the worldwide media campaign for more information.

'Don't anyone misunderstand what I'm telling you,' continued Graham. 'We're into damage limitation. What began well is now an unmitigated disaster that could get even worse if a Homeland group tries to save its public ass by burning ours.'

Irvine wasn't feeling comfortable anymore, either. He was burning with frustrated anger at having everything he'd made successful—something the president himself had openly praised—endangered by incompetent assholes such as James Bradley and Charles Johnston. And it would be destroyed, Irvine knew. Damage limitation meant abandoning Operation Cyber Shepherd as a deluded aberration, which was how his father's enterprise had been labeled and discarded. Irvine understood at last the deputy director's almost disinterested response to his previous night's phone call. Conrad Graham had formally approved Cyber Shepherd and briefly basked in the initial presidential praise; now he had a lot of distancing to achieve to prevent himself from becoming a victim of its debacle.

Graham's curt demand—'You have something to say?'—brought Irvine abruptly out of his reflection. He had to justify the operation, he determined; save it by convincing Graham that the situation wasn't as desperate as the man clearly imagined it to be.

Irvine stepped cautiously out onto the verbal tightrope between restoring faith in Cyber Shepherd and keeping safe from Johnston and Bradley anything about Vevak and Hydarnes. 'We can recover,' he declared. 'We're following a new trail on a known terrorist Internet route. One of the targets is careless, hasn't bothered to hide himself inside a host computer because he's working through a darknet, an underground, no-questions-asked, hidden-identity site, and believes he's safe. Which he isn't. We're not in a position to move yet, but we will be very soon. We've already discovered a connection from Malmö, in Sweden, where we believe his group is based, with another cell in England. The indications are that there's something being planned.' Irvine paused, not anticipating any understanding from either Johnston or Bradley, but hopeful at least of some recognition from Harry Packer or Conrad Graham.

It didn't come. Instead Johnston said, 'What the hell interest is any of this to us!'

'A potentially British-headquartered terrorist group is planning an action of some sort,' patiently finished Irvine, depressed and disappointed in equal measure. 'A British MI5 officer is holding us to ransom over access to detainees who conceivably know not just where al Aswamy's hiding but where other American targets might be. Sally Hanning's lost her ransom threat. It's ours now. So are as many detainees as we want.'

'Oh, yes!' finally acknowledged a beaming Conrad Graham. 'Now we've got her by the balls, and I want them squeezed hard to get us out of this mess.'

Charles Johnston said, 'I've got yesterday's postponed meeting with her scheduled in an hour. I'll enjoy doing it.'

'You *and* Jim,' insisted Graham, the smiled satisfaction gone. 'Nothing unilateral anymore, remember?'

Jack Irvine couldn't believe he'd made the impression he'd hoped.

Sally gave no reaction because there was none to give: she was neither surprised nor angry at the reversal. The tables simply had to be turned back as quickly as possible, and from her experience so far of the two men confronting her, she didn't imagine that would be too difficult. Except that they were the monkeys, not the organ grinder, and from what they'd already disclosed in their bullying eagerness to intimidate her, it was upon Jack Irvine and his Facebook intercepting team at Ford Meade that those tables had to be turned. Whatever else there might be for her to learn depended upon what Johnston and Bradley had been told, which she didn't imagine to be a lot.

'You haven't spoken yet to my director-general?' she prompted mildly.

'I will,' said Johnston heavily. 'But knowing how closely you liaise, I didn't think it essential that he was the first to be told.'

That was a lie of Pinocchio proportions, Sally recognized: Johnston obviously imagined it would be easier to intimidate her than to verbally confront David Monkton. Which suited her perfectly: always an advantage to be underestimated, she reminded herself. 'I appreciate the courtesy of your telling me in advance, but as I've made clear from the outset, the decision about detainee exchange has to come from London.'

Bradley gave an overly pained grimace. 'We want a detainee on a plane now!'

'I'm sure you'll make that clear to my director-general.' Sally smiled. 'I'll reiterate it, of course, when I do speak to London. I'm as anxious as everyone to get this resolved: I certainly don't want any obstacles to our continued co-operation.'

'We want a response by tomorrow, better still before this day's out,' repeated a tightly red-faced Johnston. 'You seem to be having difficulty understanding that continued co-operation depends upon an immediate detainee release.'

Neither of them was infuriated enough yet to let anything slip, but she was getting there, Sally decided. 'There's no misunderstanding. The problem, as it's always been, is that extraordinary rendition is politically very contentious in the UK, as it is here.'

Johnston said, 'There's a terrorist cell in the UK that we can lead you to, for Christ's sake! You really think you've still got a bargaining position!'

Getting closer, Sally thought. 'Since the three concerted attacks, we've stepped up everything at GCHQ. I'd expect them already to have picked up something of what you're indicating. And there's the wider seine net of Echelon, but anything extra that NSA has would obviously be a bonus.'

Johnston visibly smirked. Bradley actually snorted in derision and said, 'You really don't understand, do you! The only way you're going to get anything about a UK attack is through us, and the only way you're going to get anything through us is by putting one of your prisoners on the flight we've already got fueled and crewed at Andrews air base.'

'In fact,' quickly took up Johnston, 'I don't think there's an exchange limit anymore. We want them all.'

'Something else to take up with my director general.'

'He won't be surprised,' said Johnston, the smirk still hovering.

Another snippet, gauged Sally; in addition to this pantomime, separate political pressure was being exerted. Enough, Sally decided. She had to find out more, but this wasn't the place and these weren't the men to provide it. 'You've made yourself very clear. I'm grateful.'

'Which we expect to be, too, ASAP,' said Bradley, a bully imagining he'd won.

Sally didn't hurry the return drive to Massachusetts Avenue, intentionally detouring twice to satisfy herself that surveillance hadn't been re-imposed. Nigel Fellowes was leaving the communications room as she approached. When she reached him, the MI5 station chief smiled and said, 'I'm damned glad I'm not in any way involved.'

Continuing on, Sally said, 'Don't you own another tie?'

'A direct threat?' demanded David Monkton.

'Unequivocal,' confirmed Sally. 'All Hollywood tough-guy stuff.'

'You don't sound impressed.'

'It's difficult to be. It'll be something NSA has picked up on, maybe from one of the anonymity-guaranteeing sites; GCHQ will know how difficult it might be to catch up. I'd guess virtually impossible. And I know there's political pressure, although I can't imagine official State Department involvement in extraordinary rendition. Johnston virtually turned political pressure into another threat, and Nigel Fellowes made it clear the embassy's in the loop.'

'The complaint at their being sidelined is at embassy to Foreign Office level, which is still astonishing if it ever leaks,' confirmed Monkton. 'It shows the panic that's going to skyrocket at the thought of something else happening here.'

'When's the flight?'

'Tonight. There's an unmarked C-130 en route to Northolt as we speak. CIA, of course. Unfiled destination.'

'Johnston said he wants them all.'

'He tried that with me. I told him we couldn't release any more until we'd finished interrogating them ourselves.'

'I'll be excluded from now on.'

'Until we find a way to get you back in,' said Monkton.

'Until we find a way back in,' echoed Sally in agreement.

'What's your next move?'

'Getting myself invited out to dinner. But before that I'm going to try to talk to a man I only know as John at GCHQ.'

'Let's hope that's enough to find him.'

It was.

That afternoon anti-terrorist police arrested the two men caught on CCTV running from the failed bombing of the London Eye. They were identified from that footage by a former IRA commander, now a Belfast city councillor, following a £10,000 newspaper reward. The two were members of the still-active breakaway Real IRA who'd intended the destruction as a pay-up warning to British Airways—one of the original sponsors of the tourist attraction—and Thames riverboat and ferry operators from whom they planned to extort operational funds.

Coincidentally, within two hours of the British swoop, an informant guided the DCR, the French internal-security equivalent of Britain's MI5, to a planning session of an Algerian anarchist group in the Paris suburb of Neuilly-sur-Seine. Among evidence recovered were the blueprints of the original Eiffel Tower attack, including the names of its unsuccessful perpetrators, and even more detailed drawings of their intended second, hopefully more successful, attempt. As with the first set of documents, every attacker named was seized by the DCR.

The time difference between London, Paris, and Washington, DC, enabled extensive background on both arrests to be established for the early-evening news that Sally watched in her embassy compound apartment. Government security ministers and spokesmen for both intelligence services appeared on every station through which Sally flicked, all emphatically insisting the arrests proved there was no organized global terrorist campaign. Without exception, the news reports also carried longer segments from other politicians and intelligence agencies criticizing the total news blackout of Ismail al Aswamy's supposed arrest. Sally stopped bothering to count the open accusations that the FBI had got the wrong man.

'Long time no speak,' brightly greeted Sally when Jack Irvine answered his telephone.

'I was about to call. You fancy the same place?'

'It's noisy enough not to be overheard.'

Irvine didn't immediately reply. Then he said, 'Eight okay?'

'Check for company on your way from Owen Place,' advised Sally, the idea prompted from her earlier precautionary drive back to the embassy.

24

RECOVERY—HOWEVER, BY WHATEVER MEANS—WAS SALLY'S SOLE objective. She arrived thirty minutes early to her already-booked table, the one they'd occupied the first time, and had almost finished her first glass of valpolicella when Jack Irvine got there. She'd worn the same indigo Gucci silk shirt, faded jeans, and Chanel pumps. She guessed Irvine had left his apartment in what he'd been wearing—holed jeans, a blank sweatshirt, and scuffed loafers—when she'd phoned. She wasn't overpowered by his cologne, either.

He smiled down, not immediately sitting. 'This time you won.'

Sally smiled back. 'By my reckoning I lost.' As he finally sat, she said, 'I didn't know what beer to order.'

'I'll stay with the wine.' He looked around at the closeness of adjacent tables. 'It's not as crowded as before.'

'Still noisy enough for us not to be eavesdropped: I checked while I was waiting. You want to make your own voice-level check?'

Irvine shook his head. 'What's there to talk about?'

'Please! I'm up to here with this morning's bullshit from Johnston and Bradley.' Sally took his twisted smile as confirmation that he already knew.

Their waiter interrupted the conversation. Sally had decided on what she'd order while she waited. Irvine ordered what he'd eaten last time, without bothering with the menu or the specials recitation. He waited for the waiter to get out of hearing before saying, 'They're not my favourite people, either.'

A way in? wondered Sally. 'Or unique, although those two are in a league of their own. You know what always surprises me? How many people like Johnston and Bradley get to be department heads or managers and wreck entire operations—hugely important, essential operations—through incompetence. That's what's happened here. If Bradley had properly organized his surveillance teams, we wouldn't have lost al Aswamy and be in the shit state we are now.' His face had tightened as she spoke, but at what?

'My operation isn't wrecked! And you know it because you also know, from today's confrontation with Johnston and Bradley, that we're onto something new.'

'I know you've got a new lead you're using to get a UK detainee you hope will lead you to al Aswamy,' seized Sally. 'A UK, not a U.S., lead.'

The waiter returned with their appetizers, and this time Irvine didn't wait for the man to get beyond hearing before he said, 'It isn't the only one.'

'Threatening America?' Sally persisted, drawing upon her earlier con-if-you-can briefing from GCHQ. 'Or something you'll have to pass on to the UK or some other participating country under the Echelon agreement as you did with the Sellafield attack: something else outside U.S. jurisdiction that doesn't get you any closer to al Aswamy?'

Pointedly, like someone believing her argument won, Sally began eating, pausing only to add the neglected wine to both their glasses. Irvine started eating, too, concentrating on his food without saying anything for several minutes.

She'd unsettled him, Sally decided. And felt a twinge of regret at doing to Irvine what Johnston and Bradley had far more clumsily attempted—and so pitifully failed at—with her. Irritably pushing the out-of-place reflection aside, she said, 'This shouldn't be a fight.'

'I'm not trying to make one.'

Had the Meade team really uncovered something separate from a UK lead: another potential attack there'd be an advantage in her learning?

'It was the asshole double act, Johnston or Bradley. Or more likely both, trying to impress each other.' Irvine pushed his plate aside. He'd eaten little.

'The same asshole double act you've still got around your neck,' Sally determinedly continued. She had to go on abrading the sensitive nerve she'd obviously touched.

'Maybe not for much longer.'

Braggadocio, to impress her? Or insider pull from his time with Conrad Graham on Stuxnet? If Johnston was sidelined or removed altogether, David Monkton would lose whatever benefits remained from his direct contact with the covert operations director. 'It's good you know Graham as well as you do, I guess.'

The waiter shared the last of the wine between them as he cleared their appetizer plates for the salad. Irvine ordered another bottle.

'You really want to spend the rest of the evening talking like this?' suddenly demanded Irvine.

She had to back off. Oddly—illogically again—she wasn't upset at the break. 'What else is there to talk about?'

'You. Me. Anything but what we're talking about now because I'm not going to tell you anything more about the UK lead, am I?'

Sally smiled what she hoped he would imagine to be a rueful smile. Maybe the time she'd spent in the embassy library hadn't been wasted after all.

Akram Malik got the positive English connection at nine fifteen Washington time that night: three words, in English and clear—*Order en route*. It came to Malmö on the multiple-shared, Russian-registered Anis address, but the English sender was Swordbearer@forevermystery.org.uk. Malik, who was working the night shift, was actually ready, alerted by the incoming-message trigger with which he'd armed his eavesdropping Trojan horse.

Burt Singleton, also alerted by the trigger, was at the younger man's shoulder when the recipient-only e mail arrived.

'Everything's coming on quicker—faster—than we could have imagined!' exclaimed Malik. It was his coup: the total justification for his selection to such an elite operation!

'Maybe too fast,' cautioned Singleton, more subdued.

'What?' Malik frowned.

'You ever caught a fish by hand? Dangled your arm into the stream until that great fat trout senses no danger from the smooth, tickling fingers that'll kill it quicker than you can hit that SEND key there?'

'Not even after reading *Huckleberry Finn*, and I'm fresh out of ambiguous analogies, Arabic or American,' complained Malik impatiently. 'You want to talk to me in words, in clear ones, that I'm not going to misunderstand?'

'I'm not happy with people on anything-goes darknet sites not bothering with cutouts or firewalls or encrypting their traffic. That's hand fishing: fishing with an *f* not *ph*.'

'We're not directly involved, for Christ's sake!' protested Malik irritably. 'We're simply going to pass on the address we've just got to the Brits. Whatever might be wrong—*if* anything's wrong, that is—it'll be for them to deal with, not us.'

'I don't like it: not anything about Cyber Shepherd. It's not what our job is. What it's supposed to be.'

'I thought our job was protecting the country from its enemies,' oversimplified Malik.

'It is. This is us becoming vigilantes.'

'Why'd you take the job? Jack gave you a choice, like the rest of us.'

'Maybe I made the wrong one.'

'You can still opt out.'

Singleton didn't respond, going back to his own station.

'You think we should call Jack?' asked Malik from the other side of the room.

'Anis is your assignment, not mine.'

'It'll keep until the morning. There might be something more.' Malik hoped the miserable son of a bitch did opt out to make room for someone with a better idea of what this specialized assignment entailed.

Sally Hanning's awareness of her own sexuality held no conceit. She didn't need a full-length mirror to know her designer tastes clothed a model's figure without a mannequin's haughtiness. But at rare moments Sally visited another part of her mind where she hid all the secrets she'd kept from the MI5 psychologists. She'd had relationships, of course. Affairs even: her first lover had been a married junior attaché at the French embassy in Ankara, when her parents had still been alive. And she'd lived with a German student during a post-graduate semester at Oxford. But she always felt herself a detached onlooker, never an eager, uninhibited participant in relationships, more satisfied by infrequent one-night stands with no more expectation than the passing pleasure of the moment. Why then was she allowing herself to think like this, letting it even enter her mind! Personal liaison of any sort at any level with intelligence agency colleagues was not just professionally forbidden; until now it had been beyond her comprehension. And logically still was. Or should be. She would be juggling with semantics trying to rationalize that the prohibition didn't apply because Irvine was an American employed in a totally different branch of intelligence gathering. So it was time to stop pointless distractions and concentrate entirely upon her assignment.

'You majored in political science?' she picked out from what she'd recognized to be a rehearsed presentation.

'No, it wasn't my major,' Irvine backtracked. 'I started out with politics. But I got caught up in mathematics, realized I was good at it, and switched. The government has spotters at all our leading universities, like I know they have at yours. I got approached, passed all the requirements, and here I am.'

His response was edited for casual encounters with someone who didn't listen sufficiently to ask the awkward questions, Sally recognized. Keep it light, she warned herself. 'Fast tracked from politics to code-breaking mathematics with a pit stop on the way to learn excellent, even colloquial Arabic! NSA must think they've got themselves an Einstein prodigy!'

Irvine sipped his wine, gaining time. 'I guess there are prodigies at Meade. I don't consider myself one of them.'

She had to let in more slack, *wanted* to give him more slack, not set verbal traps. 'How's it work? From all the whistle-blowing leaks from renegade CIA contractors, I got the impression that between the five Echelon countries—you, the UK, Canada, and the Antipodes—you hear or read every radio, telephone, or Internet message—*every* conceivable electronic communication—anywhere in the world *every* day. That just can't be done!'

Unexpectedly he smiled. 'The estimate that no-one argues with is that the figure is one point seven *billion* items every day, which probably couldn't be humanly read in a lifetime! But it can be sifted by Meade's super-computers operating at incredible speeds: the Carillon, IBM 7950 Harvest, Frostburg, and Loadstone.'

Back on safe, comfortable territory, judged Sally. 'Computers can't read.'

'They can if they're programmed to recognize trigger words, phrases, or titles.'

She was edging in the right direction, Sally decided. Why didn't she feel more satisfied? 'I thought Internet communications—even innocent ones—were encrypted in transmission?'

'They are, to patterns, which make them identifiable from hidden code exchanges, which themselves are trigger targets because they don't conform to pattern regimes.'

That didn't sound like anything she'd gathered from the basic GCHQ briefing and probably meant he was dismissing her with technical-sounding nonsense. She should, she supposed, be irritated, but she wasn't. 'Cyber Shepherd is specialized. How's it operate differently from what you've described?'

From the sudden attentiveness she guessed she was right about his dismissal. 'I set it all out at the first Conrad Graham meeting you were at.'

'I don't think you did,' she openly challenged. 'I think you left something out, something that makes this operation different from what you normally do, which is why it's a special covert project worked in conjunction with the CIA, who've let you down.'

Irvine said, 'Why don't you tell me where you learned your excellent, even colloquial Arabic?'

Sally found no hypocrisy in her own rehearsal, scarcely preparation beyond concentrating upon her own trigger word, *diplomacy.* She introduced it in her opening sentence and kept employing it, generalizing that her upbringing was exclusively diplomatic, always in the Middle East. Her mother had been Jordanian—her father's first posting had been Amman—and for a period headed the country's refugee agency working out of the United Nations. Arabic had been the primary language in the home, and she'd grown up completely bilingual. Her father's equal fluency, coupled with an Oxford double first in Oriental studies—which she'd matched in the same module twenty-five years later—kept him permanently in the Middle East. They lived successively at British embassies in Syria, Turkey, Iran, Cairo, and Lebanon.

At that moment, something happened completely without warning that definitely wasn't rehearsed, and which Sally even more definitely didn't want. She swallowed against the sudden flood of emotion that welled up, choking her, hurriedly lowering her blurred eyes to her wine as Irvine had earlier used his wineglass to avoid holding her look. He wasn't focused on her anyway, his head down as well, although ignoring his glass.

'He was MI5 station chief in Beirut at the formation period of Hezbollah, which Israel considered sufficiently threatening to cross into the country to try to destroy,' Sally forced herself on, only just managing to keep her voice even. 'No-one knew then of a supposed American move to broker a cease-fire that included Al Fatah and involved a peace negotiation: there was a lot of confusion, accusations of double-dealing and unofficial diplomacy. The British foreign secretary was touring the Middle East: he flew from Cairo for talks with the Jordanian king and government, our strongest allies in the region. Everyone had to go from Beirut to Amman, of course: it was a high-level diplomatic initiative. There was no danger: all the fighting was in the south. It turned out later that Hezbollah had informants at Beirut's air traffic control: they knew of the British diplomatic mission going from Lebanon to Jordan. It was virtually automatic that my mother travel with British diplomats, as close as she was to the Jordanian government. There was a Hezbollah ambush almost outside the St Georges Hotel on their way to the plane. My father was one of the five, including the ambassador, who died instantly. My mother was kept alive on a life-support machine, although she was technically brain-dead. I agreed to it being turned off after two weeks.'

She'd used *diplomat* or *diplomacy* eight times, Sally guessed, maybe more. All the unpredictable emotion had fortunately gone. 'Some other—' she started, but Irvine at last came up to confront her.

'You know, don't you?'

Lie, in the hope of some slip when he tried to defend his father? Or go on being honest? 'I didn't, not until I got here. You're not an MI5 target, not any target.'

'What are you going to do?'

'Nothing. What is there to do?'

'My father was blamed for the massacre; made the scapegoat for a lot of other things, too.'

She didn't want a right-or-wrong, guilty-or-innocent argument. 'There's always got to be a scapegoat. Ours have probably already been decided.'

Irvine didn't respond for what seemed a long time, eventually straightening as if surprised to see Sally at the table with him. 'I think the evening's over.'

'Were you followed, coming here?' Sally demanded, trying to restore some of the abandoned professionalism.

Irvine looked uncomprehendingly across the table. 'I don't understand . . . ?'

'On the phone . . . I warned . . . ,' groped Sally, wishing now that she hadn't bothered.

'The Volkswagen's blown a piston,' said Irvine, still vague. 'I came by cab . . . need to get another . . .'

'I've got a car.'

'I'm sorry,' he said, his hunched back to her, his voice muffled.

'It wasn't the right time. . . . It'll be all right.' They'd left a corner light on and she could see his shoulders had a soft thatch of blond hair.

'It shouldn't have—'

'Stop it,' she said, halting him. 'It's not a qualification test.'

'You going home?'

'Do you want me to?'

'No.'

'Then I won't.'

He eased himself partially onto his back but still didn't turn to her. Sally moved her arm towards him, so their bodies could touch. He didn't move. She could see he had his eyes closed.

'We kill them, have them kill each other,' Irvine blurted abruptly. 'When we think we've got a group, we infiltrate their messages and set them against other groups: create suspicion and distrust. We only move against them ourselves when they don't destroy each other. There's no proper investigation even then, not if we can take them out ourselves: no trial proof. Just what we judge from their exchanges.'

They lay unspeaking, still not touching, for a long time.

Again Irvine broke the silence. 'You're not saying anything.'

'Let's put out the light.'

25

THERE WAS NO AWKWARDNESS. SALLY AWOKE FIRST BUT DIDN'T get out of bed, ready to feign sleep for Irvine to slip out ahead of her if he showed any discomfort. But he didn't. They still weren't touching—she hadn't been conscious of their accidentally doing so during the night, either—but she was aware when he stirred, half turning on his back again before stopping, as if remembering just then that he wasn't alone.

Quiet-voiced, Irvine said, 'You awake?'

'Yes,' said Sally in a normal tone. She sensed his movement towards her and turned to face him.

'Hi.' There was a half smile.

'Hi.' Was she as ready, as prepared, as she had been the previous night? She thought so. He didn't feel out for her.

'I've got coffee but not much else.'

'Coffee's good.'

'There's a deli on the corner; we could get breakfast there.'

'Okay.'

'Do you want to take a shower while I do the coffee? I've got to shave as well; takes longer.'

'I'll do the coffee, you have the bathroom first. Have you got a robe?'

His beard line was darker than his head hair, more ginger than blond; what hair there was on his chest and shoulders was darker, too. Without any embarrassment Irvine got out of bed and didn't cover himself when he returned from the bathroom with the robe. 'You're lucky. Yesterday was laundry day.'

Sally had no difficulty with nakedness, either, and didn't contort herself getting into the robe, which did smell freshly laundered, although it still had the faintest trace of the cologne he'd worn the first night they had dinner.

'Fifteen minutes,' he promised.

'Take longer. It's still early.' And she didn't have a crowded schedule, she reminded herself. She was surprised at the neatness of the apartment, with the exception of a spaghetti-cabled workstation of what, from the obvious linkages, appeared to be three interfaced desktop computers. All three screens were blank, but their standby lights were on. The living room also had more photographs than she expected to find in a bachelor apartment, a selection of campus scenes with Princeton banners in the background. A section of one wall was occupied by a collage of family photographs and framed honour citations and awards naming Irvine's father, which Sally absorbed at once but didn't linger over, not wanting to be caught doing so by Irvine's emerging from the bedroom.

She timed the coffee perfectly with his emergence in the predictable jeans, loafers, and sweatshirt combination. She remained in his robe to drink her coffee before showering, in an equally neat bathroom, and putting on the previous night's clothes. Irvine was getting up from his workstation when she returned to the living room. 'I won't ask if there's anything new because you wouldn't tell me if there were, would you?'

'There isn't, so I don't have to answer the question.'

'Would you have answered, if there had been?'

'I trusted you last night, didn't I?'

That wasn't an answer but it gave her a way in. 'Why did you?'

Irvine shrugged. 'I just wanted to; wanted to hear your reaction, but you didn't give one.'

Legal and ethical uncertainty from someone whose father overstepped boundaries, wondered Sally, conscious of the photographic shrine on the wall? She said, 'We work in intelligence. The credo is that anything and everything that achieves its objective is acceptable until it goes publicly wrong. Then it becomes contagiously unacceptable. That's what we have scapegoats for.'

'British hard-assed cynicism!'

'Universal intelligence pragmatism.'

At the diner she ordered lox. Irvine managed four pancakes with maple syrup, insisting his waistline could stand it. Sally said, 'It looked as if it could this morning,' and wished she hadn't when he immediately said, 'What about tonight?'

'What about it?' she said, hating the gaucheness.

'Can we have dinner?'

If she said no, he'd think she was mocking his libido lapse, and if she said yes, he'd take it as an automatic invitation. 'Let's talk later, after we know what the day's going to bring.'

Sally left Irvine arranging for the Volkswagen to be towed away for repair, but was still back at the embassy compound an hour before her scheduled contact with London. As she approached the adjacent compound apartment block, Nigel Fellowes emerged from the embassy annexe, scrutinizing the previous night's clothes.

Sally stopped, returning the scrutiny. 'You waiting for me?'

'We were getting ready to call the police.'

'I was logged out.' What game was the resentful bastard playing now! 'But not back in.'

'It's not a requirement. Neither is your monitoring my movements.'

'We like to know where visitors are. Washington can be a dangerous place.'

'Did you check with London?'

Fellowes faltered. 'I was going to, after talking it through with Podmore. Didn't want to cause you embarrassment if it was a personal matter.'

It was the sort of juvenile thing the man would have done, Sally thought, maybe had done, despite the denial. 'London had my number: knew where I was and what I was doing. And it wasn't a personal matter. So the embarrassment would have been yours, Nigel. And always will be if you confront me. Get back to your cocktails and caviar and stop getting in the way.'

'I will *not* be spoken to like that!'

'You just have been.' She let in a pause, indulging herself. 'And you've got another problem.'

'What?' asked the man uncertainly.

'Your breakfast is all down your tie.'

'It's gone past Johnston's usual call time.'

'I've heard nothing,' Sally told the Director-General. 'I haven't had any calls, either.'

'They've had hours to question the one we've given them, wherever they've taken him.'

'Who is he?'

'Abu al Hurr. Born in Pakistan, emigrated to Birmingham eight years ago. Already on our watch list: we lost him two years ago.'

'Was he offered the bounty?'

'Some of what we were contributing, as well as witness protection. Wasn't tempted. He wouldn't go beyond his original arrest statement, which was that al Aswamy's set up other attacks, some definitely in the UK and America, all part of a jihad that couldn't be halted, but he didn't know anything more than that.'

'Did you sit in on the interrogations?'

'Some of them.'

'What's your assessment?'

'Fallback disinformation, in the event of failure,' judged Monkton. 'He passed a lie detector, so he believes what al Aswamy told him, which is damned clever. He stayed the dedicated jihadist until he was told he was going to America on a rendition flight. Then the act crumbled. If he'd known of a positive target, I believe he would have told us then to avoid being handed over.'

'Our deal is the UK information Fort Meade's got in exchange for a detainee, whom the CIA's now got.'

'Which I'm going to remind Johnston if he hasn't called me within the hour.'

'Let's hope he listens.'

'Worthwhile dinner last night?'

Sally's surprise at the question came with a blip of unease. 'I think so,' she managed. As always, Monkton listened without interruption as she detailed Irvine's Georgetown disclosure.

'Why withhold that?' Monkton demanded the moment she finished.

'I think it was a personal, not an official, decision.'

'The father?'

'Yes.' She had no reason for unease, Sally decided.

'Any leverage in that for us?'

Sally hesitated. 'Nothing that's obvious.'

The momentary pause was from London. 'You didn't compromise yourself, getting it?'

Fellowes! immediately thought Sally. 'No, not in any way. But I'm moving out of the embassy. There's no benefit in my being there apart from secure communication, and I don't need to live there to use that. I'll get something at the Guest Quarters service flats near the Watergate.'

The London hesitation was longer this time. 'You sure that's a good idea?'

'Very sure.'

'Don't move out until I make contact with Johnston. I want to be able to speak safely with you the moment I do.'

It had been an instinctive reaction to leave the embassy accommodations, but upon reflection Sally reassured herself it made every professional sense. The embassy was claustrophobic, limiting even, and the service apartments were much more central. It certainly had nothing whatsoever to do with Jack Irvine; she wasn't even sure she'd see him that night.

The disorienting psychological sound track played on, despite the man's medically confirmed unconsciousness: agonized screams, Arabic pleas for mercy, the slamming of metal doors, metal striking metal, all tuned convincingly louder than the supposed outside Karachi-street-language mix of Urdu, Sindhi, and Punjabi. Abu al Hurr lay completely naked where he'd toppled to the cell floor, although turned partially onto his back to keep his mouth and nose free of the overflow pools from the just-completed waterboarding. His heavy beard was flecked by convulsive vomit, and his belly was distended by the water that had been forced into it. He'd fouled himself. His body was still in spasm, his chest shuddering for breath. He was alone, unattended in the concrete-slab cell, which was bare except for the slatted trestle to which he'd been strapped. The porous face-covering and a still-dripping hose still hung from it.

'I'd admit whatever I was fucking asked rather than go through that,' said the first man.

'You and me both,' agreed the second.

Both their rubber suits were draped wetly over a chair in the glass-walled observation chamber from which they'd watched the medical examination. One was Caucasian, the other Hispanic. Neither knew the other's name nor would ever again share another assignment. Neither had before been to Guantánamo Bay or anywhere else in Cuba, nor would ever again.

'I thought we'd killed him when he stopped breathing,' said the first.

'It looked to me like the doctor injected something like adrenaline directly into his heart. Can they do that to someone without killing them?'

'If he's stopped breathing, his heart isn't working, is it?'

'I guess not.'

'The instructions were whatever it takes, at any cost, for a quick result. But if the son of a bitch dies, it'll be our asses,' warned the first.

'Maybe we should go a little easier next time. But perhaps there won't be a next time. Now we play the good-cop/bad-cop routine: offer a slice of the bounty, a razor for that facial shit, and whatever new life he wants wherever he wants it.'

'Only an asshole would say no.'

'That's what the asshole did say every time we stopped drowning him,' reminded the second man.

'They get normal television down here?'

'I guess. Why?'

'I'm watching that new HBO series about English kings in the Middle Ages. You seen it?'

The second man shook his head.

'Shit! Did they know how to live! Pussy everywhere, they could do what they liked!'

'Maybe I'll look at it with you.'

'Has he stopped breathing!' suddenly demanded the first man, turning more fully towards the observation window.

'Just stopped shaking to get air.'

'Still better call the medics back.'

'I guess.'

'You going to give her the computer address or shall I?' asked Irvine. 'I could probably explain it better.'

'She gets the address when we get what I asked for, which is *all* their detainees,' said Johnston.

'That wasn't the deal.'

'It's my deal and she knows it because I reminded her today. So does her asshole boss in London.'

'The fact that it's England is no guarantee it's a UK hit. It could simply be a route switch to something back here,' cautioned Irvine. 'We screw the Brits, they could screw us right back. We should hold off from all this macho bullshit; they need us, we need them. Let's stop fucking around!'

'The Brits started it!' insisted Bradley petulantly. 'The deal's on the table: they know what they've got to do.'

Irvine sighed heavily, irritated that Conrad Graham had relegated the meeting to this level. 'I told you I'm not going to be dragged down by either of you.'

'And neither of us are going to be dragged down by you and a cocka-mamy operation that didn't work,' said Bradley. 'And don't waste your time whimpering to your great protector on the top floor. He wants them all, just like we do.'

'The embassy switchboard said you weren't at your extension anymore, that they didn't have a forwarding number,' Irvine told Sally when she answered her cell phone.

'I've moved out.'

Irvine hesitated, deciding against asking the obvious question. 'Hear you had another confrontation with Johnston?'

'Not actually a confrontation,' qualified Sally. 'He said he didn't need to see me when I telephoned. That all he wanted to hear was what time today the other detainees were being flown out. And he refused even to take a call from the Director-General.'

In his CIA office Irvine physically grimaced. 'How about tonight?'

'I'm not sure. I'm still settling in.'

'I think we should meet.'

She hesitated. 'You *think* we should meet?'

'Yes.'

'What time?'

'Eight.'

'I'll pick you up. I've got a car that works and I know the way.'

From Tehran, Vevak's Hydarnes site came on the Halal Web site with a limited encrypted e-mail routed through Lagos, Nigeria, to a Paris Facebook account from which it was immediately forwarded to an America registration. Burt Singleton watched his embedded Trojan horse pick up the route on the already-known-and-hacked-into Paris site, satisfaction moving through him. Too soon to alert Irvine, he decided, looking up in surprise at Harry Packer's entry into the room.

'Thought I'd stop by, see how things are going,' said the liaison director. 'Don't seem to be so good, do they?'

26

JACK IRVINE POURED SALLY THE VALPOLICELLA HE'D BOUGHT ON his way home from Langley and popped the cap off the beer he raised in silent toast. 'There's a Vietnamese place on the next block, but I want to talk first, okay?'

'Okay,' agreed Sally, curious, settling back into her easy chair. If he wanted privacy, it had to be work-related. Sit and listen, hold back from prompting until he's talked himself out of what he's geared himself up to say, she determined. But she didn't have to, because instead of speaking, Irvine handed her a slip of single-line paper.

' "Swordbearer@forevermystery.org.uk," ' Sally read aloud, and smiled. 'Thank you. I don't have to tell you it won't leak—so I won't bother.'

'It's not altruism.' Irvine paused, smiling in return. 'Or anything between us, because there isn't anything between us, is there? Johnston and Bradley are out to wreck Cyber Shepherd to save themselves: manoeuvring as many fuckups as they can onto others to cover their own mistakes. It's their fight back against my telling them I wasn't going to be dragged down with either of them for what's already gone wrong. My mistake. I should have just gone around them, which is what I'm doing from now on.'

Sally was uncomfortable at the soul-baring, at being let in too close, which was ridiculous because this was what she was in Washington to achieve. 'They won't get any other detainees, which is what Johnston demanded again today.'

Irvine swigged his beer. 'They probably don't expect to; maybe even hope London will openly refuse. How's this for an escape scenario? You guys held out, to pressure your involvement here. Now you hold out again on any further releases if the guy we've got doesn't talk. Bradley losing al Aswamy and Johnston's inadequacies get buried deeper and deeper under all the recriminations. And the Brits in general and you in person end up the scapegoats for everything that's gone wrong, and Cyber Shepherd goes on record as a failure.'

Precisely as his father's diplomatic miscalculations were officially recorded, Sally recognized. 'Doesn't anyone remember what the point and purpose of the whole fucking operation was? Or is?'

'You're forgetting your own intelligence mantra. It's become a publicly known—worse, an internationally known—débacle.'

Sally smiled wryly. 'And you're forgetting it was my idea to claim that we had al Aswamy.'

'They won't,' predicted Irvine. 'And I was being gallant.'

'London thinks Abu al Hurr—if you don't already know, he's the guy you've got—is disinformation,' disclosed Sally flatly.

'Disinformation!' Irvine frowned, the beer halfway to his lips.

'He was terrified at being handed over to the CIA. Passed a polygraph test that showed he was telling the truth, that what he's told us is all al Aswamy ever told him; that's what the other three have also said under polygraph interrogation, as well.'

'Shit!'

'Spraying in all directions.' Sally poured herself more wine. Abruptly she declared, 'But I'm not going to be covered in it to become anyone's scapegoat.'

'Then we'll—' began Irvine, but halted at the competing cell phone and computer alerts. His hand over the mouthpiece but still looking at his computer, he said, 'I hope you weren't hungry.'

'Not anymore.'

———

There was no natural light, but it wasn't a cell. The walls were simulated wood—the inevitable one-way glassed observation panel distorted to merge into its surroundings—and the chairs were comfortably padded. There was no psychologically disorienting sound track. The polygraph operators had gone, but their machine and its attachments remained, although now pushed to the side of the room. Two interrogators faced Abu al Hurr across the table. Neither wore ties. One had his jacket looped casually over the back of his seat in staged, casual friendliness. Both were black. Again, neither of the two men had ever worked together, nor would ever again. Both were strangers to Cuba, to which they would never return. Abu al Hurr was in a clean orange jumpsuit. He'd been allowed three hours of sleep from the moment of his recovering consciousness. The only physical indication of his earlier ordeal was hand tremors.

'We want you to know we had no part in what's happened to you,' opened the man in the jacket. 'We're very sorry that it did, but you're here with us now, safe. We're not going to hurt you. We want you to believe that, okay?'

The Pakistani grunted, head lowered to avoid looking directly at either man. Both waited for more. Nothing came.

The first man went on, 'We're your way out, out of all your problems. We're responsible for what happens to you now, not the British. In England you were going to go on trial, be jailed for ten, fifteen years, maybe even more. Some slime pit where every day white racists would hurt you more than you got hurt today. You want to think about that—worse even than today?'

'Stop! Don't want to hear!'

'That's what we're talking about,' broke in the second man, leaning forward over the intervening table. 'We're going to stop it all . . . stop everything. Here's how we do it. You tell us every single thing al Aswamy told you about the attacks he set up, where and when they're going to be, and we give you enough money—we're talking millions here, Abu—to live in luxury for the rest of your life wherever you choose. And to make sure it's a long and very happy life, we give you a new identity, new everything, and make sure no-one ever finds you.'

'I don't *know* any more than I've told you! You know I don't!' pleaded the man. 'All he said was that he was going to lead more attacks. He wouldn't say where.'

'So you asked him!' seized the first man.

'Course I asked him.' Al Hurr hesitated as he looked up for the first time. 'I told him I wanted to go on fighting the jihad against Satan's people.'

'What did he tell you!' urged one of the interrogators.

'What I told the others . . . that there were more people . . . other "armies," he called them. That we could only fight once.'

The short-sleeved man thrust himself exaggeratedly back into his chair. 'Abu al Hurr, let us help you, for God's sake! It wasn't easy for us to get you out of where you were earlier. We made ourselves responsible for you, promised we'd come to an arrangement. You keep on lying that you don't know anything more, you're strapped back on that bed and they're drowning you again, and maybe this time they'll manage to do it.'

'No! Please no!' It was an agonized wail. He began to cry.

'Tell us what we want to know!' demanded the first man.

'I don't know anything more than what I've told you!' screamed the man. His face was puce and he was choking on tears that mixed with the uncontrolled flow from his nose, both shaking hands stretched out imploringly.

The interrogators thrust up together. Struggling into his jacket, one said, 'You had your chance, Abu. You blew it.'

A guttural noise broke from the man, a much deeper choking than before, and his face became a deeper purple seconds before he pitched forward, hitting the table edge before crashing sideways. Blood was mixed with the spittle that bubbled from his mouth.

The first man said, 'Oh, fuck!'

His partner was at the door, banging at an alarm button.

From where he crouched beside the Pakistani, the first man said, 'He's not breathing. I can't find his heart . . . I mean a beat.'

The second man stood back from the door as two medics burst in. One fumbled a defibrillator onto al Hurr's chest and administered the first shock without warning his partner. Calming, warning this time, he gave ten further bursts before sitting back on his haunches to look at the two interrogators. He said, 'My name's Matt, not Jesus.'

The second man said: 'This'll cause a shitstorm.'

Irvine unthinkingly made room for Sally to position a chair so she could look over his shoulder, his concentration entirely on his terminal. She realized at once that Irvine's screen was remote-access-linked to Fort Meade, the curser moved by someone there. But it was a fleeting awareness, like the recognition of an unintelligibly encrypted message. What truly shocked her was hearing the slow-drawl voice from NSA almost casually identify the Iranian intelligence service at the same moment that the remotely moved cursor rested on an account including the name Hydarnes and immediately afterwards mention the Halal Web site, described to her during her telephone cramming session with GCHQ's John as the unattainable Holy Grail of Western intelligence eavesdropping.

'. . . didn't have the Nigerian router,' the anonymous voice drawled on. 'But I'd isolated the Paris account during the earlier run I followed. Then came the familiar transfer. And silence.'

'So who—and where—is smartman@deathtrade.org.mil?' said Irvine.

'We do know it's military, which frightens the hell out of me,' came the Fort Meade voice.

'You and me both,' said Irvine. '*Mil* is a restricted military designation on which we also know there's an Iranian intelligence transmission. Somewhere, somehow, Tehran is inside a U.S. military installation or facility.'

'Including them all, the global count will be in the thousands . . . tens of thousands. But it could be a bot hacked into an ordinary account any-where.'

'My instinct is that it'll be hidden in something genuinely military.'

'I wouldn't expect us to agree, would you?'

Irvine shifted, discomfited by Singleton's aggression. Refusing to re-spond, he said instead, 'What's organized?'

'You can see for yourself it's straight encryption: short enough for a direct order or target identification,' said the voice in time with the dart-ing cursor. 'Marian's already arrived. Shab and Akram should be here soon. We'll try for algorithms on SHA 2 as well as 3, see if 3 can justify its setup costs. We'll generate a random number search in tandem. But this is pure mathematics-based decryption, and we know it'll be good because we know the source. It isn't going to be easy.'

'We've got the destination account,' said Irvine. 'You're putting a code search through a numbers run?'

'That's what I called you about: everything else I've started is routine.'

Irvine hesitated. 'You run a code run from there. I'll do the registra-tion search from here, where the Pentagon is.'

'You going into the Pentagon?'

The predictable objections, Irvine recognized. 'It's justified.'

'It's illegal.'

'Iranian intelligence is using a U.S. military designation. That comes well within our remit.'

'Not if it's inside a civilian shell.'

'It is, by my judgment.'

'You're authorizing it?'

'I'm authorizing it. And doing it.'

'Are you coming up?'

'Nothing I can't do from here, and you've got everything else covered up there, haven't you?'

'I guess.'

'Thanks for getting it organized from your end.'

'I thought that's how we're working now.'

Irvine hesitated again, suppressing the sigh. 'Yeah, that's how we're working now. Keep me up to speed.'

'You going to ring bells?'

Another predictable demand, thought Irvine. He was surprised it hadn't come up sooner. 'Let's give ourselves a little time to narrow the search field.'

'Time is what we don't have.'

'Which is why I'm going into the Pentagon right now.'

'It'll be a botnet, even if it's military.'

'There might be a subcatalog indicator.'

'You're clutching at straws,' accused the voice.

'There'll be a lot of codes, too many for me to handle alone.'

'You giving the formal authorization for the access-code search to be conducted from here?'

Irvine sighed openly this time. 'I already have.' Would Singleton be recording this exchange just as formally?

'We'll keep in touch.'

'We'll need to.' Irvine started slightly at Sally's presence beside him, the smile uncertain. 'Well, you wanted to know it all. Now you do.'

And she wasn't going to miss one iota of the opportunity, determined Sally. 'It's a hell of a lot at one go. It makes al Aswamy almost irrelevant.'

'That guy's anything but irrelevant.'

'How long have you been this deep in a Vevak Web site!'

'Almost from the beginning: more than a year, operationally. Took me a long time before that, virtually from the conclusion of another CIA project I was involved in.'

'Stuxnet.'

'How did you know I worked on Stuxnet?'

'I didn't,' Sally admitted. 'It's the only computer-intrusion operation I know about.'

'I want to believe you.'

She couldn't lose him, not after getting this far! 'Then believe me! Johnston called you a whiz kid, which had to mean with computers and implied you'd worked with the CIA before. Stuxnet's public knowledge: the Israelis openly admit co-operating with the CIA, building a mock-up of the Natanz installation.' She could see he wasn't convinced. Where the hell was her way back in? 'We've already identified where the risks to Cyber Shepherd come from, and it isn't me. And you can take that personally as well as professionally.'

'Johnston and Bradley don't know.'

That was inconceivable because . . . oh no, it wasn't, she corrected herself; it was totally conceivable from someone with Irvine's history. Quietly, all indignation gone, she said, 'Jack, how many people *do* know?'

'The guys at Meade, obviously: they have to know.'

'Who else?'

'You've seen the way Langley works! How Bradley and Johnston fucked up. How al Aswamy's surveillance fucked up.'

'Langley doesn't know?' she persisted, determined to get a definitive answer. 'Conrad Graham?'

'He signed off on an operation to combat radicalized terrorists before they organized themselves to attack us. Or any other Western target. He knew me, knew what I could do.'

It was so feasible, so understandable: a relationship formed during an earlier, hugely successful operation, two men with differing agendas, one elevated to high authority welcoming another potential coup, the other providing—and initially proving—how that could be attained by word-of-mouth undertakings, no need for specific details. The credo in practise: anything and everything that achieves an objective is acceptable. None of which affected her attitude or her thinking. She'd gained her personal objective far, far above and beyond any expectation, including her own. Sally said, 'But you've told me. Shown me.'

'I already told you I don't know why I did.'

I believe I do, she thought. 'You've no cause for worry.'

'I've got things to do,' Irvine announced, stirring himself.

'I want to stay.'

He shrugged. 'Why not?'

Sally was bewildered at the ease with which Irvine hacked into the Pentagon Web site and just as easily worked his way through their sub-sites until he remarked it was NSA technicians and operators who'd recommended its design and installation. He explained, 'And fifteen-year-old kids still get in and put the country on war footings.' In the first hour Irvine forwarded what Sally estimated to be in excess of three hundred Pentagon entry codes to Fort Meade for supercomputer comparison against Smartman@deathtrade.org.mil. By 5:00 a.m., when Irvine called a halt, Sally guessed he'd downloaded more than a thousand, in addition to whatever registrations had independently been logged at Fort Meade. None had disclosed the Vevak recipient address.

'What are you going to do?' asked Sally.

'Start again tomorrow.'

'You going to tell someone at CIA?'

'I don't know.'

'You should—know, I mean. And tell someone.'

'It's late.'

'We should go to bed,' she agreed.

They came together like longtime, familiar lovers, each knowing the other's wants and pleasures, he unhurriedly undressing her and savouring her nakedness, Sally taking her time to undress him, tasting his body. They kept the pace, touching and feeling and luxuriating in each other, waiting for each other, and arriving together. They stayed locked together in sleep and awoke anxious for each other, and again it was perfect.

When it finally ended, Irvine said, 'I'm safe with you. I know that.'

Sally didn't speak, quieted by the knowledge that for the first time she hadn't stayed apart, uninvolved. She'd *made* love.

27

IN THE WASHINGTON TRADITION—AND SPEED—OF POLITICAL BUCK passing, the responsibility for al Aswamy's claimed seizure was shuffled all the way up to 1600 Pennsylvania Avenue. From there the White House chief of staff passed it straight back to the internationally besieged State Department with a demand for a politically and publicly acceptable explanation for the continued official silence. Encouraged by the implied presidential authority, the State Department convened a Homeland Security breakfast session restricted to directors and their deputies of all of its component agencies, who with one voice embarked upon another Washington tradition, the scapegoat hunt.

Each lined up behind the FBI—enraged at what it insisted to be illegal encroachment upon its internal U.S. jurisdiction and daily pillory ing by an even more enraged *New York Times*—to denounce the CIA's handling of the al Aswamy search as negligent, incompetent, and leaderless. None risked openly identifying the hapless Conrad Graham as the obvious sacrifice for authorizing Cyber Shepherd. But the tuned-in Graham already knew that CIA director Admiral Jack Lamb was privy to the intended career assassination of Graham, himself: despite Graham's persistently memoed requests, he'd had no prior consultation with Lamb during the two-day, White-House-and-back runaround.

Based on how the criticisms had so far been voiced, Graham believed that he could face down the other agencies. His uncertainty was in publicly confronting someone who was not only a political appointee but also someone with the inherent support of fellow admiral and Homeland Security director Joshua Smith. But one word—*political*—lingered in Graham's mind as he looked beyond the assembled directors to the White House and State Department staffers, none of whose expressions or body language matched the increasingly obvious satisfaction at the blame-fest that Joshua Smith was encouraging.

The specific insistence was for a public and politically acceptable explanation, Graham reminded himself. And the fixed-faced, unimpressed professional diplomats were the arbiters. For the second time that morning Graham pushed aside the temptation to totally scrap his intended counter-attack and improvise instead upon Jack Irvine's unexpected phone call minutes before he'd entered the meeting. But there wasn't enough information from what Irvine had hinted at. And whatever Graham speculated wouldn't fit the White House remit, which hadn't been addressed by anyone. That had to be his escape route.

And still wasn't being addressed, Graham recognized, as FBI director Frederick Bowyer, with unembarrassed hypocrisy, demanded the CIA resolve a CIA debacle and that they publicly identify and discipline the inept officers responsible to restore public confidence. That having been done, the pursuit of Ismail al Aswamy had to be transferred to the FBI, whose investigation it should have been from the outset.

What little doubt Graham had of his total abandonment came with Joshua Smith's invitation to Lamb—Jack, not Mr Director, the courtesy title by which he'd addressed every other agency head—to respond.

The debacle, unquestionably the fault of the CIA, had tarnished his recent appointment as its director, declared the grey-haired, smooth-faced Lamb, each word carefully selected. He intended a complete overhaul of operational procedures to prevent future failures and welcomed suggestions from all the Homeland Security agencies. He'd had no personal involvement in, nor did he endorse, Operation Cyber Shepherd, which had been initiated before his appointment. Specific details and answers to all the criticism would be provided by his deputy, Conrad Graham, who had approved the project.

Graham didn't hurry assembling what little counter-argument he had with the lawyer's acumen with which he'd graduated from Harvard. He intentionally waited for shifts of impatience from those around him before abruptly declaring, 'I'm disappointed that so much time has been wasted without a single, constructive suggestion for what we've been brought together to provide.'

The shift in mood now was to startled surprise, the most visible from Admiral Smith. Hurrying to build upon it, Graham went word for word, line by line, through every accusation, logically insisting on the disarray that self-serving individual exculpation would cause, doubling the political and public clamour they were meant to allay.

Continuing to draw upon his lawyer's training, Graham mentally composed an alternative as he demolished the arguments of others, encouraged by the now-visible reactions of the State Department and White House contingents. The Homeland Security announcement should be neither apologetic nor an admission of fault or failure, Graham asserted. Rather it should illustrate a considered, objective anti-terrorist investigation that had prevented a totally innocent man from being wrongly accused on circumstantial evidence provided by a closely allied Western intelligence service. That totally innocent man had been released. The inevitable demands for an identity would be enormous, conceded Graham. But they could be rejected on the grounds of fairness: innocent or not, the man's life would be ruined by public exposure. The statement should make clear that no Homeland Security component had any knowledge of how the original story of Ismail al Aswamy's seizure appeared in *The New York Times*. There should be reassurance, insisted Graham. It should be made clear that obviously not every resource had been assigned to the misled investigation. Independent, parallel enquiries had guaranteed the unremitting hunt for Ismail al Aswamy continued and was lawfully led by the Central Intelligence Agency, responsible for external intelligence.

It was a decision for Homeland Security whether publicly to admit CIA failings, continued Graham, reaching for his briefcase for the prepared photocopied performance warnings to both Charles Johnston and James Bradley. Sliding the copies along the table for individual distribution, Graham read aloud his five-day-old replacement recommendation for both men that had been ignored by Admiral Lamb. He also offered his written requests to Lamb for a pre-conference briefing at which he had intended to outline every point he was making that morning. Apart from the two men whose replacement he'd recommended, the CIA's failings were not those of incompetence but of too little adjustment time for a newly appointed director.

Neither had Operation Cyber Shepherd failed. It had proved the outstanding anti-terrorist success he'd anticipated when he'd originally authorized it.

'And which it will continue to be, with other anti-terrorist activities as well as hunting down al Aswamy,' Graham concluded, intent on the response from around the table.

Jack Lamb was looking for guidance from Joshua Smith, whose concentration in turn was on the murmurs among the White House and State Department group, some of whom were exchanging scribbled legal-pad notes. More messages were passing between other directors, too.

The FBI's Frederick Bowyer broke the confused impasse. 'So there's been no mistakes! No-one's done anything wrong!'

'Just the normal internal glitches of an ongoing investigation,' agreed Graham, defeating the intended sarcasm.

'You really think *The New York Times* is going to buy it?'

'You were as misled as a lot of other people in the beginning,' guided Graham, conscious of two of the White House staffers openly smiling. 'You're genuinely sorry and you'll make it up to them with a lot of exclusives in the future, starting with the confirmed arrest—or whatever the outcome—of al Aswamy.'

One of the smiling men offered what Graham guessed to be a written suggestion to Joshua Smith, who avoided the look of his fellow admiral and announced, 'I think that satisfactorily resolves the immediate problem.'

Graham gauged that he—and Operation Cyber Shepherd—had survived by a whisker. A hell of a lot—probably everything—depended upon whatever Jack Irvine had tried to indicate.

Irvine's mind worked to mathematical conformity: in Irvine's world everything, ultimately, had logical, deducible answers. Numerals and lexigrams and symbols and their algebraic substitutes could be disarranged or scrambled into labyrinthine codes and ciphers, but eventually the rules of mathematical certainty applied, irrespective of whatever language concealment or ambiguity in which they might additionally be cloaked. At that moment, on the car journey to Fort Meade, Irvine struggled for an algorithm to the last twenty-four hours. But couldn't find one.

There was no hypocrisy in giving Sally the England-routed IP he'd initially withheld to force the London prisoner exchange: that was the deal, the domain address for a prisoner. But disclosing his Vevak intrusion—letting her watch his unsuccessful search—wasn't part of any deal. So why had he let her in so completely? To impress her, get her into bed? No! he rejected, feeling a positive flush of anger. He'd been virtually unaware of Sally's presence throughout the hunt for smartman@deathtrade.org.mil. Any intrusive thought of sex would have risked a repetition of his first-night humiliation, making it doubly unthinkable. Why then? Why not? was his immediate mental response. Sally Hanning—possibly the best lateral thinker he'd ever encountered—was an officially co-opted, top-security-cleared British intelligence officer who'd practicably contributed more to Cyber Shepherd than any CIA counterpart; she had the professional right to know. But there was one obvious caveat: Was it above and beyond Conrad Graham's professional right?

No, Irvine forced himself to admit, seeing the first of the Fort Meade signs in the far distance. There'd been every reason to withhold the Vevak coup from the incompetents with whom he'd originally been burdened. But not for keeping it any longer from Conrad Graham. His father's mistake had been to work virtually alone and . . . Irvine's mind blocked at this moment of awareness. Was that the algorithm he needed, the answer to how—and why—he'd behaved as he had last night? Had he told Sally everything as he now planned to tell Graham everything to protect himself from mistakes that had disgraced his father? A lot of factors contributed to that mathematically logical equation. Withholding the Vevak breakthrough from Conrad Graham had been dangerously arrogant, as Sally had implied. But on his way from DC that morning he'd made the first move to rectify that by calling the deputy director. When they identified smartman@deathtrade.org.mil, having a Trojan horse stabled in an Iranian intelligence site could be presented as a new coup, not something he'd worked on since Stuxnet.

Personal risk averted, Irvine decided, taking the first turnoff. What about the risk to Operation Cyber Shepherd? A confrontation, Graham had called that morning's encounter with Homeland Security high-command directors and their deputies. Irvine wished he'd had more warning, had time to properly produce a justification for Cyber Shepherd if one was demanded. Suggesting the strongest lead to the vanished al Aswamy without disclosing details of the smartman interception wasn't enough. Revealing his being embedded in Vevak would certainly have been. But it would have been a disastrous mistake. It would have been leaked— destroying everything—within an hour of its being announced to a full Homeland Security gathering, even one limited to directors and deputies. What *would* swing it would be deciphering the IP code to identify a Vevak source inside a U.S. military facility. Which was what he was at Fort Meade to do, he reminded himself as he located a parking space close to the sprawling complex.

As he entered, Irvine should have been warned by Singleton's reaction to his arrival, but his mind was still on his reflections during his drive over. Without any greeting or question from Irvine, Singleton said flatly, 'Nothing.'

'Not from *anything* I sent last night?' demanded Irvine, disappointed as much by the announcement as the tone.

'I told you, nothing.'

Marian Lowell said, 'We're still running programs on at least half of what you downloaded. And on the encryption.'

'There'll be more from the Pentagon today,' said Irvine.

'You're blatantly breaking the law,' accused Singleton.

'There's a Homeland meeting going on right now in DC with Cyber Shepherd in the crosshairs,' declared Irvine, stopping at Singleton's station, 'I've told Conrad Graham there's potentially something big.'

'You tell him you're hacking into the Pentagon!' persisted Singleton.

'Not from a cell phone on an interstate!' It sounded more like avoidance than the sarcasm he'd intended.

'I've officially registered an objection with Packer.'

'That's your right,' acknowledged Irvine, looking further around the room. 'It's the right of all of you, if you feel like Burt. Just as it's your right to resign from the entire project.' It was a gamble, but Singleton was becoming more of a nuisance than the help Irvine had expected. If Cyber Shepherd survived, maybe it should re-emerge with a fresh team. Adjusted at least.

'Your decision,' confronted Singleton.

'Why doesn't everyone examine their commitment, take time to consider what you want to do?' said Irvine, his temper gone. 'I'm going to continue downloading from the Pentagon while you think about what you want to do. Take your time. I'm the sole Pentagon intruder, the person accepting full responsibility for what I'm asking you to do as the result of my actions, okay?'

Irvine was embarrassed as well as angry as he turned to his terminal, conscious, too, of the discomfort among the rest of the group. No-one spoke, and he had the impression of their moving as quietly as possible, not wanting to attract attention. Malik and Barker silently left the room together, he guessed either for the supercomputer rooms or the number generators. Singleton and Marian concentrated fixedly on their screens.

Irvine's own concentration during the night had been on access code banks of military bases and facilities within the United States. Now he switched overseas, most of which were annotated alphabetically, which made easier his cursory initial subject comparisons or similarities with the smartman IP, before downloading for the more detailed supercomputer scrutiny. Quickly Irvine became oblivious to everything and everyone around him, as he had in the earlier pre-dawn. Just as quickly he lost count of how many codes he'd downloaded.

Awareness of time went, too, but as it passed, an incipient doubt began to nag. Was he wrong insisting smartman@deathtrade.org.mil needed the operational cover of a military installation or facility? Or could it function through some darknet bot—or series of bots one inside another, like a matryoshka doll—as Burt Singleton argued? It was practically immaterial: the Pentagon searches were programmed on supercomputers functioning at thousandths of a second, with parallel random-number programs. There were no other ways of getting the access code. Nor was there any wasteful manpower diversion. It came down to pride: Who was right, he or Burt Singleton? Which was . . . He was abruptly conscious of his shoulder being shaken and of Marian's voice repeating his name to break through the concentration.

As she said, 'I think you'll want to see this,' and gestured towards her computer, Akram Malik turned from the telephone Irvine had not heard ring and said, 'It's Langley, for you.'

28

'I'VE BEEN WAITING,' GREETED DAVID MONKTON.

'The statement was only broadcast thirty minutes ago and I had to get to the embassy,' retorted Sally from her communications cubicle. As usual she couldn't gauge anything—impatience or irritation or curiosity—from the monotone that sounded more like a public-address announcement than a human voice.

'I've scanned you the full transcript.'

'I've already got it in front of me. It seems to have covered all the points.'

'You heard from Langley?'

'No,' said Sally. 'Have you?'

'No.'

'I'm going to wait for them to come to me.'

There was a brief pause from London. 'How long?'

'Until tomorrow, at least.'

'No longer,' insisted Monkton.

'Anything from GCHQ?'

'Too soon.'

GCHQ had only had the intercept for five hours, Sally accepted. But that wasn't any longer her major preoccupation. Would Irvine keep that morning's promise to share whatever he got from the Vevak penetration? It was a test of sorts, she supposed; she'd pass on the memorized Hydarnes domain address if she suspected he reneged, but hoped he wouldn't. Keeping to what she could discuss with the Director-General, she said, 'We need something soon. We don't want another Sellafield.'

'Sellafield was prevented by you,' reminded Monkton, although almost dismissively. 'I'm surprised you didn't get an advance of today's announcement, after the co-operation you've been getting.'

Sally, in turn, was genuinely surprised at the passing twitch of discomfort. She had nothing to feel uncomfortable or guilty about: what had happened between her and Irvine was quite separate—totally unconnected—from what she was doing professionally. 'We're the obvious "friendly intelligence organization" supposed to have named an innocent man as al Aswamy. I don't know what the curve's going to be, but there'll be one.'

'You think the communiqué is going to defuse all the hysteria?'

'No,' said Sally at once. 'It'll just re-direct it. Which might, in fact, be the curve.'

'That's the way I see it. It's why I want your impressions the moment you form them. We've kept up so far—been ahead, a lot of the time. That's where I want it to stay.'

'That's the way I want it to stay, too.' She believed she had a good chance of achieving it, although she didn't expect to see—maybe not even to hear from—Irvine that night. He'd warned before he left Owen Place that morning that he'd stay at Fort Meade until they'd broken the Vevak encryption. Or was he staying down there for another reason? Could he have known about the Homeland statement and used Fort Meade as an excuse to be out of DC when it was issued? It was Irvine who'd suggested that London—with her the most likely focus—would be targeted as a diversion from America if the ruse backfired. Could he have already known about today's announcement, taken part in formulating it?

'You think Abu Hurr is the innocent man?'

Sally blinked the reflection away. 'I can't see how they could manipulate that, but who knows?'

Sally didn't expect a direct response to the rhetorical question, but the silence lasted so long that had they not been talking on a secure line, she would have imagined they'd been disconnected. Then, abruptly, Monkton declared, 'We need to talk specifics.'

The voice had risen above the normal blandness for the first time. 'What specifics?'

'We had to bulldoze your acceptance into the working group?'

'Yes?' agreed Sally cautiously.

'Was that resented?'

'There was a general understanding that it was professionally justified, I think.' Where was this going!

'By Johnston?'

'You, the Director, were the person with whom he was prepared to co-operate, not me.'

'Bradley?'

'He lost al Aswamy. He followed wherever the senior officer led, kept his head down whenever we met.'

'So you weren't accepted by him?' pressed Monkton.

'It didn't arise, not in any practical way.'

'As it did in a practical way with Jack Irvine?' Monkton's voice, which had subsided, grew stronger again.

'It's obvious from what I was able to give you earlier today that he's co-operating,' said Sally without any hesitation.

'Did you use the father's disgrace?'

'It came out in conversation, when I told him about my parents. I didn't *use* it.' She shouldn't have qualified it like that! Sally thought immediately.

'When I asked you, you told me you weren't compromised.'

'I'm not.'

'Is there a personal as well as a professional relationship between you and Irvine?'

'I don't consider that to be a question I should be asked, nor one to which I need to reply.'

'You just have replied,' said Monkton. 'So I'll ask you again, are you professionally compromised?'

'No.' He'd withdraw her, Sally guessed, recite all the prohibiting regulations, even though technically they didn't apply, and order her immediate return. Which she didn't want to do, not yet. Could she refuse, postpone it at least? Argue she needed time to pack up or insist upon the long-overdue vacation? She smiled in sudden, belated awareness. She had an irrefutable argument for staying where she was. She had access to the Vevak's Holy Grail Web site.

From London Monkton broke another pause. 'Don't confuse your priorities, Sally. Don't ever do that.'

It was the first time he'd ever called her Sally, she realized after they'd hung up. As she crossed to her parked car, her vibrating phone signaled another surprise.

'Motherfucker!' exploded James Bradley, thrusting unannounced into Johnston's office, trailed by Johnston's protesting secretary. Johnston waved the woman away and told Bradley to close the door. Bradley ignored him, standing instead with his legs spread, hands imperiously on his hips. The secretary closed the door on her way out.

'Which son of a bitch ordered this!' demanded Bradley, waving a piece of crumpled paper in his hand.

'I don't know what you're talking about,' said the covert operations director. 'What is it?'

'You didn't have this sent! Weren't involved!'

'What is it, for Christ's sake!'

'I'm off the active field register, off covert ops. Re-assigned to a fucking desk job in Personnel with a lot of fucking clerks. That's what I've been demoted to, a fucking clerk!' Bradley became aware that his jacket was unbuttoned and hurriedly re-fastened it to form his protective shell.

'Haven't you seen what Homeland just issued?'

'I've been reviewing the whole al Aswamy thing, trying to find anything we missed.'

Johnston pushed the two-page printout across the desk, saying nothing while the other man read. It took several minutes.

Finally looking up, Bradley said, 'What the fuck's it mean?'

'It means total bullshit and that everyone's bunkered down and that there have to be internal executions, yours and mine, to account for all the mistakes so far.'

'You?' questioned Bradley doubtfully.

Johnston picked up another sheet of paper, fluttering it like a flag, and let it fall back onto the desk. 'My authority to initiate covert activity has been indefinitely suspended. All such potential action must be submitted for the signed approval of Admiral Jack Lamb.' He sighed. 'I'm a fucking clerk, just like you. But as I'm keeping the title, I'm going to be responsible for all the other covert fuckups in the future.'

'What are you going to do?'

'Be a fucking clerk. I'll keep my grade—which you'll do, too, don't forget—on which my pension is calculated, and which I'll draw at the first available retirement opportunity, which I've already calculated to be eight years, six months, and four days. That's more than enough time to find a house on a golf course somewhere in the sun.'

'They can't do this!' declared Bradley, the anger resurging.

'They can and they just did.'

'Not to me they won't. I'm not rolling over to die without taking others with me.'

'You do that, Jim. You create a bloodbath all of your very own.'

'I will. I know where enough of the graves are to dig a lot more.'

Irvine was already at Owen Place when Sally arrived, although he'd told her on the phone he didn't expect to get there until seven thirty. It didn't occur to either of them to kiss, embrace in any way. He already had his beer open, her wine poured.

She said at once, 'What did you break, the IP code or the encryption! Tell me it was both!'

'So far we've got neither?'

'Then why are you back? This morning you said—'

'You've seen the Homeland statement?'

'Of course.' So he had known!

'Bradley and Johnston are officially gone, although Johnston keeps the title. Graham's in personal control of Cyber Shepherd, which puts him on a very thin line because Homeland want it scrapped and him sacrificed with it. Your detainee is dead. I'm ordered to a breakfast meeting with Graham, eight a.m. tomorrow; that's why I'm back and why I asked you to come here, where the computers are for me to be properly linked with Fort Meade. That brings you right up to speed with what's not in the communiqué, so sit down and drink your wine. And I think you look terrific.'

Maybe he hadn't known about the statement in advance, she thought, her mind switching between her personal and professional satisfaction. Don't confuse your priorities, she reminded herself. There was a lot to distill from what Irvine had said, maybe even things, inadvertently or otherwise, that he *hadn't* told her. But which she had to discover—now—before they became engulfed in the obvious confusion that existed at Langley. 'Where did Abu Hurr die?'

'I don't know. Or how, although that's kind of obvious.'

'You told Graham about the Vevak penetration?' she asked, conscious of his looking for the third time at the blank-eyed computers.

'Not yet.'

'You have to.'

He smiled briefly. 'Lecture time?'

'Reality time.'

'Tomorrow. It's how I'm going to save Cyber Shepherd. And Conrad Graham.'

She couldn't lose access to the Vevak intrusion! 'What about you?'

'What?' He frowned.

'You'll save Cyber Shepherd, sure. But look at it objectively. Cyber Shepherd's sensational. Stuxnet got Graham the deputy directorship, which now hangs by a very thin thread, according to you. Shepherd's his triumphant way back, with an expanded, dedicated unit. Where are you going to be in it all?'

'Making it work, like I did with Stuxnet.'

That was an exaggeration, Sally knew. 'You sure?'

'What's your point?'

'Cyber Shepherd is your baby. You should get the credit, not have it taken from you.'

'It won't be taken from me.'

The moment to sow the seed, judged Sally. 'GCHQ haven't made any progress yet; I'd be surprised if they had. But I'll know the moment they do, which will be the moment you'll know, too.'

'GCHQ's *your* baby.'

'Trust means sharing everything, doesn't it?'

'I guess,' said Irvine, looking at his terminals again. 'It's going to be another long night. We could order in.'

'Last night was even longer. You order in. I'll go back to the apartment tonight.'

Irvine came fully back to her, frowning. 'What's the problem?'

'Near exhaustion.' Sally smiled. 'Tomorrow night it won't be.'

'Your solemn promise?' He smiled back.

'My solemn promise.'

It was eight forty-five when she pulled out of Owen Place. Her fleeting impression was of imagining the surveillance, but as that thought came, Sally picked up the white Honda that had followed her earlier to Irvine's apartment. She kept to the shortest crosstown route, not trying to evade her tail, and stopped directly outside Guest Quarters for the doorman to park her car in the underground garage. From the darkened lobby she watched the Honda pull in farther along towards Watergate. What level of professional intelligence utilized a visibly obvious colour such as white for its surveillance vehicle? wondered Sally. If the outside street weren't so dark, she'd probably have been able to make out the head-bobbing doll on the windscreen ledge.

29

CONRAD GRAHAM SAT UNMOVING, BOTH HANDS FLAT AGAINST his desk as if needing its support, his expression halfway between bemusement and outright disbelief. When they came, the words were spaced, reflecting both. 'You're—reading—Iran's—intelligence—transmission!'

'*One* site,' carefully qualified Jack Irvine, encouraged by the reaction.

Graham's secretary answered the intercom instantly. Graham said, 'No calls from anyone. *Anyone*. No interruptions whatsoever,' and snapped the machine off as he moved to lock his door, with the other hand clicking on the outside red warning light of a restricted meeting in progress. He didn't bother going back behind his desk, perching instead on its edge. 'From the start! I want everything from the very beginning, right up to now, this moment!'

'Are we being recorded?' asked Irvine, syncing his presentation to the other man's attitude: straight down the line as far as possible, layman-level techno-talk to gloss over how long he'd been a cuckoo in a Vevak nest.

'Absolutely not!' guaranteed the deputy director earnestly. 'Just us: no notes, no automatically triggered disks, nothing.'

'I guess it goes back as far as Stuxnet, when I asked myself if we did the unthinkable then, why couldn't we do the unthinkable again. Just differently this time. And better.'

Graham was swinging his hitched-up leg like a metronome, keeping time, an inviting smile permanently fixed.

'Easier thought about than done,' continued Irvine, introducing his timeline-covering caveat. 'With Stuxnet we tried using Iran's Halal Web site, although eventually we had to infect technicians' personal PCs to introduce the worm into the Natanz centrifuges.'

Graham nodded sagely, as if he remembered; Irvine was sure he didn't. Graham's participation had been practical espionage, organizing and supervising infiltrated field agents.

'We're being straight with each other, right?' demanded Irvine. 'Everything in the open: There won't be any changes of mind, no misunderstandings? Not like it's been since we lost al Aswamy?'

'What!' Graham frowned, the smile slipping.

'There was some hesitation from a couple of my team, in the beginning. About legality.'

The derision spluttered from the other man. 'For fuck's sake, Jack! I'm the guy that's backed you from the start, remember!'

'Just clearing the point.'

'We're talking about terrorism, finding a known Iranian terrorist leader, saving Operation Cyber Shepherd and us with it! Stop jerking off about legality.'

Irvine almost wished a recording were being made. 'I spent a lot of time, months, years in fact, surfing Halal and the criminal and suspect darknets—cyber back alleys where anything and everything goes—and hacking into those that featured regularly—'

'What about normal NSA stuff . . . you fix some sort of dispensation . . . a moratorium?'

Irvine shook his head, ready for the question. 'The majority was in my own time: borrowed just a little from NSA, as well as the facilities. Expanding what we've now got from a NSA breakthrough, too: their discovery that some terrorist groups—not Al Qaeda in the beginning—were hiding in, and behind, Western social Web sites. That widened the search but ironically concentrated it: Was Vevak adding things like Facebook to their Halal and darknet communications to their cells in the West?'

Irvine paused. 'It took me almost a year to come up with the answer, which was yes!'

'They're using Facebook!'

'Along with millions and millions of other people!'

'How!' demanded Graham.

'A shared user, single-named domain umbrella account, no linked contact between sender and recipient, each recipient with separate subcatalog address known only to their Control, Vevak.'

Graham laughed aloud. 'It's basic intelligence tradecraft, with a twist . . . a cyber dead-letter drop! We used it for years, still do, when it fits the circumstances. The Russians, too. Goddamn! Nothing's new!'

'Cyber dead-letter drop is good,' flattered Irvine. It was going well, better than he'd hoped. Wrong to relax, though, as wrong as it would be to offer much more without prompting. Question and answer from now on: Graham's encouraging questions, Irvine's limited answers. 'You with me so far?'

'In step all the way. You get al Aswamy through Facebook?'

Shit! thought Irvine. Maybe he could manoeuvre around the answer, although it meant abandoning the intended brevity. 'I didn't fully understand al Aswamy's importance at that time, had no way of realizing then the size of his operations. At that stage I only knew it was initiated by Vevak, not even that Hydarnes was a shared account. The first intercepted post indicated a recruitment drive, nothing more. We sabotaged that, believing we were destroying potential terrorist cadres and their trust in each other. What I didn't realize was how central, literally, al Aswamy was to the combined international assaults: that he was the coordinator. The trigger messages directed to Britain and Italy were under different subcatalog accounts: that's what fooled me.' Again he'd gotten himself into position more easily than he'd imagined. 'I've got a point to make here, out of context with others I want to flag up later. We passed on, in accordance with the Echelon agreement, British- and Italy-designated transmission. It was the Brit, Sally Hanning, who jointed all the dots together; if she hadn't, the Washington Monument and Rome's Colosseum would probably be piles of rubble, and Britain would be dealing with its own Chernobyl. And we've got Sally Hanning here with us in DC.'

Conrad Graham stared across the desk, blank-faced and unspeaking for several moments. Then he said, 'What *is* the point you're making?'

'We're talking survival: your word. We need her with us if we're going to survive.'

Graham's face opened in feigned understanding. 'I already built that insurance into the announcement if we have another Abu Hurr fuckup. Any sort of fuckup.'

Whatever it took to get her included, Irvine consoled himself. 'She's also a hell of an operator. She'll contribute.'

'Let's get back to what's important,' urged Graham impatiently.

'Abu Hurr's dead.'

Sally decided against telling Monkton that she already knew. 'Under torture?'

'Heart attack during interrogation were Conrad Graham's words.'

'Same things,' insisted Sally. 'What else did he say?'

'It was an accident which they regretted. He hoped the co-operation would continue. What do you think of Graham?'

'A damned sight more than I thought of Johnston or Bradley, professionally. I need more personal contact to go much beyond that.'

'I hope you'll get it. He guaranteed you're part of what he called the team.'

'To be sacrificed if there are any more big mistakes?'

'That's how I read it.'

'What pressure does Abu Hurr's death in U.S. custody give us?'

'Unquantifiable, at the moment. I don't know—and don't expect to be told—in whose custody he physically was. Could be a dozen different rendition countries. Graham's line was that Abu al Hurr didn't exist, had never existed.'

'What did you tell him?'

'Nothing. And you're right about Graham being professional.'

'How?'

'There was a white-noise eradicator at his end of the telephone; there was nothing on the recording here when we tried to play it back.'

'Which means you weren't compromised, either.'

'All's not totally lost.'

Sally smiled in anticipation. 'Did Johnston believe Abu Hurr existed?'

'Vociferously so. And we got the registration of the CIA's rendition plane, even if we didn't get its flight plan.'

Who was the more professional, Conrad Graham or David Monkton? wondered Sally. 'When are you going to let Graham know?'

'When it serves a useful purpose: *our* useful purpose.'

'Anything from GCHQ?'

'They haven't cracked a message code yet. But there was a subcatalog link that they're working on. Now that I know you're physically in the communications room, I'll have the link sent immediately so you can take it up with GCHQ.'

The GCHQ discovery was already waiting, under her designated Eyes Only restriction, when Sally emerged from her cubicle. Conscious, as Monkton clearly was, of Nigel Fellowes's pervasive presence, Sally held back from any outward reaction in front of the communications room technicians, merely asking to be reconnected to London. From the security-guaranteeing Thames House she was patched through to Cheltenham and was relieved to be connected to the surprisingly co-operative John.

'This was random?' Sally pressed at once.

'Totally. We're still only treating it as a possibility that there's a link to the message code.'

'That's not sufficient. We've got to be absolutely sure,' insisted Sally. Where's the supposed close co-operation? she thought, irritated.

'I don't need to be told that!' said John, abruptly indignant.

'What's the possible connection?'

'Mil,' replied John with obvious reluctance.

'Smartman@deathtrade.org.mil?' queried Sally, quoting what she'd memorized from Irvine's computer.

There was a momentary silence. 'Yes.'

'Which ends the doubt?'

'Yes.'

Sally didn't bother to conceal the sigh. 'Could NSA have missed the transmission?'

'It's possible. We haven't been in contact yet.'

'Don't. I'll liaise from here.'

'Could this be as important as Sellafield?' the man asked at the end of the briefing.

'It could be even more so.'

She was ahead of everyone still involved in Operation Cyber Shepherd, Sally calculated, in a position, even, to take a lead that Jack Irvine and Conrad Graham would have to follow. Was the gamble worth it?

'That's it, right up to where we are now,' declared Jack Irvine, echoing Conrad Graham's initial response, as the uncertainty finally left him. He'd done it! He was well past any time-frame challenge on his Vevak penetration: from now on it was forward not backward examination, and he had that as clearly arranged in his mind as he'd planned everything else. 'And it gives us a hell of a problem.'

Conrad Graham had gone back behind his desk as Irvine had come to his obvious conclusion. At once the man came up from head-sunk contemplation. 'What problem?'

'Being able to make proper use of it,' said Irvine flatly.

'You're not making sense!'

'I thought we were talking about survival: keeping Cyber Shepherd intact. How long do you imagine we'll be able to do that after you tell all those different Homeland Security agencies who want to stake you out naked in the mid-day sun what I've just told you? If I've got half-right what you've told me of yesterday's meeting, I'm betting it'll be seconds before it leaks to every major television and media channel in the country—and no longer than a minute before I lose my Vevak window.'

Graham looked across the desk in undisguised astonishment. 'For Christ's sake, Jack, stop being such an asshole!'

'I'm being practical. No matter how well you pitched it and how well you talked up national security, all any of them are concerned about is stopping the al Aswamy shit from falling on their individual fiefdoms.'

'You really think I'm going to tell a single one of those motherfuckers!'

Once again Irvine came close to regretting there wasn't a recording. 'How *are* you going to handle it?'

'I tell you what you do. You keep intercepting and cracking Vevak codes and leave the implementation of what we do to me.'

Too vague, Irvine recognized at once. 'You're going to keep me in the loop, aren't you?'

'We're equally dependent upon each other, aren't we, Jack, joined at the hip? You survive, I survive; I survive, you survive: the perfect partnership.'

'It'll be daily contact?' questioned Irvine uncomfortably.

'Much tighter than that. I want a running commentary as things happen, the very moment they happen. Joined at the hip, don't forget.'

'Okay.' Irvine shifted in his seat.

'Just before you go.' The other man stopped him. 'You say nothing of this came up *during* Stuxnet? It was all long after?'

'Long after.' Fuck it, Irvine thought.

30

SALLY IGNORED THE INSTINCTIVE TEMPTATION TO CALL IRVINE from the security of the communications room, reluctant to establish the personal link on a call she knew would automatically be recorded and logged. She didn't detect any surveillance on her roundabout drive back to her apartment. Irvine picked up her call immediately, but she didn't let him get beyond a greeting, breaking in to insist they meet at the George-town restaurant at eight thirty, if he wasn't returning to Fort Meade. She was encouraged when he told her he wasn't.

'What's the problem?' Irvine demanded.

'There isn't one. This is an insecure line.'

'I've got stuff to tell you.'

'Tonight,' she stopped him, reminding herself that it was she who was breaching tradecraft.

It took her less than thirty minutes to change and find a Hertz loca-tion in the phone book, and a further fifteen to study from her apartment window the three potential surveillance vehicles outside.

She set off on foot, identifying the awkwardly slow-moving dark blue Honda that had been stationed outside Guest Quarters. She timed her move as the car was halted by a stoplight at Foggy Bottom, suddenly turning into the metro as if making a last-minute decision. She took a train con-veniently already at the platform, needing to switch services twice to ori-entate her direction before finally returning to street level and the Hertz rental office at Commonwealth Avenue. She rejected the first offered Toyota because it was red, settling for the dark green, which the clerk told her was more frequently rejected because of the bad luck associated with the colour.

Sure of Irvine's preferred route, she positioned herself as close as possible on the Arlington side of the Key Bridge, able to isolate the easily recognizable and newly repaired Volkswagen long before it completed its descent from Langley. She let four following vehicles intervene before pulling out behind them. By the time they got close to Owen Place, the gap had reduced to three. Once, a black Ford, braked heavily approaching Irvine's turning to increase the separating distance.

Sally continued on, finding an unrestricted parking lot in a parallel street three blocks farther on. It took twenty minutes for her to return to Owen Place on foot. The black Ford was parked twenty yards from Irvine's building. The driver was the only occupant, slumped against the headrest to make himself inconspicuous. Sally noted the registration, as she had of the Honda earlier, walked back to where she'd parked her car, and drove unhurriedly back across town to Georgetown, still arriving sufficiently ahead of time to linger over coffee on an M Street outdoor café while she chose her observation spot.

Just before eight she got in position with an unobstructed view of the Italian trattoria. Irvine was early but still hurried, tossing his keys to the parking valet as he went quickly inside. Sally remained where she was. The black Ford with the number she knew arrived as the restaurant door closed behind Irvine.

Sally had expected to confirm the renewed surveillance, but not observation as clumsy as she'd experienced so far that evening. It worried her: it wasn't right.

Sally's mind was still on the surveillance as she entered the restaurant, although she registered that tonight's table was closer to the rear and spaced farther away from adjoining tables than the other they'd occupied, which was good. Irvine had ordered their usual wine and was already drinking it instead of his customary beer. 'Hey!' he said, and reached out towards her as he stood. Not until Sally automatically responded with a brief hand contact and said 'Hi,' did she feel the awkwardness of the greeting. She guessed Irvine was discomfited, too, trying to cover the moment by insisting they order at the same time as Sally's wine was poured to limit any more interruptions.

As the waiter left, Irvine sniggered. 'That was ridiculous, wasn't it?'

Sally laughed back hesitantly. 'How about I go out, come back in, and we start all over again?'

'You might not come back. I'd understand if you didn't.'

'Maybe I should stay.' This infantile, schoolkid repartee was even more embarrassing, but Sally decided to go with it.

'That's what I'd like you to do.'

She had to stop it, get back on track. Feeling no hypocrisy, she said, 'Let's talk about progress on Smartman and what happened at today's meeting.'

Irvine seemed physically to straighten, helping them both to more wine. 'We're stonewalled on Smartman.'

'Why aren't you at Meade then?'

'It's routine now: computers working in milliseconds to programs that there's enough people down there to load.' Irvine didn't look directly at her. 'We'll break it; of course we will. We expected too much, too soon.' He looked up. 'So it made better professional sense to be here.'

As artless as the greeting, judged Sally. She actually welcomed the waiter's return, breaking the atmosphere it seemed Irvine was striving to create. When they were alone again, she said briskly, 'So let's hear about Conrad Graham.'

For a moment Sally thought Irvine was going to continue in the direction she didn't want. Instead he said, 'Yes, I should, shouldn't I?' and launched into what she quickly realized to be a near-chronological account of his encounter with the deputy CIA director, the punctuating pauses as much for recall as to eat. Sally didn't interrupt, not even during the hesitations, wanting Irvine to completely talk himself out. It took a further fifteen minutes, but Irvine finished a very different person, someone she gratefully recognized in preference to the gawky man who'd first confronted her.

'He didn't challenge you about Stuxnet until the very end?' Sally said, gauging Irvine's need for reassurance.

'And it didn't amount to a challenge, more like he just wanted to hear it again, specifically.'

'There's no way he can prove the contrary: no surviving records, documents, stuff on computer hard drives?'

'No.'

'You're sure?'

'Positive.'

'You've gotten away with it,' declared Sally. 'He needs you, even if he may not fully believe you.'

'You think?'

'I know.' Hurrying on, she said, 'And I'm still part of it, included in everything?'

'Part of it.'

'But not included in *everything*?' she demanded, inferring the qualification. Could it be that they didn't have the Smartman transmission that GCHQ had intercepted? Far likelier from that remark was that he was holding back.

As if aware of her doubt, Irvine said, 'You're completely in as far as I'm concerned.'

There was more she had to establish, to be sure, thought Sally. 'Who else is going to know about Vevak?'

Irvine hesitated. 'Conrad Graham. Me.'

'You're not making sense imagining you can control it between the two of you.'

'He's going to handpick his field people. Don't forget how recently he was director of covert operations: he's got a lot of loyalty where it matters.'

'We're not talking field level here.'

'You have any idea how many different agencies with fuck knows how many separate agendas with the CIA at the top of their hit lists make up Homeland Security!'

'You just spent an hour telling me.'

'It gets to Homeland Security, it gets to the national media—the international media —that quick.' Irvine snapped his fingers.

'There's got to be an inner group, a leakproof caucus.'

'Graham openly confronted Jack Lamb, who's a retired admiral: humiliated the man. The director of Homeland Security is Joshua Smith, a retired admiral. You know what the Wedge is?'

'No,' said Sally, who did, but wanted a moment to consider her own strategies.

'It's Hoover legacy, carved—and forever sealed—in stone: the barrier that J. Edgar drove permanently between Pennsylvania Avenue and Langley when he was refused the combined directorship of both the FBI and the CIA. They don't co-operate on *anything*: they compete, on *everything*, inside and outside their specified jurisdictions.'

Sally knew it was true. It added to some of her concerns but ironically resolved other lingering doubts. 'You genuinely believe there aren't any records of your meeting?'

'He'd be recording himself, wouldn't he?'

Irvine was on the periphery, in an esoteric adjunct of espionage, Sally reminded herself. 'I want you to make me a promise.'

'What?' He frowned.

'That from now on you'll tell me everything that happens between you and Graham.'

'I've already told you that's our deal.'

'Not just the obvious things: asides, remarks, or his doing something you don't expect . . . don't understand.'

'You frightened he'll try to use me?'

'I *know* he'll use you, if he believes he has to. And that will be after he uses me.'

'I can look after myself.'

Would Irvine's naïve father have believed that, descending from the diplomatic mountain into the terrorist gutters? wondered Sally. 'I know you can,' she soothed, another decision reached. 'So you've already picked up the surveillance?'

'What surveillance?' said Irvine blankly.

'It's back on, on both of us.' She passed her scribbled note of the Ford registration across the table. 'It followed you all the way from Langley to Owen Place, and from Owen Place to here. It's outside, right now.'

'I don't believe you!'

'Go take a look: the black Ford four spaces back towards M Street. I followed it, following you. There was a tail on me, from Watergate, but I lost it.' She wouldn't tell him about the trailercraft inconsistencies, not yet, nor about her conversation with John at GCHQ.

'Graham can't deny it: we've got the proof,' said Irvine, gesturing with the slip of paper.

'You've just given me a list of Homeland agencies this long!' said Sally, arm outstretched. 'It could be any one—or several—of them in the circumstances you've described—'

'We can find them from the registration!' broke in the man, angrily insistent.

'The majority of Homeland Security is intelligence,' reminded Sally patiently. 'Intelligence surveillance vehicles aren't identifiably registered to their organizations. It'll be a shell-company ownership hidden inside another shell. And maybe it's not intelligence at all but another Homeland affiliate that doesn't operate the way they should.'

'I don't understand.'

'Professional vehicle observation is never single-manned. The attempted tail on me was, which made it easy to lose him: I simply ducked into the metro knowing the driver couldn't abandon his car in the street—certainly not one in the vicinity of the White House. There's only one guy in the Ford outside.'

'Who then?'

'I don't know,' admitted Sally honestly.

'What are we going to do?'

The mind-set she'd worked so hard to inculcate, Sally recognized, satisfied. 'Be aware of it all the time, even when we can't identify it. Turn it back on whoever's initiating it, if it serves any purpose: run a false trail they'll misconstrue.'

Irvine had become introspective as Sally spoke. Now he looked up. 'I'm trying to think who else it might be.'

'And?'

'It can't be Iranian.'

'No, it can't,' she agreed, keeping any condescension at the suggestion from her voice.

'What about your people?'

The possibility hadn't occurred to her. Now it did, and Sally accepted at once that it answered virtually every discrepancy. There was practically as much animosity in London between David Monkton's MI5 and the MI6-supervising—and antagonized—Foreign Office as there was here in Washington between Conrad Graham and Homeland Security. That was the reason she hadn't phoned Irvine from the legation communications room. It had been a diplomatic requirement to register her apartment address at the resentful embassy, and she'd been followed from Guest Quarters to Owen Place, which would have identified Jack Irvine. The begrudging Nigel Fellowes would have been the first to volunteer for an MI6 stakeout—persuading as many of the MI5 *rezidentura* as he could to join him—but there still wouldn't be sufficient manpower properly to staff it, which would account for there only being a driver in the pursuit cars. So would something else, Sally abruptly acknowledged. Maybe MI6 weren't involved at all. It was David Monkton who'd initiated—and persisted with—the talk of her being compromised that had led her to admit the relationship with Irvine.

Sally smiled across the table. 'That's a very clever suggestion! I *want* you to give Graham the number, see what or who it might bring out of the woodwork.'

Irvine was silent for several moments, again not looking directly at her. 'Who's going to leave first?'

'What?' asked Sally, openly curious.

'I guess you can't come back now, that maybe you didn't intend to after. . . . Just tell me what you want to do.'

'I've got another rental in the stacker on M Street. You can drop me off on your way to Langley in the morning.'

'I'm confused!' complained Irvine, finally looking at her.

'I know you are. We need to talk about that.' She needed to talk to Monkton, too; hopefully going home with Irvine would provide the reason to do so if the surveillance was still in place.

'I'm estimating 250 characters, 270 tops,' declared Burt Singleton.

Marian Lowell shrugged. 'There's no way we can estimate the numeric equivalent. And there could be multiple word significance in the switch between Latin additions to the Kurdish, and the Urdu in the Pashtu. We've identified twenty-four numbers, which include eight repetitions that we can't match, and six different common Iranian languages—on an IP address in Roman script—and got ourselves nowhere. This is one of the most difficult codes I've ever encountered.'

'Okay, so they've got great cryptologists.'

Neither looked away from his or her individual station as they talked, instead scrolling intently through the latest supercomputer downloads from the search programs being operated by Barker and Malik from a separate SHA logarithm annexe.

'I thought we were supposed to be the best.'

'It's got to be a binary code,' insisted Singleton. 'The recipient's already got the first half with which our intercept meshes, to make a whole.'

The woman frowned but still didn't look away from her screen. 'Or is it the key, enabling this to be read?' She paused. 'You believe what Jack said on the phone, that this is continuing as an active operation?'

'I told you all that he told me,' avoided Singleton awkwardly. 'I'd like to know what's kept him in DC. He's supposed to be running all this, not leaving it to us.'

'Is he coming up tomorrow?'

'He didn't say.'

'Any regrets at not quitting when we had the chance?'

'I think I'll drop by Hank Packer's office tomorrow,' said Singleton, again avoiding direct answers.

A new download registered on their screens.

It took Sally a long time to come down from the lovemaking, which had been as good as ever, and which she didn't want to end until it absolutely had to, which made what she needed to say as important to her as it was to make him understand. She said, 'That was wonderful.'

'More than wonderful.'

'But now we must talk.'

'I made a mistake and I'm embarrassed about it: wasn't thinking properly. I'm sorry.'

'What we're doing, this assignment, won't go on forever: I won't be here forever. While I am here, I want this to go on, and I hope you want it to as well. But we're not making commitments.'

'No.'

'Are you offended, shocked?'

Irvine shook his head. 'No commitments is what I want, too.'

She was doing the right thing, keeping the GCHQ discovery to herself, Sally decided. She wasn't abandoning him. She'd share it when the proper moment came: when everything was in place and couldn't be ruined by internecine ambition and ego wars. Waiting until then meant she had to be included in everything.

31

SALLY'S DECISION TO WITHHOLD THE GCHQ INTERCEPTION
wavered during her night-time stirrings, ending in a moment of awaken-
ing guilt at treating Irvine with the arrogance with which she believed
he'd kept the Vevak penetration from Conrad Graham. Just as quickly
came the justifying contradiction. There was no comparison between her
holding back GCHQ's Smartman interception and what Irvine still
hadn't told Conrad Graham. So why was she seeking one? It was ridiculous to feel—even to imagine   guilt, because guilt about anything she
did or had to do was unprofessional, an unacceptable relapse in the profession she supposedly practised. It was not one that allowed morality at
any level or for any normal reason.

The self-correction made—and proper professionalism restored —
Sally acknowledged that to stay ahead, where she believed she now was,
she had just slightly to adjust that day's schedule. Which sadly didn't
allow for any early-morning repeat of the previous night's lovemaking.
She eased herself carefully from the bed and managed to shower and dress
without waking Irvine.

'Why so early?' he protested as he emerged from the bedroom.

'England's been awake for hours. GCHQ might have something.' She
was keeping the exchange honest, speaking to Cheltenham ahead of Monkton, reflected Sally, so she was being truthful and at once wondered why
she'd needed that self-reassurance.

'You know there's been nothing overnight from Meade,' said Irvine, gesturing to his silent computer bank.

'I want to be up to speed before today starts officially here,' said Sally uncomfortably.

'If there's nothing moving at Meade, I'll stay here, after seeing Graham.'

'Let's talk either way. There might be something from my end.' And she'd be manipulating all the moves.

Sally was an hour ahead of her usual time, but the traffic was just as heavy. She drove, keeping an eye on her rearview mirror, introducing one detour, but didn't pick up any followers. The embassy car park was as unexpectedly crowded, forcing Sally to an outer bay. On impulse she took a circuitous path towards the building, searching for the two surveillance vehicles of the previous night, but found neither. She didn't see the waiting Nigel Fellowes, either, until she was well past the staff entrance.

'Earlier than ever!' he greeted, smiling. He wore a new, unstained Eton tie that predictably clashed with the brown suit.

Was it pure ineptitude, or did he want her to know he was monitoring her embassy visits? Either way, it was an opportunity to utilize. 'Didn't you say something about early birds when I arrived?'

'I didn't think you were taking any advice from me.'

'You're right, I'm not,' she goaded.

'Which is unfortunate.' Fellowes flared at the mockery. 'I could have given you a lot of help: the embassy could have provided a lot of support.'

'About what, specifically?'

'Specifically about the danger of arrogance and blind over-ambition,' the man tried to mock back.

Fellowes really shouldn't have been allowed out by himself, Sally thought. 'The downfall of so many.'

His stick-on smile slipped. 'Have you any idea what trouble you've caused in London! It's all hell let loose back there: absolute hell.'

She shouldn't waste too much more time. 'What car do you drive, Nigel?'

The MI5 station chief was briefly speechless. *'What!'*

'Your car? What make is it?'

Fellowes still hesitated, finally stumbling, 'Jaguar. British of course. The flag and all that.'

'Not a Honda? Or a Toyota?' There was no point in correcting the man about Jaguar's corporate ownership.

'I don't understand– ' Fellowes started, but stopped abruptly. 'We're not riding shotgun for you, Sally. You told London you didn't need help or intrusion from us, remember?'

Why, then, had he been skulking in the entrance-hall shadows this early, watching her? She'd warned Fellowes that his surveillance had been detected if he or the MI6 *rezidentura* were involved, which was sufficient. 'It's good to know it's not you: I didn't want the embassy caught up in what's likely to happen because of it.'

'What's that!' demanded the man, the concern immediate.

'Nothing you need to be concerned about: you're safely separated from it all, don't forget. Best to keep it that way.'

Sally settled expectantly into her soundproof cubicle with plenty of time to spare, judging the encounter with Fellowes an additional bonus in a still-to-come carefully manoeuvred—and hopefully fruitful—day. It was a short-lived aspiration.

'Nothing,' flatly declared the GCHQ conduit she still knew only as John.

'There's surely something!' blurted Sally.

'We've had Smartman exactly forty-three hours, forty-two minutes, and Anis@mukhtarbrigade.ru twelve hours, six minutes!' retorted the man, irritably pedantic. 'It's not Scrabble we play here, you know!'

'It wasn't a criticism,' soothed Sally, smoothing out the Hydarnes transmissions on the narrow ledge in front of her.

'We know it's Iranian because of Hydarnes. But the encryption is as clever as hell. It doesn't conform to any mathematical rule, which ultimately it has to.'

'Help me,' urged Sally, lost.

'At the moment we're working on the principle of it going back to wartime cryptology,' predicted the code-breaker. 'Onetime message pads. The recipient already possesses the crib to transcribe the once-only encoded message he or she gets: neither the code nor its key is ever used again. New code, new crib, every time: nowhere for us to start, no comparisons we can make between a repetition of symbols, numbers, algebra . . . between any damned thing.'

'Shit,' broke in Sally.

'Mountains of it. Just to make it more difficult, that one message needn't be complete. It could be split, first half in the initial encryption, next part in another code. And that division needn't be limited to two separations: it can be divided three or four times, impossible to read without its specific individual key. And it still doesn't stop there. You want to make it *really* difficult, the deciphering—although it might translate into what appear to be comprehensible words or phrases—can turn out to be meaningless because those words or phrases represent algebraic numerals or symbols that need a totally different codex. And you've guessed it—that second mutation is onetime, too.'

'You telling me it's unbreakable?'

'I'm telling you it can't be broken in hours. For this stuff you can forget speed-of-light supercomputers and number crunching.'

After a momentary silence from both ends, Sally broke it. 'Could these two messages be to different recipients?'

After another pause John said, 'A lateral thinker!'

'One or two?' persisted Sally, caught by an attitude quite different from her previous exchanges with the man, particularly over Sellafield.

'We're expecting there to be two, using a shared IP,' reluctantly conceded the code-breaker.

'Remind me again what a *shared* IP means.'

There was a discernible sigh. 'Sharing the same domain address.'

'Could it be more than two senders?'

'Of course.'

Sally's eyes fogged, cleared, then fogged again from the intensity with which she was staring down at the side-by-side printouts. But it was not the absolute concentration nor the further silence that unsettled her. It was a freakish sensation, which she later thought akin to hallucination, of not recognizing something from the shapes of symbols and number outlines burning into her mind. She squeezed her eyes tightly shut to refocus, clearing her vision and the impression with it, only partially registering the words from GCHQ.

'. . . from Fort Meade?' Sally heard.

'I'm sorry, I missed that?'

'I asked what progress Meade's made on Smartman and Anis,' repeated the man impatiently. 'That's why you've called, isn't it? That's the arrange-ment . . . ?'

It was, Sally accepted uneasily, surprised the demand had taken so long. 'Like you, nothing.'

'*Absolutely* nothing at all?' queried the man disbelievingly.

Sally's unease deepened at the assertiveness: she wasn't leading any-more, not keeping control of the exchanges. 'Not as of last night. It's still only six in the morning here. I'll come back to you around your three this afternoon.'

'I need to speak direct, technically,' said the man briskly. 'They might have some progress that would make sense to me but not to you. They've had more time, after all.'

'It'll be better if you wait,' insisted Sally, confronting a situation—and an attitude—she hadn't anticipated. 'My being here's sensitive. It took a lot to get this degree of co-operation. It'll jeopardize it—give the impres-sion you and I aren't working fully together—if they get a direct approach.'

'Don't be ridiculous! There are things impossible to communicate through you . . . things you wouldn't understand. Call me this afternoon, after I've spoken to them.'

Sally's reaction was immediate. She overrode every communications-room protest from other users demanding priority connection to Thames House, repeating the insistence to reach David Monkton. He cut her off with 'Stay there' after less than a minute, leaving her in what she accepted as an appropriate punishment sweatbox, uncertain if she'd explained sufficiently.

It scarcely mattered, Sally concluded, edging the cubicle door ajar. Cheltenham wouldn't agree to what she'd pleaded with Monkton to achieve. She—and technically GCHQ because their officer had trusted and worked with her—would be circumventing an internationally negotiated and agreed-upon operational procedure. Could she recover to stay involved? She thought she could. She'd lose all direct co-operation from GCHQ, but hopefully Monkton could retain that at some level. And Irvine was still at Langley, maybe not even going down to Fort Meade; if there was a reason, they'd arranged to speak before he left, so she'd be able to tell him about Anis before any GCHQ approach. Definitely recoverable then. What about David Monkton? She hadn't . . . Sally's mind was suddenly seized, the reflection broken—as it had been less than an hour earlier—by the side-by-side Vevak transmissions still set out on the cubicle ledge.

There *was* something, a connection between the two that she should be seeing, questioning—which was preposterous. How could she, someone knowing nothing of the techniques or craft of code-breaking, imagine—because that's what she was doing, imagining a significance without being able to see or say or work out what it was—when the interceptions were defeating the best mathematically trained minds in American and British cryptology. And yet . . .

The linkup signal jarred into the cubicle, startling her, and Sally almost dropped the headset fumbling it back into place.

'It didn't go well,' announced the Director-General. 'They're not prepared to breach international protocols, which I didn't expect them to be, no matter how important we consider this individual operation. Co-operation and participation, particularly with NSA, is how they work. It's their ethos. And there's more to it than that.'

'Like what?'

'The man you've been liaising with, John Poulter, is short-listed for the deputy directorship, largely on the strength of his involvement with Sellafield. It got GCHQ a prime ministerial commendation, which more than balanced all the problems in 2013 when they had to admit receiving one hundred million pounds from NSA for circumventing American law; they didn't like being labeled poodles or being exposed by renegade spy-agency contractors. They want distance from us.'

'As bad as that!'

'The best I could do was to get them not to send their Smartman questions to Meade for twenty-four hours, to give you time to fix things at your end.'

'Thank you,' said Sally, chastened and not liking the feeling.

'From now on I must be the first person you speak to professionally in the morning.'

'You will be.'

'Your remaining where you are depends upon it.'

'Thirty guys in the unit,' spelled out Conrad Graham. 'Know them all personally from my time at Covert Operations: vouch for every one of them. No private agendas, no fuckups. All of them thought Johnston was an asshole: dodged any assignment with him in charge knowing it would fuck up.'

'I wish it had been organized like this from the start,' said Jack Irvine, meaning it. It was his first contribution in the thirty minutes it had taken Graham to set out the CIA organization he'd put into place to re-establish Operation Cyber Shepherd.

'I wish a lot of things had been organized like this from the start,' came back the deputy director heavily. 'This is how it's got to be between us personally from now on, Jack, everything out on the table.'

Irvine said, 'That's how I want it to be, too. Definitely how it has to be.'

'Got six guys already working on the review.'

'Review?'

'Going right back to your very first memo, before Operation Cyber Shepherd even had a name, before I left Covert Ops.'

Irvine remained unmoving, stretched easily back in the enveloping chair opposite the deputy director, cold cups of coffee on the low table between them. 'You think something got missed? That there was a mistake before al Aswamy was lost?'

Graham shrugged. 'Could have happened. It'll do, until you break that goddamned Smartman encryption.'

'My entire team is on it with me. It's a bastard: the worst we've come up against in a long time. I'm going up to Meade when we're through here.'

'Nothing my guys can work on with you?'

'Not from the encryption.' Which was a qualification, not a lie. The only people who could work on what Marian Lowell had told him about the GCHQ message minutes before the Graham meeting were at Fort Meade, not Langley.

'What then?' Graham frowned, recognizing the reservation.

'Surveillance is back.'

There was another shrug. 'The list of those stacked up against us is too long for a realistic sweep. We've got to live with it.'

'It's a pain in the ass.'

'Don't let it be. What about your team? You got enough working with you up there?'

'We're not working bulk. Computers do the donkey work, and I've got all the facilities I need available at Meade.'

'What about the doubters you talked about in your team?'

'Not any longer. A hundred percent behind it.' Burt Singleton was working as hard as everyone else now, maybe even harder.

'The review I've started?' pressed Graham. 'The file is complete, isn't it? Nothing's at Fort Meade that needs factoring in?'

'Nothing,' guaranteed Irvine, who'd ensured every connecting link with Stuxnet had been eradicated. After he'd irrecoverably wiped it clean, he'd dropped the computer hard drive holding the Vevak discovery into the Mediterranean during a farewell Israeli R&R in Herzliya.

'We need to keep the Hanning woman locked in with us,' continued the other man. 'She could be our get-out insurance if there's a problem with Abu al Hurr's death.'

'Yes,' agreed Irvine tightly.

'I'll call her.'

Sally snatched up the apartment telephone on its first ring. 'I've been waiting.'

'Things took longer.'

'Where are you?'

'On my way to work,' said Irvine, awkward with the necessary ambiguity on an insecure line.

Sally hesitated. 'We arranged to speak first.'

'There could be something.'

'New or old?' demanded Sally, concern flaring.

'New, from the Brits. I don't know anything more than that.'

Two-faced, cheating bastards, Sally thought. 'I got an indication when I called this morning. That's why I wanted to talk.'

'I'll come back tonight.'

'Don't if there's something to work on.'

'If there is, I'll call.'

'Do that, either way.' Her phone rang again the moment she put it down.

32

SALLY PASSED UNCHALLENGED THROUGH LANGLEY'S OUTER security on her MI5 accreditation. At the CIA complex an escort waited to take her through the identity-recording barriers to the executive level. There, another escort, female this time, was at the arrival elevator to take her to the deputy director's suite. Conrad Graham was at the open door, beyond the double-banked protective ring of personal assistants and secretaries. The deputy director, immaculate in a jacket, knife-creased trousers, and stiff-collared shirt, solicitously guided her to an already set visitor's chair before going to his pristinely uncluttered, authority-demarcating desk. No coffee was offered. No secretarial notetaker, either. There'd be an automatic recording system, Sally knew, remembering Monkton's noise blank-out.

He didn't intend to review past mistakes, Graham began, the presentation obviously prepared. Getting al Aswamy topped the recovery agenda. To achieve that he'd assembled a handpicked CIA task force, with SEAL and SWAT backup. She was officially to be part of that task force, at the epicentre of Operation Cyber Shepherd. He'd cleared that seconded appointment an hour earlier in a telephone conversation with David Monkton. An office was being made available to her at Langley. She'd have direct access to him at all times, through the Watch Room if it was out of hours; until al Aswamy was in a body bag, nothing was out of hours.

Graham extended a closely cupped hand. 'This is how we'll have the son of a bitch Aswamy, like we got bin Laden, okay?'

'Okay.' Sally nodded, hoping it hadn't sounded like mockery. It was a composite performance of every spy movie she'd ever watched—with borrowings from a few crime series.

Graham shook his head. 'Let me hear some real feedback!'

He wouldn't like hearing that she still believed herself the convenient sacrifice to disaster. 'This is where I want to be, at the centre. I think I can make a contribution,' she said, accepting that she sounded like a programmed talking doll.

'The media problem's getting bigger—closer—by the day.'

Could the publicity be her nemesis? wondered Sally; she'd proposed the original press manipulation. 'They're being fed leaks. Being briefed.'

'We couldn't survive the shitstorm if they learned about Abu Hurr. Neither of us could.'

Was he talking personally or of their separate organizations? 'Did you discuss it with my director-general?'

'It's your input I'm looking for!'

'I'll give it to you when I've properly thought it through.'

'And after you've spoken to Monkton.'

'Of course after I've spoken to Monkton!' shot back Sally, determined to end the exchange on her terms, not his. Feeling no hypocrisy she went on, 'The shit we're trying to recover from was dumped by too many people trying to follow too many personal agendas.'

She hadn't expected an open admission that there was no NSA-linked CIA investigation, but at no time during this meeting had there been any reference to Fort Meade or Jack Irvine. The logical question risked an awkward as well as predictable answer, but she needed to ask it. 'Jack Irvine's obviously part of this inner group that I'm now a part of.' There was no reaction from Graham at the mention of Irvine's name. 'Who else? No one. This is a no-mistakes troika, Jack providing everything from NSA, your input—that's Monkton's guarantee, total British input—and me co-ordinating it all from here, at Langley.'

'You know Jack from way back, of course,' chanced Sally.

'What's he told you about that!' demanded the CIA deputy sharply.

'Nothing operational,' said Sally, immediately detecting the suspicion. 'Just that you and he worked together. Stuxnet is public knowledge: there was an obvious connection.'

'He did good there. He's got to do even better now.'

It would be a mistake to push it any further. 'Do I get to see my office?'

'Tomorrow. On the same floor as Jack's.' Graham extended his cupped hand again, crushing it closed this time. 'That's what's going to happen when we get the bastard.'

Graham might already be fantasizing about the Hollywood biopic of al Aswamy's seizure, but she didn't think he was a good enough actor to have carried on this long without an indication she'd have recognized. So Graham *didn't* know about her affair with Irvine. Which he would have if he'd been responsible for the surveillance. 'Thanks for bringing me in.'

'You've got a part to play.'

To my script, not yours, instinctively thought Sally.

And she thought it again, although from a different perspective, at Monkton's reaction to her account of the Conrad Graham meeting. 'There's nothing we hadn't already anticipated.'

Sally said, 'I'm briefing you on the meeting, not making a plea!' She'd decided against telling Monkton of his apparent failure to convince GCHQ to hold back its approach to the NSA and was further disconcerted by the attitude she was confronting now.

'Good,' said the Director, clip-voiced. 'You're embedded now as deeply as it's possible to be. And I did promise the total co-operation to provide you with as much protection as possible. You do, of course, have the added protection of your personal involvement.'

Sally's discomfort was at the communications cubicle's constrictions, not Monkton's reference to the affair, until it struck her that the man's surprising acceptance of a relationship with Irvine was prompted by Monkton's expectation of precisely such professional benefits. *'Hopefully,'* she qualified pointedly.

'That's for you to ensure.'

'Our response—yours and mine—to Abu Hurr's death needs to conform if it's leaked, which is very likely in a bear pit like this.'

'He died in U.S. custody, not ours.'

'Custody we facilitated on a rendition flight.'

'We made Abu Hurr *available* to U.S. authorities here in London after the Sellafield investigation discovered he had illegally entered the United Kingdom from America, which he'd *legally* entered on a still-valid student visa from Pakistan. He was still legally our prisoner: we were preparing indictments on terrorist charges. He had committed no offence in America. We had no awareness before handing him over that he would be repatriated to America, which was not discussed and certainly not agreed upon with Charles Johnston during any of our recorded contacts. Abu Hurr's death made pointless any Foreign Office protest about the episode to Washington.'

'That won't be an easy message to pass on.'

'Paraphrase it. Be subtle.'

She'd deserved that, Sally conceded. 'I'll try.'

'Don't use Langley communications for our conversations—'

'I know I'll be monitored!' broke in Sally, although keeping the impatience from her voice.

'—unless there's something you want to be intercepted.'

'I've thought of that, too,' assured Sally contritely.

She'd come through the revelation of the affair with Jack better than she'd expected, Sally decided, making her way out of the embassy. Her cell phone rang the moment she turned it on in the parking lot.

Irvine said, 'I've been trying to reach you! I'm on my way back.'

'What is it?'

'Owen Place. An hour.'

Sally left the car at Guest Quarters and used the metro route, confident she cleared her trail. She got to Owen Place with time to spare and checked for a stakeout, which she didn't detect. She waited fifteen minutes after Irvine arrived and was sure he hadn't been followed, either.

'So what is it?' she demanded as she entered, anxious to guard against misspeaking from the beginning.

'GCHQ are holding out on us!'

Not enough! 'Holding out how? On what?'

'An interception we didn't make, although we did provide the original IP: we left it alone, believing it didn't have any U.S. relevance. Your guys are obviously assuming we got it, and they're limiting what they're telling us! What do you know about it?'

As little as possible, Sally warned herself. 'Just that it's new; that they were having trouble. Let me see it so you can explain what more you need to know.'

Irvine frowned, for a moment hesitating, but finally went to his computer bank. Sally was at his shoulder when the post came on his screen, glad she wasn't in his eyeline to see her startled reaction.

It wasn't a Smartman message; the connection went beyond the Hydarnes source. And at last she thought she knew what she was seeing in all the other domain names, despite this one's being different!

33

THE DOMAIN IP WAS KERMANI@IMAGEMAKING.ORG.YE. THE CON-
cluding YE designated Yemen as the registration country. John Poulter's
covering e-mail said they hadn't intercepted it until it was forwarded on
Facebook from Riga, Latvia's capital, to their blanket-monitored Malmö
site. Nothing indicated its continuing on to the UK; they suspected a
memory-stick transfer. GCHQ was currently defeated by the encryption.
Was Operation Cyber Shepherd encountering similar difficulty? Or had
it made progress? If it had, however small or inconclusive, GCHQ would
welcome the immediate guidance beyond the terms of the Echelon agreement, on the basis of their earlier co-operation on Facebook channeling.
Had Fort Meade considered onetime message pads unexpected—even
bizarre—as such antiquated cryptology might appear at first?

Sally's primary concentration was upon the intangible Facebook post—
counting and comparing letters, every time with the same result except
for the identity—but at the same time she was also trying to resolve her
other uncertainties. The most important of which—personal and professional in equal measure—was that Jack Irvine hadn't been lying to her
about their lack of progress. Nor had John Poulter lied to Monkton. GCHQ
had intercepted a total of four, not one Facebook transmission beyond NSA's
original Smartman trawl. And Poulter, suspecting Fort Meade was hang-
ing back, was spreading his bets, hoping she might provide more information on one and Meade on the other.

Monkton was right, although not exactly from the same perspective. She was definitely at the operation's centre. For an uncertain period, maybe—exactly just how long still depended on a lot of variables over the next twenty-four hours—but momentarily she was in a position of not just knowing all that was going on but possibly, even, of manipulating it to her advantage. And Irvine would never, ever, know how she'd juggled her professional and personal integrity.

What about the variables, one above all others? Not a variable, Sally at once corrected herself: a hypothesis that had taken some time to get clear in her mind and still risked her being ridiculed by John Poulter. Would her awareness of his NSA approach be sufficient to persuade the man to restore her open access to Britain's eavesdropping facility even if he ridiculed what she was going to suggest? From variable to hypothesis to yet another conundrum, to go with too many others.

She could, of course, do the whole thing differently: put her suggestion to Monkton for him to propose. But that risked exposing the Director-General to humiliation if the idea was laughable, as well as—an equal if not more essential consideration—losing her Sellafield-gained reputation for innovative thinking if it provided the way forward.

'Did you know about it!' repeated Irvine, impatient at the time she was taking hunched over his screen.

Why didn't she put her theory to Irvine? There wouldn't be any humiliation if he laughed it away: it could become their personal joke, something for both of them to laugh about. For the same reasons that she wasn't going to involve Monkton, she acknowledged, with customary self-honesty. Avoiding the question, she said, 'Mirza Kermani was an Iranian revolutionary: assassinated a shah. You didn't have his name as a trigger word?'

'I just told you we didn't have anything,' said Irvine, the impatience growing. 'You'd have known if we had.'

Sally pushed aside the faintest twinge of guilt. 'And you haven't responded directly to the Kermani discovery?'

'With what! We've got nothing to respond *with*!'

Except pride, Sally thought, recognizing like for like. Which was a passing thought: she could move the pieces around the board to position herself even more firmly at the epicentre. 'I can sort the differences there seem to be between you and GCHQ through Monkton, but not now. It's three o'clock in the morning in England!'

'This will be the end of your being here—of everything—if it's not sorted. Graham would have already nailed you to the barn door if he knew GCHQ were holding back.'

'Let's not tell him then.' Sally smiled.

For the first time since that awkward first night, the lovemaking wasn't good, although both of them feigned otherwise, and yet again Sally was awake long before Irvine. She waited until she reached the living room to put on their shared bathrobe. It was instinctive to stop at the sentinel line of black-faced, standby-lighted computers. The touch of a key would wake the master screen, instantly showing what might have come from Fort Meade over the past few hours. If there had been progress, everything could be affected—changed entirely—and need complete re-evaluation to keep her ahead. Sally snatched back the reaching-out hand, as if the firewalls had physical, burning heat. Irvine had described his protection as impregnable: talked of self-destruct programs against intrusion supplemented by specialized connection USBs that instantly garbled unauthorized entry. But she wasn't hacking *in:* she was already there, officially accepted. She simply wanted to wake a hibernating machine. Her hand twitched but stayed tight to her side. It was wrong to become impatiently over-confident, to take risks that didn't need to be taken.

Sally pulled the robe more tightly around her and pushed farther into the room. With its photographic display, it was, she realized, far more complete than her initial impressions. There was even a picture—the location unidentifiable from its background—of a boy of about nine she presumed to be Irvine gazing up admiringly at his white-haired, immaculately uniformed father. Not simply a family collage, Sally decided: there was only one, an indistinct picture of the woman who had to have been Irvine's mother. It was a shrine, an homage, to an adored man.

'Did you know him? Did your father know him, I mean?' Irvine was unashamedly—bizarrely, it immediately seemed to Sally—naked, as he had been the morning after their first unfulfilled encounter.

'My father would have, obviously. I knew the name, that's all. I don't remember ever being in his company. I was away in England, at school and college for a lot of the time.' She hadn't wanted this, didn't want it.

'He was betrayed—cheated—by people he trusted.'

'Is this what Shepherd's all about, surrogate revenge?'

'No!' denied Irvine, red-faced.

It was lightening outside, dawn maybe in another hour. Around nine now in London. 'I'm glad, because that would have been confused thinking, and there's already some confused thinking that I've got to sort out, remember?'

'I'm not on a surrogate revenge trip!'

'I believe you,' lied Sally. 'I need to get dressed now and do my job.'

Which she was on her way to do when the news break came on the Volkswagen radio.

Irvine said, 'That's not going to affect anything, is it?'

'Sounds like stage posturing,' dismissed Sally.

Which, by itself, it was. But at that moment—and for a further hour to follow—she didn't know how a cruel chance would be over-interpreted and re-fuel the terrorist hysteria on two continents.

Sally's dismissal of the car-radio news flash was based solely on sound-bite extracts from Giovanni Moro's first public court arraignment in Rome, which in addition to radio coverage was televised live. And for which, knowing Italian law permitted personal opening statements, the murdered politician's grandson had meticulously prepared.

The beard and moustache had gone. The hair was almost militarily short. The tie was muted grey. The shirt was pale pink, to appear white on-screen by avoiding the strobe-light glare. The well-tailored suit was businessman black. The voice in which he announced he would defend himself ("against lies and hypocrisy with truth and honesty") was clearly audible but not strident. The rehearsed opening statement was measured, free of histrionic tirade. The fundamentalist clichés were restricted to martyrs (jihadist warriors), Satan or satanic (the USA and its Western acolytes), and crusaders (Western opponents or oppressors).

The United States of America was powerless to confront or defeat the forces of Allah. The wrath of God was continuing what had begun ("but thwarted by deception") with the attack upon Rome's Colosseum and England's nuclear facility. It would engulf the West in blood, war, and devastation. For every fallen martyr ascending into paradise, a hundred crusaders would die to descend into hell.

From the live television and radio recordings it was possible to fix at precisely 11:32 a.m. the moment Moro declared, 'Today is the Armageddon against infidels.'

It was also the precise moment two suicide bombers simultaneously detonated their backpacks in the second and third carriages of a train as it entered Madrid's Atocha terminus. Sixty-three people, including the bombers, died instantly. A further thirty-six died on a train stationary at the opposite platform. The explosion almost completely ripped off the roof of the still-moving third carriage, although it remained intact and attached at one end as it flattened sideways into a massive scythe that sliced waist-high along the entire length of the platform upon which people who'd escaped the direct blast still stood or huddled, too shocked or dazed to move. Thirty died on the platform. Twenty more were among the total of fifty-five from the two trains who died later in hospital. More than a hundred were permanently maimed.

At 11:55 a.m. an unwitting Sally was connected from the British embassy communications facility to GCHQ's John Poulter, who was also totally unaware at that time of the atrocity.

'I've discussed everything with your director-general,' declared John Poulter stiffly.

On the point of rejection before she'd spoken a word, Sally thought, attuned to the tone. She had to restore her relationship with the man, which meant convincing him as quickly as she could that he had more to lose than to achieve by blocking her out. 'I know. And thank you for the twenty-four-hour concession with the Smartman transmissions, which Meade hadn't intercepted. Neither had they seen Kermani until your post to them.'

After an initial silence from England, which Sally took as a good omen, Poulter said finally, 'You're sure of that?'

'Positive. And as of this moment they're making no progress with Kermani.'

'What about Smartman?'

'Nothing that makes any sense. Meade believes you're holding back. If I told them this morning another interception was coming and you sent it within, say, half an hour, it would reassure them you weren't—iron out all the uncertainties.'

'Yes, it would, wouldn't it?'

The rejecting tone wasn't there, but had it gone sufficiently for the question she had to ask next? Risking it, Sally said, 'You aren't, are you—holding anything back?'

'Why would we?'

Not the answer she wanted. Avoid Poulter's promotional concern, she decided. 'Because of the problems in 2013 when the CIA contractor defected: the Prism Project and GCHQ's Tempura programme?'

Another silence. Then Poulter said, 'No, we're not holding back. Something's being set up: that much is clear from the amount of electronic chatter, quite apart from the coded transmissions we're intercepting but can't read. And wherever the hell it's planned for, we've got to stop it.'

'Send all the Smartman material to Meade an hour after we finish talking. They'll know it's on the way.'

'An hour from now,' accepted Poulter, moving to close the conversation.

'There's more I want to say!' stopped Sally. 'I'm glad that we *are* talking, as we were before.'

'We've got an atrocity to stop.'

Let him have the justification, thought Sally, satisfied. 'There's something else.'

'What?' demanded Poulter, the impatience returning.

'Start from Anis@mukhtarbrigade.ru. Compare it to Mohammed@homagebridge.ye. Then to Nek@dangerrange.ng. Follow that with Swordbearer@forevermystery.org.uk.' She paused. 'You seeing anything?'

'No,' said the man flatly.

'Go on to Smartman@deathtrade.org.mil to Kermani@imagemaking.org.ye.'

'For God's sake, make your point, Sally!'

'All IP addresses in every domain name are created—with the exception of Kermani—from the same letters in the first NSA interception, Anis@mukhtarbrigade. Ignore the country registration letters. What about the numeric ASCII code. Why can't the real terrorist messages be encoded in the IP domain address with the recipient maybe having a crib—the modern equivalent of a onetime numeric message pad—that you've actually been working on?'

After a snort of derision, Poulter said, 'Absolutely ridiculous! Absurd!'

'Why? Because it's technically impossible? Or because it's something you've never considered or encountered before?'

'Mathematics has rules: conformity.'

'All the domain addresses we're talking about have a mathematical rule.'

'What!'

'You at a station?'

'Yes.'

'Split your screen and load Kermani and Smartman and Swordbearer side by side.'

John Poulter became silent. So did Sally. She could hear his breathing; twice there was a heavy inhalation, as if he were about to speak, but he didn't. Then, suddenly, there was a faint sound of what she hoped was realization. The man said, 'It's an understandable impression.'

'It's a lot more than an impression,' insisted Sally, emboldened. 'All domain addresses are composed from identical Roman-alphabet lettering, although each make up different words. All vary in length and in the number of intervening decimal dots. In the longer addresses, the same letters are repeated.'

'So they're the code we've got to break?' It was a genuine question, not sarcasm.

'I think they make up coded messages. But acknowledging that these guys aren't amateurs, I'd expect they'll be as intentionally misleading as whatever the supposed, currently indecipherable message will turn out to be.'

'What do the NSA team say?'

The flattery of honesty, Sally decided. 'I risked your ridicule in preference to theirs.'

'I like our working together again,' Poulter said.

So did she, decided Sally; one hurdle crossed, two more to go.

Harry Packer stared down at the loan rejection letter, his stomach—and his mind—hollowed in despair. It had been his last resort—all the other already-tapped sources run dry—and the fucking bank, which already had 30 percent of the house, wasn't just refusing to extend by another $5,000, but was demanding a reduction on the existing debt in a month. And that was the limit Rebecca's lawyer had imposed in his letter the previous day before initiating court proceedings for back alimony.

He needed a miracle, Packer knew, and there were no such things as miracles.

34

THE COINCIDENCE THAT WAS TO CAUSE SO MUCH CONFUSION and as many misconceptions was the arraignment in Rome of Giovanni Moro—with his earlier Basque terrorist associations—coming on the same day and time as the Spanish atrocity, which was instigated by an Algerian-based Al Qaeda affiliate and totally unconnected with al Aswamy or the Colosseum attack. The misinterpretation, never fully corrected, was compounded in less than an hour by Al Jazeera's transmitting an Oran-sourced suicide video identifying the bombers as two more American, ex-army converts disaffected by their combat tours in Afghanistan.

Italy's publicity-eager justice minister provided what was initially accepted by American and European governments—and the international media—as official confirmation of the continuation of the al Aswamy jihad. Utilizing the adjust-as-required adaptability of Italy's legal system, the minister suspended Giovanni Moro's court appearance and announced on television a re-opening of the investigation into Moro's terrorist activities. Madrid immediately accepted the Italian invitation to participate.

Presented with a better-scripted opportunity than he'd prepared for his fifteen minutes of dubious fame, Moro improvised that his court declaration had been planned in the event of his capture. Rome's announcement of his trial a week ahead of its opening had given the Madrid bombers their simultaneous time frame.

Sally emerged for a brief, in-between calls respite from cubicle claustrophobia to the Italian foreign minister's voice-over reaction to mobile-phone footage of the Madrid carnage, preparing her for the conversation she would be having with David Monkton. He, predictably, was unemotionally monotone, rejecting pre-conception and the invited hysteria from nervous Downing Street support staff anticipating parliamentary demands for Italian explanations. He told Sally he was awaiting reports from the Rome embassy *rezidentura,* as well as inevitable approaches from Italian and Spanish counter-intelligence. She was to keep in closer touch—from her CIA office, to establish her presence there—in case any positive associations were established.

Sally was confident by now that she'd mastered navigating Monkton's psychologically unnerving habit of listening without interruption, although it was still unsettling hearing only the echo of her own voice. Prepared by the earlier conversation with Poulter, Sally concentrated upon establishing herself as the conduit between Poulter and Irvine, minimizing—without being obvious, she hoped—how she would fulfill the role. She was sure, she insisted, that by positioning herself between both men she'd learn most of what each was working on, thinking as she gave the undertaking that it was guaranteed from Jack.

'Impressive,' allowed Monkton.

'We're not there yet,' cautioned Sally, getting the qualification in ahead of the Director-General. How long would it be before he demanded to know why she hadn't first discussed it with him?

'You sure Poulter's going to co-operate?'

'I can't be, not totally. I'd put it at seventy-five percent. But we're in a much better position than we were,' said Sally, satisfied at how her argument was echoing back to her. 'And I'll still have the NSA team input—which should provide a double check on how much or how little Poulter's telling them as well as me. But I'm as sure as I can be that I've persuaded him of the professional benefits of talking things through with us first.' She felt a twinge of unease at how close she'd come to saying *me* instead of *us.*

'Greatly influenced, as he obviously was, by your recognizing the domain similarities, which neither he nor the NSA team isolated?' pressed Monkton.

Here it comes, thought Sally. 'It might lead to nothing.'

'Poulter appears to believe it could.'

'When we next talk, I'll have a reaction from the Fort Meade team,' Sally tried to hurry on.

'They'll be receptive because of Poulter's response.'

Honesty time again, Sally recognized. 'I'm going to imply the domain repetition was the reason for Poulter's direct approach, which in future will come through me. That's how I get to be the go-between.'

'So everything depends on your being right!'

'Not at all,' refused Sally, ready for the cynicism. 'Poulter knows now that in addition to whatever GCHQ discovers, he can get either through Jack or me what's going on at Cyber Shepherd and Fort Meade at a finger snap, without having to wait for communication through official channels. He's not going to endanger a source like that even if there's no significance in the domain names. Neither is Conrad Graham—who also needs all the help he can get to survive—going to throw away a back-door route to GCHQ if the domain peculiarities turn out to be nonsense.'

'And if it's anything but nonsense, you're more valuable as a continuing participant in Operation Cyber Space than as a convenient sacrifice.'

'That's occurred to me, too.' Sally wished that hadn't sounded so smug.

'You've worked it all out very well,' congratulated Monkton, after the briefest of pauses.

No rebuking criticism at all? wondered Sally. 'Thank you.'

'I don't believe I could have offered a better, more worthwhile, contribution. But in future I want to hear in advance, not after it's been initiated, about anything as potentially important as this. Which I thought I'd already made clear.'

It would be a mistake to fall back upon her prepared defence, Sally decided. 'I understand.'

Conscious of having been at the embassy far longer than she'd

anticipated—and now officially part of the CIA's Cyber Shepherd group—
Sally for the first time openly called Irvine from the communications room,
startled after Monkton's monotone calmness by Irvine's agitation.

'Where are you! All hell's broken out! Graham's been summoned by
the Director: we're on conference standby.'

'I'm on my way,' promised Sally, following Monkton's example by
refusing to be caught up in the Madrid frenzy.

And continued to refuse even when she learned more about Madrid, at
Langley, insisting what she had to say was still more immediately important.

'That's what Poulter wanted, to know if we'd isolated the domain peculiarities?' Irvine blurted the moment Sally finished her edited explanation.

'Yes.'

'Why didn't he ask outright?'

'Didn't fit the normal patterns, I guess. Which it doesn't, does it?'

'No,' agreed Irvine, concentrating on the quartered screen he had dis-
played in front of him. 'But why didn't we pick up on it! It's there, right in
front of us!'

'*Because* it's there, right in front of us: *too* obvious.'

Irvine logged on to Fort Meade as they talked, his screen now turned
sufficiently for Sally to read as he wrote. Sally hadn't expected Irvine's un-
questioning acceptance and was curious of the Fort Meade response. It came
from Burt Singleton, who dismissed the suggestion as idiotic.

Irvine ignored the dismissal, ordering a decrypt effort to include a
search for matching IP variations in earlier suspect traffic on file. He'd
join them, Irvine advised, directly after a CIA review of the Madrid attack; he wanted any relevant material copied back right away.

Sally's initial thought was that Irvine was physically stretching when
he leaned back into his seat until she realized he was offering his computer reply to John Poulter's original approach. It was a courteous recognition of what Irvine referred to as "a curiosity"—which Sally considered

another way of saying idiotic—upon which they should "clearly and jointly co-operate."

'Okay?' he asked.

Theirs was a united aim: she wasn't cheating or manipulating anyone, Sally assured herself. 'We got this far because John Poulter trusts me, expects me, a member of the British service now seconded here, to be our link. I think that should be acknowledged, made official from this end.'

'You're right,' agreed Irvine, adding her name to the message as the Cyber Shepherd conduit.

She'd jumped all the hurdles, Sally decided; she wished she could see the finish line.

Only one office—unoccupied—separated Irvine's CIA accommodation from hers on a mezzanine floor directly below that of Conrad Graham. It was windowless and sterile, fitted with a desk and matching chair, with another against the side wall against which a single filing cabinet was also set. The computer was on a wheeled, metal side station, at that moment to the immediate left of a desk bare except for a green internal telephone beside a black handset with its dialing-instruction booklet alongside. The computer came on at a touch of its power button. She was invited to select her own password. She chose Selwa, her Arab name, interspersing the Roman script with the numerals of her birth year. Acceptance was instant. The telephone manual warned no calls could independently be dialed. Being channeled through the switchboard guaranteed the stipulated security. As it guaranteed a verbatim transcript to go with the record that would be kept of any Internet communication on the supplied computer, Sally pragmatically accepted. But which, absurdly, she wasn't supposed to realize.

Her quick annoyance was not at the assumption of her naïvety but at how slow she'd been not to understand Monkton's earlier remark about using the acknowledged monitoring as a misinformation conduit if the need arose, which was not, as nothing the man ever said was, a casual throw-away line. The CIA's switchboard responded instantly. The London connection was just as swift. The line was echoingly clear, with no blur of interception. She told Monkton she was happy with her CIA office. He said he was glad. The Madrid investigation was ongoing; the Washington embassy *rezidentura* could handle background checks on the two American bombers. He had a fairly comprehensive dossier from Rome and offered Sally the opinion he was formulating. Sally agreed it could fit the facts so far available, and that maybe the Italians had over-estimated Giovanni Moro. Monkton hoped there'd be some developments soon from her complete CIA inclusion. Sally said she hoped so, too.

Conrad Graham's summons came as an already-alerted Irvine arrived at her door. On their way to the floor above, Irvine said, 'It's measuring ten and rising on the Richter scale.'

Which was how the deputy CIA director presented it, in the beginning actually slapping the desk in frustration. 'Madrid's ours, had to be ours! It's overseas, CIA's remit. It's part of the al Aswamy operations, our remit. But Admiral Joshua Fucking Smith has assigned it to the FBI because investigating the bombers' background will be *in* America, the Bureau's jurisdiction. And it's being publicly announced. Homeland is determined to bury us, take it all away. Sons of bastard bitches!'

They'd tentatively talked about what to offer Graham before Sally left Irvine's office to examine her own, and she waited for him to open the discussion, but he said nothing.

'Well!' Graham demanded.

'That's good,' tempted Sally. 'Takes the pressure off us.'

'What the hell are you talking about?'

'I was talking to London when you called,' expanded Sally. 'Director Monkton doesn't believe there's a Madrid connection with al Aswamy. Or Giovanni Moro. We're not getting that guidance from Italian intelligence. According to all our *rezidentura* sources in Italian intelligence, the justice minister didn't get any briefing to justify what he said on television. We're putting significance on the suicide videos: there's no reference whatsoever to al Aswamy or any of the attacks al Aswamy organized. Nor was there in what Giovanni Moro originally said in court. He only claimed the association *after* being told Madrid was the reason for the trial postponement.'

'Is London going to go public with that?' Graham smiled, his frustration easing.

'I don't imagine so, not this early,' said Sally. 'But you'll get all the guidance that I get.' Enough was on her monitored call for Graham to be convinced of everything she was telling him, she reflected, looking invitingly to Irvine beside her.

'There's something else we're working on with England that you should know,' picked up the code-breaker.

Sally was impressed at Irvine's domain summary, actually giving her the liaison credit but not over-inflating the potential in his argument against Graham's making a premature disclosure of something that could turn out to be nothing.

'And nothing goes beyond this room,' insisted Graham sourly. 'We give Smith anything we haven't got already in a zipped-up bag, the son of a bitch will screw us, like he's done today.'

Irvine didn't call from Fort Meade, which was the arrangement they'd made after the Langley meeting, and Sally was glad, hoping it indicated progress. She waited until after midnight, though, filling the time listening to the BBC World Service, from which she learned that the following day's *New York Times* carried a sidebar linking a man named Abu al Hurr with their Madrid bombing story. Hurr was believed to be one of the attackers arrested at the UK's Sellafield nuclear plant. The Pakistani passport upon which he'd entered England contained a still-valid student visa to the United States, where he'd failed to take up a post-graduate course at Rutgers School of Engineering in Piscataway, New Jersey. Piscataway was also the town in which James Miller, one of the confirmed suicide bombers, had once lived.

35

ALERTED BY THE FIRST EDITIONS OF *THE NEW YORK TIMES,* THE entire Trenton FBI field office, led by Agent-in-Charge Ben Hardy, traveled overnight the forty-three miles to Piscataway to establish a task force. By 8:00 a.m. that task force was supplemented by a further ten agents and technical support staff from the New York and Baltimore field offices. By then the Trenton party had identified twenty-five senior staff and practical instructors from the Rutgers mechanical, chemical, and civil engineering faculties—some already awakened during the night by catch-up media enquiries—who'd possibly had personal contact with James Miller during his time there or who had knowledge, however hearsay or trivial, of Abu al Hurr.

A substantial amount of information was available on Miller, who'd actually attended Rutgers. He'd enrolled in an aeronautics course under the Pell rehabilitation bursary for Iraq and Afghanistan veterans. He'd served in a Rangers division in both conflicts; in Afghanistan he'd been awarded a Purple Heart. He'd been twenty-eight at the time of his Rutgers enrollment in October 2012. A first-semester notation from his practical instructor said that Miller hoped to qualify as a helicopter technician. Further instructor notes showed an early if average aptitude had deteriorated into erratic behavior and absenteeism. Miller was also officially warned—on two occasions dismissed the sessions—on suspicion of excessive alcohol use. His medical and psychological assessments gave no indication of post-traumatic stress disorder. Urine and blood tests, however, disclosed alcohol and cocaine abuse. He received written cautions about his behavior and treatment recommendations. He'd listed his religion as Presbyterian. The absenteeism worsened after eleven months, and he finally dropped out completely three months later. The only address in the personnel file was a rooming house off Sidney Road.

Only very limited documentary material, all supplied by the man himself, was available on Abu al Hurr. No-one questioned at any faculty knew anything about the man. Hurr's entry application listed a home address in the Kohati Gate district of Peshawar, Pakistan. There was also an address on the Abbottabad campus of the Peshawar University of Engineering & Technology, from which he had provided Grade 1 graduation documentation in macro-electronics. He had applied to Rutgers for a postgraduate degree in applied electronics. A personal reference letter from a Professor Sohail Khan, who described himself as Hurr's tutor, praised the man for his outstanding academic dedication and described him as wishing to return to research electronics after commercial employment in engineering posts in Germany and the United Kingdom. He'd given his age as thirty four in his application, which was dated July 20, 2013.

Seizing the advantage of the day, Hardy had ten agents in place at the end of Friday prayers at the Masjid An-Noor mosque in Piscataway's Hoes Lane. Neither the imam nor any of the worshippers recognized James Miller from his Rutgers registration photograph or from the name. The imam volunteered, however, that an American had come to the mosque to discuss the Islamic faith whom he'd not now seen for several months, maybe even as long ago as a year. From their conversation the imam believed the man had served in the American military: he'd talked of living on a military disability or discharge pension while undergoing unspecified medical treatment. The imam did not believe the man was local: at the last of the three meetings he'd talked of moving on. As far as the imam could remember—"I'm afraid I've got a very bad memory"—the man hadn't said where he was going. Because of that bad memory—not wanting to lose a potential convert—he'd kept a reminder note of their meetings in his diary. It took him almost thirty minutes, going back through crammed entries as far as December 2012, to find the man's name: Milton Kline.

A well-rehearsed Ben Hardy—with the benefit of an already-established acquaintanceship from close-by Trenton—personally headed a Bureau diplomatic visit to Piscataway police headquarters. It was carefully timed to take place exactly one hour after a placating telephone call from FBI director Frederick Bowyer to minimize traditional local-police resentment to federal law intrusion. Which it did. James Edward Miller's rap sheet was laid out in readiness for Hardy's arrival at the police headquarters. It recorded three incidents of Miller's being taken into protective police custody for public drunkenness, which is not a prosecutable offence under New Jersey State or local law. On each occasion, for the same reasons, a man named Milton John Kline was also taken into protective custody.

By mid-morning the FBI's technical division had installed a complete communications unit, including satellite facilities, in the temporary field office in former laundry premises off the main street. From there the emerging information, including Abu al Hurr's Peshawar connections, was relayed to FBI headquarters on DC's Pennsylvania Avenue for follow-up investigation. And from there Ben Hardy received Director Bowyer's congratulatory call:

'You've done good, Ben. Damned good.'

'Thank you, Mr Director.'

'The unit I transferred over from Baltimore—find out if there's anyone among them who's got an asset, a friend, on the inside at Fort Meade. I need to know what's going on there.'

'I'll get onto it right away.'

'I know you will, Ben. That's why you're team leader.'

Elsewhere, Operation Cyber Shepherd did not progress as productively.

'Did we know about Piscataway?' demanded Sally, without any time-wasting preliminaries, the moment she was connected to David Monkton from the embassy communications room.

'Nothing to make a possible connection until yesterday and even then—and as of now—there's no positive confirmation,' heavily qualified Monkton. 'Algerian intelligence recovered a partially burned American passport and some papers—we don't yet know what sort of papers—in the name of James Miller. Algiers messaged MI6, believing Six was handling Sellafield; it wasn't passed on to us until late yesterday. Now—this call—would have been my first opportunity to tell you.'

That wasn't a sufficient enough answer to her question! 'We knew about Abu Hurr's American visa. When did we know Rutgers Engineering School was his intended college?'

'Not until about a week ago, and then it wasn't relevant. Abu al Hurr was dead—America's problem—and Madrid hadn't happened. What's your point?'

She should have been told: its relevance was hers to decide. 'Finding al Aswamy—destroying whatever jihad he's trying to direct—has virtually become secondary here to the infighting between the FBI and the CIA and God knows who else in Homeland Security. The *Times* leak is part of that disarray: agencies playing off against agencies. I need to know as much as possible—even things that don't seem relevant—to stay as closely involved as I am. Which could be the wrong place with the wrong people if Abu Hurr's death becomes public.'

'I'm expecting a call from Conrad Graham. You already know what I'm going to tell him about Abu Hurr. He's not going to like it, which puts you on the scapegoat list. You ready for that?'

Instant improvement, Sally judged, taking her time to factor the *Times* disclosure into the question. 'I might even find a way to use it.'

'You should have been told about Piscataway,' conceded Monkton. 'It was a mistake.'

'Is there anything else I should be told?' persisted Sally, maintaining the criticism while accepting that was the closest the man would come to apologizing.

'No.'

'We need—I need—to be distanced from the *Times* disclosure,' insisted Sally. 'What was Algeria's distribution?'

There was a hesitation from London. 'Wide. "Reply all" to MI6, CIA, Spain, and Italy.'

'Simultaneously?'

'Yes.'

'Timed?'

'Afternoon: three ten.'

Sally used the pad in front of her to calculate the comparative time adjustment between North Africa, London, and Washington, DC. Allowing herself a two-hour error variation, the CIA would have received the Algerian advice by 5:00 p.m. their time the previous day. She'd been at Langley then. Remained there for a further two hours, been with Jack Irvine and Conrad Graham—Conrad Graham, who'd been enraged at having the Madrid bombing taken from Operation Cyber Shepherd. Today he'd be apoplectic when Monkton told him MI5 were washing their hands of Abu al Hurr's rendition. 'I hope the *Times*—or any other media outlet here—doesn't have any more surprise leaks: there's too many sources in Homeland Security.'

'There's not a lot you can do about it.'

Sally thought there might be something but decided not to mention it at that time. Instead she said, 'Except go on being very, very careful.'

'Does being very, very careful apply to personal situations?'

Sally frowned sharply at the unexpected tangent. 'If it becomes necessary.' Would she be as careful as she was making out? Of course she would! Whatever there was with Jack would always be secondary.

'Your Langley telephone could have a lot of listeners.'

'Could!' echoed Sally, irritated at the remark. 'Most certainly *will*. Which I'm unlikely for a moment to forget. Or neglect.'

'Neither will I. That's why we'll repeat this conversation on the Langley line later today, to ensure no-one's disappointed. I'll put in some caveats about over-interpretation and some reminders about Sellafield to enhance your input value from an external agency with a focus not solely confined to Cyber Shepherd. It'll put us on the right footing if we need to find different workplace friends.'

Monkton's hadn't been a casual remark, Sally corrected. He'd been thinking laterally, as she would have been if she hadn't been distracted by his personal question. 'I'm calling Poulter directly after this.'

'Get back to me if there's anything I should know. If I don't hear from you, I'll give it at least an hour before I follow up to let him know we've talked, to reassure him he's not risking his professional future coming back to us.'

None of the interceptions were so far decipherable, but among the other cryptologists was a palpable satisfaction at the gradual, letter-by-letter unpicking of the Hydarnes IP codes. After his earlier breakthroughs, Akram Malik felt irrationally isolated from the centre of things monitoring the targeted Action chat rooms of Moscow Alternative. He looked unnecessarily at the wall clock he'd consulted four minutes earlier, impatient with Irvine's posting restrictions, hoping today wasn't going to be as fruitless as the previous two—more than two, he corrected. There hadn't been any responses to the Shamil25 bait for fifty-six hours, which didn't sync with the increased volume of Facebook-routed traffic the rest of the group all around him were huddled over.

He hit the log-on key at Irvine's stipulated moment, between hour-designating 2 and 3 to avoid its appearing timed. Shamail25@akhoulgo.org.ru registered on the screen. So intent was he upon it that Malik didn't properly hear the acknowledgement of another letter identification, although he recognized Shab Barker's excited voice.

His concentration broken, Malik looked instinctively at Barker's triumphant 'And another!' When Malik looked back, Redeemer was on his screen.

Inshallah.

Malik: *Inshallah . . . and at last.*

There was no immediate response. Then: *Arranging a wedding is more difficult than arranging a funeral.*

Redeemer didn't talk in proverbs—even paraphrased!—immediately remembered Malik, but he had to follow the theme here. *My friends anticipated the wedding.*

Redeemer: *Sometimes such things have to be cancelled.*

Had Malik's greeting been too impatient, irreverent even? A shared domain, he remembered, conscious again of the different style: this could be a different Redeemer, a rival faction perhaps. *That would cause great sorrow. Many have prepared gifts.*

Redeemer: *The gifts list is changed.*

Malik: *They surely still have to reach their destination.*

Redeemer: *Inshallah.*

Malik moved to speak, but the disconnection came even before the traditional invocation. Turning into the room, Malik announced, 'We've got a problem.' That I may have caused, he thought.

In the heightened back-watching atmosphere of the competing Homeland Security agencies—coupled with the TV and print media descent upon the town—the CIA inevitably learned of the FBI invasion of Piscataway before it properly awoke. By mid-morning Conrad Graham, in direct contravention of the law prohibiting American spying on Americans, had two CIA, not NSA, technicians in place. By noon they were successfully eavesdropping on the FBI's temporary-field-office communications. From those intercepts Graham heard of the identification of Milton Kline and of Bow yer's intention to establish, with Homeland's tacit agreement, an Abu al Hurr task force in Peshawar, which was also, technically, in contravention not just of American but Pakistani law.

Since the American invasion of Afghanistan in 2001 and the discovery in 2011 of Osama bin Laden, the CIA has built its *rezidentura* in neighboring Pakistan into its largest overseas presence in the world. Graham assigned a six-man priority response team from the Islamabad embassy to pursue every monitored lead from the former Piscataway laundry before the FBI task force boarded their scheduled flight to Pakistan from Washington's Dulles Airport.

By mid-afternoon, Washington time, Graham was already getting preliminary but encouraging Eyes Only reports, wondering as he read how long it would be before Frederick Bowyer publicly staked his claim to Cyber Shepherd leadership.

It wasn't a long wait.

36

BUT GRAHAM NEVER IMAGINED IT WOULD BE ON PRIME-TIME TV news. Or trailed in advance to maximize the viewership figures.

It was stage-managed by FBI director Frederick Bowyer, a heavy-bodied, small-featured man who invited the comparison with the Bureau's founder by bringing his thinning hair over incipient baldness. Against the background of a flag-draped photograph of the president, Bowyer declared major success against the jihad being waged against the West. FBI agents, employing the traditional fast-track technique of J. Edgar Hoover in times of national crisis, had in less than twenty-four hours confirmed the extent of the global terrorist conspiracy. Direct connections had been established between the Madrid bombers and Abu al Hurr, a known associate of Ismail al Aswamy, the Al Qaeda mastermind of the attempted attacks on the Washington Monument, Rome's Colosseum, and a British nuclear facility. Evidence indicated that al Hurr, in U.S. custody after that failed British attack, was an equally important Al Qaeda figure who had gained a place on the Rutgers engineering faculty as a post-graduate student. Within the next twenty-four hours Bowyer expected further information from an FBI task force in Piscataway, New Jersey, about the cell created there by al Hurr and Americans James Miller and Milton Kline, both of whom served in the U.S. military in Iraq and Afghanistan, where they had been radicalized. Another task force was at that moment en route to Peshawar, in Pakistan, where al Hurr was understood to have other known

Al Qaeda associates. Bowyer also anticipated progress from the interrogation of al Hurr in the ongoing hunt for al Aswamy. These Bureau successes would seriously hamper al Aswamy's terror campaign.

'That was totally unbelievable!' said Conrad Graham in genuine surprise. He added more bourbon to his glass, again gesturing to Sally with the bottle between them on the desk.

'Beyond total.' She shook her head against the repeated offer, all irritation gone at being summoned from the floor below by the deputy director to watch the transmission. 'You think he actually tries to *do* a Hoover impersonation there!'

Graham snorted a laugh. 'He'd look even more ridiculous than J. Edgar in a little black dress.'

'Homeland's Joshua Smith can't have authorized this.'

'Bowyer wouldn't have moved without some sort of approval. My guess is that he got carried away.'

Which she couldn't imagine David Monkton ever having done. Or drinking three fingers of bourbon at a time, which was another surprise of the evening. 'He's brought Abu al Hurr into play.'

'Personally identified with him,' enlarged Graham. 'No longer our concern.'

No apoplexy after all, thought Sally. 'Something that shouldn't go unrecorded, though.'

'It won't be,' reassured Graham. 'What's the latest from GCHQ?'

'Slow but going in the right direction,' said Sally, continuing the myth of not knowing her conversations were being listened to. She was anxious now to get back to the incomplete transliterations from Meade and GCHQ that she'd been comparing when Graham called.

'Nothing I can use then?'

'Use?'

'Fred really did get carried away up there in the limelight.'

'Even associated himself with a dead man.'

'And he should have waited until he heard from his task force in

Peshawar,' said the deputy CIA director, who'd heard from his own more strategically posted team three hours earlier.

'Did you see the television!'

'Yes, Mr Director.'

'Whad'you think?'

'Very impressive, sir.'

'Your input, Ben, won't be forgotten.'

'Thank you, sir.'

'You got any news for me?'

'Our guy's Jimmy Lowe. Grade five, good agent. Lives on the same street as a NSA guy named Packer, an administration executive.'

'I remember him now from Homeland sessions,' said Bowyer. 'Tall guy, never contributes. I never expected to get this close.'

'Neither did I,' acknowledged Hardy. 'Both are Friday-night poker players. Jimmy's cried off tonight, of course.'

'No, he hasn't,' hurriedly corrected Bowyer. 'Tonight Jimmy plays better—or worse, if it suits the purpose—than he's ever played before. What's he know already about Packer?'

'Divorced about three years ago. Wife got the two kids and the guilty husband's alimony that Packer tries hard to supplement from the Friday-night games but usually doesn't.'

'Here's what I want. I want to know everything about how Irvine's team works, how close they are—or aren't—to al Aswamy. I want to know everything they're doing about the Madrid attack, and what this gal Hanning passed on from the interrogation of al Hurr before the Brits passed him over to us. I particularly want to know all there is about her, too, including how to get her into the sack.' Bowyer hesitated. 'You get the picture of what I want?'

'I'm sure I do, Mr Director.'

'And as quick as you've organized everything else so far, Ben, okay?'

'May I ask a question, sir?'

'What?'

'Is the Bureau leading the investigation now?'

'There'll be a statement tomorrow.'

'You got misled at the start,' sympathized Conrad Graham.

'Each is greatly resented; none will be forgotten,' threatened the man.

'Nothing came from the CIA,' quickly reminded Graham.

'That's accepted. We don't like being misled. We're not being misled again, are we?'

'That's for you to decide when we're through talking.'

'Yes, it will, won't it?'

'This guidance isn't too late for tomorrow's paper?'

'There's plenty of time to go into everything.'

'That's what I want to do, go into everything,' said Graham.

37

FOREWARNED, SALLY STAYED UP FOR THE BBC WORLD NEWS report of the following day's *New York Times*, which studio commentators variously described as staggering, disgraceful, scandalous, and unprecedented, all of which Sally considered understatements when she got her copy on her pre-dawn drive to the British embassy.

The coverage dominated the front page, the story Sally knew to be based on Conrad Graham's unattributed leak, separated from Frederick Bowyer's press conference—illustrated with a smiling photograph of the FBI director—by a feature headlined "Unacceptable Chaos." Across five columns above all three articles ran a three-inch-deep strap disclosing the death in U.S. custody of Abu al Hurr, described as the Pakistani-born leader of the attack upon the British Sellafield nuclear facility.

Sally did not read in detail until she reached the seclusion of the communications room, concentrating first upon what had come from the deputy CIA director. The introductory paragraph promised important developments in the fight against what was now unquestionably an organized global jihad. Progress in those CIA developments had been seriously impeded by the grossly inadequate investigation of another agency suggesting a connection between James Miller, one of the Madrid bombers, Abu al Hurr, and an Al Qaeda cell in Peshawar, Pakistan. That time-wasting, false, and totally unsubstantiated claim was solely based upon the coincidence of Miller's having studied at New Jersey's Rutgers University, at which Abu al Hurr had been offered an engineering-faculty place he had never taken up. Hurr had been accepted on the basis of completely false, forged information. He was unknown in Peshawar and had no connection with its university. The two men had never been contemporaries at Rutgers. There was no evidence of their ever having met. In conjunction with other intelligence agencies, the CIA had also dismissed the claims of conspiracy between Giovanni Moro and the Madrid bombers.

The separate strap story said that a pathologist's report was awaited to establish the cause of Abu al Hurr's death. He was understood to have denied leadership of the nuclear-facility attempt to British interrogators or any knowledge of intended terrorist attacks the CIA believed to be imminent. It was not known how Abu al Hurr was transferred to U.S. custody or the whereabouts of the man's death. No statement or explanation had been forthcoming from British authorities.

The *Times* opinion column demanded immediate explanations from the CIA and FBI directors before a public hearing of the Senate Select Committee on Intelligence. The enemy confronting the FBI and the CIA were the jihadists, not each other. Both directors and both agencies needed reminding of their remits and of the boundaries of their responsibilities. The director of Homeland Security should also appear before the committee to account for how such an appalling situation had been allowed to degenerate to the point of endangering America's internal security.

'How much advanced warning did you get?' asked David Monkton, the moment Sally was connected.

'None, not in any detail. What's the reaction back there?'

'The inevitable. A question already tabled in the House. It'll completely dominate prime minister's question time. Our story stays the same. We made Abu Hurr available for questioning in the UK, nothing—and nowhere—else. There was never any discussion and certainly no agreement about rendition. I've already asked through the Foreign Office for an explanation from the U.S. embassy of how he got there. I've already briefed our ambassador there, so don't get involved. How's it otherwise going to affect you?'

'Personally, I'm still working it out. At the moment I think Graham's been damned clever, which surprises me. And makes me question my judgment of the man up to now. He's got the FBI and the two admirals who were ganged up against him all on the rack at the same time. Everyone will know Graham was the source, but if he can face down his accusers, he could emerge the kingpin, which puts me very definitely in the right place.'

'This promised development is a code breakthrough, right?'

'I can't think what else, but I haven't heard any justification of that from Meade. I'll speak to them before calling GCHQ.'

'And then call me directly afterwards,' insisted Monkton. 'I can't be caught out on this.'

None of us can, thought Sally. 'It'll probably be from Langley.'

'We'll speak carefully.'

It was still only 6:45 A.M. Washington time when Sally emerged from the communications room to find Nigel Fellowes very obviously waiting in the outside corridor.

'Here before dawn again!' greeted Fellowes. 'What ever happened to beauty sleep!'

'I didn't pick out your car behind me,' challenged Sally. Why this ambush? she wondered, her curiosity piqued.

'Parking-lot arrivals log, timed four forty-five a.m. Much simpler.' Fellowes smiled easily, looking at *The New York Times* under Sally's arm. 'We need to talk.'

'Monkton's already briefed your ambassador,' assured Sally, shifting the newspaper.

'Not directly about that,' qualified Fellowes, gesturing towards the newspaper.

'What then?'

'I'm not breaking London's rules of engagement, trying to encroach on forbidden territory. But I think you've been dealt a pretty shitty hand.'

'Not a difficult judgment to reach,' encouraged Sally, conscious of the attention from some of the other embassy staff in the corridor.

'I've got friends, assets of sorts, in the Agency. And in the Bureau.'

'I'd expect them to think of you as an asset, too.' And be disappointed, she thought.

'You're being targeted,' declared Fellowes flatly.

'You sure about that, that it's against me personally?'

'As sure as I need to be.'

Was she going to be challenged about herself and Irvine? Sally abruptly wondered. 'Why?'

'Inter-agency rivalry that's all over the paper you've got under your arm, is what I think. Only a lot worse. Homeland Security's too diversi-fied to work effectively, properly: everyone's staking their leadership claim, and there's the proof of it, right there in your hand.'

He wasn't telling her anything she didn't already know—he was prac-tically quoting verbatim from the paper as well—but she hadn't antici-pated danger beyond the tight circle into which she'd inveigled herself, the circle that very much included Jack Irvine. 'Targeted how, exactly?'

Fellowes shrugged. 'I don't know. Can't find out in any precise detail. Discrediting exercise, possibly: CIA having to bring in British help.' Hur-riedly he added, 'That's a pure guess. Another guess is that the Madrid leak in this morning's *Times*, resurrecting Abu Hurr from his unmarked grave, is part of it; maybe even a preliminary to more unspecified leaks.'

Sally's concentration was absolute now. 'Did you get any steer on Abu Hurr and Madrid?'

'Within an hour of it arriving at Pennsylvania Avenue. That's why I wanted us to talk like this.'

'Did you speak to London about it?'

'No way!' snorted Fellowes. 'Forbidden territory, remember? Hands off, stay-away order signed by Director-General David Monkton himself. Which I'm ignoring talking to you now, putting myself at your mercy, in fact.'

'Why?' demanded Sally, returning to the recurring question.

'Not from altruism, believe me! From complete and utter self-interest and preservation. I don't know what's being mounted against you personally. But whatever it is, it won't stop at you. It'll ripple out to encompass the *rezidentura,* which I head. I don't want to be caught up in any part of what you're involved in: of what happens to you or Cyber Shepherd. I give you as much unofficial warning and help as I can—like I'm doing right now—I survive. I follow hands-off orders, I'm applying for jobs as a parking warden anytime soon. I don't like the choice.'

All the dots joined up to make a picture of sorts, conceded Sally. 'I'm not sure I've even got a choice.'

'I'm putting myself at your mercy.'

'It'll stay between us. I want to survive, too.' Which—or whose—safety was she worried about, hers or Jack Irvine's? Or both of them? She wasn't sure of the answer.

For an organization in potential turmoil, outwardly Langley appeared as tranquil as its surrounding landscaped woodland. The customary taciturn escort—reduced by now to just one—delivered Sally to her room. The intercom sounded as she entered. An anonymous aide said Conrad Graham would see her and Irvine in two hours. They were to wait for his call.

Irvine answered his Meade number on its first ring. 'I hear you're coming down?' she said.

'In about two hours.'

'I heard that, too. I'm at Langley.'

Irvine hesitated. 'How is it there?'

'Quiet. What about you?'

Instead of answering, Irvine said, 'You spoken to Poulter yet?'

She should have called from the embassy, Sally thought, annoyed with herself: Why was she suddenly so concerned about their affair becoming known? 'Not yet. What's he told you?'

'Can't reach him,' said Irvine shortly. 'He's at meetings.'

'Since when?'

'Early breakfast this morning, London time.'

Long after the *New York Times* disclosures, calculated Sally. 'Anything else?'

'Redeemer's gone quiet on us. Withdrawn.'

'I'll see you here in two hours.' I hope, she thought. She had a lot to do before then.

'This isn't a blame game,' assured Frederick Bowyer. 'Far from it. You understand what I'm saying?'

'I think I do, sir,' said Ben Hardy.

'You weren't part of any over-reaction.'

'Thank you, sir.' For as long as he had a better use, thought Hardy objectively.

'I need some inside leverage to make the Bureau's case before any official enquiry or committee,' reluctantly conceded Bowyer 'What's happening with Packer and our guy?'

'Jimmy's set up an additional game for tonight. Says Packer's flaky but doesn't want to press too hard and spook him. Today's *Times* has got to be the only other thing on tonight's table apart from cards.'

'I don't want to spook him either, but I need to know what's going on inside Meade and that special joint unit that's running with the Agency: know the problems, the weaknesses that need plugging. They're definitely there. It lost al Aswamy, for Christ's sake!'

'I'll talk to Jimmy right away.'

'You got all the numbers to call me on, Ben.'

'I have, sir.'

'That's ridiculous! Doesn't make any sense!' argued Sally, exasperated, abandoning any thought of being able to get back to Langley from the embassy to meet Graham's deadline. At that precise moment she didn't give a damn. Nor did she care that from all the security checks and monitors her movements would be traceable in and out of Langley and the British embassy like a puppet on elastic strings.

'I agree,' said Monkton, as always frustratingly calm.

'We *know* there's going to be an attack! GCHQ withdrawing the specially agreed instant exchange like this could let it happen!'

'A point I made personally, more than once, to the Director himself. To be told that all special arrangements had ended: that exchanges would revert to Echelon procedure unless outstanding circumstances arose.'

'Outstanding circumstances like a fucking massacre we were too late to prevent!'

'I gave that warning, too, without the profanity.'

'You want me to apologize?'

'No.'

She would have found it difficult, thought Sally. *'Why!'* she demanded, anguished.

'The Director is new and GCHQ has been caught up too often in exposure and embarrassments of the sort that required the previous incumbent to resign, which his replacement doesn't want to do. And today's *New York Times* looks just like one of those embarrassments.'

'Is everyone there thinking more about appointments and promotions than what they're supposed to be doing!'

'Questions like that don't solve our problem.'

'How much higher can you take it to get it reversed?'

'I've already trodden on too many sensitive egos on this to have kept open receptive doors and ears. I've copied to GCHQ's director and the foreign secretary the warning I've sent directly to the PM, so far without even acknowledgement from anyone.'

'It's got to be overturned, reversed!'

'Give me something to do that with.'

38

SALLY WAS AN HOUR LATE GETTING BACK TO LANGLEY AND DIDN'T care, twice ignoring her ringing cell phone until the third call as she was finally parking in the overflowing CIA lot.

Irvine got as far as 'Where the——?' before she stopped him with 'I'm here, on my way up.'

He was waiting at her office door. 'Graham's in meltdown.'

'It'll get worse,' predicted Sally, 'GCHQ have closed us out, frightened by the *Times* coverage. It's strictly Echelon from now on except in extraordinary circumstances.'

'We're in extraordinary circumstances right now!' insisted Irvine.

'I've been in one ever since I went back to the embassy.'

'I've told Graham you're here; he already knew,' said Irvine as they went up to the next floor.

'The all-seeing electronic eyes and movement logs,' said Sally sourly.

'This better be a damned good story!' greeted the deputy CIA director. His face was mottled red. The bourbon bottle of the previous night was gone, but Sally guessed it had been within arm's reach minutes before they'd arrived.

Turning the threat back on the man, she said, 'It's anything but good.'

Graham's face got redder as he listened, shifting awkwardly in his empowering executive chair. When Sally finished, the man said, 'I'll get on to Monkton.'

'That's who I've been talking to for the past three hours,' said Sally impatiently. 'And he's talked until there's nothing left to say to the GCHQ director, who's adamant they're going back to the official information-exchange system. Monkton's gone direct to the prime minister, but as of an hour ago heard nothing back.'

'What are the assholes worried about?'

'Today's *New York Times.*' Sally looked directly at Graham, whose colour, which had started to recede, flared again.

'The Senate intelligence committee *are* convening an enquiry session.' Graham steadily held Sally's gaze. 'It's being announced sometime today.'

'That'll frighten GCHQ even more.'

'I'll still call Monkton,' stubbornly persisted Graham, turning to Irvine. 'What's this shit from Meade?'

'Our best Vevak source—someone whose darknet transmission we could read because they weren't encrypted—has closed down. The Brits were actually getting more than us. That's why today was important: we could simply have switched to their interceptions—'

'Whoa!' stopped Graham. 'How come they're getting more than us?'

'They're blanketing a domain routing through Malmö, in Sweden, for what appears to be something directed at the UK. Some of the material that cross-referenced with us didn't come on our Hydarnes route. Vevak's obviously got another darknet we're not into.'

'Why's our source closed down?'

'We'll never know,' said Irvine. 'Could be he was careless or arrogant or both by not encrypting: got punished for it. We don't believe our close-down came from the guy we were used to: it was a totally different style, although he or she used the same domain name.'

'What the hell are we left with?' demanded Graham.

'Only what we've already got and still can't get a positive lead from.'

'And the Brits have got more that they won't share?' Graham formed his fingers into a steeple that reminded Sally of the man's earlier histrionics.

Irvine hesitated, caught by the tone in Graham's voice. 'We think they might have,' Irvine replied cautiously.

'You know one of my favourite remarks?' asked Graham with strained rhetoric. 'Made by Richard Helms, one of the best CIA directors the Agency ever had. Called the CIA the president's bag of tricks. We've already pulled a rabbit out of that bag proving with Cyber Shepherd that despite Iran's nuclear non-proliferation bullshit, they're still sponsoring Al Qaeda with communication facilities on darknet channels.'

'I'm having difficulty keeping up with you,' lied Sally.

'We got an attack coming that we can't do anything to stop, we've got to turn it over to people who can,' declared Graham. 'We've got to give Operation Cyber Shepherd over to the Brits.'

'Motherfucker!' raged Irvine, fury trembling through him. 'He can't! No! Shepherd's mine! I can do it. He's got to let me do it.'

Sally waved Irvine down into his chair, at once accepting that the outburst confirmed a lot of her earliest impressions, which saddened her. 'He can do it and there's unarguable justification that he should. It isn't—can't be—personal. If GCHQ have a better chance, a more definite lead, they've got to be given it. The only objectives are to stop attacks happening. If they crack the code that does it, it becomes the extraordinary circumstances they built into their back-channel refusal. So we'll get it, too.'

'But it won't . . . ,' started Irvine, but stopped. Awkwardly he finished, 'We don't know they have a more definite lead!'

But it won't *be me*, thought Sally, mentally completing what Irvine had started to say. 'You gave Graham enough reason to believe they have.'

'Graham's covering his ass. He passes it over, it's not his responsibility anymore, is it? He's squeaky-clean, every which way.'

'Yes, he is. So are we.' But she would have had no personal part—no personal recognition—in the successful conclusion as she'd had at Sellafield. But for her this wasn't a private crusade, as it was for Irvine.

'Bastard!' said Irvine, appearing physically to deflate as the anger subsided. 'You going to speak to Monkton?'

'After he's spoken with Graham and gotten back to GCHQ.'

'I'll wait to hear the reaction before going back to Meade.'

'How do you think your guys are going to take it?'

'As I'm going to take it, by not giving up.'

'I didn't imagine you would.' She hesitated, wanting to satisfy an uncertainty. 'You know Graham well, don't you?'

'I thought I did.'

Sally ignored the self-pity. 'My first impression wasn't that he was a drinker?'

'How'd you know he was?'

Was?' she queried, ignoring the question.

'He developed a problem during Stuxnet. Went into a programme just afterwards, straightened himself out. And you didn't answer my question.'

Irvine sat forward in his chair, suddenly demanding. She shouldn't have started this conversation, Sally acknowledged. 'Just a guess. We watched Bowyer's press conference together: I thought he was a little high, that's all. I didn't know it had been serious.'

'You telling me he's relapsed, got too drunk to function properly! To make proper decisions?'

'Don't try to run with that, Jack! You'll be the only casualty.'

'Was Graham drunk?'

'No! And I won't testify to anyone or any enquiry that he was. He's right in doing what he's doing!'

Irvine remained strained forward for several moments, staring fixedly at her. Then he said, 'Isn't it time you called Monkton?'

Sally did so from her Langley office, cautioning Monkton where she was, for the first time unconcerned at an unrestricted exchange's being monitored.

'Who's idea was this?' at once demanded Monkton.

'The deputy director's. He says, quite rightly, it's the responsible thing to do. What's GCHQ say?'

'They want to know what the problem is.'

'They're the problem, cutting off the direct exchange.'

'They think they're being manoeuvred into something.'

'Jesus! You've got to go over their heads: get a directive from Downing Street!' Sally insisted once more.

'I don't need to be told what to do!'

'That wasn't impertinence. It was despair!' Perhaps it hadn't been such a good idea to be uncaring of the CIA telephone monitoring.

'Have GCHQ got all the US intercepts?' asked Monkton, clearly echoing a GCHQ demand.

'All of them,' said Irvine, listening at Sally's shoulder, before she could repeat the question.

'Who's that?' demanded Monkton.

'Jack Irvine, in charge of the Fort Meade unit.'

There was a hesitation. 'They must immediately be sent anything new that Meade get, even though their source appears to have dried: nothing held back,' said Monkton, repeating what Sally guessed to be another GCHQ insistence.

'They will be,' undertook Sally, at Irvine's begrudging nod. As exasperated as her lover, Sally said, 'Wouldn't it be easier to go back to how it was!'

'That's the manoeuvre they're frightened of,' disclosed Monkton.

Ben Hardy personally reached Frederick Bowyer on the FBI director's cell phone after trying two of the other direct lines the man had provided in addition to the Pennsylvania Avenue headquarters numbers. Nervously, Hardy at once blurted, 'You said I was to call anytime, sir.' It was just after 8:00 p.m. The noise of people, laughter, was in the background.

'And now you have, Ben, so it must be something you think I want to hear.'

'Is it all right to talk?'

'I'm walking to the den now.' The noise faded. 'So what is it?'

'Jimmy played hardball tonight. Cleaned Packer out and ended up with two hundred dollars of his markers before Packer packed in, which Jimmy did as well. Bought Packer bad-luck drinks and put the arm on as much as he felt was safe. Packer got as nervous as hell with the conversation Jimmy was pushing. Then the news came on the bar TV, with the enquiry announcement, and Packer says that Jimmy should talk to a guy named Bradley, who was the original CIA field supervisor whose crew lost al Aswamy. Bradley got sent into the boondocks because of it. Word now is he's going to be the enquiry sacrifice and is crying foul—'

'Which I think is a cry we should listen to.'

'I thought you might think that. That's why I had Jimmy get a number.'

Sally accepted lateral thinking as a convenient phrase for others to label her unusual reasoning, but it wasn't something of which she was mentally or even physically conscious, like having a process or a formula she could summon at will to confront situations. To Sally it was simply the *way* she thought. Not until she entered the intelligence service did she actually acknowledge that she viewed and assessed things differently from most people. In her first year at Oxford she'd briefly thought she might have a cognitive problem because her logic was so often at variance with that of others, while even earlier, at prep school, she'd been worried about being judged mentally deficient like characters in Charles Dickens's Victorian novels for being left-handed, which she was.

She considered her recognition of all the Hydarnes-sourced IP domain addresses as being transliterated from original Arabizi as more a fluke than unusual or even supernatural clairvoyance, which was how Irvine had

exaggerated her suggestion in the first exhilaration of even partial deci
phering. And how she thought of it again now as she sat before her computer in the stark Langley office, asking herself how she could possibly
make another contribution.

The simple, as always self-honest, answer was that she couldn't. Monkton hadn't called back and there'd been no update from Irvine at Fort Meade.
The only addition to the evening TV news announcement of the Senate
enquiry, which she already knew about, was of a promised CIA statement
the following day about Abu al Hurr's death. Leaving Sally with the choice
between an empty evening at her Watergate service apartment or an ump-
teenth re-examination of the GCHQ and Fort Meade downloads on her
Langley computer. She chose Langley for its secure telephone link to
Irvine. Who would already have used it to call her if there'd been any breakthrough. They were now relying on GCHQ to provide it, from whatever
else—whatever new—GCHQ intercepted. Irvine could be right, of course:
there was no proof they *had* anything new. It was a surmise, from the British withdrawal, which was a result of career fears. There could after all
be something among all the mathematical hieroglyphs she was looking
at. Careful, Sally warned herself. If there were, she'd already accepted it
wasn't she who'd have the eureka moment. How close, though, could GCHQ
conceivably be? She could gauge—or at least make a calculated guess from
what she had in front of her—that directly hidden in every intercepted
Vevak Facebook post was the partial transliteration.

Sally closed her split screen to concentrate entirely upon the British
cache, remembering as she did so that it was GCHQ who'd snared both
Kermani and Smartman. With that came the further recognition that Kermani was the only interception whose domain address was in the name of
a known Persian historical figure, the shah assassin Mirza Kermani. Was
using the revolutionary's name significant? Or was she trying too hard?

There had been three encoded Kermani messages. The first according to date and for which GCHQ had sought American help had transliterated from the original Arabic into twenty-four Roman letters and

numerals. Nine—AANBLEEYE—were potential decryption. Still encoded
were WIQQFDNCMLN59NM. She knew from the time she'd spent at Irvine's side that single letters were rarely if ever repeated in translation after their first use, and that some single letters represented a block. Some
letters and figures were meaningless decoys. Digital dots and separations
could also have letter significance. Until at least half were decoded, it was
usually impossible to separate a string into comprehensible words. After
thirty minutes she gave up trying to make sense out of the first block of
nine. Kermani's second message ran to forty-two letters, numbers, and digital characters. There were ten hopeful decodes—ICEOUFLUIS—and
thirty-two failures.

With eye-blurring concentration Sally worked for a further two hours
through every English-collected message from Kermani, running over
into Smartman, Anis, and Swordbearer exchanges shared with Fort Meade,
before finally abandoning the effort, acknowledging the pointlessness.
She briefly considered telephoning Irvine's direct Fort Meade line but abandoned that idea, too, grateful to finally get to her Guest Quarters apartment, too tired to bother with food.

At exactly 3:00 a.m. by her illuminated bedside clock, Sally came
abruptly and fully awake, the awareness complete in her mind. She couldn't
be right. It had to be an aberration, a fatigue-induced hallucination that
she could check unbeknownst to anyone when she got to Langley in the
morning.

She lay open-eyed in the darkness for another fifteen minutes, isolating it again and again and becoming surer every time that she was remembering correctly, before throwing off the bedcovering. It *was* the
morning. Why was she waiting?

39

IT TOOK JUST FIFTEEN MINUTES FOR SALLY TO CONFIRM SHE hadn't been hallucinating and only another ten for her to assess the significance of her realization. Four a.m. in Washington, DC, was 9:00 a.m. in London. David Monkton answered his direct line on its first ring.

'I know the British target and believe I can confirm the American through it. We'll know for sure when we run some numbers through Fort Meade's computers.'

'Where are they?' monotoned Monkton.

'The RAF base at Waddington, Lincolnshire, and a USAF base somewhere here.'

'From Waddington drones are flown against Al Qaeda IS and the Taliban in Afghanistan and in Pakistan.'

'As well as in Yemen and Somalia,' expanded Sally.

'What makes you so sure?'

'The first intercepted Vevak message in the Kermani group, the one for which GCHQ asked for NSA's help,' listed Sally. 'Waddington's post code, LN5 9NA, was hidden in the encryption.'

'Is that all?' pressed Monkton.

It was impossible to discern the doubt, but Sally guessed it was there. Not hiding her irritation she said, 'I think complete postal coordinates in an encoded Iranian intelligence communication for a British air base from which drone attacks are mounted against Al Qaeda IS and Taliban targets justifies a security alert!' She was breathless, jagged voiced, when she finished.

'So do I,' punctured Monkton in three words.

Shit, he'd off-balanced her again, Sally acknowledged. 'And would be doubly justified when we uncover the zip code.'

'It's your four thirty in the morning,' Monkton unnecessarily pointed out. 'You're surely not proposing to wait until Fort Meade wakes up to run your zip-code search when GCHQ is fully operational right now!'

Sally smiled in anticipation of her recovery. 'No, I'm not proposing that! I'm sure about Waddington—and glad you agree with me—and believed alerting you was my first priority. The Fort Meade unit *is* awake: they're working a twenty-four-hour rota. With their technology they'll do in minutes a search that would physically take me hours and still risk a mistake or an oversight. If there's a match, GCHQ get the complete package, which keeps to our agreement, and if there isn't, they get what's applicable to them, to England, without wasting their time.'

'Logically argued,' conceded Monkton after a pause. 'Next question: When?'

'We don't have that, not yet. But we can be in place, ready, ahead of any attack. We're not expecting it to be a long wait, are we?'

'Not if the indicators are right. You—and Meade—have got an hour.'

'Thank you.'

'And well done. Once again.'

Sally recognized the drawl but couldn't remember the name, which wasn't offered in return when she identified herself. He said he'd wake Irvine, but Sally suggested he run the check first: she could be wrong.

'You got the zip?'

'Two, off the Internet: 89018 and 89070,' offered Sally. 'Try 070 first: I'm guessing it's base-dedicated.'

'Give me your number.'

It was Irvine who called back. 'We located both: 070 in the third Kermani post, 018 in Swordbearer's first. It's definitely Creech Air Force Base at Indian Springs, Nevada. And you should take up clairvoyance as a profession.'

'I'll think about it as a career change,' dismissed Sally.

'Who else knows?'

'Monkton. But he'll leave you to tell GCHQ when I tell him it's definite.'

'I'm on my way down.'

'I'll be here.'

'And congratulations.'

Which was the word Monkton used when she called him back, twenty minutes short of his deadline. So why, she wondered, wasn't she feeling more satisfied? It didn't improve even when she made a connection they could follow to get the date for the attacks.

'Bradley fell over himself for a breakfast meeting, so I came down myself; so it made sense to carry on personally,' said Ben Hardy. He'd taken a chance arriving at Pennsylvania Avenue unannounced, but so far it looked as if he'd pulled it off.

'Absolutely,' agreed the FBI director.

'He's one hell of an angry guy.'

'What's he got to say?'

'Everything and anything you want to know about Operation Cyber Shepherd, I guess,' exaggerated Hardy.

'Let's hear it!'

'Devised by Irvine—first name Jack—whom you know from Homeland meetings. Comes with heavy baggage. Father was the U.S. ambassador to Lebanon who almost caused a Middle East war trying single-handedly to get Hezbollah, Fatah, Hamas, and Israel all tucked up in the same bed—'

'And skewed a presidential election here because the Jewish vote didn't go to the incumbent's second term re-election,' broke in Bowyer, remembering.

'The link continues, after a fashion. Irvine's a computer geek. Worked in Israel with Conrad Graham perfecting the sabotage of Iran's nuclear development.'

'How's Cyber Shepherd work?'

'It hits terrorists before they hit their intended targets: simply takes them out.'

'Now there's a lot to think about,' mused Bowyer.

'You spoken to Graham?' demanded Irvine before he entered her office, ignoring his own. He'd jogged from the parking lot and was breathing heavily.

'Tried to, when he didn't contact me,' said Sally, who'd known Graham would have been aware from the omnipresent internal security of her nocturnal return. 'He's unavailable until mid-morning, which is a bonus. I've got an idea of how to find out when they'll hit.'

'How?'

'Smartman@deathtrade.org.mil. Isn't that where he'll be, but where you couldn't find him: hacked into a military base?'

Irvine shook his head in bemused realization. 'Shit, yes! He's got a botnet in a computer somewhere there.' In his excitement Irvine pulled up from the only other chair to lean over the desk towards Sally. 'That's it! We're gonna get him!'

'No, we're not, not that easy. We'll only get one shot. One mistake— the vaguest hint that we're looking, know where to look—and we'll lose him, lose everyone: those in England, others elsewhere, *and* the Hydarnes access.'

Irvine eased back into his chair, the euphoria gone. 'The concealment will be good, the best. We know it will.'

'The best. But you've got to be better because you've got to do a lot more than just find it. When you do—and get past all the obstacles—can you hack into him: put a botnet inside a botnet to see everything that passes between Smartman and Hydarnes without their knowing you're there?'

'Yes.'

Almost too quick, worried Sally, and wished she hadn't. 'Have you done it before?'

'Yes.'

'Then we can stop it all, like we did before.'

'What can go wrong!' clichéd Irvine, confidence returning.

'That one mistake.'

The objections were immediate and predictable. With Irvine listening—and prompting—from her side, Sally openly spoke to Monkton from her monitored CIA line, wanting to prepare the overhearing Conrad Graham for the inevitable disagreement to follow. For the first time she consciously welcomed Monkton's unnerving silence for the uninterrupted opportunity it hopefully provided to persuade the man that for them to get the attack date, there should be no immediate response beyond the Internet search for Smartman.

'It's a virtual certainty that Smartman is embedded somewhere within the Creech IT system, reading everything. He might even be an airman serving *on* the base. So there can't be any abrupt and visible military buildup of men or equipment,' Sally warned. 'Absolutely paramount, no electronic communication containing any reference—the slightest indication—to what we know. Every communication has to be handwritten on non-electric equipment and hand-couriered. Both GCHQ and NSA have established beyond doubt that domains have been shared on at least two darknet sites. Jack, who's with me, has already advised GCHQ to sweep Waddington's entire IT systems for a duplicate of what we're sure is a Smartman botnet at Creech. Technically GCHQ can get into Smartman's hack and read his traffic. That's how we'll get the date.'

For the first time ever betraying an emotion—incredulity—Monkton said, 'You're guessing, an absolute and utter guess, that Smartman has hacked into a Creech IT system! You're proposing, on the basis of that absolute and utter guess, that America—and we, here in the UK—do nothing in the hope that, first, you're right; secondly, that Irvine's unit will find the intrusion; thirdly, that they'll be able to invade it without being detected and finally get a date for the attack. And only then, according to your reasoning, do we do something about trying to protect ourselves!'

'No!' denied Sally desperately. 'I don't know the geography around Waddington from here. There must be a base, facilities of some sort, close enough covertly to move in personnel and equipment with helicopter support to bring defence in within minutes.'

'You're proposing a variation of Sellafield all over again,' accused Monkton. 'But at Sellafield we had our defence *inside*, waiting, as well as outside.'

'So far al Aswamy, Al Qaeda, Iran, whoever the hell all these people are, have lost in everything they've attempted. But still won,' fought back Sally. 'They haven't caused any real damage or physical harm, but they've still generated global hysteria. Here's their cherry on the cake: hitting the two places from which they've been hit and thousands killed. This is their pièce de résistance. We can't just prevent it. We've got to get al Aswamy and all the other jihadists and publicly arraign them—publicly show they've failed and can only posture.'

There was a silence now Sally didn't welcome. Monkton said, 'Your reasoning is skewed, Sally. And all this is academic anyway. I promise I'll put your thinking forward, but it isn't our decision, is it? We elect people who know better than us to decide things like this.'

'That argument didn't work at all, did it?' sympathized Irvine at the end of the exchange.

Neither did Irvine's when he tried to make the same, now rehearsed pitch to the already-rehearsed Conrad Graham, whose rejections were familiar to both. 'And now this operation can at last be properly organized,' completed Graham. 'Pending the findings of the congressional enquiry, the president's appointed me acting CIA director. I'm already operational. And very much in charge of Operation Cyber Shepherd.'

An hour later the CIA issued its Abu al Hurr statement. It included, in full, a medical certificate signed by two doctors attesting that the man died from an aneurysm rupture of the aorta. The autopsy also established that the aneurysm was a long-standing and obviously undiscovered condition. Concluding the long-running and misleading coincidences, Algeria arraigned a captured terrorist from their leading Al Qaeda faction who'd confessed to involvement in the Madrid atrocity committed by James Miller and Milton Kline. It had, insisted the man, been a single act, unconnected with any other Al Qaeda or jihadist activity.

John Poulter's telephone call, patched through from Fort Meade, halted Irvine and Sally as they were about to leave Langley. Poulter said that after some reconsideration, GCHQ felt the circumstances required the closest and direct co operation. Irvine told the other cryptologist he felt the same and was glad there'd been a rethink.

On their way to the Owen Place safe house and its secure computer links to Fort Meade, Irvine said, 'I've got a good feeling about how this is going to turn out.'

Sally wished she had, too.

40

CONRAD GRAHAM'S PARTING INSISTENCE THAT IRVINE REMAIN instantly available—which Graham also demanded of Sally, who didn't intend on going anywhere—meant Irvine's staying in Washington, which Sally welcomed on every level. She hadn't expected to miss Irvine as much as she had during his Fort Meade absences and balanced her conscience twinge with the professional recognition that his secure Owen Place computer bank would give her unrestricted access not just to his own unit's eavesdropping but to all Cyber Shepherd traffic with GCHQ as well. And it wouldn't stop there. Her minimum twice-a-day conversations with David Monkton and morning and afternoon sessions with Conrad Graham would provide an overview of each of the drone-base protections that began at Waddington and Creech within two hours of the attack alert.

Sally was relieved that voices in addition to hers had echoed her concern at an obvious military buildup at either air base. Only a dozen officers—men as well as women, commanded by two undesignated wing commanders—were to be moved onto the Waddington base. All but two would be military communication specialists and technicians with closed-circuit contact with the outside Special Forces and military defence units. The other two were IT experts who would liaise with outside GCHQ colleagues, supplied with their owners' or users' bona fide IP domain codes to pick their way as quickly as possible through every base computer mainframe, desktop, laptop, and connected cell phone for Smartman@deathtrade.org.mil. The force waiting outside was to be divided between four neighboring RAF bases—Coningsby, Cranwell, Digby, and Holbeach—all within five minutes' helicopter flying time of Waddington.

Concealment of an outside military reaction force was more limited in Nevada, but from the planned schedule appeared already to have been effectively prepared. Nellis, ten minutes' helicopter time from Creech, was the only nearby holding area of sufficient size, but there had already been a Pentagon announcement of a desert survival training exercise to cover the encampment, under canvas, of two hundred SEALs and Special Forces only a mile from Creech. The inside command contingent was to be made up of twenty officers, again male and female, who were to enter in twos and threes during that early evening and night. Five were the core segment of a fifteen-strong Meade IT sweep team—independent of Irvine's unit—hunting Smartman.

'Looks like you were right again about avoiding a too obvious military buildup,' lightly mocked Irvine.

'It's not about who thought what first. These are obvious precautions,' dismissed Sally.

'What if we don't find Smartman?'

'You're more qualified to answer than me. I'd want to look all over again, until we do find him.'

'So would I.'

Sally nodded towards the screen upon which they were receiving a simultaneous, Pentagon-provided television feed from both bases. 'It looks good—secure—set out like that. I'm guessing three days, tops, before there's some sort of leak.'

'I'm not concerned about a few locals seeing a convoy moving around the Mojave Desert: the military do that all the time. What we've got to worry about is Smartman or someone else in the jihad having a lookout position from which they can make the connection. So I'd give it a little longer than three days.'

'Just a little, not a lot longer.'

Sally kept her reservations to herself at Cyber Shepherd's enthusiastic acceptance of GCHQ's suggested decryption pattern because the evidence appeared unarguable. Her reluctance anyway came down to the same unease that she'd had before but still couldn't translate into words that others might accept.

The British assumption was that the intercepted Iranian messages were predicated, like the darknet chat-room exchanges, on Arabic proverbs and aphorisms. Their recommendation was that decoding should be approached using selections—or combinations—of each as crib grids. Following that principle, two codes had been transliterated in the preceding twelve hours. One, from Kermani, was from the encryption in which Sally had located the Waddington post code that led to Creech.

It read, *A mosquito can make a lion's eye bleed.*

The second was another original GCHQ intercept from Smartman. The transliteration was *One tiny insect may be enough to destroy a country.*

'The Brits have made the breakthrough,' declared Irvine, one of the few among the assembling groups to remain subdued.

'Have they?' questioned Sally, matching Irvine's mood, which she guessed to be chagrin at the proverb idea not coming from him after his having supplied the chat-room lead.

Irvine looked at her curiously. 'The attacks are against drone bases. What do Al Qaeda and the jihadists call drones? Mosquitoes. How else can you read it?'

'Not even encoded. How do you read insects bringing down countries?'

Irvine's curiosity deepened into a frown. 'Reinforcing the mosquito analogy, maybe; we know GCHQ have a second Vevak source, although they haven't gone all the way back as we have with Hydarnes. There could be different recipients.'

'I'm not arguing with the transliterations. It's the interpretations—our interpretations—that I'm not sure about.'

'Give me another one,' demanded Irvine.

'I don't have another,' openly admitted Sally, not liking the inadequacy or his head shake of disappointment.

'Then until you do find one, we've got to go with what we've got.'

That evening, thirty-six hours after the alert, the first security review was held on a conference-link video between the Creech and Waddington commanders, each with their staff officers—the Americans from Nellis, the British similarly hidden at RAF Cranwell—as well as David Monkton, John Poulter, and an unidentified Foreign Office official at GCHQ, and Conrad Graham, Jack Irvine, and Sally Hanning at Langley.

The military overviews were presented by an unidentified U.S. colonel staff officer and an equally anonymous British wing commander, both in undesignated fatigues, against aerial backgrounds of both Creech and Waddington. At Creech, one thousand men, predominantly Special Forces from all three services, made up the immediate defence and were already in place. A further five hundred were on standby at Fallon, Nevada's third air base. At Waddington, five hundred Special Forces were stationed at the four conveniently close bases. High-altitude American E-3 Sentry surveillance aircraft were already permanently airborne over Creech and Waddington; their look-down radar provided horizon cover over 320 kilometres. A minimum of four helicopters—the normal daily average in and out of Nellis—were currently airborne, as were two at Waddington. That cover would be maintained from regular base fleets on twenty-four-hour rotation pending the attack. Throughout the available darkness of the preceding thirty-six hours, a helicopter wing of thirty gunships had been assembled at Creech—fifteen at Waddington—and concealed in hangars. The moment of the attack would trigger the launch of an additional ten troop-carrying helicopters from Fallon. A further two hundred troops would be helicoptered into Waddington from RAF Digby. Psychologically disorienting sound systems had also been brought into both bases under cover of darkness, as well as additional mobile radar equipment, ground lighting, and television relay equipment. Electronically, from its beginning and throughout any engagement, Creech and Waddington would be beneath an electronic shell, inside of which, from both ground and E-3 radar, the attempted incursion would be visible and recorded.

Sally thought what followed was an anti-climax given the military preparations, with their illustrated backgrounds, including photographs of the latest covert-operations Sikorsky MH-53 helicopters and even some older, Vietnam-style, open-side gunships. John Poulter, whose obvious self-confidence was in contrast to the uncertain man she remembered from their Sellafield encounter, said the successful GCHQ reading of seemingly innocuous Facebook transmissions unquestionably confirmed the imminent attacks. Sally positively rejected the half-formed thought that Jack Irvine's contribution lacked the presentational confidence of his British counterpart's.

Conrad Graham waited until the television screens blanked and the technician controller confirmed the sound system was off before saying, 'I thought that went pretty well. I could have made the presentation myself.'

'I expected you to be the spokesman,' said Irvine.

And I wish you hadn't been so dogmatic, thought Sally protectively.

Graham said, 'I want us to crack the attack signal.'

'That can be your moment,' said Sally.

'You're right!' said Graham, too absorbed in his biopic fantasy to detect the sarcasm.

Memory-stick-terminated decryptions from both Fort Meade and GCHQ were waiting for Irvine when he and Sally got back to Owen Place. GCHQ had another Kermani post—*Who does not think that his fleas are gazelles*—that Fort Meade had not intercepted. They had, though, transliterated another insect encryption—*When the ant grows wings, it is about to die*—from Swordbearer. Sally spent more time poring over an Anis message—*Death rides a fast camel*—because it wasn't insect referenced.

Irvine didn't break her concentration until Sally finally thrust herself back into her chair, sighing. 'Well?'

'The attack's getting close,' suggested Sally. 'But that's too easy: it's all too easy to make that conclusion.'

'It's—' started Irvine, closer to the computers, but then he erupted, 'Found it.'

Sally came forward to read the screen and said quietly, 'It could be Graham's moment.'

41

SMARTMAN@DEATHTRADE.ORG.MIL WAS EMBEDDED IN THE DESK-top of the executive operations officer of Creech Air Force Base and was loop-connected to the base commander and two other executive officers and was separately backed up in the man's personal laptop.

As he read the initial Nellis-relayed alert, more to himself than to Sally, Irvine said, 'It would have gotten into the mainframe through the less secure laptop. That's how we got the Stuxnet worm into Iran's nuclear installations at Natanz and Bushehr.'

After a transmission pause of several minutes, a second e-mail came, requesting a Skype conference. Irvine said, 'The sweepers are frightened to go in.'

Sally said, 'They should be.'

Before Irvine could reply, another e-mail, this time addressed directly to him, said a helicopter was on standby from Creech to Nellis: they could be talking in ten minutes. Irvine said, 'Ten minutes wasted!'

'Frightened people make mistakes,' warned Sally.

Irvine e-mailed that he would be waiting, continuing on with a longer secure post to GCHQ suggesting that despite the time difference in England, John Poulter be awakened to listen to the impending Skype discussion via remote access. Still not pausing, Irvine separately forwarded to England the brief details of the Smartman discovery before copying the complete file to his Fort Meade unit, who were to make direct contact with the sweeper group. In the interim they were to prepare alternative Smartman algorithms. Finally he called Conrad Graham. It took Irvine several minutes to convince the acting CIA director that the Owen Place computer system was more secure than any at Langley, and that everything he'd set up to remain in DC on Graham's orders was concentrated in his security-guaranteed apartment.

'You expect me to come there!' demanded Graham.

'I don't expect that at all. I'm keeping you in the loop is all. And which I'll continue doing, with whatever devolops.'

After a silence Graham said, 'You think there's going to be something moving tonight?'

'At this stage I haven't any idea what's going to happen tonight.'

'I'll be here. Call me every half hour.'

'That won't be possible,' refused Irvine. 'I'll call you immediately if there's a definite reason and in between times otherwise.'

Irvine's telephone sounded as he replaced it. He was expecting it still to be Graham, but John Poulter said, 'Thanks for the invitation.'

'Sorry you won't be able to see as well as hear.'

'You going in right away?'

'Of course. You briefed your guys at Waddington on what I just sent?'

'They've worked from the bottom down: done all the officers and middle ranks already, official equipment as well as personally owned stuff. Looks like you've got Smartman all to yourself.'

'No second chance if something goes wrong, then?'

'That's another way of putting it,' agreed Poulter.

'You'd better connect up.'

Nellis linked exactly on time. Irvine initiated the Skype from Owen Place to ensure total privacy apart from the British connection. Momentary interference rippled across the screen, but suddenly it cleared. Irvine didn't recognize the face.

'Will Fisher,' identified the man. He was clean shaven, about thirty-five, compensating for his premature baldness with a tightly clipped, full, black beard.

'You did good, finding it,' at once praised Irvine.

'You coming out?'

Irvine paused, frowning. 'Will, I'm almost three thousand miles away; don't know how short a deadline we're looking at! And you're already there.'

'It's your operation,' pressed the man.

'And it's your expertise: you're the guys who sweep the Oval Office and all those other secret basement places where the president holds his crisis meetings. You know all the traps and tricks, which I don't, not completely. This time you've got the official IP codes and passwords to both hacked machines: no official firewalls in the way. And you've got Smartman's complete IP, too. I'm risking breaching the no-contact insistence for Fort Meade to come to you with anything else you might need.'

'Give me every detail of what you want,' said the man, resigned.

'Our own botnet beside Smartman's, in both the desktop and laptop. I want to hack into Smartman's bots, get everything he's got there. I want his hard disk memory, for what's already on it and whatever's to come; to be there for whatever's to come is the most important. And I want his contacts lists to gauge the possible size of the assault.'

'That all?'

'Don't forget flash drives,' added Irvine, ignoring the sarcasm. 'We'll need everything recorded, as you go—'

'In case I mess up.'

'Nothing and nobody's going to mess up. Is there CCTV in this officer's room?'

'Yes.'

'Re-align it so we get it in pictures, too. I want a digital feed to here.'

'Which do you want first, desktop or laptop?'

It was a professionally valid question, Irvine acknowledged, briefly considering it. 'Smartman will have put firewalls into his botnets, if he really is a smart man. And cutouts on his hacked way in. But the desktop was his ultimate target, so let's make it ours, too.'

'Should we risk direct commentary from Creech to you, for the record to be maintained?'

The communication clampdowns were against written interception, thought Irvine, but he'd already ordered two minimal breaches.

'I've arranged a direct line from Fort Meade, and I want the CCTV relay to watch what goes on from here, which is already too much. You make your own record, as you work.'

'You didn't wish him good luck,' said Sally, as the screen blanked.

'Maybe I should have. But professionals shouldn't need luck, should they?'

She might once have made that sort of remark, conceded Sally. She wasn't sure she'd have done so as casually now.

'It's a total lockdown,' complained Frederick Bowyer. 'But it's within the United States: I've the right, the authority, to know!'

'Yes sir, you have,' agreed Ben Hardy uncomfortably. Being summoned personally to Pennsylvania Avenue and involved in one-to-one conversations like this was unquestionably a professional elevation. But he was unsettled at what appeared to have become an obsession with the director, which had earlier precedents.

'I want you to go back to Packer. Give the impression it's semi-official: Bureau concern at suggestions from other agents about Packer's personal difficulties. Unfortunate if NSA internal security got involved, that sort of approach. You just want to talk it all through with him, colleague to colleague. Get the idea?'

Hardy shifted awkwardly. 'I think so, sir. But that's how Jimmy Lowe tried it, and I got knocked back at the last minute.'

'So don't get knocked back this time. If the son of a bitch still tries it, tell him it's more serious than you thought, and that it's your responsibility to talk to NSA security after all.'

The executive operations officer's desk had been cleared of everything except the desktop. That was manoeuvred for its screen to be the central focus of the CCTV's relayed feed to Irvine's Owen Place installation. Additional lighting whitened everything almost too brightly. Will Fisher was completely visible, but everyone else moved in and out of the shot: sometimes there appeared to be disembodied arms and heads. Without sound the CCTV's view was ghostly surrealism, heightened when an unattached hand and arm came in and out of the frame. More of another body but without a head offered Fisher a combined microphone and ear-padded headset attached to a telephone.

'The direct line to Meade,' said Irvine. His hands twitched across an imagined keyboard, the real one deeper in on the table in front of him. Abruptly aware, he pulled them back, rubbing one over the other as if he were washing the impulse away.

The familiar unattached arm and hand deposited a yellow legal pad and pencils beside Fisher. Already written on it were the officially registered entry codes and passwords to the desktop and laptop. Mouth moving in silent acknowledgement, the man began scribbling number selections, stopping with a block of ten.

Irvine said, 'Meade's first-try algorithms, if Smartman doesn't let us in.'

Sally hoped he wouldn't keep up the commentary.

Theatrically Fisher spread the fingers of both hands, interlaced them, and then cracked them like a concert pianist about to perform. The icon-packed screen illuminated at the registered entries. Fisher splayed his fingers again. He reached forward confidently.

The attempted entry got as far as *SMA* before the screen seized solid. After a pause the icons vanished, replaced by the smiling face of Ismail al Aswamy as a screen saver. It remained there a timed second before diminishing into a receding dot that vanished into oblivion.

The screen was a flurry of different body movements until Fisher reappeared with the desktop. He stared, face crumpled in fury, at the screen, then turned it towards the CCTV camera. It was blank.

'Fuck!' said Irvine vehemently.

'They'll know we found it,' said Sally quietly. 'Al Aswamy himself will know we found it and that he beat us again.'

42

IT BECAME, LIKE SO MANY BEFORE IT, ANOTHER MOSTLY SLEEPLESS night, which, Sally reflected, probably gave Irvine preparation time for his impressively measured responses to the varying reactions he encountered. His first response was to relegate Conrad Graham to last on his priorities list. While he waited for Will Fisher's helicopter to arrive back at Nellis, Irvine briefly outlined the disaster—which scarcely required a long explanation anyway—to Burt Singleton at Fort Meade. The concentration had to be upon attack-abandoning Facebook posts between their known jihadists: he asked for their suggested algorithms list to be copied to Owen Place. In the longer conversation that followed with John Poulter, Irvine repeated his abandonment expectation, in spite of which he was continuing the Creech sweep, initially focusing on the connected machines of the base commander and the other two executive officers to discover from their hard drives what sensitive material had been accessed by the Smartman intrusion. The two Smartman-infected machines, the flash drives, CCTV film, and Fisher's seconds-long commentary would be shipped to Fort Meade for forensic investigation. The hard drives of both computers would confirm what al Aswamy's group had obtained. GCHQ would get complete details immediately when they were available.

'No doubt now that it's al Aswamy,' said Poulter.

'Or that we've lost a way to trap him a second time.'

'At least it won't get into the public domain.'

'I'm not taking bets.'

'What do you know about the firewall?'

'Nothing. I'm waiting for Fisher to arrive.'

'You think Smartman could really be a serviceman on the base?'

'A visually activated firewall, you mean?'

'It's technically possible,' Poulter pointed out. 'But I was thinking more about the degree and depth of personnel background checks that have been carried out at Creech?'

It hadn't been mentioned during the military overview, Irvine remembered. 'I don't know. I'll find out.'

'We're almost through the staff personnel checks here. We had to be careful of accusations of racism; so far it's a total blank. And we'll keep the equipment sweep going, of course.'

'Let's talk again tomorrow—' Irvine paused. 'Or rather, later today. Sorry to have woken you up for nothing.'

Sally was listening intently enough to pick up the resurging self-pity, which irritated her after Irvine's unexpectedly imposing performance so far, but since al Aswamy's firewall appearance her greater concentration had been upon re-adjusting her misconceptions, which was probably the greater cause of her annoyance than Irvine's poor-me lapse.

She'd allowed the unimaginable and let herself be guided—or rather misguided—by the interpretations of others instead of rationalizing and thinking as she should have done, Sally acknowledged, the anger burning through her. None of the conveniently appropriate proverbs and aphorisms had been backward-looking at past drone attacks upon Afghanistan or Pakistan or Iraq. That wasn't—wouldn't have been—the Arab mind-set, which she knew, had always known, but hadn't brought into any analysis. She'd become complacent—arrogant—hypnotizing herself with incomprehensible hieroglyphs instead of thinking at least like a surrogate Arab upon the intended meaning of their translations.

So how, belatedly, would a surrogate Arab think? Or better still, how would a committed jihadist think? mused Sally, halting her reflections as Will Fisher appeared on the screen.

Irvine said, 'I want everything, second by second, but before you start, this isn't an inquest looking for guilt. You were up against the best, and that's what they are, the best. Anyone would have lost him.'

Fisher's lips moved, without words. Then he said, 'Thank you. I'm still sorry.'

'We watched but obviously couldn't hear. So tell us . . .' At Sally's nudge, Irvine added, 'This is a British colleague beside me, Sally Hanning.'

Fisher nodded at the introduction but didn't speak, looking briefly down from the Nellis screen at what Sally guessed to be self-defence reminders. They'd tried to anticipate everything, insisted the man strongly. To prevent a Smartman firewall from being triggered by a laptop power surge to the larger machine, they'd disabled the Wi-Fi from which both operated and charged them instead from heavy barrier USBs. Flash drives were installed in both to duplicate any transmission and to download the Smartman botnet's hard drive and contact list if their hack succeeded. Both machines registered negative to electronic testing for built-in Wi-Fi. Fort Meade had provided ten potential algorithms' entries for the Smartman bot. Fisher had attempted the first. The screen had frozen after three letters. The keyboard had seized solid, too. So had the screen and the keyboard on the laptop. Fisher's impression had been of a fraction of time—he hoped it would be measurable from the flash drives—before the face appeared on both screens.

'The keyboard!' demanded Irvine. 'Was there any change in the keyboard tension between the legitimate IP and password entry and your attempted hack?'

Fisher frowned, hesitating. 'We were watching the laptop, not operating it.'

'That wasn't my question. What about the desktop?'

There was another pause. 'I wasn't conscious of any difference; again, milliseconds, which might be on the flash drive. The hack was over in milliseconds, too . . . then it was solid, like a rock.'

Sally waited but when Irvine didn't continue she said, 'I looked hard at the image of Ismail al Aswamy in those few milliseconds. I thought there was some lip movement. Were there any sounds . . . any words?'

'There was something,' confirmed Fisher more confidently. 'I couldn't make it out as a word or words . . . the volume receded with the image.'

'Maybe forensic will get it off the flash drive, be able to enhance it,' suggested Irvine.

'I . . . we,' Sally corrected quickly, 'we need to hear it, know what it was.'

'He appeared to be laughing,' offered Fisher hopefully.

'He had every reason to,' said Irvine bitterly.

Irvine twice postponed their promised return to Langley, finally arriving there with Sally after midnight. They parted in the elevator, Irvine to go up one more floor to Conrad Graham, Sally to speak to David Monkton from her office.

'Just like that!' said the man, incredulity in his voice. 'Why did they attempt the hack in situ? Surely it would have been safer in forensic surroundings with the specialized equipment they're subjecting the computers to now, when it's too damned late!'

It arguably had been a mistake, conceded Sally: Jack Irvine's mistake. 'They had equipment. The Meade sweepers are the best.'

'No, they're not! They were beaten, in seconds from how you've explained it. It was the golden—possibly the *only*—chance to get ahead of them. Now it's gone!'

'Irvine's sure they'll abandon the attack.'

'What do *you* think!'

Sally isolated the change in tone from incredulity to dismissal of Irvine's opinion. 'It would be the obvious thing to do: which may be why they won't do it.' She needed to fit the receding image of Ismail al Aswamy into its proper place among all her other re-considerations and re-examinations.

'Or delay so that we believe they *have* abandoned it and then strike, and to guard against that would require us to keep God knows how many military service groups on indeterminate standby! Or they could shift to another target we might not find out about in advance where they won't fail, as they did with the Washington Monument, the Colosseum, and Sellafield! It's got to be stopped, not moved on!'

'They could do all of that. And probably more,' agreed Sally wearily.

'We've got to stop them winning!'

They hadn't won, not yet, but it wasn't worth the argument. 'I know that, too.'

They didn't speak much on their way back to Owen Place. Irvine said the bourbon smell still beat all the peppermint breath cleansers Graham had chewed, and that the acting director had already been mad at the intelligence committee's acceptance of a formal enquiry into the death of Abu al Hurr, which was a waste of time because the body had already been cremated. He'd made a lot of noise about the loss of the Smartman bot and was going to call another televised conference later in the day. The failure had to be contained at all cost. Sally limited herself to saying Monkton was furious, without going into pointless detail.

Both were too exhausted to think of lovemaking, but Sally remained awake long after Irvine fell into a snuffling sleep, running like a film clip through her head the decoded Vevak transmissions she'd memorized practically word for word, just as she'd memorized the smirking, vanishing face of Ismail al Aswamy. That unquestionably was how he'd been, Sally determined: smirking arrogantly, mocking. . . . Sally stopped the mental slide show at the word she'd been searching for, fixing its place. That's what Aswamy had been, what all the underlying intentions of the encryptions had been—mockery. Why? What was it that made the man so contemptuously sure that this time he'd properly succeed—even if they'd broken the codes or found the targets? The firewall wasn't enough, even though it had self-destructed. Al Aswamy had posted his own image, said something: she had to know what that word or words were to analyze the derision. What was there she could deduce? They wouldn't abort. That was part—the entire point and purpose—of the contempt. No matter what precautions were taken or protection emplaced, al Aswamy and Vevak were sure they couldn't be stopped. But how could they be so confident! It couldn't be the timing, whenever that might be. Everything was in place, every contingency anticipated, both bases ready to be cordoned off in minutes: impenetrable according to the military briefing Obviously they'd still be better protected if they had the date and were able to get enough men inside, confronting the onslaught, not catching up from behind. Was the timing in the codes, like the mockery? Or was there something she was still missing, the way she'd missed so much else until now? She didn't know; couldn't think. The date and the derision; she had to know— work out—the date and the reason for the derision. What—or where—was the significance? Date and derision, echoed in her head, like a mantra. Date and derision, date and derision, was Sally's last conscious thought before she finally drifted to sleep.

43

AND WERE THE FIRST WORDS THAT CAME INTO SALLY'S MIND when she awoke. And stayed there like a taunt as she showered, anxious to get to the embassy to speak to Monkton, knowing she'd need his support. Irvine came into the kitchen as she finished making coffee.

Sally said at once, 'Al Aswamy won't abort the attacks.'

Irvine stood staring at her for several moments, not speaking. 'How'd you know?'

Sally sipped her coffee, glad of the rehearsal, but conscious of Irvine's visible bemusement as she talked.

He remained silent again for several moments when she finished, as if expecting her to say more. When she didn't, he said, 'That's it! Nothing more?'

'It's how an Arab thinks.'

'Not these Arabs. They're jihadists first, Arabs second; militarily trained zealots don't attack a target they know is expecting them, not even if they're assured of paradise if they die doing it. You try to argue this at today's assessment, they'll laugh in your face, and it'll be difficult for me not to laugh with them. Think about it from every which way, Sally! None of it makes sense. There's nothing to support it.'

'I'm leaving ahead of you. I want to speak to Monkton from the embassy.'

'Do that. I really want you to: for you to be ordered not to do it.'

'When will we get Meade's preliminary reports on the computers, know what al Aswamy said?'

'That's not going to convince anyone, darling! We don't know if he said *anything*!'

The *darling* word jarred but didn't block out *date and derision*. 'When?'

'I'll know when I get to Langley. There should be something today.'

'I'll come directly there from the embassy.'

Sally detoured to Watergate for a change of clothes, using the delay to rethink her approach to the MI5 Director-General. She hadn't expected Irvine's outright rejection, though he'd tried to couch it, an oversight she shouldn't have allowed. She hadn't properly gauged how it would sound, lacking any supporting facts or evidence, because she was back thinking the way she always thought—automatically thought—which made logical sense to her but hardly ever to anyone else.

Sally changed a phrase or two of her original argument but basically it remained the same, and Sally was aware from the pitch of Monkton's voice, though it had reverted to its customary monotone, that he wasn't accepting her insistences any more readily than Irvine.

'I don't know why Ismail al Aswamy believes he can carry it out!' admitted Sally, answering Monkton's repeated question. 'But I'm convinced he's going to: that the attack's still on.'

'Are you suggesting something nuclear, the final proof, despite all the denials and permitted weapons inspections, that they've got the capability?'

'I'm not ruling it out nor ruling it in,' said Sally, inwardly cringing at the vacuity of what she was saying. 'At most I'm arguing against a premature withdrawal of everything that's in place at Waddington and Creech. If I'm out-argued about Creech, please keep Waddington on standby.'

'For how long?'

'Until it happens and we can put up some sort of resistance—save lives!'

'You're asking a lot.'

'To achieve a lot.'

She'd half expected Nigel Fellowes to be lurking outside the communications room, which seemed to have become his habit, and was glad that he wasn't there as she left. It had started to sleet heavily as she hurried across the parking lot, and with Fellowes in mind she remembered his initial warning of winter's arrival when October turned into November.

Her cell phone sounded as she reached her rental car. Irvine said, 'Graham in an hour: something we didn't expect. And the conference linkup is at three. What did Monkton say?'

'That he'd think about it. But he didn't forbid it. What about the computers and flash drives?'

'Nothing.'

'The son of a bitch is denying any knowledge or involvement, of course,' said Conrad Graham. 'I'll push it as far as I can, make sure every goddamned person on the Senate intelligence committee hears what he tried to do. Bowyer will survive until the next president'—Graham snapped his fingers—'then good-bye, Frederick fucking Bowyer. And until then the leash will be short enough to strangle him.'

'I never doubted Harry Packer for a moment,' admitted Irvine.

'You didn't have cause to,' Sally pointed out. 'It was he who wouldn't co-operate with the FBI and instead blew the whistle to NSA security.'

'He put himself in the position to be compromised . . . blackmailed,' said Irvine. 'He'll be out.'

'Bradley won't.' Graham smiled in anticipation. 'He should be, sure. But I'm going to keep that little cocksucker in his little coop, and I'm going to refuse a resignation or any application for premature retirement, and I'm going to have monitored every single move he makes, up to and including every time he takes a leak.'

'Do you think it could have been Bradley—or someone in the FBI— who put that surveillance on us?'

Graham shrugged. 'Could be. Who knows? You think you're still being tailed?'

'No, as a matter of fact I don't.' Sally hadn't bothered to check that morning or for two or three days, or nights, prior to that. She hadn't thought about Nigel Fellowes's warning of being targeted, either.

'Now let's hear about this cockamamy attack theory of yours,' demanded Graham.

The preliminary damage assessment arrived from the National Security Agency an hour before the televised conference linkup. It was separated into two sections. In the first, the potential harm of Smartman's sideways intrusion into the Creech commanding officer's computer was described as an incalculable disaster. Intelligence information held on the desktop included the identity of all civilian suppliers and contractors to the base, making them potential terrorist targets; forward-planning proposals against Al Qaeda and jihadist training camps in Mali, Yemen, and Somalia; allied-country over-flight co-operation; and intended drone and pilot capability at both Creech and Waddington over the following six months. The contact list had the restricted e-mail addresses— some containing the unlisted or security-restricted telephone numbers—of top-echelon officers at the Pentagon and the British Ministry of Defence. The second, much smaller section was devoted specifically to the failed Fort Meade attempt to isolate the Smartman botnet. The cutout laptop would have been the self-destruct trigger for the desktop, but the forensic examiners believed its destruction programme had a reverse function if the desktop were swept first, which had been the case. Destruction had been absolute, in both machines, leaving no electronic fingerprints. It had taken maximum volume enhancement to obtain audibility from the indistinct sounds from Ismail al Aswamy's receding image. Even then the sound was difficult to distinguish. It sounded like the repetition of a single English word: the most likely was *conquest*, but that was not definitive.

The NSA also included two successful interceptions over the previous twenty-four hours. The transliteration of one from Kermani read, *A promise is a cloud; fulfillment is rain.* Anis's post was decoded as *Better a thousand enemies outside the tent than one within.*

Once again Sally divided her attention, listening to—and analyzing—the exchanges between England and the Nevada air base, but at the same time assessing what she'd speed-read from NSA, seeking anything to support her insistence that Creech and Waddington remain on high alert. But she couldn't find it. She thought Anis's thousand-enemies post could refer to the Smartman hacking—further derision of the hacker still serving on the base—but Sally accepted that suggestion would be overwhelmed by the Creech commander's assurance to Irvine's previous day's prompt from John Poulter that every serviceman's background had thoroughly been cleared. And there was nothing she could utilize from the minimal NSA report on the two infected machines.

'I have already notified the Pentagon of the gravity of the loss,' the Creech commander was telling London. 'And having now learned the seriousness, I imagine you'd like to terminate this discussion to do the same with your Defence Ministry.'

David Monkton took the question. 'We haven't discussed the armed forces disposition at both bases.'

No immediate response came from either base. One finally came from an undesignated wing commander at Waddington. 'What's to discuss? It wasn't ever going to be a physical attack. They've achieved a victory that's going to take us months, years, to recover from, and we've wasted hundreds of thousands on a pointless military exercise that we've got today to start standing down.'

'Don't!' declared Sally, hoping the strength of her voice would disguise the plea. 'They have achieved a victory. But they haven't stopped. There will be an attack. And if the military is stood down, their second, public victory will be the destruction of both bases from which their most feared and hated weapon, drones, are deployed.'

'How do you know this!' demanded the American base commander.

Sally breathed in deeply. 'It's my assessment, my judgment, from monitoring from an Arab mind-set every decrypted terrorist message since this jihad began.'

'Assessment!' echoed the wing commander disbelievingly, looking to those on either side to share his bemusement. 'I was told you were a brilliant intelligence officer, but now I learn you're really a witch: someone who reads the runes.'

'My officer was responsible for preventing what would have potentially resulted in serious nuclear contamination over a considerable area of England. And was the first to realize—and prove—that we were confronting a full-scale jihad,' said Monkton defensively. 'She has a unique ability to interpret and anticipate and should be listened to, not mocked. If the decision is to stand down Creech, I will recommend my government maintain a substantial force at Waddington.'

'I am trying to prevent another incalculable disaster,' said Sally, hearing the despair in her own voice.

'Lady,' said the American, unmoved by Monkton's intrusion, 'we've all had a hell of a time; now we're suffering the strain. It's over now.' He scrambled through the printouts. 'Here's what the guy told us himself: conquest. That's what this was, his conquest. He won. We lost.'

'No!' said Sally in abrupt realization, close to sniggering. 'That's not it, not it at all. And I know when it's going to happen.'

'What the hell are you talking about now!' demanded the man.

'I'm talking about 1979. November fourth, 1979, when Iranian students took over your embassy in Tehran and for 444 humiliating days held Americans hostages. Which Iran called the conquest of the American spy den.'

'That's exactly what they called it,' said Irvine, although more in confusion than confirmation.

'And tomorrow's November fourth,' said David Monkton.

'That's when they'll attack,' declared Sally.

44

SALLY SAID SHE'D SLEEP THAT NIGHT AT HER SERVICE APARTMENT, and Irvine didn't try to dissuade her, neither wanting tension they couldn't prevent from being a barrier between them. Although there'd been no prior arrangement, Sally detoured to the embassy on her way from Langley. David Monkton was still at Thames House.

Sally said, 'I wanted to thank you for today.'

'You absolutely sure the attack will be tomorrow?'

'As sure as I can be.'

'But not absolutely?'

'Can we ever be?'

'Graham called. Told me about the FBI business.'

'It didn't get in the way.' Should she tell him about the strange warning from Nigel Fellowes of being personally targeted? No, she decided. That hadn't gotten in the way, either: nothing more than Fellowes's posturing at being left out. Too much had been in the way if he *had* been involved.

'You got any idea about tomorrow?'

'It'll obviously have to synchronize with the eight-hour time difference between Nevada and Lincolnshire.'

'Which end of whose day?'

'Evening of November fourth in England, I'm guessing,' said Sally. 'Although that *is* a guess: America's the Great Satan, where they'll want to make the headlines and get the television coverage. And the most damage, of course.'

'That's sensible reasoning.'

'There's no point now in the military hiding away.'

'They're not going to,' disclosed Monkton. 'They're moving in over-night, at Creech and Waddington. Men and armour as well as aerial cover. It's going to be a suicide attack.'

'Which they'll know: expect. And which I don't understand   can't even guess—and not being able to do either worries the hell out of me.'

'You're starting to speak like an American,' mocked Monkton.

'But still thinking like a surrogate Arab.' I hope, she thought.

Sally hadn't expected to sleep, conscious that the televised conference feed was opening at one minute past November 3 midnight— eight hours earlier on America's West Coast to maintain the synchronicity—but she had, dreamlessly. By six she was on her way to Langley, sure she'd guessed correctly that the assault would be during Waddington's evening or night, Creech's November 4 day. She decided against suggesting her reasoning as she entered the room in which she expected to spend most of the day. She'd told Monkton it was up to him to pass it on.

The command teams had changed locations at Creech and Wadding-ton, both now relaying from operational rooms against wall-mounted, aer-ial, blown-up photographs and maps of the respective installations. Each room also had a large, central ops table with scale models of both stations. Low-voiced operational staff tried to appear occupied in both, but neither the Creech commander nor the Waddington wing commanders were there.

They hadn't fixed a meeting time at Langley, but Sally was surprised Jack Irvine wasn't there. Conrad Graham came into the room at ten and said, 'Hi,' his concentration on the ops-room screens.

Coming back to her but nodding back towards the pictures, Graham said, 'I think I saw the movie.'

And you're going to be in the sequel, anticipated Sally. 'It might be a long day.'

Graham looked fresh and alert, showing no alcohol fatigue. 'A television feed was put in overnight to the White House Situation Room.'

Graham would *definitely* be in the movie, decided Sally. 'Has the president been told what's already been lost from Creech?'

Graham nodded. 'Sure as hell glad it wasn't me who had to be the messenger. A second examination's discovered there's even more gone than we were told yesterday.'

Could that be what was delaying Irvine? Sally wondered. 'You heard from Jack?'

'He's staying in touch with Meade for any fresh intercepts. He says there should have been some more reaction to our knowing of Smartman's penetration by now.' Graham looked back to the television. 'How long do you really think this day's going to be?'

Sally decided against leaving Monkton to spell out the time variations between Waddington and Creech. 'The attacks have to be simultaneous, but the eight-hour time difference between Creech and Waddington has to be allowed for. It won't be until England's afternoon: maybe even in the evening.'

'No reason to hang around here, then?' said Graham.

There wasn't, Sally accepted. There might still be something more she hadn't recognized in the already-intercepted Hydarnes transmissions.

But there wasn't, and by Creech's noon—8:00 p.m. on November 4 at Waddington—Sally's concentration was flagging. Conrad Graham was already there when she got back. So was Irvine. He would have walked right past her office, she realized. But the door had been closed and he wouldn't have expected her to be there.

He smiled. 'There's nothing new. No claims on any Middle East outlet, either. It doesn't make sense.'

'That's the play, isn't it? We're not supposed to understand it.'

Beyond Irvine, Graham looked at his watch and said, 'In England it's already—'

'Eight thirty at night. I know.' On the live video feed Sally saw that all of yesterday's participants were in their seats and wished she'd returned earlier. Monkton didn't acknowledge her arrival.

'Perimeter checks are routine; we've just completed the fifth. There's nothing—no-one—around,' said one of the Waddington wing commanders.

'Our airborne helos aren't seeing anything, either,' picked up the Creech commander sardonically. 'The high-altitude surveillance plane says the surf's good on Venice Beach, but there's nothing much happening between there and us.'

Conrad Graham shifted in his seat and immediately shifted back to how he had been sitting, looking at his watch again. David Monkton was looking directly at her face, his face as expressionless as his voice usually was. Sally hoped her face was just as blank. From the wall-mounted clock behind the MI5 chief, Sally saw it was nine fifteen.

Graham got as far as 'I think—' before an alarm light burst red next to the wall map in the Waddington ops room and a metallic Tannoy voice said, 'We've just been hit! There's burning, a fire—!' A Klaxon blared.

As it did in the Creech command room. Telephones rang and the Tannoy voice said, 'We're under fire—! Two explosions by the control tower . . . there's another!'

The commander grabbed the base loudspeaker pod, shouting over the erupting noise, 'Where? How many? I need a situation report . . . someone tell me where they're coming from!'

'I don't know! I can't see any attackers . . . just strikes,' said an unidentified woman.

'It's a UAV,' intruded an astonished English voice.

'What the hell's a UAV!' demanded someone.

'Unmanned aerial vehicle . . . a drone . . . a miniature goddamned . . . a drone,' came a reply.

'They're hitting us with drones!' said an incredulous voice.

Mosquitoes that could sting a lion's eye! thought Sally at once; al Aswamy was attacking with remotely controlled drones, still mocking them.

The Tannoys became over-amplified, building up echoing noise in the operations rooms, where an even higher, yelling cacophony could be heard over it. Sally isolated the American commander demanding outside vision, and suddenly on a television screen next to the map display a live picture appeared of a section of the base. And with it a picture of a crumpled but still identifiable helicopter about the size of a car tire that she'd seen being flown by children in London's Hyde and St James's Parks, easily controlled and flown from cell phones that hadn't then needed the GPS directional guide that those she was seeing now had required. The helicopter was visibly scorched by whatever improved explosive device had been carried on it. As her eyes focused more intently, she picked out miniature wrecks littered around the ground. Some were lodged in the buildings they had set alight. Groups of firefighters, dragging hoses, were dousing buildings as they ran between them, hindered by larger squads of fully kitted, bewildered soldiers seeking unseen enemies.

There was a babble of confused, conflicting shouts and demands, too. 'Can't shoot the fucking things down . . . came in under the radar . . . Jesus H. Christ, what a mess . . . fire trucks, need fire trucks . . . beat them with our own helicopters . . . fly over them, take them out with our downdrafts . . . blow them off course . . . drive them down . . . helicopters have got to fan out, find the sons of bitches who're operating them . . . got three . . . we've detained three guys . . . laughing . . . they're laughing at us!'

Mocking them! Sally thought again. Irvine tried to pull away from Sally snatching at him for attention, and when he finally looked away from the screen, she reached farther across to grab at Graham.

'What's a cloud?' she demanded. 'In computer-speak but in my language, what's a cloud!'

'In your language, where computer data's held, stored,' said Irvine, still trying to pull away.

Tugging again at Graham, Sally demanded, 'That extra material from the commander's computer we didn't know about yesterday? Was it the storage location for Creech's past computer traffic, maybe even future planning . . . tactics?'

'I don't know.' The man frowned.

It took almost thirty minutes to reach the Creech operations room, only finally succeeding by telephone because they weren't responding to their conference voice link.

'I haven't time!' the commander yelled at the executive officer relaying Sally's demand to talk.

'Tell him this isn't the attack. This is a decoy!'

'What?' demanded the man, finally coming to her.

'You and Waddington aren't the real targets. You're decoys. They're going to attack your computer storage.'

'How did you know?' asked Irvine fifteen minutes later, when the first confirmation came of the ground assault by a twenty-strong terrorist group upon the storage facility at Ellsworth Air Force Base near Rapid City, South Dakota.

' "A promise is a cloud. Fulfillment is the rain," ' quoted Sally. 'The last of Kermani's intercept: his attack instructions.'

A total of 350 cell-controlled, GPS-guided mini-helicopters—aerial platforms—were launched against the Creech and Waddington air bases. All were commercially purchased, either in toy stores or online. They were all eight-rotored—like their military drone equivalent used for surveillance and reconnaissance—with a flying capacity of just over seven miles. The adaptation to carry the IED incendiaries—a lot made from chemical fertilizer—was minimal, as was the majority of the damage. A bicycle storage shed and half a latrine block at Waddington were burned out, and the fire caved in the roof of a sports hall at Creech.

The firefight at Ellsworth Air Force Base caused much more damage because the attackers penetrated the outbuildings of the bunker—the *cloud* in Internet parlance—of the Creech computer traffic. There were no life-threatening American casualties, but eight of the attackers were killed. One of them was a still-bearded Ismail al Aswamy.

The initial celebrations that night were limited to the three of them. Conrad Graham invited them to his suite, where the alcohol choice extended well beyond bourbon, even to wine for Sally. Graham toasted her and said she'd done a hell of a job, and Sally pointed out that the death of al Aswamy didn't mark the end of jihad terrorism. Irvine said it was inevitable that Vevak would take down their Hydarnes site, but they'd get another access in time. They stretched to a second round of drinks—although Sally declined because the wine was sweet—and managed to escape after another half an hour.

Sally left her car to ride home with Irvine. Neither spoke until they were crossing the Key Bridge. Then Irvine said, 'It is over as far as you're concerned here, isn't it?'

'I don't know,' avoided Sally. 'I haven't spoken to Monkton yet.'

'It will be.'

'It always had to end, didn't it?'

'I don't want it to.'

'I don't want to talk about it tonight.'

'Tomorrow then.'

'Tomorrow,' agreed Sally, to end the conversation.

The difficulty had evaporated by the time they reached Owen Place. There was no talk of food, of anything. They walked, unspeaking, directly to the bedroom and came together as if angry, Irvine ripping her shirt as he pulled it off. There was no foreplay and they started to make love still angrily but then locked, in frozen fear, as the apartment door crashed open and noise and running feet and men hustled in.

The light went on as the bedroom door burst open, with them both still joined.

'You've got every reason to hate us for doing this, buddy, but it's for your own good,' said the man at the bedroom door. 'Sorry to you, too, lady.'

45

CONRAD GRAHAM OBVIOUSLY HADN'T LEFT LANGLEY AFTER THEM.
He had a bourbon blush but no slur when he asked Sally how she'd torn
her shirt. It was the only thing Graham said—refusing all their shouted
demands as Sally had refused his—before handing them first-edition
copies of that day's *Washington Post*.

Jack Irvine was instantly identifiable from the four-column, five-inch-
deep photograph that accompanied the story headlined 'NSA Spycatcher
Defeats Al Qaeda Jihad.' Sally's image was far less clear. Her body was
half hidden behind his, and her face was partially obscured by a hand gesture he'd been making when the picture had been snatched of their leaving Owen Place together sometime over the previous week.

The coverage was padded out by archival material—as well as an
official ambassadorial photograph—of Irvine's father's Middle East debacle. Irvine was described as NSA's leading code-cracker, who'd worked
on the Stuxnet sabotage of Iran's nuclear-development project before de-
vising the entrapment operation of Ismail al Aswamy, whose importance equaled that of Osama bin Laden. Intelligence analysts judged the
death of Aswamy, the mastermind of the failed attacks on the Washington
Monument, Rome's Colosseum, and a British nuclear installation, as a
major Al Qaeda setback. A further and equally devastating defeat for the
jihadists was the degree of co-operation and information from thirty of the

fifty-eight mini-drone operators in exchange for shares in the multi-million-dollar bounty, coupled with witness protection.

Sally was not identified by name and was referred to only as the English intelligence agent who had been seconded to the American operation after foiling the British nuclear attack. The details of the attacks on Creech and Waddington were limited to their being incendiary assaults—with no reference to mini-helicopters—that had successfully been repelled. Al Aswamy's death had occurred in a separate attack on another, unnamed military installation.

'Where—how the fuck—did they get this!' exploded Irvine. 'It's . . . I . . . Oh, fuck . . . !'

'There were leaks at Creech, of course,' said Graham. 'I authorized a media release limited to what you see there, and which is all that's running on the wires. I obviously didn't mention you by name; I didn't mention anyone by name. Or say anything about Stuxnet. Or your father.'

But the story would open the way for the biopic, thought Sally. She said, 'Nearly all of it was put together in advance, ready for a hook to hang it on. It's got Fred Bowyer's fingerprints all over it.'

'I neutered him,' insisted Graham.

'Not sufficiently,' accused Sally.

'I'll find the source,' promised Graham. 'Whoever it is, I'll find the son of a bitch and hang him by the balls with piano wire.'

'I lived once through what happened to my father,' said Irvine. 'I guess I can live through the repetition.'

Was there an element of satisfaction, son restoring the family name? wondered Sally. The outrage had been short-lived.

'Your father isn't the point, why I hauled you two out of bed,' said Graham. 'GCHQ intercepted some chatter. The ayatollahs are issuing a fatwa.'

Irvine sniggered an uncertain laugh. 'You can't be serious!'

'NSA wants you in a protection programme. So do I.' Graham looked at Sally. 'You're going out of Andrews in two hours on a military flight, courtesy of the CIA. Until then you're staying here. We're returning your rental car, picking up all your stuff and bringing it here; you can change your shirt.' He went back to Irvine. 'Your guys will have cleared out all the technical stuff from Owen Place by now; your personal things are being brought here, too.'

'I don't want to go into a protection programme!' protested Irvine. 'Fatwas only apply to Muslims. It's sharia law, doesn't apply to me. Who's going to get to me inside Fort Meade, for Christ's sake!'

'You work at Fort Meade, you don't live there, and even if you did, you still wouldn't be safe,' insisted Graham.

'Killing you would re-establish the jihad,' said Sally quietly. 'And to the jihadist it wouldn't matter whether you're a Muslim or not. That's what they do, manipulate the Koran.'

'No!' yelled Irvine.

'It's not a choice,' insisted Graham. 'We're keeping you alive.'

Sally changed her shirt when her luggage arrived. Irvine stayed as he was. They stacked everything in his soon-to-be-abandoned office to make enough room in hers for them to wait for their transport to arrive.

'It's not going to be permanent,' said Irvine. 'Could be over in just a few months.'

'Sure.'

'We could keep in touch: there'll be channels.'

'You know we can't, Jack.'

'When it's all over, I mean.'

'It hasn't begun yet.'

'If it hadn't happened, this threat, would you—?'

'I don't want you to finish that question,' stopped Sally.

'It was hypothetical.'

'That's how it stays, hypothetical.'

'I want to tell you—'

'I don't want you to finish that either.'

'I don't believe I have to.'

Two escorts arrived at the door to take her down with her luggage, waiting outside after they collected it. Sally said, 'None of the usual good-byes fit, do they?'

'No, I don't suppose they do.'

'Just good-bye then.'

'Yes, just good-bye.'

They remained looking at each other for several moments, not touching. Abruptly Sally turned away towards the waiting escorts. She said, 'Let's go.'

Conrad Graham was waiting in the expansive Langley entrance hall. Two unmarked 4x4s were drawn up directly outside, and several more plainclothes escorts waited around them.

Graham said, 'Another ending might have been better.' He hadn't bothered with peppermint candy.

Sally shrugged. 'You're probably right.'

'You really did do a hell of a job.'

'I need a favour,' ignored Sally.

'You got it.'

'Let me know who leaked to *The Washington Post.*'

'Like I said, you got it.'

Sally didn't think he would, but there was always the outside chance.